THE
MATRIARCH
MATRIX

MAXIME TRENCAVEL

978-0-9993350-3-1 Paperback
978-0-9993350-2-4 Ebook

Library of Congress Control Number: 2017954439

Edition 2.0.0.0
Published by Tail of the Bird Books, Larchmont
www.tailofthebird.com

Please visit the author's web site for behind the scenes background, historical comments, and more.
www.tailofthebird.com
Trencavel, Maxime. The Matriarch Matrix. Tail of the Bird Books.

À mes deux filles.
Que leur monde soit celui de la paix et de la tolérance.

✍

To my two daughters.
May their world be one of peace and tolerance.

PREFACE

In 1994, the world's oldest temple, dating back to the end of the last ice age, was discovered in Turkey. Why would a hundred or more tribal hunter-gatherers build a site of religious worship? What of their words have passed into our times?

In 2014, the Daesh, also known as ISIL, overran the lands of the Ezidis in Sinjar, Northwest Iraq. They killed many thousands. They took thousands of women and girls as sex slaves, many sold in markets. Today, as many as three thousand are still unaccounted for.

In 2022, the story of *The Matriarch Matrix* links these and other historic events that are emblematic of our troubled times and our past. The heroine is a survivor of the Daesh kidnappings and enslavements. Her story and that of her ancestral matriarch portray a mythic and metaphoric parable of how mankind has evolved, or not. Only her love will lead to the truth.

At times, the story is dark and intense, reflecting what has actually happened to oppressed people, especially women, across time all over the world. May we learn from stories like this so we can strive to make our daughters' world better.

I would like to thank all the women who have helped with the critique and editing of this story—one that I hope helps you reflect upon our world.

PART I

Let's be companions, the two of us.
Let's go to the Friend, my soul.
Let's be close intimates, the two of us.
Let's go to the Friend, my soul.
Let's go before this life is over,
Before our bodies disappear,
Before enemies come between us.

—Yunus Emre,
thirteenth-century Turkish poet and Sufi mystic

PROLOGUE

Somebody should tell us, right at the start of our lives,
that we are dying. Then we might live life to the limit,
every minute of every day. Do it! I say. Whatever you want
to do, do it now! There are only so many tomorrows.

—Pope Paul VI

Our present has happened in the past from where our future appears. Our lesson learned from the voice of the object.

The voice called for her to save us all. But tonight, there can be no peace. Neither lamb nor sheep can I be. For I must be the wolf to save her. No matter what she has said.

So here I must stand. Our last stand on this desolate pier jutting into the tempest of an angry Black Sea, the tears of a darkened, sorrowful heaven pelting my face.

Finger on this detonator. One flinch and a kilometer of this world will vaporize. All because of this black object, for which we have been chased, shot, and bombed in our quest to solve a mystery that burns deep in both my dreams and those of the man who is going to kill us now. That is, if I don't kill us first.

To my left stands Jean-Paul, once Father Sobiros, now an armed biblical archeologist who has done his best to assuage my "alien origins of religion" hypothesis. To my right is Zara, once a Kurdish freedom fighter, who has personified the Neolithic goddess of my dreams.

In front of us is the object, the one of my family's legends, the one of the matriarch of so many millennia gone by, the one that has changed Zara in the profound spiritual ways she has long sought, wrapped in six kilos of the most explosive material in the world. I cannot do what Zara has asked me to do, to her and to the object. I just can't. Not after what she and I have been through together.

Next to the object is the man who hired us, Alexander, who looks extremely annoyed we didn't quite deliver this supersized stone, this black object, under the terms he wanted, and who has just raised his hand.

No. Alexander's snipers just shot Jean-Paul. He's down and not moving. Follow her plan exactly, she said. No deviations. No matter what happens. Poor Father Sobiros.

I yell, "Alexander, tell them to stop or I'll detonate the object. You lose. I lose. We all lose."

Alexander yells something in Russian into his lapel mike.

No. Please, no. His sniper shot Zara, twice. My heart skips. Stay focused, she said. No matter what happens, I have to stay patient, obedient to her plan. Yes. She's scrambling on the floor to grab her rifle back and rolls over with her hand on a grenade launcher.

There ends the sniper. Clearly Alexander is beyond annoyed as he aims his pistol at Zara's head. Okay, Zara. I would follow you to the ends of the earth and beyond, but I have to save you first. If only one person can walk out of this, it must be you. I don't care what the voice said.

Click goes the detonator to normal mode. And where's that pistol Zara gave me? Here it is. What did Zara tell me to do? Release safety, check. Pull backwards on the top slide until a click is heard. No click. Come on, faster, before he shoots Zara again. Oh, how I love her… Focus, Peter. Okay, slide it back harder. *Click*… too late.

Alexander has shot Zara directly in her chest, her Russian protective vest shattered for good this time as she yells, "Peter, shoot him! Rapid-fire rounds into his chest, like I showed you."

"One more move and the first round has Alex written all over it," I assert, as bold as I can be.

"Peter, my boy. Tell me, did you dream last night that you would be killing me today?" asks Alexander, still focused, with his gun now aimed at Zara's scarf-covered head. "Because if you didn't, then Zara here will die needlessly. Your choice, Peter. Kill me and kill Zara at the same time, or simply release that button and blow us all up. What did your dreams say you would do? Mine said you're not the kind of person to kill."

"Peter, shoot him. Ignore him. It doesn't matter if I die. You know what will happen if he puts the object halves together. You know what the voice told us," Zara says weakly as she slumps to the ground.

"Peter, my dear boy. You have been a loser, a failure so many times in your life up to now. Did I not say you and I were more alike than different? Be a winner this time. Be a winner with me. We both need the object intact. Put down the detonator," pleads a fatherly Alexander.

I can do this. I can do this. No, I can't. I can't kill. It's not in my DNA. What do I do? What do I do?

"Peter, my boy," Alexander says softly. "Spare Zara. We can all see how deeply you care about her. I do not want to shoot her either. I care about her too. So, put down the gun. Put away the detonator, and you and Zara can walk out of here."

Zara makes one last appeal to me. "Kill him, Peter. Let him kill me. If you love me. If you truly love me, let him kill me."

What do I do? In every option spinning through my head, Zara will die. If only Zara and I could touch. When we touch, her soul and my soul together, everything becomes clear. And through her, the voice is so clear. How can I let her be killed?

"Okay, Alexander, here's what we're going to do…"

CHAPTER 1

You can't go back and change the beginning, but you
can start where you are and change the ending.

—C.S. Lewis

Parkside, San Francisco, California
8:20 a.m. GMT–8, April 28, 2022

The fog. The fog billows by. The fog that surrounds during the night slowly retreats. So too begins the morning retreat of the infamous San Francisco fog, slowly but surely back into the Pacific, only to return once again every night. And so it has been for Peter Gollinger since he was born. The wet blanket of billowing fog all night is all his mind knows.

Half-awake, half still in the fog of a traumatic dream, in a full sweat, he bolts up out of bed, yelling, "I can't kill. I can't. What do I do?" Dazed, he looks at his clammy hands held out in front of him, shaking, gripping something.

Heart rate beyond tachycardic, clammy hands in tight fists, he looks around in panic for someone. "Where is she? Forget where, who is she? Oh, I wish, I wish I could remember these ordeals of my nights."

Stumbling to his small bathroom, so tight his knees hit the wall when he's seated on the squeezed-in can, he turns and looks around his one-room studio rental, the highest room in one of those pastel-colored stucco box houses that line the streets of this part of San Francisco.

"Did I just remember a dream? Did I just dream of a gun? I hate guns. Why would I dream of things that scare me?"

He sighs again, looking at his war zone of a bed with the pillows bunched up and tossed about, the sheet and blankets in twisted spirals, flung in all directions. He glances back into the oval mirror over the sink in his small bathroom. He brushes back his sandy brown hair, with vestiges of the blondness of his younger days. He tries to smile to show his dimples, but he can only frown as the bags under his eyes signal the fatigue his nightly dramas bring. "If only I could get a restful night. Even once every new moon would do," muses Peter.

A mug full of microwave-heated imitation gourmet coffee and Peter is ready to start his day at his dilapidated desk, perpendicularly placed next to his one window that provides just a peek of his precious Pacific fog. The walls of his tiny place are bare save three posters, ones that remind him of someone who meant so much to him. The newest with all the Starship *Enterprise*s, from the 60s to the seventh of the reboot series. Another with all the alien gods and goddess of the *Stargate* franchises. And one emblazoned with the *X-Files* motto: *I want to believe.*

He clasps his MoxWrap around his wrist like a lucky rabbit foot. He needs some luck to go his way again. He could never have afforded one of these, but one day last year, MoxWorld Holdings sent him one free. Totally free, with no service fees, even. He won one of those contests where he answered a series of questions. Somewhat personal questions, but free is free.

MoxWorld clearly demonstrated to him why they were the worldwide leaders in all things digital. Out of nowhere, they even sent him a free upgraded unit last week. Other than the quite pleasant tingling feeling he gets from the occasional upgrade, what's not to like?

He had to play a promo ad to activate this unit:

"The device sitting on your wrist now will change your life. For the better. The MoxWrap is simply revolutionary. Thin, flexible, and available in your choice of seven sizes that allow custom molds around any adult's arm. Lighter than the now-obsolete smartphone, with the comfort of a terry-cloth wristband, the MoxWrap contains the power of a personal command center. With solar-assisted batteries, the run time vastly exceeds all previous options. You could be in the wilderness for days, and as long as the sun shines, you will have around-the-clock minicomputer power through its satellite links to hectares of processors, the largest databases in the world, and infinite memory capacity. Triple the bandwidth and burst speeds of the best alternative technology allows for applications never imaginable until now. Congratulations on a smart decision."

He taps his lucky rabbit foot surrogate and the associated processor unit on his desk beams up a screen as well as a virtual keyboard hologram. Keyboards are the instruments of his music. Of his magic. For he is an editor. A copy editor, making the written work of others that much better.

He reads his messages, deleting all but the flagged one from MoxMedia he has kept for two days. Fingers tapping the desk, he waits for a message from his managing editor, Jerrod, with news of his bonus, as well as—maybe—an offer to become permanent and no longer a contractor. He rubs his MoxWrap again, wishing for luck.

He picks up an old-fashioned picture frame on his desk that holds an equally old-fashioned photo print of a woman. Someone else no longer in his life, who meant so much to him. She is attractively and tastefully posed, with her long dishwater-blond hair in a ponytail cascading down the front of her open plaid shirt, which is tied at the bottom, covering her sports bra. Her raggedy blue jean cut-offs accent her lovely tanned legs, which slip right into her grey woolen socks, encased in her medium-height brown hiking boots. She was picture-perfect, his goddess at the top of Mount Shasta.

Catching himself lamenting about what once was, he puts a tank top and shorts on his lean runner's body, one of average height for an American. Within minutes he is jogging down the Great Coastal Highway alongside his beloved Pacific Ocean. Running in the fog is his best therapy for the fog of his brain, trying to resolve what he cannot fathom during his dark dreams.

Walking up to his studio room after his morning ritual outing, he hears his MoxWrap sound. "Argh. Bus to the Angel's Rest nursing home will be here in fifteen. Pappy will be so disappointed if I'm late. And Dr. Beverly. I hope she liked the final edit of her book."

A quick shower and he pulls on jeans and a black t-shirt emblazoned with a yellow banana slug, mascot of his alma mater.

Looking out the bus window at his native California, Peter sees a land of cars, about sixteen million of them. People like Peter, who do not drive, who do not even have a driver's license, who are creative in finding public transportation options—they are reducing society's dependency on fossil fuels, the destructive addiction to gasoline that has governed global politics since the Second World War. As he rides the No. 397 bus from San Francisco to Daly City, he ponders. How many wars have been fought, in the name of God, in the name of democracy, in the name of whatever is painted to be "just," to ensure that the oil flows and is affordable? Peter wishes someone could change this.

He taps his MoxWrap to watch the MoxMedia morning news program. The world-renowned newscasters Rhonda and Sahir blare out the latest global events on this Friday morning. "Coming up on MoxWorld News AM: In Washington, the president defends the previous administration's America First policy as conflicts around the globe continue to escalate. The Great Depression of 2020 has left the country with such an unprecedented deficit that it can no longer afford to be the world's policeman.

"In the Middle East, the price of oil fell through its previous floor of twenty dollars per barrel as the Arabic Confederation last night launched an invasion into Iran, while they amass troops at the Turkish border near Kobanî. Recall that back in 2020, the catalyst for the creation of the Arabic Confederation and the New Kurdistan out of the former Syria and Iraq was the price of oil tumbling below twenty-five dollars per barrel, sending the region into chaos once again. In Moscow, the Russian president issued terse warnings of military reprisal for the downing of three more Russian fighters in Turkey's latest challenge to Russia's no-fly zone over New Kurdistan, the two-year-old union of the Kurds in former Iraq and Syria. In the South China Sea, warships from China, Japan, and the Philippines face off. In Europe, the Great Recession continues to take its toll as France and Germany retrench spending again for the rest of 2022, announcing their inability to fund NATO obligations. More after these messages."

Seeing Rhonda, with her salmon-colored blouse and lips tinted peach with lipstick from her signature makeup collection, now being advertised on his MoxWrap, makes Peter think of his sister's commentary on how the CEO of MoxWorld controls women through the fashions of his female newscasters.

Peter arrives at Angel's Rest, where Pappy has convalesced for the past four years. As the only grandson of Nikolas Gollinger, Peter carries a deep unspoken obligation, the only heir to the family mission his grandfather has passed along— their calling, their quest, their pursuit, their ancestral commitments.

Jenny at the front desk knows Peter very well, given how frequently he visits. Even the attending physicians do not come as often as Peter. "Good afternoon, Mr. Gollinger," says Jenny teasingly.

"Jenny, it's just Peter," he banters back playfully.

"Mr. Gollinger is finished with his breakfast and is expecting you…Peter, Mr. Peter. Oh yes, Dr. Fontaine is here today. She would like to talk with you. Could you stop by her office?"

With a smidgeon of concern, Peter asks, "Anything out of the ordinary, Jenny? Is he okay?"

"Oh, no worries about Mr. Gollinger. I think Dr. Fontaine is looking for another special favor from you," replies Jenny with an uncharacteristic schoolgirl-style giggle as she dials the intercom. "Dr. Fontaine, Peter Gollinger is here. Shall I send him down? Okay, he's coming down now."

With that, he is reassured and wanders down to the office that Dr. Fontaine uses when she is visiting patients at Angel's Rest. He sees her waiting in the hallway outside her office. She's more than an inch shorter than him, seeming even shorter as she wears sensible black shoes with the slightest of heels, which complement her brown hair, up in a tight professional bun. She wears a white physician's coat tailored for a woman, unlike the flat draping ones for men. The coat is open and Peter can see she wears a white cotton blouse and grey wool pencil skirt underneath. It does not escape Peter's attention that this is the first time he has seen her in a skirt, however businesslike, and not in dark slacks.

"Peter, please come in and sit down," says the doctor as she waves him in.

Out of habit, Peter goes to one of two chairs on the patient side of the doctor's desk. He looks at her business cards on the desk. Assistant Professor of Clinical Geriatric Psychiatry, UC San Francisco Medical School.

After hanging her white lab coat behind the door, which she closes, Dr. Fontaine opts to sit in the other patient chair, facing him with her legs crossed, top one pointing at Peter. "Once again, you are my hero. My savior. I finished reviewing all your changes and suggestions to my latest manuscript...our latest manuscript. You are simply a genius with ideas, thoughts, and words," Dr. Fontaine says.

"Dr. Fontaine, of course—you deserve the best a simple editor like me can offer."

"Peter, we're behind closed doors now. Remember, you can call me Beverly when I'm not on rounds or with patients," she replies with a smile. "You're a special person. And I mean not just your editorial skills, but your compassion. I've never seen anyone visit their dearest family member in a convalescent home more than you. I think your visits have helped prolong your grandfather's life, or at least improve the quality of it."

"How is he doing, Doctor...uh...Beverly?"

"Dr. Elfante, your grandfather's physician, mentioned to me on my last visit that your grandfather is doing well, considering the severity of his condition. Having been a smoker for most of his life has taken its toll on his lungs. He's a real fighter, though. He's determined to live for some greater purpose. Your visits are vital to his sense of purpose, Peter. You are his best therapy."

"Beverly, I cannot thank you enough for advocating that my grandfather not be given antipsychotics. That would be the end of him, at least his spirit. He really wants to be cognizant in his last days."

"Peter, I'll be candid. My colleagues and the nurses are afraid of his restless nights, his dreams, and how unsettled he is every morning. Dr. Elfante and I had a long discussion about the situation, and I convinced him, after much personal observation, that your grandfather is not endangering himself or other patients. He's not violent or clinically deranged. He's just very anxious about trying to grasp his dreams."

Beverly shifts in her chair, leans on her left elbow with her fingers to her lips. "That said, he seems to have confided in me more than he does in Dr. Elfante. These dreams seem to be an issue that he's been grappling with ever since early childhood. Smoking was one of the ways he had been coping with this disorder."

Beverly pauses, coyly smiles, and adds, "He's been very candid about how your grandmother had helped him cope. As he felt more comfortable talking with me, he described her administration of a special palliative care. He confessed that prolonged passionate interactions with his wife helped him more than the smoking. At first I dismissed his comments as reflective of male wish fulfillment typical in men of his generation."

A little flushed, Peter purses his lips, then asks, "How much has my grandfather talked about his dreams and what he's trying to solve?"

"Your grandfather's dreams are suggestive of a prior traumatic event, but his life history doesn't suggest he has directly experienced or witnessed such an event. His condition could perhaps be the subject of another paper. Carl Jung would have suggested that your grandfather's dreams are a sign of great personal transformation trying to emerge—his search for a greater context, one with a greater sense of purpose and destiny."

"Bev, I'm not making the link between what you're saying and my grandfather's affliction."

"The collective unconscious is part of our mind that is shared with other humans, common to all humankind, and stems from latent memories from our ancestral past. Perhaps in your grandfather's case, his dreams are trying to bring out some ancestral traumatic event."

With a smile she adds, "Freud, on the other hand, would call his dreams 'wish fulfillment.' There is a forbidden or repressed wish, which may be a result of guilt or taboos imposed by society or family. The dream is the way to transform that wish in a nonthreatening way. It's an attempt to resolve the repressed conflict."

Peter shifts in his chair as he reacts to the mention of conflict. He debates discussing the dream from last night that he can't seem to remember.

Peter is saved by the intercom buzzing. It's Jenny, who says, "Dr.

Fontaine, it's Mrs. Fitzgerald again. She's having a fit and the staff nurse is requesting that you come as soon as you can."

Beverly stands up to get her white coat from the door, pauses, and turns back to Peter. "I'll catch up with you in your grandfather's ward. We have to talk about the book that I'll need your editorial help with," she says before running down the hallway.

Walking down to his grandfather's unit, Peter reflects upon Beverly's propositions. Maybe his grandfather will have further wisdom on the subject, he muses as he enters his pappy's room. A single room, as the restlessness of his dreams has precluded his peaceful cohabitation with another elderly patient. His grandfather is slightly elevated in bed, with an oxygen mask over a nasal cannula, indicating he is under duress.

"Pappy, how are you today? Needing a little more oxygen this morning?"

Taking off his mask, Pappy, a bit short of breath, says, "Peter. My boy. A little late today, aren't we?"

"I was talking with Dr. Fontaine about a new project she's working on."

"Oh, the good doctor. Why can't I have her as my physician? She'd be so much better than that Dr. Elephant. She's so much more compassionate and understanding."

"So I gather, Pappy. You two have been spending some quality time together."

"I was simply trying to get her to understand how best to provide me comfort."

"So I've heard, Pappy. How was your night? Anything clearer?"

"The same. What I would give for a peaceful night. Peace. Even the partial peace your grandmother provided. It isn't so much to ask," Pappy groans. "As always, I awake knowing I dreamt something very important, but I cannot piece it together. Ninety-four years of this. Ninety-two, if you don't count the years I couldn't speak. And what about you? Can you remember anything?"

Scratching his head, Peter stares out the window. "The same agony of not being able to put my finger on that important something." He turns and shivers. "A darkness. An emptiness. A void. That is, except for a gun."

Pappy lurches up, very focused. "Peter, my boy, this is very important. Tell me more."

Peter moves closer to Pappy and helps him lean back to rest. "You know how it is. Everything is so fuzzy. I've never remembered anything from these nightly torments. But strangely, the past two mornings it's different. Maybe a gun, and a woman. Dark hair?"

"Yes. Yes! Gun and dark hair, Peter," Pappy gasps. He puts the oxygen mask back on. "I've waited. Thirty years. For you and me. To have the same dream. And you needed to save her."

Shaking his head, Peter stares down at his pappy's aged hands holding his mask on. "I'm afraid I can't save anyone. Even in my dreams."

"Everything has changed now that I know you and I have dreamed the same images," exclaims Pappy.

Peter pauses, processing that revelation. "Pappy, I was just down the hallway with Dr. Fontaine, discussing the psychology of dreams. But she explained things in such a simple way that I now understand how these theories might relate to our disorder. She says ours are anxiety dreams. That our minds are acting out some repression. Jung says it's a sign that we're trying to transform. We're driven by something repressed that happened to our prehistoric ancestors."

Peter stares at his grandfather. "What repressed conflict are we seeking to resolve? What transformation are we seeking?"

Pappy takes Peter's hand. "Peter, all we have is our family tradition to guide us. Please, repeat it for me. That is the so-called repressed conflict of Dr. Fontaine."

Peter gulps. Looking serious, he says, "The long-tailed star came from the sky, and our lands became ice, and winter became forever. Only the giants of the reindeer dominate. The bright star that never sets will be your guide. Watch for the long-tailed star."

"Good, my boy. The second part, now."

"And be wary of the giants, the Reindeer People, for when they arrive, you must flee and seek the mountains."

Pappy, assuming the patriarchal appearance that has commanded Peter's life, says, "The third part."

Nervous, Peter continues, "Follow the black object, for this will guide you as you search for your new life."

With deepening aggravation, Pappy gasps and admonishes Peter. "Boy, you must—you must not change anything. We have recited this from the beginning of our line. As far back as my great-grandfather, and he said as far back as his great-grandfather, we have passed down these oral traditions. We must preserve them." Pappy gasps again, and Peter helps put the mask on him.

From under the mask, Pappy mutters in slow, broken phrases, "Follow the vision. And words. Of the black object. For this will guide you. As you seek your new land." He stops and waits for the oxygen to rebuild in his blood, then nods for Peter to continue.

Peter mentally rehearses and finally recites, "Fourth part: Man and woman. Only as two together can you find peace. The object can save. You might see in sleep, might hear."

Pappy rests his head back and gasps. After several tense minutes, he removes the mask. "Peter, forgive an old man if he repeats himself every time you visit. But I find that if I don't keep repeating myself, at my age I will begin to forget. And my grandfather pounded into my head that we should never forget.

"He made me promise to find the meaning of this object, as I have made you and your father promise. He said what has happened in our past will guide us in what will happen to us now." He pauses to breathe. "And, my boy, you have been faithful to this quest.

"When I was a boy, we had only books to help us solve the mystery of this object," laments Pappy. "But that little Austrian burned the ones my father and I needed to find to continue our research, our study. It was my Austria too, and yet he burnt our books. How were we to find this object? What did we have to compromise for this quest? What line did my father cross to save us all?"

A very dark pause passes between them as the aged man runs his tongue along the inside of his mouth. "His death would be in vain if we could not make progress in finding the object. Our family name would be exonerated if you could find it, Peter."

Pappy pauses again, in deep reflection, with a look of regret mired in pain. "After the war, I met your mother's uncle, James, who was just like me. He suffered the dreams. The dreams that haunted both his parents' lineages as they did mine. And we searched together. But postwar Europe was a mess, Peter."

He stares out into the hall and spots Dr. Fontaine looking busy across the way with some charts. "And then your grandmother found me. She was a nurse. Part of an American relief program. She recognized the dreams. Her grandfather had them. And she knew what she needed to do to help me through the nights, through the next morning."

Pappy pauses. "Were you able to make any progress in your search last week, my boy?"

Peter grimaces. "I thought I had a lead, like so many I've had over the years. The professor I studied under at Santa Cruz, she has so many useful resources and contacts. When you're an editor, it's amazing the doors that open to those who want your services. Her latest contact had traced a possible pre-Neolithic site that might tell of where the object may lie—Tell Abu Hureyra, fifty miles east of Aleppo. The Gollinger luck strikes again. The site is thirty feet under Lake Assad. As if I could assemble an underwater excavation team. Besides, given what's happened today, with the Arabic Confederation staging an impending attack on Turkey from that area, I don't think I'm going to get anyone over there to help with recovering this source."

"Peter, keep trying. You are now our ancestors' only hope. I wish I could fund you. I spent our entire family fortune chasing the object. But I have taken both families' words and traditions and passed them to you. You have a more complete set than any of us ever had," Pappy concludes, taking Peter's hand again.

"I thought your father was going to solve the mystery. I was so proud of him when he was accepted into the archeology program at Cambridge. When he came back, I introduced him to your mother. I thought she knew what your father needed, just like your grandmother did."

Pappy pauses, taking a break for oxygen. "But she couldn't handle it anymore. Once you and your sister were in school, she told your father that he had a choice—her or the object. Your father stopped searching, stopped teaching you the traditions. It didn't make his pains any better. It just got worse. I didn't tell him he failed. I told him I failed him. And you."

"And Ma blames you for his death," Peter says with tears forming. "I loved Pa. I love Ma. I think I understand why it was so hard for her. Sarah said the same thing to me."

Pappy peers down at his hands. "I'm so sorry. She was a lovely girl. I thought you two would...I thought she was so much like your grandmother. Even better, as she shared your passion for history and discovery."

"Pappy. Sarah, Ciara, Tara—all of them keepers according to Ma's definitions. All of them left me because of my pursuit of this mysterious object. At this rate, you'll never have great-grandchildren for me to pass these traditions down to. My sister's like Ma. She doesn't want to learn them. Says it's just a man thing."

"My boy, we are close. Our dreams last night. Close. Close as they have ever been. It's time for you to be introduced to something. Your granduncle James wanted to pass a written document on to you, but your mother refused to give it to you for fear that you'd end up like your father. James and I agreed we would only show you when you found a good woman as your partner. I thought once you married Sarah..."

"Pappy, I'm trying my best to move on from Sarah. Evidently, I'm not the kind of man who could provide the protection, the security, a woman like her desires."

"That's what your father said. That is, until your grandmother had the good sense to introduce him to James's niece, your mother." Pappy coughs. "My boy, it is no secret that I am slowly dying. We cannot wait until you find that woman you are to meet. The dream we had must be the signal. Please, in that drawer, you'll find James's document."

Peter opens the drawer in the closet and finds a metal cylinder, like a mini thermos, with air lock seals. He opens it to find a small scroll. Animal skin parchment, with drawings looking like Hs. These progress to two abstract figures with their hands in front of them, forming an H. Alongside the H, another tall male figure with a long face, long ears, and large dark eyes points to a long-tailed star. Alongside this man, a smaller female points to an oblong shape under a series of dots. A third female figure has one hand pointing at the series of dots and the other at an angle of sixty degrees. Adjacent to the figures is an area with some sort of characters.

"What is this, Pappy? How old is it? What is this part, writing?"

"What you're holding is faith. My faith. Now our faith. When James showed me this parchment, my faith was renewed. It's a dialect of Akkadian cuneiform. Right after the war, carbon dating was just being introduced to the archeological community. Through my war buddies, we got a sample of this tested." Pappy pauses to catch his breath. "It's four thousand years old. Four thousand."

Stunned, Peter sits on the side of the bed. He stares at the parchment and his mind races with the possibilities. He takes several snapshots with his MoxWrap and turns towards Pappy, asking, "Do you believe in God?"

Looking down with a dour expression, Pappy responds, "My boy, with what I saw—with all that happened—there could not be a God." He pauses and sighs. "At least, not one who loves us."

"Hence why Ma wanted to distance herself from you," Peter laments. "She so wanted me to believe, to have faith. To have faith in her God. But your faith, this animal skin in my hands, is my faith too. These are aliens, Pappy. These are aliens who met the Akkadians in 2000 BCE."

Pappy holds his hand out so that Peter can hand him the parchment. He turns it upside down and sideways and says, "It could be Akkadian Halloween. It could be aliens. It could be God's angels." He gives the parchment back to Peter.

"Your father was working on translating the cuneiform. It's an old form and a rare dialect from the northernmost reaches of the empire. He became lost in dozens of interpretations when your mother forced him to stop. It's now up to you, Peter. In this digital age, in a world that is interconnected, maybe it's you who will find the answer."

"Mr. Gollinger, how are we doing today?" says Dr. Fontaine as she enters the room. "Did Peter tell you? He's offering to work with me on a new book on religion and the psychobiology of the soul. With what you've passed along to him, his talents will be especially invaluable to me."

Pappy glances at Peter and gives a thumbs-up. "Go for it, my boy. She's a keeper, this doctor."

And the nonagenarian Gollinger takes the doctor's hand so he can rub her palm. "And, Doctor, could you do me a favor and take my grandson home with you tonight? He's behind on his ancient obligation to make more Gollingers who can continue our search for our precious object."

Beet-faced, Peter just wants to crawl under a bed somewhere and hide. But the good doctor turns and takes his hand into hers and says, "I have to say, with your grandson's killer dimples, his eyes that emote an adorable innocence, he is handsome. But if I married him, I would lose my best editor." She winks at Peter and says, "We couldn't do that, now could we?"

She then spies the parchment in between hers and Peter's hands and says, "May I?"

She gently examines the antique animal skin, carefully scanning both sides, then looks at Peter and says, "I have to wonder if this is related to your grandfather's dreams. I would love to learn more. But I have to get back to Mrs. Fitzgerald and adjust her medications again." She leaves, writing notes down on her clipboard.

"Pappy, exactly what did you tell her about Grandma? From Beverly's, I mean Dr. Fontaine's recounting, she thinks sex is the treatment protocol for your condition," Peter jests.

"My boy, I've surmised that you've already found out that sex helps. It calms your nerves so you can grapple with what the dreams, and your inability to remember the dreams, do to you."

Shaking his head, Peter exclaims, "Ma says you told her she had to have sex with Pa every night, in the middle of the night. She thought you were just passing along ancient male power plays over women, so she resisted your ideas. Dr. Fontaine more politely said this is another case of male wish fulfillment. I can't believe sex is the only solution to our problems."

Pappy shakes his head too. "Peter, do not mistake my words. I should have said passionate bonding, not necessarily sexual bonding or, more crudely, physical penetration." Pappy pauses for oxygen. "The touch of passion creates bonds between you and your mate. Bonds that create dialogue. Bonds that will help the two of you decode the dreams. You need to talk about what you're coping with in order to make any progress in understanding what is happening."

Pappy stops to catch his breath, and then he says in a fatherly way, "I think you need—the tradition requires that you are paired with a woman. A good woman to find the answer to our traditions. The answer to that scroll."

A frown passes over Peter's face as he ponders his failings with Sarah. "How do I know what makes a woman 'good' according to your definition?"

His grandfather closes his eyes, and a warm smile lifts his mouth. "You will know, my boy. You will know first from her touch, her smell, her voice and the sounds of her heart. And only then can you know her with your eyes."

Closing his eyes too, Peter tries to remember Sarah's touch, her smell, but he can only remember the shame, the failure of discovering her in their bed with that alpha male muscleman. Everything he is not. And that deep pain wells up, and water seeps from the corners of his closed eyes.

"My boy, are you all right? Did you have one of those damn flashbacks?" asks Pappy.

"I'm sorry, Pappy. I just had one of those moments. I'm okay."

Pappy stares somberly down at his hands. "I've had those moments for near eight decades now only to have failed my father. Peter, please don't let me fail you as well. Please."

Scrolling his MoxMail to find that message, *the* message, Peter says, "Pappy, I have the solution. I'll apply for the junior editor position with MoxMedia in their Middle East correspondence unit. I'll have access to all of MoxMedia's resources to find the object. I've been sitting on this invitation to apply for a couple of days, wondering whether I have what it takes. I won't fail you, Pappy. I'll make sure I have what it takes."

CHAPTER 2

*I talk all night long with a dream image. About the tales
of my pain; Thus my sleeplessness comes from these tales.*
—Amir Khusraw,
thirteenth-century Sufi mystic and poet

9620 BCE
Northern shores of the Black Sea

The woods. The low-hanging fog. Or to these three hunters, the low-hanging cloud that makes finding their prey that much more difficult. In the fog, they effectively only have ears to listen for their prey. In contrast, their prey has eyes, ears, noses, and animal ESP, which pierce through the fog, and so do those who hunt them.

It is Orzu's birthday. Born on the seventh day of the sixth moon, he has seen seventeen cycles of the sun. In a few more sun cycles, it will be time for him to find a wife. His grandfather, Parcza, has taken him and his sister Illyana into the woods so Orzu can master the art of providing meat for his family. Parcza doubts whether Orzu will ever become a good provider for a new family, for Orzu has yet to kill during the hunt, any hunt.

Illyana, on the other hand, is a natural-born hunter. But Parcza knows that the young men of the village will not be selecting Illyana based on her hunting skills, for she has become a very fetching young woman, at fifteen cycles of the sun. Two sun cycles ago, her breast buds began to blossom and she begrudgingly had to alter her clothing to accommodate these changes, asking why she needed to dress differently than Orzu.

Orzu has taken point, softly and slowly moving forward in the dense undergrowth of the forest. They have gone farther north than normal as the lands near their village seem depleted of game. He peers back at Parcza to see if he is doing well in his grandfather's eyes. Parcza has been a surrogate father for Orzu and his sister. Six sun cycles ago, the Reindeer People, the giants of the north, took their father as a slave; they took their mother and their grandmother too for unspeakable reasons. Thus, Parcza has done his best to mother them as well as father them.

A shuffle of a leaf, and Orzu stops, holding his hand up. He lifts his bow and draws the arrow shaft back, just as Parcza coached him this morning. His arrow has a normal stone head for smaller game. He and his sister have a few special arrows for larger game, with a very shiny black stone that is extra hard and sharp. Parcza found these on the Reindeer People's arrows and spears after they massacred a nearby village, and he kept a collection for their use. Parcza is holding a spear in case they are the hunted, as these woods have two types of animals—the ones much smaller than they, which can be killed by arrows, and the ones larger and sometimes hungrier than they, which may or may not be deterred by their spears.

Orzu scours the forest for the source of the sound, and he sighs in relief. It's a rabbit. Unlikely to jump at them and rip their limbs off. He aims along the arrow shaft as he watches the rabbit nibble some leaves and wiggle its nose. Orzu finds it cute. He'd rather have it around the house than dead. *I cannot kill this animal*, he thinks. *It is not right.*

Whoosh. His trance is broken as Illyana's arrow splits apart the head holding the cute wiggling nose.

"Orzu, what were you waiting for?" Illyana admonishes as she goes to retrieve the carcass, which is convulsing as if the head were still attached. "What were you thinking of? Inviting the rabbit home to dinner?" Parcza glances at Orzu, shakes his head, and goes over to Illyana, congratulating her on her fine kill.

As Orzu leans down to look at the animal oozing blood, Parcza begins his next lecture, one especially for Orzu. "Your ability to kill with one shot is vital to your survival, and the survival of your family. Not only do we need to eat meat many times each moon cycle to be strong, we need to be ready to defend against attacks, by animals and by the giant Reindeer People."

Orzu and Illyana have only seen the Reindeer warriors once—the night when they raided their old village several sun cycles ago. Parcza came to their house to hide them and their mother while their father joined the other men of the village to fight them. Orzu remembers seeing the Reindeer warriors lift two men of the village at a time and throw them a distance further than ten strides. They towered over the tallest of the villagers by nearly three heads and could lift boulders seemingly with ease.

Orzu held his dear Illyana tightly and covered her eyes as they hid in a secret compartment and watched the Reindeer warrior search the rest of their house. As the Reindeer warriors assembled their new slaves, Orzu's mother, Thara, gasped, seeing her husband terribly wounded, captured as a slave. Overwhelmed by her sense of love, she abandoned their hiding place to go to her husband's aid and was grabbed by a warrior and defiled in front of her hapless husband.

Parcza escaped with the two children out the back way into the woods, knowing the warriors would come back to search their house again. Illyana saw more, much more, than Parcza had wanted her to. But she was strong. She told Parcza that she wanted to learn to hunt, learn to kill, so she would never have to hide again. And so Illyana came with Orzu on this hunt, and every hunt.

"Orzu, your sister asked the right question. What were you thinking?" Parcza asks in utter dismay. "You had a clean shot. Your draw was perfect, as was your aim."

Looking at the ground, Orzu meekly replies, "Parcza, isn't it true that the Reindeer Giants kill indiscriminately? They kill animals not only for food, but for their pleasure, just like they kill their slaves when they are no longer useful. I heard they drink their blood and eat parts of their body."

Parcza nods. Illyana purses her lips in disgust at the thought.

"Thus, Parcza, if I kill for my training, am I not like them? What separates me from them? Killing is not good," says Orzu.

With anger in his eyes over Orzu's dangerous logic, Parcza gives a stern recounting of the ills that the Reindeer People bring. "Orzu, do you love your sister?"

"Yes, of course," Orzu replies, putting his hand on her head, "I love her with all my heart."

"Orzu, you love my rabbit in a kettle more than me as you can't kill one yourself," a smiling Illyana rebuts.

With the most serious face, Parcza reminds him, "Orzu, if taken, you will work to your death lifting stones that weigh more than an entire village to make their pyramids. I have not taken you there to see these giant structures, which stand more than twenty men tall, as the horror of our men dying on their feet is too much for even me to bear. Mark my words, Orzu, the horror of what they would do to Illyana is far, far worse."

Illyana peers at Orzu with distress. Even though she had only nine sun cycles of age that tragic day, she has nightmares of her mother's screams at the unforgiving hands of the Reindeer warriors.

"Orzu, you may not want to kill to save your own life. But maybe you'll need to kill to save your sister's, if you love her." Parcza pauses, then adds ominously, "Be clear on what would happen to her if she were caught. They do not care how young she is. Orzu, listen to me. They will make your sister dress in ways that are meant to incite lust. They will teach her to paint her lips and tint her eyelids. They will teach her how to make potions for lust and delirium. With what she will be forced to do, she will long for someone to kill her. Orzu, you would kill to save your sister from such a fate. You would and you must, just as she would do for you if you were to be enslaved."

Parcza pauses, his eyes growing moist. "They took your grandmother too," he says with a crackle in his voice. "I tried to follow her as they took her to their pyramids. I heard her crying in the night as they hurt her, but I couldn't free her. I was tormented for numerous sun cycles, until I got enough villagers to come with me to rescue our women."

He pauses to collect his thoughts. "Finally I saw her. With her lips painted and eyelids colored, clothed in ways against her raising. Holding her hands were the children she bore for her tormentors. The oldest was on his way to being a giant, already your height, Orzu, in only a few cycles. I will never forget his face. Like his mother's, but so long and distorted."

He wipes away the tears forming in his eyes. "Then she saw me. She said to go. I should have killed her before, but now it was too late."

Parcza stops again as he sees his grandchildren are stricken.

Illyana has hidden her face in her hands, which are covered in rabbit blood. With the red staining her cheeks, she cries at Orzu, "You must kill. If you can't kill the bastards, then you must promise me that you will kill me before they do to me what they did to Mother." She glares at Orzu. "Promise me that." Orzu nods and hugs Illyana.

Taking a deep breath to inspire her inner courage, she takes out the three arrows, their points made of extra-sharp hardened black stone, from her quiver and holds them out to Orzu. "Big brother, rest assured, I am not solely dependent on you to save me. I can shoot three of these deep in the chest of any Reindeer man in less than the count of three. Unlike you, I have learned from Parcza how to be a warrior. I will not be taken."

Parcza changes the topic. "Orzu, it's time to recite the tradition. As my grandfather has passed to me, as his grandfather passed to him, I pass to you. So start."

Orzu is caught off guard and stutters, "Tens and tens of cycles ago, the long-tailed star came and our lands became cold and winter came. The giant reindeer dominated…"

Orzu stops as Parcza slaps the back of his head. "You must memorize it word for word. If you change it, your children will change it. And their children will get the wrong message. Their survival depends on it. The children of the children of your grandchildren—their lives depend on your knowing each word precisely."

Illyana pipes up, reciting the tradition in just a few breaths. "Tens upon tens upon tens of cycles of the stars ago, the long-tailed star came from the sky and our lands became ice, and winter became forever. Only the giants of the reindeer prospered, because of the power from this star. Thus, the forefathers of our forefathers' forefathers moved away from the land of the ice. We prosper as we move farther away each generation. Keep looking for lands rich in animals to hunt, water to fish, grass to harvest, and settle there. Make alliances with neighbors for safety. And be wary of the giant Reindeer People; when they arrive, move away from the direction of ice to seek safety. The bright star, the tail of the bird, will be your guide. Watch for the long-tailed star, which came from the direction of the bird. For when it returns, lands will again become winter, and the lands and animals and even man will change again."

She sticks her tongue out at Orzu and then recites it backwards: "Again change will man even and animals and lands the and winter become again will lands, returns it when for." She grins.

Parcza pats Illyana's head in approval and says, "Orzu, that's another reason why you need to keep your sister safe. For only she will be able to teach your children the tradition."

Observant of Orzu's gaze at the loose leaves lining the forest floor, Illyana gives him a little hug. "Don't worry. You will find a woman like Mother. I know all the young girls of the village. I'll find you a good woman. I'll even tell her what a great provider you will be. But that means you need to improve your hunting game, big brother."

Their grandfather smiles at the exchange, then stares towards their home many days' hike away. "Up until your time, our family has survived for generations because we follow this tradition. Now we have our backs to the vast lake and things have changed. But you must understand these traditions—act on them, or pass them to your children so they can act on them."

Lost between jealousy of his sister's keenness with words and weapons and his poor comprehension of the oral tradition, Orzu asks, "But what do these words really mean, Parcza?"

"The Reindeer People came into the lands after the long-tailed star came. For cycles and cycles, they expanded their lands and their numbers by taking from our kind and breeding with our women. Their women are barren, so they need ours. Even their daughters born by our women are mostly barren, so they need to steal our women constantly to reproduce. This is why they have so little regard for females, as they are just objects, mere breeding vessels to them, and why we should fear them so. They worship the sky where the long-tailed star came from. It is said they gained their size and their power when the star landed out of the heavens. Our family has survived up until now as we have always moved away from the Reindeer People. That star we see at night, the tail of the bird in the milky streak, it is our reference point of where we need to move away from. Do you understand?"

Orzu and Illyana nod.

Minutes later, evening starts to come and the stars emerge through the dissipating fog. Parcza points up to the sky and shows them the three brightest stars in the milkiest, cloudiest part of the night. "See the bird? The star at its tail? Always remember this star, and when you're in danger, move away from it. Tell your children to watch it each night and flee if the star with the long tail returns, for the Reindeer People were born of that star. The next may bring worse to our kind.

"After the raid that led to the death of your parents, we fled from the tail of the bird, and we moved our house near the vast lake—the lake that we cannot see across. The surviving villagers followed us, as they have no traditions. We are now cornered if the Reindeer People move in this direction. If we need to move again, then you or your children or your children's children will need to cross the lake. I know not what is there. But you must find out what is on the other side, prepare your family for the journey, and remember to find the tail of the bird and move in the other direction."

Parcza moves to give them a hug when the bushes rumble. A boar taller than Illyana leaps at them, knocking Parcza down as he brings his spear around defensively. Orzu instinctively pushes Illyana back behind him and stabs his spear at the boar repeatedly, at the neck and then the chest. He checks to see that Illyana is okay, then goes to Parcza, who is bleeding from a shallow thigh wound.

Illyana rips some of her clothing, exposing her legs, to make a bandage to tie around Parcza's wound. They help Parcza stand, and they all look at the boar, writhing in pain as it dies in front of them. Illyana stares at Orzu and says, "So you cannot shoot a little rabbit, but you can maim a monster boar." She hugs her big brother with renewed respect.

Orzu makes a cane for Parcza to use while Illyana carves up portions of the boar to take back to the village. Parcza puts his arm around Orzu for support and pats his head. "So, you will make a good provider for your family after all."

The three of them look for a place to make camp for the night, with Parcza using both his cane and his spear to steady his walk. In the camp, Illyana smokes the boar meat in preparation for the several days of travel ahead. The next day, they break camp at dawn and head through the forests, back to the village. Orzu is at point with his spear, with renewed confidence after his boar kill. Illyana helps Parcza navigate the debris of the forest floor.

Then the bushes rumble again. Orzu, with spear ready, scans for the next boar. But this time it is no boar. He stands four heads higher than Orzu, with massive pectoral muscles and sculpted abdominals showing through the open-hooded feathered cape he wears. Underneath a large bird's-head headdress, his face is long, his ears are long, and his eyes are dark and piercing as he looks at Illyana and her exposed legs.

Parcza rushes forward with his spear but irrationally stops short of spearing this Reindeer warrior, as he recognizes the face. The face of his wife. He cannot kill his wife's son.

And with that momentary delay, the fraction of a second of hesitation, the massive warrior rips the spear from Parcza's hands and tosses it to the ground. "I am the great Tureal, grandson of the King Anneal, great-great-grandson of those who are descendant from the stars."

He surveys the three and recognizes Parcza's face. "You. I remember you. My mother fled from you to seek the joy of my father's loins. She screamed in pleasure and pain, as only a real warrior like him could have so pleased her." He hits Parcza in the groin with the butt of his spear, sending him to the ground howling in pain.

Whoosh, whoosh, whoosh. Illyana plants three of her black-tipped arrows deep into Tureal's perfect left pec. She smiles, as she has exacted revenge for her mother and grandmother.

Much to her shock, Tureal lunges at her, ripping the arrows from his chest, and grabs her by the waist, turning her upside down. He rips her already-shredded lower garments off and examines her, as Illyana screams in pain. "Good, you are a virgin. My finest warriors will fight over you, and you will become the prize for the strongest of—"

He is interrupted by Illyana's screams. "Kill him. Kill him. Like you did the boar. Don't let him take me."

With haste, Orzu interrupts Tureal's attempt to possess his sister as he thrusts his black-tipped spear at Tureal's neck. Thrust after thrust is glanced to the side as if Tureal were swatting flies. Tiring of the game, Tureal rips the spear from Orzu's hands, turns it around, and spears Parcza in the gut. Tureal turns to leave with the struggling Illyana, who has begun to recognize the futility of her situation.

And so she decisively screams to her brother, "Kill me. Kill me. Kill me now. Don't let them do to me what they did to Mother."

Orzu has drawn his bow with a black-tipped arrow. It will slice so clean and fast, maybe she won't feel it, Orzu hopes. Tureal has torn her upper garment open so that her breasts are exposed. And Orzu has a clear aim at her heart. Just let those fingers loose and it will be a clean kill.

But he hesitates. As Illyana hysterically screams to kill her, Orzu's mind races. *I can do this. I can do this. I can... No, I cannot. I cannot kill. It is not right. What do I do?* And time slows to a crawl.

Illyana cries, "Orzu, you promised to kill me. I'm not the rabbit. I'm your sister. If you love me, if you truly love me, kill me now."

Orzu stares down the arrow at his sister's heart between her breasts. And he searches inside for a voice, the voice that will tell him what he should do. What is right? As Illyana continues to scream and cry, inside him it is only silent, empty, and dark.

CHAPTER 3

A country can't be free unless the women are free.

—Abdullah Öcalan,
imprisoned leader of the PKK,
recognized as a terrorist organization by the US,
NATO, and the EU.

Mountains outside Siirt, Turkey
12:40 p.m. GMT–8, April 28, 2022

"He didn't die in vain, Zara."

Two dark-haired women stand high, overlooking a green valley, beyond which there is another mountain, and another behind that. These are the northernmost peaks of the Zagros Fold, a 1500-kilometer creation of the Arabic tectonic plate smashing into the Eurasian plate twenty million years ago. They form a crown around the lands known today as the Fertile Crescent, extending from southern Turkey through northern Iraq, along the border with Iran and down to the Red Sea.

But for these two women, the only importance of these mountains is the safe haven they have provided for the people known as Kurds, who have found shelter and safety in these alpines for thousands upon thousands of years. Who until two years ago were the largest ethnic group in the world without a country.

The taller of the two women wears a grey outer gown over a full-length purple dress, black belt, sandals, and headscarf, the latter decorated with colorful embroidered flowers and carefully wrapped around her oval face, tucking away her shoulder-length dark brown hair. On her wrist is a simple wind-up watch. Her almond-shaped dark eyes are fixed on the horizon, where she still sees the village.

"Didn't he? Die in vain?" replies Zara. "I told my little brother not to join the PKK. We needed him at home. He was the last man left in my family. And now, there is only me, my mother, my grandmother and, thank Xwedê, still my great-grandmother."

Putting her hand around Zara to comfort her is Peri, who in contrast wears a formfitting red cotton top covered by a loose beige sweater, black cotton capri pants, and tan sandals with sequins matching the ones on her sweater. Her black hair is pulled into a ponytail, with two stylish twists on each side of her face. And on her wrist, at the adamant request of her friend, nothing. No MoxWorld devices at all.

"He died while trying to get the women and children of that village, the one you imagine seeing on the horizon, up into the mountains as government troops searched for the PKK," Peri states calmly. "He died a hero."

"And what good are heroes?" Zara laments. "Especially when they are dead."

Zara walks along the mountainside through the lush green vegetation of spring. Patches of red, purple, blue, and yellow flowers litter the landscape. She bends over to pick a number of red ones.

"My mother lined his room with poppies of this color after his death five years ago. The color of the blood shed by the men of our family."

Following her best friend as she walks, as she always has, Peri asks, "Then why did you insist we meet here, if his memory brings back such pain?"

"Because you want me to help the Anatolian Kurdish separatists. There is a price one pays. My little brother did," the taller woman replies, her long earlobes peeking out from her headscarf in the gust of wind. "I don't agree with separatism. I believe we should work out a peaceful solution. One that would better the lives of Kurdish women. Equality for all as we saw in Rojava.

'wives.' As your commanding officer, I couldn't let them take you."

"As my friend, you couldn't," Peri replies as she punches her friend's left shoulder. "Does it still hurt where you took the bullet instead of me?"

Zara pretends to wince and smiles as she replies, "Well, you did the same for me."

"Yeah, but that one missed me as I shoved you aside." Peri punches Zara again in the same spot. "That's why I followed you into your YPJ unit. We were there to save the Rojovan Kurds in Syria, like we did the Bashur Kurds back home in Iraq. And now, after the non-Kurdish Syrian and Iraqi factions united to form the AC, the Arabic Confederation, the Kurds finally have won their nation. At least the Syrian and Iraqi Kurds."

Stopping to gaze upon the horizon again, but this time looking southeast, Zara says, "I miss my mountains back in Duhok Province."

"Well, I miss my mountains east of Hewler. And they are prettier than the ones in Duhok."

And that is what best friends are for. Getting you to smile when you talk yourself into a slump. And Zara smiles. "Don't tell me about pretty and Hewler. I had a bad dress day there when I was a teen." She pulls her scarf tight around her head again. "My grandmother made sure I was appropriately corrected." She laughs.

With a sly look on her face, Peri says, "If you help the nearly fifteen million Kurds here in Turkey, they can unite with the other Kurds, including our friends in Duhok and Hewler, in the New Kurdistan. One nation of twenty-three million who can freely speak, teach, and practice their Kurdish traditions without prosecution."

She turns Zara to face her, and with a very somber expression she states, "But that can only happen if you talk with the big man. What do you call him? Sasha?"

Eyes closed, a big sigh, and a series of little breaths. She reflects upon the plight of her people. Hundreds of years of oppression, torture, and institutional violation of women. Her family, her friends, herself included. Finally, Zara replies, "It's been nearly four years. He knows I want nothing to do with him."

"He wants to talk with you. He'll get the Russians to back the Anatolian Kurds. Come on, the Chinese backed the moderate factions in old Syria and Iraq, which led to the formation of the Arabic Confederation. Rumor is, after the Americans backed out, your Sasha got his Russian buddies to back the Kurds in Syria and Iraq, which allowed them to form New Kurdistan. With your word in his ear, he'll do it again for the Kurds here in Turkey."

The proverbial lightbulb goes off, and Zara squints and peers into her eyes. She opens up Peri's loose sweater to get a better look at the tight fit of her red cotton top. And she sighs again.

"You saw him, didn't you? What did he ask you to do? You didn't, did you?"

"What do you mean?" Peri gasps, closing her sweater around her bust. "He was a gentleman. A little lecherous in the way he looks you over...and where he put his hands when he said goodbye." She pauses. "Come to think of it, maybe he was not such a gentleman."

"Peri, don't be naïve," yells Zara. "Monstrous men like him have only two purposes for women. And if you're lucky, you're only a sexual object to him. I wasn't so lucky."

Silence again. Zara takes Peri's hand. "If you promise me you will never meet with him again, I will consult for those who wish to form the Anatolian Kurdish State. Stay away from Sasha."

Arms folded, covering her bust, Peri pleads, "With the AC forces threatening Turkey's border this morning, the time is perfect for the Kurds in this region to declare independence. The Turkish army will be split between chasing us and defending the southern flank."

Clasping Zara's hands in hers, Peri adds, "You know full well without the advanced weaponry from MoxWorld Defense Industries and the Russians, the Anatolian Kurds will be crushed within months of their declaration of independence. The slaughter will be worse than Kobanî in every one of our cities. Remember what Saddam did to our families, our villages? Was that all in vain, what we fought for?"

Zara looks afar. Adjusts her scarf again. Drapes her grey outer gown tightly around her body. "It's one thing to have your body taken away from you to do with what they wish. It's another when they own your soul. I have taken both back. I live in complete submission to Xwedê and only serve Him now."

"And Xwedê will watch the Kurds be slaughtered once again," Peri insists as she pushes Zara's headscarf off her head. "Unless Xwedê offers better military technology than your Sasha, Mr. Alexander Murometz, all the mothers of this region will be putting poppies on the graves of their sons, their husbands, their uncles, and now, their daughters."

Her piercing eyes darken, like the grey clouds above that blot out the sun. The grounds go dark. The winds pick up. Silence as the two women stare at each other, neither one willing to give ground as the winds swirls around them, lifting the edges of Zara's scarf into the air.

With pure black circles for eyes, Zara pulls the black cloth back around her head and asserts, "Tell the regional commander of your new Anatolian Kurdish State to give this message to Mr. Murometz. If the great giant will not protect them, I will hunt him down and shoot him." She pokes Peri's forehead with her index finger. "In the head. One shot. In those words, exactly. Sasha will recognize those as my words."

And Peri pokes Zara back in the forehead several times and then laughs. "You need to lighten up. You promised you would shop with me for our jelli eidi, our end of Ramadan dresses." She pulls open her sweater, tugs on her red cotton top, accentuating her form, and gives a salacious smile. "And you are going to get something that will make men's tongues drop out this year, yes? You know we are not getting any younger. Two unmarried women in their midthirties. What's our chance of finding a good man to share the better part of our lives with?"

"None," Zara affirms as she looks at Peri's feet, then at hers. Peri now has soft feet with pedicured nails and gloss. Hers? Weathered skin, natural nails. And scars. The worst on the bottom. It took her months to learn to walk again with only a slight hint of what had happened. But it took her years to cover the scars within her.

"Since when did you do that to your feet?" asks a worried Zara. "What happened with you and that giant man?"

"He had me meet Rhonda, who gave me a fashion makeover," says Peri, pointing to the gloss on her lips. "I can do the same for you when we get our drop-dead gorgeous holiday dresses."

Zara's alarm goes off. One p.m. "Time for Dhuhr prayer. Will you join me?"

"You know I am not as devout as you," Peri states as she looks at the rough rocky ground. "Although there's that time you asked the whole unit to pray before the assault on Tell Abyad. We didn't lose anyone through the whole campaign. Maybe your prayers saved them."

As she looks for a mat of grass to pad her knees, Zara replies, "I only wanted the more religious members of our unit to understand that when we liberated the women in the Daesh-held villages, when we abolished the parts of the Sharia law that oppressed women, we were not acting against Xwedê or the words of the Prophet."

"That's why I followed you and still do. You made tangible, made real for our soldiers the teachings we learned in our Peshmerga training. Were we not told that a country cannot be free unless the women are free? Under Kurdish rule, women have equal say in political rule."

Watching Zara as she searches for a soft place she can pray, Peri taps her on the head to get her full attention. "Remember our Peshmerga training about Jineology? 'Without the freedom of women within society and without a real consciousness surrounding women, no society can call itself free.' You made us recite this each morning. You made that idea come alive in your unit."

A stretch of arms upwards, a gaze up into the sky, and Zara finally replies, "And the other principle I asked everyone to recite. 'Woman's true freedom is only possible if the enslaving emotions, needs and desires of husband, father, lover, brother, friend and son can all be removed. The deepest love constitutes the most dangerous bonds of ownership.'"

She shakes her head and laments, "And what has that done for us? Forty percent of Kurdish women in Anatolia still cannot read. I tell you the solution is not political, not religious, certainly not military technology, but simple economics. History is all about the power of economics. Our people have been suppressed due to economics. The lands we grew up in are rich in resources others want. Economics aside, most of our unit joined to escape the patriarchal traditions of rural Kurdistan."

Nodding her head in agreement, Peri affirms, "Firya escaped an arranged marriage, Beri and Rana evaded honor killings. Me, I ran from my abusive husband who was thirty years older than me. Being sold at thirteen for a dowry and a box of gold is not an honor."

She stops, peering deep into her friend's eyes. "And you, Zara. What were you running from?"

Alone higher up the mountain, Zara seeks respite from that question. She is still running.

She misses her mountains in Duhok Province, formerly northern Iraq, now part of the country of New Kurdistan. Who is she fooling? She misses her walks in her mountains with her father. Who is she fooling again? She misses her father. Peace for her was found in those mountains, walking hand in hand with her father.

"Why did he have to kill himself? He had peace with me," said little Zara, the girl deep inside big Zara, a memory she fights so hard to repress.

She cannot fault Peri for asking. As her second-in-command, Peri always asked the right questions, and on her watch, they brought the unit through the war with only a few wounds. Including hers.

Atop the mountain, she finds a modicum of solace in the high air, the blue sky, the early moon rising on the horizon. The purest silence. The essence of her inner peace.

Mehhhhh. Mehhhhh.

She scans around for the impolite intruder upon her peace.

Mehhhhh. Mehhhhh.

And she finally sees them. Two newborn lambs, near a crushed crate down near a ravine. A few minutes down a treacherous rocky precipice, she sees their problem. Their mother recently died in the crate. Their sibling also died, likely shortly after birth. She sits down near the precious babies. A black one, a white one. They come to her, and she takes them into her lap, warming them with her body heat. It does not take much more than a minute before they have decisively adopted her. Maryam, Zara's mother, will be very pleased, for Zara is now a mother.

Licks to her face, nature's biology, genetic destiny come forth as her warrior façade subsides, leaving but a warmth and a glow. And their eyes. Those of utter innocence. After what seems like hours, the mountain girl in her recognizes she needs to head home before nightfall enwraps the high terrain. Looking at the climb needed to get out of the ravine, she sees that her two little ones cannot make it out without her help. What can she do? She needs both hands to climb. And there are two. She removes her scarf, which forms a makeshift baby carrier on her back. The lucky lambs are not only adorable, but little enough to fit.

Atop the mountain again under blue skies, she looks at them more closely. Two little girls. If they were older, she would make them walk all the way home, like her father did to her. But getting home by Asr prayer takes priority. And she double-times it down the mountain as only a girl who grew up in the Kurdish alpines could.

As she gets to the edge of her great-grandmother's home village, she puts her new baby girls on the ground so they can learn to walk with her. She gives them their first motherly lesson. "Don't go chasing after the first boy lamb that wags his you-know-what at you. He'll make promises that fill your heart and soul. But they're only promises. And promises are only there to be broken. Like your heart. And if you are lucky, only your heart."

On the way back through the village, they come upon a house with a woman crying hysterically outside the entry steps. A little older than Zara, Kilda, once a girl who Zara's grandmother babysat, points into the house, screaming away in machine-gun Kurdish. Kilda's daughter, Waja, thirteen years old, had been betrothed to a man twenty-five years older. Kilda explains, "Waja escaped from her tormentor, the man who paid her father for her body as his third wife. And this man wants his property back."

Zara reflects. Waja is about the same age as her aunt Leyla and Peri when they were essentially sold off by their families. None of these marriages worked, and the poor girls were left suffering and traumatized by their supposed husbands.

Screams of a young woman come from within the house. The kinds of screams Zara knows all too well.

Zara's eyes darken. Piercing black. She turns to Kilda and hands her her new furry daughters. Now with two lambs in her care, Kilda quivers at the sight of Zara's burning eyes. Even fiercer than those of the incensed brute inside, who is physically beating a lesson into her daughter for fleeing their lawful marriage.

Before the crying woman can stop her, Zara rushes into the house. Crashes and thuds precede a bloodcurdling scream, and running out of the house comes a man in his forties, with a purple eye and a bloodied nose. He turns and yells Kurdish obscenities back into the house, which results in Zara throwing his pants onto his head. As Zara comes out of the house, he goes running.

Zara comes back out and sits on the doorstep with Kilda. Her knuckles bloodied, she winces as she holds her right pinky, which hurts like it might be broken. She says to a bewildered Kilda, "You should tend to Waja. She needs her mother at this moment."

She holds her little lambs to her rapidly pulsing chest, careful not to get her blood on them. "You are fortunate. You are born with innocence and submission to Xwedê. Do not stray."

CHAPTER 4

Start by doing what's necessary; then do what's possible;
and suddenly you are doing the impossible.

—Saint John Paul the Great

Parkside, San Francisco, California
7:10 a.m. GMT–8, May 4, 2022

The fog blankets the house where Peter oversleeps his 6 a.m. alarm. Cold, damp, opaque, and yet ethereal in how the real and the imagined mingle in its mists. But for Peter, his fog, real or imagined, is not one of love, but that of the cursed.

In the emptiness within his soul, he cries, "Please help me. What do I do?"

And the man who can pull together others' words so they sing cannot even find the words to cry out his angst as he rolls through the twists and turns of sheets and blankets.

Thud. His body, rigid and cold as Death's scythe, hits the floor.

"Oh my God. My little sister. She's in trouble," Peter screams as he bolts to his rickety thirdhand desk to find his MoxWrap, tapping in panic on the call icon of a young woman wearing long golden metallic swirls in her blond hair, accented by similar earrings. "Pick up. Pick up. Please."

And then he sees the time in Shanghai: 12:04 a.m. tomorrow morning.

Women and men governed together as equals. I want you to think about the consequences of what you ask of me now."

"They only want your advice. You do not have to take up arms."

"They want my connection to him," Zara replies, pulling her silk scarf closer around her oval face. She throws her poppies with the wind gust, which sends them flying a hundred meters as if they were little balloons.

Silence as they walk by a more crimson-red set of poppies. Peri bends down and picks some and hands them to Zara.

"I do not like that shade of red," Zara says as she drops the crimson reminders of "him" and crushes them under her sandal.

"Why do I follow you, Zara?" asks the disturbed Peri. "You are so complicated. Poppies are poppies."

"Why did you follow me?" retorts her friend.

"You were the only woman to beat me in the Peshmerga training camp," says Peri, slapping Zara's shoulder with the back of her hand. "You were the best. The American military advisors knew that too. You were only second to me in attracting men of all sorts…mostly the wrong sort, unfortunately."

Zara winces. "Don't mention that American. He's history to me."

Peri slaps her shoulder again. "And when you punched out that boy, Zengo, who you followed into the Peshmerga, you were my hero."

And that gets Zara to stop. She stamps her feet. Her hands form fists by her sides. "He should have told me rather than hide his deceit. Men. Their failed promises. Their lies. Chlamydia is not something you hide. Nor is a family and an adorable wife safe at home away from the war zone where you have seduced an unwitting local girl into thinking she would marry you after the next campaign, and the next, and the next."

Rubbing her finger across her teeth, Peri smiles. "I'm sure Mr. Chlamydia still remembers you too, with his two front false teeth."

She takes Zara's hand, looking at the scars across her knuckles. "And this one here is from the teeth that you knocked out from that Daesh ape who grabbed me when we were on patrol outside Kobanî."

Taking her hand back, rubbing across her knuckles, Zara says, "They kidnapped women in the villages they took to make them their so-called

Sheepishly, he shuts down the call, hoping he didn't wake up Michaela.

The fog from the night clearing, both outside and inside, and with microwaved instant coffee finally in hand, he scans his MoxMail. Nothing from MoxMedia yet. Ouch. But then there is his landlord's gentle reminder that his rent is due, and one from his boss, Jerrod Olson. He opens the last one, hoping Jerrod has mercy in mind and is going to give him a surprise bonus for his exceptional work for nearly two years as a contract copyeditor for the *Journal of International Geo-Archeology*.

Oh, the trauma. Oh, the inhumanity. I'm fired again. I was right in what I edited. Why doesn't Jerrod see that? Why is the author always right? Even when they're wrong?

The irony of it all. I finally had a job that would have made my father proud of me. The son he always wanted me to be. Another few months, and I would have gotten my year-end bonus and maybe a perm position, in which I would have had full access to the resources and people I need to complete his and Pappy's search. A full-time employee.

And so, he puts his head to the desk with arms around his aching brain. He finds relief from his dream-impaired thoughts as he goes for his run along the Pacific, up to the Golden Gate Bridge. Better than Pappy's smoking, but certainly not as good as passionate bonding. But he reflects on Dr. Bev's male wish fulfillment comment and makes do warming his heart with the image of little Peter sitting in the lap of his pa while he reads the newest findings in archeology. They shared the love of discovering the new in the old of the past. And his brain energizes with the memory of Pa's words explaining the nuances of the *Star Trek* franchise.

His chest fills with pride at the memory of winning a summer internship in the newly created Near East department of the Asian Art Museum after his junior year in high school. But with that thought, the darkness always returns. He ran into the house to tell his pa the great news. But the darkness began. The gun. In his mouth. The blood. His eyes open in despair. And Peter sank to the ground and cried. His mother's God left him that day, and so he left God.

Blond. It was blond that shone through the darkness. He could see his mother's hair glistening as her fingers wiped his tears away at his father's funeral. Only her touch could breathe warmth into his beleaguered soul as his clammy hands clasped hers and they watched his father's casket lowered into the ground.

How am I going to pay the rent if I don't ask Ma again? What am I going to tell her? Should I pretend nothing happened?

Back at his little studio, he peers out his window with that precious view of the Pacific and sees sunlight peeking its way through the fog. Maybe there's hope after all.

Blond. It was blond that caught his eye as Sarah asked him to coffee that night at the Aliens R Us Society meeting. He picks up Sarah's photo, puts it in the trash bin, but then pauses, taking it out and placing it facedown on his table. His mother still holds out hope they will get back together, but Peter knows better, for he edited Sarah's first book.

A long shower. Cold one at that, given what he thinks he dreamt only minutes ago. A close shave this morning because he will be meeting his mother for brunch, hand held out, begging for more rent money. Those "eyes of innocence" stare back at him in the mirror. What was Dr. Fontaine talking about? All those eyes got him in Manhattan was mugged at gunpoint late one night coming out of the subway. Naivety, not innocence, beaconed his eyes to all would-be thieves.

He looks in his closet. A collection of banana slug shirts. He takes out a navy one with Sammy the Slug in his blazing yellow glory holding his anthropomorphic hands out with boxing gloves on.

The smell of negative ions is so distinct to the Pacific. He knows, as he spent time in New York. The Atlantic just didn't smell the same. As he exits the pastel-pink-and-white-trimmed stucco house hosting his little studio apartment to go on his morning run, Peter is relieved he snuck by his nice landlady's door without being asked about the rent. In his wallet, he has a ten and six ones. Just enough to get to brunch with his mother and back. Hopefully with a rent check. Being fired could not have come at a worse time.

Down the street, a fifteen-year-old brown minivan is in the process of moving in or out. An early-forties woman in a tight beige spandex top and carmine knee-length skirt waves him down. Mrs. Harrison. Her colors and mascara are perfectly coordinated with MoxFashion's guidance for this week. "Peter. Perfect timing."

"Why, Mrs. Harrison? Are you moving?"

"Yes. Come inside, please," she says.

Once he's inside, she elaborates. "The terms of my divorce weren't so good. My husband—my ex, that is—really took me for everything. Do you believe it? I have to pay him alimony," she says, brushing her dark blond hair back, exposing her ear.

She thumbs through a stack of papers and shows Peter three. "But enough about my problems, I wanted to show you Melinda's third-round acceptances into Stanford, Princeton, and Harvard. All came within the last two days. And to think, a year ago, all three schools rejected her. If it hadn't been for your editorial help, your coaching, your confidence building, she would have wasted her gap year. You are a godsend, Peter. You are." And Mrs. Harrison takes Peter by surprise with a big hug.

She pulls back, looking at his UC Santa Cruz t-shirt, and purses her lips. "You're so brilliant. Why didn't you go to any of those schools?"

Dimples aglow, feet shuffling, hands in pocket, Peter replies, "That was more than a dozen years ago. How could I have chosen differently? I loved UC Santa Cruz. How could I proudly wear Sammy the Slug if I didn't accept their offer?"

"I wish I could pay you for your help, Peter, but this divorce has stretched all my finances. Melinda and I have to move to a smaller place not far from here. But I can offer some home-cooked meals. You look like you might be tired of the microwavable cuisine bachelors subsist on," says Mrs. Harrison as she puts her right foot towards Peter, wriggling it to get his attention.

But Peter only sees her large tabby cat, coming by her legs to curl around his. He bends down to pet this descendant of the saber-toothed tiger as Mrs. Harrison says, "Maybe you'd like a little cougar in your life, Peter? It's very common these days."

He looks up at her innocently. "No, no, Mrs. Harrison, I couldn't take care of your cat. Well, maybe babysit him until you can get settled in your new place."

To his surprise, she kneels down with him, making sure he has the best view of her, and pinches his right cheek while gazing into his eyes. "You are so adorable. Those eyes. A woman could lose herself in them."

"That was good, Mrs. Harrison," Peter retorts. "I read the first chapter of your manuscript. You have a latent talent for being a romance writer, not that I'm an expert on that kind of fiction."

Placing her hands around the dimples on both sides of his face, she replies, "Call me Amelie, Peter. Maybe if we partner on all things romance, I could pay you with the royalties for my first book?"

Removing her warm hands, Peter nods, pursing his lips. "I tried editing romance novels. My ex-girlfriend started writing them just after I won a set of MoxWraps. She took a test on hers that said she was a natural for writing that genre. I couldn't relate to the alpha male heroes. Chiseled faces, glistening pecs, and the bulging shorts. But she could. We made the fateful move to the Upper West Side in Manhattan to further her writing career. And things changed. I guess that's why I found her in bed with a man just like that. Ex-Army Ranger sniper, ex-NYPD, and now assistant head of MoxWorld USA security. Everything I'm not."

Again to his surprise, she kisses him on the forehead. "And maybe some women have grown out of that alpha male type. My ex was one. And look where that got me."

Out the open door, an old white pickup truck can be seen pulling up, and out exits a large man, chiseled face, day-old stubble, perfect chest-to-torso ratio, tattooed arm, dressed in a tight-fitting grey compression tank partially covered by overalls. He yells, "Of course you would be trying to seduce someone too young for you just a week after our divorce papers were final."

Amelie bolts up, straightening her top. "You should show this young man some respect. He helped your daughter get into Stanford, Princeton, and Harvard. Something that you couldn't do."

Barging in the open door, reeking of alcohol, the worst, cheapest kind, he pulls Peter up by his hair and leans his rough face into his. "An intellectual, huh? Take my advice, she isn't worth it. Don't fall for her act. I did."

"Randall," Mrs. Harrison yells. "Get out of here. Haven't you hurt us enough?"

And Randall lets go of Peter and grabs his ex-wife by her top. He growls, "I'm here for my daughter. She shouldn't be living with you. You've missed paying my first month's alimony already. What kind of role model are you, parading around like this?"

And the big man strikes her, drawing blood. And what is he thinking? Peter, that is. For he grabs this man, who must be fifty percent bigger than he in all dimensions.

"Mr. Harrison, you need to sober up and come back later. It would be best for all."

"Oh, Mr. Egghead here thinks he can talk me into leaving. And let him try to be a role model for my daughter? Not happening," he yells, shaking Peter's hand off him.

And that gene activates, the exact one that wrote in the margins of that pristine, pompous professor's paper about how wrong he was regarding the Black Sea hypothesis. Out of Peter's mouth comes, "You know that one to two percent of our genes come from the Neanderthals. But in your case, you must be at least fifty percent. You should leave nice homo sapiens ladies alone so our species can keep evolving. Crawl back to your cave, why don't you?"

Whap. Something very hard rips Peter's skull. Barely standing, wavering to and fro, Peter feels warm fluid drip down his hair onto his neck.

Looking up from the redness streaking through the beloved slug on his t-shirt, Peter tries to focus as his glasses have gone flying. And then Peter sees it. Randall Harrison had a gun in those overalls. A gun now pointed at his face. A gun with his blood on it.

And he stands there frozen in time. There he was at 157th and Broadway, staring down the barrel of a gun. There he was in his father's den, staring at the gun in his bloody mouth. There he was in the forests, staring down an arrow at…at his sister's chest. Frozen forever in time.

But it is her screams that snap him out of it. With an iron grip on her top, the drunken, crazed caveman drags poor Amelie towards the bedroom, yelling he is going to collect an advance on the alimony she owes.

Words won't save him. Words won't save Amelie. What can he do? He taps on his MoxWrap, looking for 911. What is he doing? She needs him now. And the welterweight editor, the alien-loving omega male sci-fi guy, tackles the monstrous caveman.

Whap. Well, his tackle is more like a ping-pong ball against the side of an elephant as Peter flies backwards to the floor. Maybe he's merely stunned. Maybe he's petrified by a haunting flashback. But for sure as he looks up, he's staring once again into the darkness of a gun barrel. Maybe there's a glint of a bullet. But that's the last thing he sees.

∾

"And what do you think you were doing, young man?" asks Samantha Gollinger. "I didn't raise my son to be a ruffian. And certainly the Gollinger men weren't born to be the hero type."

The bright white institutional lights of the urgent care clinic burn his eyes only a modicum less than his mother's words do his ears. He is trapped here waiting for the neurologist report stating that he does not have a concussion. Fortunately, he only smells bleach and antiseptics, with no trace of sulfur, gunpowder. He hasn't been shot. But his ego sure feels like it, trounced first by that Neanderthal and now by his archetypal helicopter-parent mother.

The woman dressed in the latest MoxFashion cashmere slip dress in Rhonda's recommended beige, with carmine trim and a gold cross dangling from her neck, resembles his ex, Sarah, but a couple inches taller. Come to think of it, so did all of his girlfriends.

And then the stinging. She has licked her fingers to wipe his right temple clean, near the caveman's steel club strike. And with all of her finger-administered moist salves, that warm feeling, the relaxing opening and peaceful sensation, overcomes him. She did the same at his father's grave, the only action that could stop his near-hysterical crying. He needed her healing.

"My father was not an overgrown lout. Nor was your father, my George. Look at your frail pappy. You all were born with the genetics to be civilized men. Better suited to being librarians than adventurers. But you all fancy yourselves Indiana Joneses without the panache, fantasizing about your next archeological dig, which will reveal the truth behind that inane family mystery," Samantha admonishes, brushing her blond locks back behind her ear. "What were you thinking, tackling that idiot?"

Peter glances around but cannot find her. He asks, "Where is Mrs. Harrison, anyway?"

"You mean Amelie?" his mother mocks with eyebrow raised. "She came by to see you while you were getting your head examined. Apparently your MoxWrap dialed 911, and the police arrived shortly after you tried to play hero. We're supposed to go to the local station and give a statement when we're through here. You know, if you're going to save a damsel in distress, maybe you should pick a younger one. Although at least she has the sense to be in tune with Rhonda's colors of the week."

And Samantha brushes her cheek, showing she has the same hue as the MoxMedia anchor babbling away on the screen above about the rumors of the Kurds in Turkey forming another new nation. "Men like you should be finding a woman who can take care of herself."

"I wasn't dating her, Ma. I helped her daughter get into Stanford and a couple Ivies."

She ruffles his hair on the side opposite the wound, in her best emulation of her husband's attaboy. "And that, you are good at. Not that physical hero stuff. Since you broke up with Sarah, you really have been acting strange. The protein shakes, the push-ups, sit-ups. Did you tackle Amelie's ex because he represented the ex-Ranger Sarah left you for?"

Now his head hurts even more as he remembers the day he moved his worldly goods out of Sarah's place, ready to come home to his beloved Pacific. And the new man was there. His rectangular, high-cheekboned face screamed security, strength, and bad boy sex. His distinctive double-clefted chin could launch a thousand ships. And his gun, big and bad as he cleaned it on the table, watching Peter's every step as if to say "one false move" with anything to do with his Sarah—not Peter's, but his—and that gun would be discharged into something vital of Peter's.

And again, a gun in Mr. Harrison's hand. One he didn't even see until too late. A pistol whip administered by Randall the Neanderthal. If only Peter could have been born with their body type—big, tall, structured.

A perceptive Samantha interrupts his self-flagellations with her motherly advice. "I didn't marry your father because he was a muscle-bound knight and could protect me from dragons. I married him because he partnered with me equally, loved me for my failings as well as my aspirations, and would be a wonderful father to wonderful children. Like you and Michaela."

With dour face looking beyond his mother's shoulder, Peter laments, "And look where that got him. And us."

And that stern mother look washes over Samantha's face as she puts her hand under his chin, squeezing his now dimple-less cheeks. "We've been down this road before. We need to move on. He didn't abandon us. He loved us. He loved you. And do I need to say for the umpteenth-thousandth time that you should ignore that daft grandfather of yours? Your father didn't fail us. And you are not failing because you haven't found that stupid object."

"Pappy showed me Uncle James's parchment. Why didn't Pa tell me? Why didn't you tell me? I could have taken up where Pa left off years ago," Peter laments.

A big deep breath and then a long sigh as the stern hovering mother deflates. Fighting the inevitable has come to a head today. Her son will be the inevitable's next victim unless she says the right thing. She wraps her fingers around the gold crucifix she wears.

Kissing his forehead, she says in a softer voice, "My son, my family, your father's family, we're different. We're plagued by some bizarre notion that we can find the special, the ultimate in saving mankind. The truth is, only through our Lord can we find that salvation. You must believe me. Christ was our savior."

Seeing she's not making a dent in her son's already dented head, she adds, "I know how much the pain of your father's death has led you to believe aliens created God. Sometimes a traumatic incident drives one closer to God and other times further away. I am not going to debate you again on this subject. But listen to your great-grandmother Camilla's wisdom on the topic of these family legends. She taught me that if the men in our generation cannot solve the mystery, then they need to focus on procreation. No different from what our Bible tells us, except in that the next generation or the ones after might live in a world where these mysteries can be solved."

Clasping his hands over his ears as he sits on the edge of the examination table, Peter moans. "And now comes the 'where are my grandchildren?' discussion."

She kisses his forehead. "Don't dismiss what a good woman in life brings. And think about how successful you'll feel when you see your children master the family oral traditions and show you where that tail of the bird star is at night. Teaching our next generation, raising them to be even better than us, is equally or even more fulfilling than our own personal successes."

Silence. Well, the noise of the urgent care unit still rattles and clanks in the air, but the two are quiet. A little buzz on the wrist, and Peter glances at his MoxMail. "Ma. I got it. I got it. MoxMedia accepted my application, and they say I should be expecting more information shortly."

"But what about the job you thought Jerrod was going to offer you? A bird in the hand is always better."

"Uh, Ma, he fired me this morning."

"Seriously, Peter? Again? Can't you call him up and beg like you did the first time he wanted to fire you?"

"Ma, don't you understand? The number one company to work for in the world just invited me to come and interview. Well, part of the number one company. MoxMedia. They're looking for a copy editor in their Middle East news group, and they're interviewing a highly select group of candidates at their new San Francisco office. I can chase my family legends, your family legends, and you won't have to loan me more rent money…after this month, that is."

She fully expected his rent payment remark. Why else does a son ask to see his mother at the same time each month? But the protective, concerned mother in her says, "Peter, please don't tell me you're going to have to run around with your keyboard over there. With the re-emerging war stance between Turkey, Russia, and the Chinese-funded Arabic Confederation, you'd be in the middle of what might be the next world war. What did we just say about not being the hero type?"

"Ma, you just rattled off all the reasons why this is the best editorial job in the world right now. If only the journalists would invite me to visit the region, but they always put the junior editor in a four-by-four cube, shielded from the real world. There's no way you'll see me running around out there with bombs falling all around, Ma. That's so not me. That's for the war correspondents, whose words I will be making dance."

"But didn't your sister call that company's CEO evil? He's a Russian crook, no?"

"Ma, that's only malicious rumormongering. Alexander Murometz is no crook. He's the most successful global entrepreneur of this millennium. He is a giant among giants. His MoxWorld Holdings spans the globe like no other multinational company ever did before. Your MoxWrap is a prime example of his brilliance."

"I don't know, Peter. Wouldn't calling Jerrod back and begging be better? You read all those stories about how devious that CEO is and the unethical practices that made him his fortune. And you're so vulnerable right now. Just waiting for another male figure to follow, like you did with that president you voted for."

"Gossip, Ma. Idle gossip. Fake news from jealous competitors. Mr. Murometz will be a great man to work for. You know these huge complex corporations. I'll never even meet the man. But mark my words, Ma—today, Peter Gollinger is going to turn his life around. No more perennial loser. No more moping about Sarah. I'm going to do something that's going to make a difference in this world."

A beep sounds and the holographic image of another woman appears, blond hair flaring out, wearing a red nightshirt emblazoned with a big white S.

"Hey, bro. OMG. Are you okay? What did you do?"

Sheepishly, Peter says, "I'm okay. Just a little cut on the head. Well, a bruise on the cheek too."

Samantha interrupts, "Your brother tried to play knight in shining armor to a divorcée whose ex decided he was in the way."

Now noticing her mother, Michaela tries to sort out her frazzled blond strands as she says, "Hi, Ma. Don't be hard on him. He was my knight in flimsy armor. You remember the time you fetched Peter from the emergency room when I was in middle school? He defended my honor then, too. Against really bad odds. But his broken arm and ribs healed fast."

Peter's not-so-little sister turns to him and asks, "So I'm not interrupting another one of those 'where are my grandchildren?' talks?"

A little chuckle and Peter replies, "Yes, you missed her not-so-subtle grandkids innuendo, but she hasn't had the subtle monthly 'Michaela the Stanford grad is so much better than you, the Banana Slug school grad' discussion."

"Why, big bro, she's right. Little sisters can always best their big brothers. And Pappy knows it too. I can even say the precious family words backwards. 'Save can object the. Peace find you can together two as only.'"

Eyebrows raised for sibling sparring action, Peter asserts, "Well, Little Miss Stanford Showoff, if you have to know, I was just letting Ma know that your super editor brother has just been asked to interview with MoxMedia."

Eyebrows furrowed in alarm, Michaela replies, "You wouldn't. Not with that misogynistic MoxWorld CEO. You can't work for him."

Peter is very amused. He hasn't seen his sister so riled up since the 2016 election. "Admit it, sis, you just don't like male trillionaires. Like I say to Ma all the time, some things are more important than money. Like the truth. And I'll be a great copy editor for MoxMedia."

Seeing the errant strands crossing her face, Michaela straightens out her hair. "Yes, big bro. The truth that you'll be covering up some huge corporate conspiracy working in his fake news empire. But if you are going to sell out your soul to be in that crook's company, maybe you can get the MoxFashion group to help me get into Shanghai University's Paris-Shanghai Fashion Institute. They have that place locked down only for their fashion needs. I'd be happy for you to sell your soul if that means I can get into that closed club."

With a remonstrative face, Samantha intervenes again. "Michaela, you know better than to joke about selling souls. The Lord looks out for our family and our souls. And no child of mine will be selling their soul, even if it means no grandchildren."

"Okay, Ma. No soul selling. Hey, I gotta go," says Michaela. "Big bro, two things before I go. Faust. Reread it. Be one hundred percent sure of where your moral lines are before you interview. They're tricky, those Moxers. Before you know it, you'll have a blood contract with you know who."

Peter spies his mother cringing at his sister's admonitions as Michaela adds, "And Ma's sure to remind you about finding a woman after I hang up. Maybe you'd have better luck if you diversified. Go dark hair for a change. I can set you up with some super-sexy raven-haired sirens at the school here. They'd love that you're so docile you couldn't hurt a squirrel, not even if it was a rabid one about to bite you."

And with that, her image disappears.

As the discharge nurse comes and goes, with Peter signing away his life on endless documents, he asks her about the faint bleach smell. She replies a ten-to-one bleach dilution is used for cleaning up bloodstains or spills. He apologizes if he has left too many of these, and she smiles and leaves.

Alone again, Samantha says her final piece. "I'm proud of you, for getting invited to interview with the world's most successful company. Your sister's Faust comments aside, I'm sure the place is full of wonderful single women and you'll find a good one somewhere."

She brushes her blond hair back again. "And as much as I'm flattered that you like women who look like your mother, and your grandmother, Michaela is right. A dark-haired woman who can help you, who can defend herself, but who needs your gifts to find her special role in the world, you should not turn her down either."

Grasping his hands, she adds, "And by gifts, I don't mean your lack of brawn, but your heart and the wonderful words it can sing."

✧

Back in the safety of his little studio apartment, rent for this month paid by his mother as she saw him back to his abode, Peter stares at the framed picture of his ex turned upside down on his desk. His perishing pappy, his hovering helicopter ma, and even his sassy sister, all pointed the same way. He can't do it alone.

His MoxWrap sounds. What did his mother forget to tell him this time? He taps it to reveal an unexpected hologram.

"Mr. Gollinger?" a hauntingly lovely woman asks, to which Peter replies affirmatively.

"Mr. Murometz would like to speak with you. Please hold."

CHAPTER 5

And they have gone to the daughters of men upon the
earth, and have slept with the women, and have defiled
themselves, and revealed to them all kinds of sins. And
the women have borne giants, and the whole earth has
thereby been filled with blood and unrighteousness.
The Book of Enoch, Chapter 8, Verses 7–9

Northern shores of the Black Sea
9600 BCE

"Orzu, you promised to kill me," Illyana cries out as the giant
Tureal restrains her. "I'm not the rabbit. I'm your sister. If you
love me, if you truly love me, kill me. Don't let them do to
me what they did to Mother."

"Kill me. Kill me. Kill me," rings in Orzu's ears as he searches for a voice,
any voice, to guide him.

As he stares down the shaft of his arrow pointing at Illyana's young bosom,
her breasts become larger, nursing a child. Illyana is standing with lips rouged
and eyelids painted, her chest exposed.

She is screaming, "Orzu, you promised to kill me. You broke your
promise. You did not truly love me. And look at me. Defiled. Worthless. My

spirit gone. Kill me now."

"Please tell me what to do," Orzu cries out into the darkness. "I cannot kill her. I love my sister. Is not life more precious than death? Please, anyone. Speak."

As he cries, he awakens in soft, warm arms that rock him, holding his head to a soft bosom. Orzu looks into the warm, dark eyes of a dear woman who tells him, "It's only a dream. You saved me. You are my savior, and I will forever love you." She kisses him, again and again. They make passionate love and Orzu rests peacefully in her arms.

The next day, these lovers are out on a boat in the middle of the sea. Orzu and Narn are pulling in a fishing net with Orzu's son of ten cycles, An. Orzu looks back and watches his beloved wife, the savior of his soul, Nanshe, cleaning the last catch with Ki, their daughter of fourteen, going on fifteen, cycles, who has grown up to be a fine-looking young woman. A blend of her mother's beauty and the courage and spirit of his sister.

Nanshe is half a head shorter than Orzu and solidly built. She has an oval face and dark eyes, with straight dark brown hair. The perfect mate for him, the peaceful fisherman, Orzu thinks as he smiles at her. Ki is more lithe, but shows the same strength Illyana had, both in mind and body.

And he is snapped from his romantic trance by the overwhelming tugs at the net. Narn, brother of Nanshe, is almost pulled overboard but is held back by Orzu's strapping young son, An. Orzu himself places his feet firmly on the backboards of the boat. Whatever is in the net is not the trout, bass, perch, or sturgeon they normally catch, but something so strong it pulls the boat downwards to a near swamping point.

Finally he spies it, and it is much longer than he is tall. They will be swamped if they don't do something now.

"Nanshe, Ki! Shark! Help! Now!" Orzu yells.

From the side of the boat, Nanshe grabs two harpoons half as long again as she is tall. Ki grabs a club nearly her height. Nanshe rushes to the back of the boat, raises one of the harpoons, showing the musculature of her arms, waits, waits, and then drives the tip deep into the side of the shark once it surfaces near the boat. She repeats this with the other harpoon. Pulling the death stick back, she draws the shark to the back planks, and her beloved daughter clubs the head of this beast, over and over again until the behemoth is dead.

The men, relieved, pull the carcass into the boat. No small task, as this is the largest shark they have ever seen in all their years fishing. Orzu has learned from local lore that the lake was once saltier, and the shark is an ancient evolved monster from days perhaps as old as the stars. Only the largest and strongest survived the change to freshwater. Nanshe hugs her brother and then her husband, rejoicing, as shark meat will trade for a premium with the villagers and other fishermen. They are rich for the moment.

Orzu hugs Ki for her courage and then pats An on the back for a job well done. As Nanshe and Narn cut up the shark, Orzu sits his progeny down and asks them to recite the tradition, just as Parcza taught him. Ki takes after Illyana, reciting the words rapidly and trying to do it backwards. An, like him, struggles, but finally gets it. More practice. More practice always.

Even though daylight has yet to be extinguished, he asks them to point to where they think the tail of the bird star would be. An asks him how he can tell, and Orzu reminds him of the stones they have in front of their house. They align with the direction of the tail of the bird. He hugs them both and returns to steering the boat, heading in a new direction.

The killings of his youth weighed heavily on Orzu. He became a fisherman to avoid the hunt and, more importantly, the haunting image of the arrow shaft pointed between his beloved Illyana's breasts. He has become expert at navigating the lake. He knows by the season and the position of the sun where he is, and he meets with fishermen from the other side of the lake twice a moon cycle to trade and learn about their lands. And today is one of those days.

The two boats are tied together as Orzu welcomes his guests onto his boat. Nanshe has cooked a shark broth, not only as the perfect hostess, but as the perfect wife seeking the best value for the trade of shark meat, skin, and fin. She loves that Orzu tacitly understands who runs their household. Certainly her brothers understood so perfectly, as she takes after their mother.

Then comes the barter. Orzu and Nanshe have come to learn the language of the Other Siders. Their own language is richer and more descriptive, which helps them conceptualize how to negotiate win-wins, even in the Other Siders' language. Orzu wants more than the normal amount of the hardened black stones, which the Other Siders call obsidian. They offer twice the amount for half the shark. Nanshe sheds her perfect demure hostess mask and demands they tell her where this obsidian comes from as well as give them all the stones they have on the boat in exchange for two-thirds of the shark.

Reluctantly, they tell her and Orzu. The town that trades these stones is nearly a day's sail from their location to the shore on their side, and another day's sail along the coastline to the left. They come from a mountain further inland, about half a moon cycle by foot over three mountain ranges. One of the men draws a map on the floor of their boat, as Nanshe grins at Orzu because she got them the best part of the deal. Once in their boat, the Other Siders hug each other, thinking that they won the encounter.

Late evening arrives when Nanshe and Orzu reach their home on the shore of the side of the lake closer to the tail of the bird star. The walk to their home from where they anchor the boat grows shorter each year, as the lake is rising half the height of Nanshe's lower leg each sun cycle, growing ever so slightly colder all the time. They anchor at the site of Parcza's former house, which is now half-covered by the tides. The land under the water is long and shallow, so the tides come far up. Nanshe worries that someday they will need to move their house. But not tonight, she thinks as she puts her half-asleep children to bed.

In the warmth of their own bed, Nanshe leans her head against her treasured husband's chest. Orzu is proud of their obsidian trade, remarking that these stones were more valuable to the Reindeer People than enslaving him and his family. As the giants had expanded away from the tail of the bird star, they moved farther and farther away from the source of their obsidian stones. Orzu has struck a deal with them. He provides a new batch of stones each cycle, and they leave him and his family alone. Included in this deal is the safety of the home of Nanshe's older brother, Namu.

"You were so good with the deal today, Nanshe. I love you," Orzu whispers in her ear. "It was almost as good as the deal we have with the

Reindeer People. So far, our children, and your brother's children, have been kept safe. Nonetheless, we are prudent to take our children fishing with us, as the lake is the safest place for them." He hugs his beloved.

He pets her hair as he says, "Ki is taking after you so much. And after Illyana." His voice cracks as he mentions his sister's name. "Ki is getting fuller like she was. She is nearly the same age as my sister was when..." And he can't form the rest of his words.

He cries, unable to speak more. Nanshe moves from having her cheek on his chest and draws his head onto hers, stroking his temple. "I look at Ki and I see Illyana in her. I can't bear to look at my own daughter due to my guilt, my failure, my fear that I cannot save Ki any more than I could Illyana."

He murmurs, "I failed her. Not once, but twice. I could not kill. I cannot kill."

He kisses the ample bosom of his beloved Nanshe and continues, "I took more than two cycles of the sun to find the courage to search for Illyana and try to save her. I learned patience. I learned to hide. I learned to be invisible to the Reindeer People. I hid near the pyramids where Illyana was held. I watched her be taken, half-naked, between buildings. I learned to be still and wait while I listened to her screams.

"And then, as I became familiar with the times when the Reindeer People would not be around, I made my way into her building." He gasps, swallows, and in a teary voice, says, "And there she stood looking at me. Just as Parcza said would happen. She was barely covered in those pitiful excuses for garments the Reindeer warriors made women wear. Her eyelids were purple and her lips were red, not from beatings but from the color they made her put on her them.

"It seemed longer than a sun cycle that she stared at me. And I suddenly noticed she nursed a child, which I had missed at first as I stared in shock at the horror of what they had done to her. And she finally spoke. As if no time had passed since I had last seen her that day in the forest, she said repeatedly, 'Kill me.'

"And I knew that I had broken my promise. I had agonized for two cycles of the sun over my cowardice, my failure as a brother to honor her wishes. I had come back to atone for my failure. And I asked for her forgiveness."

He strokes Nanshe and searches for the courage to continue reliving the unbearable. "Illyana, no longer the young girl whom I loved so much, would no longer tease me, no longer would stick her tongue out at me. She could only say in a low, tired voice, 'Please forgive me.' And then she cried. She was so ashamed of what she had become, of what she had been made to do.

"And I asked her to come home with me. We would go far away from the tail of the bird star, as Parcza said, and make a new home far away. But she would only cry and tell me she could not go home. No man would have her."

Nanshe wipes Orzu's face of his tears and kisses his head as he continues. "I implored her, insisted that what she said was not true. I would love her and take care of her. Any man would. She was the finest young woman in all of our villages. I simply asked for her forgiveness. I wanted to make our lives right again." Orzu becomes so choked up that he cannot continue reliving the memories.

And so Nanshe continues the story. "And she cried again for you to kill the male child feeding on her breast, cried so coldly, as if the baby were a parasite. She cried that he would only grow up to enslave your sons. He would only grow up to take your daughters."

She lifts Orzu's head and looks into his eyes. "And you said you could not. You begged her to forgive you, but you could not kill." She kisses his forehead. "Miraculously, to my graces, to my wishes, to my prayers, she turned and pointed at me. Only fifteen cycles of the sun. Just like Illyana had been. And she said you should save me, for I was still pure, like she once was. That I would give to you the forgiveness that you so sought, and that she, so impure, could not."

Orzu kisses his beloved wife back as he finishes the story. "And she implored me to kill her son, kill her, and take you. I cried for a voice to tell me what to do. Any voice. And the same darkness, emptiness, and silence that left me numb and paralyzed the first time in the forest overcame me there again. If not for your love, if not for the beautiful children you bore for me, I would not have been able to go on in spite of my failure to save Illyana."

Nanshe holds Orzu's head tight to her bosom, squeezing as if her life depended on it. "I love you so much, Orzu. I fear sometimes I don't let you know how much. You have nothing to be forgiven for. Nothing." She kisses the top of his head. "I stared in fear as you turned away to leave the room, to leave Illyana in her shame, to leave me.

"But before I could cry that I was to be left there too, you turned and speared Illyana through her heart. Her lips, her eyes, spoke out that she felt your mercy. Her big brother who fulfilled his promise to his beloved sister. You put your arm around me and your hand across my face, so I would not see her die, but I knew you were merciful. She did not suffer."

They both cry. Nanshe finds her voice through her tears and says softly, but strongly, "At that moment I witnessed your courage, your mercy, and your love. I never told you what Illyana did just before you came. We had learned from the Reindeer Giants about the gods they prayed to, the gods for which they built those pyramids with the blood and death of our men. We had nothing left. Nothing that we could hope for. And so we had prayed to a god, any god, anyone who would listen to our pleas. Illyana, she prayed for someone to come and kill her, and I, for someone to save me.

"Minutes after our pleas, you came through the door. My savior. The answer to my prayer. Not only did you save me, but as I pleaded with you to do, you went to save my two brothers, who were enslaved building the pyramids, near to their deaths. You pulled them up to their feet and brought us all to safety. I learned that night there is someone, somewhere who listens to the prayers of the most debased, the most defiled, the most desperate. And for this I am forever grateful to you. And I love you, unconditionally love you. You do not need forgiveness from me or anyone else. Please know this."

Holding her precious savior tightly, she closes her eyes, savoring the love they share.

"And you showed me how deep your love was as we came back to your empty home. You took me not to your bed, but to your heart. You sensed I was not emotionally ready for you to take me as your wife. You waited. You were patient. I felt a love like you had for your sister as she wanted you to take me as her surrogate. You protected me, nourished me, allowed me to grow. And waited cycles and cycles of the sun for me to recover, for my love for you to grow, before I came to you to gently bed me. And I came to truly know love."

Following this testament of devotion, they kiss, slowly and lovingly. Sitting upright, she gazes into his eyes and summons her courage. The courage to say what needs to be said, what will either bond them more or, in her worst fears, break them.

"Orzu, your love for me will always be my salvation. And at times I fear I am unworthy of your love."

She peers deeply into his eyes, searching for a sign his soul will be merciful, as she asks, "Orzu, is there anything, anything at all that I might do that would lessen your love for me? Anything?"

Orzu, taken aback by this question, answers in a puzzled voice, "No. No, nothing. Why would you ask?"

"I have done something so hideous, so horrible, so heinous, I have hidden it from you. The shame stands between us. I feel it keeps us from truly being the closest two souls can be."

Orzu hugs her tightly and assures her that nothing could ever lessen his love for her.

She puts her hands around his head, her forehead to his, and glances down with shame. "You took me in as if I was your beloved, just as Illyana had asked. To you, I was as pure and innocent as she was the day she was taken from you. And your love for me was as it was for her. A love so good, I did not want for anything else."

She then cries and cries, and it is Orzu's turn to wipe her tears as she says, "Illyana wanted you to think I was pure. But I was not. I had been defiled and debased for more than a moon cycle the day you saw me. I had been put with Illyana because I was not enough for them. She was teaching me how to please them more, how to paint my face and dress in ways that denigrated my self-respect."

She stops in silence to gauge her husband's reaction and then continues, "I was so afraid to tell anyone. I was so afraid I would be left. I saw other captive women who killed themselves as there was no hope. I heard stories of others who were recaptured after escape. About how their relatives would not accept them. About how they were shunned, one even stoned by her family and friends. I could not bear having my brothers shun me. But I am so sorry for hiding this from you, the one I love the most."

She looks at Orzu and bravely puts forth, "I will accept my punishment for my deceit to you. If you wish me to leave, I will do so. But without your love, I would ask, as did Illyana, that you do to me that which you did so mercifully to her. Please spare our children. They are innocent of my deceit."

She cries. Orzu cries. They have cried most of the night thus far. And Orzu assures her his love for her is not lessened, but strengthened. He knew she never was impure, for the pureness of her heart is all he saw that day she was with Illyana. She should feel no shame, no dishonor, for she is his savior. He pledges that he will stand by her until their deaths. Strengthened by her courage to finally discuss her deepest, darkest pain with him, they cry more. And kiss with the most passionate love of their lives coming to them, over and over and over again.

CHAPTER 6

The source of my suffering and
loneliness is deep in my heart.
This is a disease no doctor can cure.
Only Union with the Friend can cure it.

—Rabi'a al-Adawiyya,
eighth-century Persian philosopher and mystic

7:35 p.m. GMT+3, May 5, 2022
Village outside Siirt, formerly Turkey, tonight the Anatolian Kurdish State

She stands tall and proud in her new jelli eidi, or bayramlık as is said in Turkey, holiday clothing for the Ramadan Bayramı, the feast celebrating the end of Ramadan, which in Turkey has become the Şeker Bayramı or Sugar Feast. Standing a couple centimeters taller than her grandmother, Roza, taking more after her great-grandmother Sara's height, this radiant Kurdish woman beams with glowing joy as she shows off the fruits of the last week spent shopping for her second-favorite holiday festival after Newroz, the spring new year feast.

"Grandma, you don't think this white blouse is too revealing, do you?" Zara asks. She worries that her skin tone can still be discerned through the light fabric as she tugs a little more of the blouse out of her ankle-length navy-blue skirt with modernistic white diagonal stripes, such that the light cloth does not hug her breasts too tightly.

Her maternal grandmother shakes her head, scolding herself for succumbing to the conservatism of Zara's paternal grandmother in teaching the adolescent Zara to abide by strict guidelines of modesty. Perhaps if she did show off her figure a little more at the Sugar Feast, a strapping man would find the courage to court her. In their culture, a woman unmarried by her midtwenties is destined to be a childless spinster, and her granddaughter has passed that mark by a decade already.

Roza fastens a reddish rose belt around the waist of her unwed granddaughter, then, much to Zara's surprise, tucks the blouse in, further enhancing the shape of her bosom. "Zara, perhaps you are old enough to show more of what Xwedê has provided you. Times have changed since we first talked about modesty a quarter century ago."

Losing her beaming smile, Zara frowns as she replies, "The changing times have only taught me even more that nothing good comes from not dressing with proper modesty." She untucks the blouse again to obscure her form.

"Your best friend Peri's dress allows her femininity to show in a modest, but still beautiful manner," Roza states.

Wrapping a navy silk headscarf around her oval head, long ears, and straight dark brown hair, Zara rolls her eyes. "I learned my lesson too well since my dalliance with fashion as a teen. And you don't want to know what I wore in college abroad."

Roza feigns horror at the thought as she wonders why her dearest granddaughter opts to stay at her mother's ancestral home as opposed to finding a good man as Roza had done, as her mother Sara had done, and as Zara's mother, Maryam, had done.

"I'm only teasing, Grandma," Zara assures her, seeing Roza's eyes. "I kept my legs covered to the ankles even as all the girls wore the tiniest of shorts. I kept my shoulders and arms covered even as all the girls wore spaghetti-strap tank tops or tube tops. But I am deeply sorry I lost your favorite hijab."

Zara's frown dissolves as a little smile peeks out. She twirls around in her bare feet, lifting her dress up into a perfect circle and exposing only a couple centimeters of her lower calves. "I won't be performing a Sufi whirling dance in this dress, though," Zara says, referring to her deceased great-grandfather, a Sufi imam who inspired both her mother and Zara through his poems and wisdom and the practice of the whirling dance.

The frown passes from Zara to Roza as the latter observes the scars around her granddaughter's feet. Undoubtedly, she has led a hard life, leading her to prefer tending the sheep to seeking a man in her life. "Perhaps, Zara, a pair of your mother's shoes would be better with your new jelli eidi than sandals," Roza advises, which brings misery to Zara's face.

On cue, Maryam comes into Zara's room and says, "Roza, Sara wishes to speak with you." She smiles at her daughter, who, however rough she may appear at times, is always beautiful, from the inside out, as a daughter always is to a mother. "Zara, if you are done here, please join me in the kitchen to pack the candies for the children at the festival."

They pass through the family sitting area into the kitchen. Their simple cinder block house is typical in this Kurdish region. With what Zara earned working for Sasha, she could easily have provided her mother's mothers with the largest estate known to anyone in this region. But her family has chosen to live simple, traditional lives, showing their deep regard for their faith as well as their culture. And she has chosen to tend the sheep and goats, a profession far more fulfilling than what she did for Sasha.

Mehhh. Mehhh. Her two babies, now much more robust than when she saved them, chase her into the kitchen. For they know that room means one thing: milk.

As Zara feeds her two darlings, she finally smiles. Maryam glows at seeing her Zara smiling and packs candies into little bags. "I am so happy you have chosen a lively, sharp, distinguished jelli eidi this year that isn't as plain as the ones you have chosen in the past years," she remarks. "There will be many men at the festival who will see you in your dress, men who will be interested in marrying you. You should be open to their overtures this year. I pray that in your fear that one might actually touch your heart, one who might come to know who you are, you do not lash out at them. You need someone in your life. Someone close that you can trust."

Zara can only roll her eyes at her mother's not-so-subtle suggestion. "Only bad things have come from me and men, Mama. You should know better than to suggest such a thing."

"Not all clouds bring rain, my little Zara."

Zara shakes her head. "For every misfortune, there is always something worse that can happen."

With this exchange of Kurdish sayings, silence descends on them as they finish packing the candies. Maryam pops a candy into her offspring's mouth, hoping to bring a little cheer. She points to Zara's bare feet and takes her child to her room. They pass by the house's only room for a male, Zara's deceased brother, Soran. Maryam keeps a picture of him standing next to his older sister in this room. Zara glances at the little boy with curly black hair like his late father's, standing next to her in the photo from their teenage years in Kurdistan, taken just before they left home to join the Peshmerga. A twinge hits her as she laments. So annoying some days as he followed her around like a puppy dog. But he was family nonetheless, and she misses him.

With a pair of navy pumps in hand, Maryam slides them on her sole surviving child's ravaged feet. "These should make you smile again. I know you, my daughter. You work so hard to exude a tough exterior. But that is only to protect the pain of what you hide inside. I had thought maybe you had healed yourself of that which you do not show. Why are you so glum? You were happier at the Newroz Festival only a couple of months ago."

Trying a few steps in her mother's footwear, Zara wobbles on the modest heels; she has worn only flats and sandals since her days in military boots. Scars of deep wounds inflicted upon her soles don't help matters any, and she wobbles like a Weeble. She holds her hand over her abdomen as she answers, "It's nothing more than the onset of cramps, Mama. It's better to be born a man than a woman."

Maryam offers, "PMS is not what truly ails you. In the past four years since you have come back to live with us full-time, I haven't seen you so dour. It's Sasha, isn't it?"

Zara shivers at hearing his name, which has not been spoken in this household in many a month. "I haven't seen him in the years since I came back to be with you and my family. And why does he contact me now? Because he has an urgent, dire need for me to be in his life again? What has happened is best left in the past. I'm happy being a new person. A new woman with my beloved family who is true to her faith and her upbringing."

Maryam retrieves a pair of navy patent-leather flats from her closet. As she places these on her daughter's feet, she says, "Perhaps it is Xwedê's will that you should see Sasha again. As much as I love to have my daughter at home, my lovely daughter should see the man who has done so much for her. Who loves her so much."

Fondling the flats, Zara glares at her mother. "Mama, you have no idea what he made me do. I am no longer that woman, and I'm happy for it."

Ever so subtly shaking her head, Maryam gazes at the floor. "In the old Kurdish ways, the ways of Roza's time, the ways of even my childhood, a woman must do things that she does not like, but which she must do out of honor, out of custom, out of duty to her family."

With a little stamping of her feet into the flats, Zara replies, "I am not that kind of woman, Mama. I love who I have become living with you again. I've put all that I was in the past where it belongs. To go back and see Sasha is only inviting the past to come back and haunt us." She sighs as she puts her hand on her cheek under her headscarf, rubbing the scars that mar her face.

Up onto tippy toes, Maryam hugs her. "My dear, no matter what you have done or will do, you will always be my beautiful little Zara, who I love and cherish."

Roza returns wearing her bayramlık, covered head to toe, but stylish nonetheless, with a little lace showing at her arms. "Zara, Sara wishes to see her great-granddaughter's bayramlık."

With her mother's flats afoot, Zara enters her most venerable matriarch's room. She bends down and kisses Sara's hand, placing it on her forehead as she wishes her a happy Bayram. In turn Sara offers her great-grandchild an envelope.

"Open it, my child," Sara asks.

To her surprise, Zara finds two hundred-dollar bills inside. "But why, Great-Grandma? I would have thought you would want to give currency from the new Anatolian Kurdish State. I hear they'll be exchanging Turkish bills for the new currency tonight at the festival."

The aged Sara simply smiles with an air of wisdom older than the mountains. "I hear California is very beautiful."

Looking very perplexed, Zara politely replies, "I thank you for your well wishes. However, I have never gone to California, nor do I have any intention of doing so."

With more wisdom beaming from her face, Sara signals for Zara to stand up. She is as tall as Zara, which is no surprise as her granddaughter has taken after her in more than just physical dimensions. "I glean from the look in your eyes that the time will soon be here for you." And she kisses her great-granddaughter on the forehead, leaving Zara in great mystery.

Shaking her head, Zara can only say, "I have no desire to go back to America again. I had enough of American men. And Russian ones and Kurdish ones."

"Everything is God's will. Praise be to God," Sara states simply.

"Praise be to God," Zara replies, knowing it is time for her submission.

"It is an old Sufi belief that, by knowing yourself, you become closer to Xwedê," Sara says wisely. She sees in Zara's eyes a devout believer who yet has a corner of doubt in her soul.

Zara bows her head. "In these last years alone with you and my family, I have been pious, faithful, and obedient. I have faith that one day I will be as close to Xwedê as you have become."

"You have many years to develop, my child," Sara says sagely, walking over to her window to gaze upon the sheep. "At the risk of touching what you do not want touched, you must truly let go of the past. Only what you do from this moment on matters. What men have done—to you, to those you loved, done in the name of Xwedê, citing the Qur'an—you must understand, it is not the same as your faith. The words of the Prophet brought women greater equality with men than in the times before the Prophet. His words speak of the equality of both woman and man in the eyes of Xwedê. Only cultural interpretations and male-dominated written traditions have altered the original purity of this intent."

The wise, aged woman turns to face Zara. "The mystical side of Islam we practice, Sufism, which was banned by Turkey and which, with the declaration of the Anatolian Kurdish State, we can now practice openly, was started by a woman, Rabi'a al-Adawiyya. We raised you with her influence, her belief; we should be motivated not by fear of hell, not by longing for paradise, but by love. The love of God. And through love we should seek our closeness with God. The Prophet said, 'He who knows himself knows his Lord.' And our practice of Sufism is about opening the door to love. To our love of God."

Zara kneels again, taking Sara's hand and kissing it.

"We know you love us, Zara, your closest family to survive all the wars and political killings we have endured. But until you open yourself to real love again, you will only continue to be obedient, subservient to God as our faith asks. You will not know God in the way in which you seek. You need to let go of the ghosts of your past that haunt you and open yourself. Open yourself to love that will bring you the unity you seek."

"But, Sara, I am faithful and open to the love of God," Zara pleads, confused.

Sara takes her hand to rise again. "Remember, you can learn from new books but still listen to old teachers. Rabi'a's story is a parable you should remember. She was kidnapped and sold into slavery. And each day of her slavery, she prayed to remain devout in her obedience, until one day, her owner realized she was a saint. He saw a light around her while she prayed, and freed her for fear of offending Xwedê. Even though you have been physically freed from your tormentors, you are still a slave. Free yourself, open yourself fully as did Rabi'a."

The mere mention of captivity brings weakness to Zara's knees. She recalls her darkest of days, which she has buried in the deepest recesses of her mind so they can never haunt her again, or so she hoped. "But, Sara, I find love here with you and Roza and my mother. Through you, I know some of the love of God."

Sara kisses her great-grandchild on the cheek with the hidden hideous scar. And then with the sternest of faces, she says, "Khadija married the Prophet when she was forty. You still have a few years until you are her age, and you can still find a good husband as did she. One who will help you find what you yearn for. One who will help you understand what you need to touch, to find in yourself."

Zara leaves her great-grandmother's room in deep perplexity. Did they all conspire to have the same talk with her today, only in different ways? Never before in her life has her maternal family put so much pressure on her to marry. Why now? Why did Sasha try to reach her now? Did he talk with them all? The thought boils her blood as she pulls her red pickup truck out of the shed.

Mehhh. She kisses her babies goodbye and helps her three mothers safely inside the truck cab. And as the sun begins to set, Zara drives them to meet Aunt Leyla, who keeps an apartment in the city of Siirt. The custom-built truck is one of only two gifts she has kept from her days with Sasha.

Out of the corner of her eye, Zara spies a MoxWrap hiding under her mother's sleeve. "Mama, why are you wearing that device? Did we not discuss never, ever using these instruments again? He can track us now."

In the front seat next to Zara, Maryam tries to hide the device under her right hand as she says, "But Zara, I only wanted to ensure we are in constant contact with your aunt. She says people in town are wary of the public festival for fear of possible attack by the Turks seeking to reclaim the new Anatolian Kurdish State, or by assassins from the Daesh offshoot groups operating from within the Arabic Confederation seeking to destabilize the new country."

From the backseat, Roza says, "Maryam is right. We need to stay in contact with our family. I cannot forget those days when Turkish helicopters came from the skies decades ago. The sound still haunts my generation."

"And dearest Zara, perhaps you were too young to remember Saddam's helicopters when they attacked us in Duhok Province," Maryam exclaims, her voice cracking with terror.

Zara shivers at her own memories of the helicopters, and the men who led her father to his death. She reaches over to turn her mother's MoxWrap off.

But it's too late. As if the conversation were prophetic, the distinct throbbing of air pounds their ears. Dust whips up around them as a helicopter descends, taking a parallel path to theirs and shining lasers into their windows. Zara recognizes these as laser microphones, listening in on their conversation, which has turned into gasps.

The beast from the sky speeds up and then lands, blocking the road. Zara engages in emergency braking maneuvers. Men in dark uniforms jump out of the helicopter and surround the car.

Zara spies the same horror on her mother's face as she had when her father was taken away to be tortured. Maryam stifles a scream.

Zara finds her backup gun under her seat but looks at her terrified family and weighs the consequences of a firefight. One pistol versus three heavily armed men. Three years ago, there'd have been no question. But she has not fired this gun since then. She puts it away to save her family, for she will need to submit her body again to save the ones she loves most.

The dark man next to Zara's window yells something in Russian, tapping the glass.

Maryam screams again as Roza holds on to Sara, shielding her from the eventual bullets.

Looking around at her family, who have lived out this scenario too many times in their lives, Zara says, "Stay in the truck. You will be safe if I go with them."

As Zara leaves the truck cab willingly, perhaps sacrificing her life for theirs, Maryam screams out, "I can't bear losing you too. Is Xwedê not satisfied with taking my son and my husband? Must he take my only daughter as well?"

CHAPTER 7

On a day when the wind is perfect the sail just needs to open and the world is full of beauty. Today is such a day.
—Jalāl ad-Dīn Muḥammad Rūmī,
thirteenth-century Persian Sufi mystic

6:50 p.m. GMT–8, May 6, 2022
Pacific Heights, San Francisco

Astonishing. Mr. Murometz is calling him personally on his MoxWrap. *The* Mr. Alexander Murometz.

He stares spellbound at the elegant, strikingly lovely Asian face on his MoxWrap as he waits. She is quite becoming with straight, shiny shoulder-blade-length black hair, fine and silky. She wears deep peach lipstick with matching stone drop earrings. Wow. Maybe his mother was right. Maybe his sister was right—he needs to diversify with a raven-haired Asian siren. Her visage, so sensually different from his last girlfriend's, hauntingly echoes something in the deepest reaches of his psyche. Is she the dark-haired woman from his dream?

"Mr. Gollinger," she says in what he hears as a dreamy voice, "I'm transferring you to Mr. Murometz."

"Mr. Gollinger. I'm so happy I was able to catch you," says Mr.

Murometz, a man in his late sixties with thinning white hair. "I want to express how much I have wanted to talk directly with you after having seen your job application. I apologize for the extremely short notice, but I hope you can come interview with us at my office in San Francisco tomorrow?"

Peter stutters, "Why, yes, Mr. Murometz. This is probably the most important interview of my life."

"Very good, Peter—may I call you Peter?"

"Why, of course, Mr. Murometz. Please call me anything you want."

"Then simply Peter will do well between us. Tomorrow you will meet Mr. Chapwell, who will run you through a standard interview. We have to be consistent with everyone we interview, abiding by your country's laws. Please be patient with him and bear with the process, as he is only doing his job, which he does well. Rest assured, Peter, you need not worry not about the results of his tests. For certain, you and I will talk by video conference afterwards. I apologize for being so short on time here. I have a dinner engagement waiting for me."

"No worries, Mr. Murometz. I'm tremendously honored you called."

"Good. See you tomorrow, Peter." Alexander Murometz signs off.

And the oh-so-lovely face comes back. "Mr. Gollinger, sir, can you see me clearly?"

"Yes, I can. Very clearly," Peter assures her.

"Mr. Gollinger, I'll be in the lobby of our office in San Francisco at eight thirty a.m. and will bring you to our Head of New Talent Assessment, Mr. Harlan Chapwell the Third. After meeting Mr. Chapwell, I'll bring you to our videoconference suite to continue your conversation with Mr. Murometz. Is that okay with you?"

"Yes, of course," Peter affirms. "Eight thirty a.m. sharp in the lobby. Do you mind, is this a suit-and-tie type affair?"

"Mr. Gollinger, wear whatever you believe is appropriate to show your true self. That's all we're looking for," she says with a smile that could make the North Star look dim. "Good night, Mr. Gollinger. And I will see you tomorrow morning."

"I love you. You haven't deceived me. You loved me. You are my savior. I will stand by you until the day we die," mutters Peter as he hugs the woman of his dreams. A woman with lovely dark hair. His diversification from blond.

He rolls and rolls in passionate embrace, in the greatest bliss any night has bestowed upon him.

Thud. Once again, he's on the ground wrapped in a sheet. He clears the sheet from his face. How bad are things? When you wake up finding out you've been making love to your pillows, it is pretty bad.

As daybreak emerges through the fog the next morning, Peter goes through his daily routine, looking at his haggard face in the mirror. Bags and angst wrinkles. On his morning run along the fogbound Pacific, he reflects. What a dream. Why is it now he is starting to remember these dreams? And this one is yet another version of that dream he can't recall. Something emotionally deep? Crying? Lots of crying and this woman. A dark-haired woman again. He's ready to cry too. He shakes his head, which has its habitual haze, fog, and ache.

He throws icy water on his face as he looks in the mirror again. Out of the closet he gets a smartly starched and pressed white shirt, the one he thought he would be wearing at his wedding with Sarah. Looking in the mirror as he buttons up, he thinks something is missing. He goes to his closet and gets a UC Santa Cruz tie, in a tasteful navy with a cute little yellow banana slug on it. Still missing something. Ah, the cap. He finds his navy UC Santa Cruz cap with a bigger banana slug emblazoned on the front. Now his ensemble is perfect.

"The lovely lady said, 'Mr. Gollinger, wear whatever you believe is appropriate to show your true self.' And this is my true self," Peter says as he pats Sammy on his lightly padded belly.

Five minutes before 8:30 a.m., Peter enters the lobby of MoxWorld USA, which, like the other big digital giant in the city, sits within easy access to Interstate 80 and 280, BART, and the airport. MoxWorld wanted to make their headquarters at least as commuter friendly. The building is the antithesis of grandiose. Not much color. Bluish hue. But everything is tall inside. MoxWorld knew its workers were virtual and global, so there is no need for minion offices and cubes, which he strategically didn't tell his mother. No need to get her worried that he would be assigned hazardous duty in lands afar.

A black monolith dominates the lobby. In the midst of a glistening pool, the twenty-five-foot towering stone overwhelms the senses, measuring eleven feet wide and three feet deep, surrounded by gushing fountains. No other design element adorns the walls save the simple enigma of the corporate logo, which looks like a connect-the-dots outline of a bird diving downwards. With Mr. Murometz's money, empire, and global influence, he certainly could have picked anything he wanted for a logo. As Peter continues to scan, he sees no reception desks, no security guards, just a few stone blocks for sitting on in the waiting area. Odd.

"Hello, Mr. Gollinger. Welcome to MoxWorld USA," the lovely Asian lady from the night before greets him. "I extend Mr. Murometz's personal and deep appreciation for coming on such little notice. Your dedication to your work has been noted. I see you're admiring our lobby. Clearly, we at MoxWorld are unlike any other US-based firms you may have encountered."

She waves her hand and says, "And this is how MoxMedia welcomes its esteemed guests like yourself." The blank walls of the lobby light up with screens of news and programming from around the world, with Rhonda dressed in black-and-coral trim with her perfectly done hair, bright coral lips and perfectly matching makeup front and center.

Peter is too distracted by the aura of the room to digest the text scrolling under Rhonda's image: "Russia poised to invade Georgia. China sinks Japanese destroyer in the South China Sea. Arabic Confederation overtakes Iranian Persian Gulf ports. Turkey's Prime Minister warns the AC that any border crossing will result in war. Are we on the precipice of world war?"

Instead of watching the news, Peter stands in awe of his hostess—long, lithe, and taller than he by an inch or so. This morning, she sports deep coral lips accented by spiral coral earrings and matching eye shadow. Her makeup resembles that worn by Rhonda and dozens of other female anchors, whose faces are now emblazoned around the room. Peter reflects on his sister's outburst. What kind of man is this Mr. Murometz that he commands his female employees to coordinate their colors on a global basis?

This philosophical thought aside, he admires her long silky hair, pinned back on one side with a matching coral-and-red pin in the shape of a lotus. She emanates sheer elegance in her black Mandarin dress with coral lace trim. He studies her face. Not the almond-eyed, fair-skinned and pointed-chinned face of classic Chinese models, nor the soft, delicate, dollish beauty of modern Chinese media stars; but underneath her makeup, which tries to connote a reserved, delicate femininity, he sees the sharper lines of a certainly determined woman.

Looking down, he cannot help but notice her dress's long side slit, which reveals her very trim, shapely legs. And adorning her lovely feet are black lace-and-suede sling-back shoes. Two-inch heels. Very elegant and sensible. If she had worn three-inch stilettos, Peter would have no respect for her whatsoever. His girlfriend before Sarah, Ciara, was a physical therapist who educated him on the foot and calf distortions caused by heels and how to remedy them.

She walks ever so wispily towards him. He extends his hand to shake hers, and she clasps both her hands around his in such a way as to ensure he sees no ring on the left hand. "Mr. Gollinger, my name is Mei. That's Mei with a tone that starts high, goes low, and comes high again."

Still in awe, Peter notices that her arms match her legs. Long, very trim, shapely, muscular but not bulky, and oiled. All with the perfect tan. "Thank you, Mei. I am so honored to be here. What's your last name? I didn't catch it."

His hostess simply smiles. "It's just Mei. Do you know what Mei means in Mandarin, Mr. Gollinger?" Peter shakes his head no. "It means simply beautiful."

Peter wants so badly to agree with her as he rolls his tie between his fingers to distract himself from what he's really thinking. Is she the one? The one in his dream?

"Mr. Gollinger, what is that cute little yellow thing on your tie? And on your cap too?"

"Oh, he's Sammy the Slug. The mascot from my university. He's thirty-six years old and still going strong."

"Cute, Mr. Gollinger. Simply cute. Please follow me, and I'll take you to Mr. Chapwell's office."

Peter trails behind her, transfixed by her legs, which seemingly float her across the room. Peter searches for any way to distract his mind from what is clearly a hyperglandular response. Mrs. Harrison didn't evoke this kind of feeling. His nostrils have flared. What's happening to him? As a visceral storm begins to envelop him, it makes Peter wonder how he can concentrate on his interview with currents of raging hormones swirling about.

They enter Mr. Chapwell's office. A perfect corner-windowed suite, except these are not windows, but perfect virtual replicas that display whatever the office's occupant desires. Today, the office sits in the middle of Harvard Square.

"Mr. Gollinger, please let me introduce you to Mr. Harlan Chapwell the Third, Head of Talent Assessment, MoxWorld USA," says Mei. "I'll leave you two gentlemen to your work and wait by the Out of Town newsstand."

Peter takes the sole seat in front of Mr. Chapwell's desk as Mei takes a post in the corner.

"Very good, Mr. Gollinger," says the staid man in the conservative bespoke light grey pinstripe Savile Row cashmere suit. "I'll be asking you a set of questions, after which we will run you through our standard battery of tests, which every candidate across the globe has taken. Let us start with your education."

Looking at Peter's tie and cap, Mr. Chapwell, stiff like a mummy in his heavily starched white Egyptian cotton shirt, starts with, "I can see without looking at your resume that you attended University of California Santa Cruz. Why there, instead of more prestigious institutions like Stanford, Berkeley, UCLA, or an East Coast Ivy?"

With a quick glance around, Peter spies the diplomas on bold display behind the third Harlan Chapwell's head. Princeton undergraduate, summa cum laude. Wharton MBA in organizational behavior. Harvard PhD in neuro-psychobiology. And the "defend the underdog" gene in Peter activates.

"Mr. Chapwell, those are all fine schools. Unquestionably, they've produced some of the finest leaders in all walks of life. I, however, loved UC

Santa Cruz. I loved the spirit of the students and the professors. We had freedom to think, but in a rigorous way. The school fostered us to seek out innovation," Peter asserts as he peers intently into Mr. Chapwell's eyes for a reaction.

"And most of all, I loved the ability to hike in the redwood forests. In the damp morning fog, the banana slugs would all come slithering out, and I would silently commune with them." Peter would have thought this would cause Chapwell to wince. But nothing.

Unfazed, Mr. Chapwell takes note and says, "And your strengths and weaknesses, Mr. Gollinger. Be candid."

"Oh, candor is my strength." Peter beams. "Clearly my strength is telling the truth and doing what is right."

No response from Chapwell other than, "And your weaknesses?"

"Telling the truth and doing what is right," Peter spits out rather cheekily.

"And are truth and righteousness the reasons why you were dismissed from your last job, with the Journal of International Geo-Archeology, Mr. Gollinger? Your job history makes you look more like a loser than a winner. A perennial loser."

Peter smiles and replies, "Oh, you must have spoken to Jerrod. I saved his author from enormous embarrassment and public ridicule. As I explained to Jerrod, that author clearly ignored the last decade's evidence refuting the Black Sea flood hypothesis. Another noted scholar hypothesizes a major meteor strike in the Black Sea around 9,000 BCE may have caused the legendary flooding, wiping out the advanced civilizations thought to have lived on the northern shores."

No response whatsoever from Mr. Chapwell. Instead, he throws a real curveball. "Mr. Gollinger, our reference check indicates a checkered history. Is there a reason for this?"

Peter is caught off guard by that one. "Mr. Chapwell, I thought companies conducted reference checks after the interview was completed. It seems you have a full census already."

"Mr. Gollinger, when you pressed the button to accept our invitation to interview, you agreed to the 2,785-word terms of agreement, which stipulate that you allow us to conduct reference checks and mine our data sources on you," Mr. Chapwell states in his matter-of-fact manner.

With that, Peter tries his best to turn the situation around. "Of course any of my references from my brief stint in New York won't be good. You know how those stuffy East Coast types simply don't understand native Californians. My best references would come from the emancipated, the open-minded, the free spirits whom I have helped establish their voices as writers and authors."

No response from the ice-cold, rigid Mr. Chapwell, which bothers Peter to no end. So Peter takes the verbal duel one step further. "Mr. Chapwell, I don't see any response from you. Nada. Is this normal, or is it true that the Ivy League sucks the life out of you lest you fail to be awarded summa cum laude?"

Bull's-eye. Mr. Chapwell is clearly not amused as he ends the questions and asks Peter to take a series of tests on the screen in front of him. Peter wonders why no more interview questions. He is quite proud of his clever answers just as his father taught him to defend himself in a world built on socioeconomic status and stereotypes.

While Peter starts taking the tests, Chapwell stares at a screen of his own, watching his answers and periodically glaring at him. "Mr. Chapwell, most interviewers go away at this point and leave the beleaguered candidate alone to suffer their fate in the deafening silence of solitude," proposes Peter.

Mr. Chapwell affirms that observing him is part of the evaluation. Oh. Now Peter knows for certain he's going to flunk the interview. He feels that big F painting itself on his forehead.

"Mr. Chapwell, might I ask if there's a time limit for these tests?"

"No," said with no emotional or physical cues.

Five hours later, Peter finishes. He is bewildered by the odd, crazy, sometimes twisted tasks and questions he completed. An SAT would have been akin to adding one plus one compared to this. Oddly enough, he is not tired; quite the opposite, he is surprisingly refreshed after these exercises.

Chapwell lets him know he will have Peter's results later this afternoon and waves to Mei to get him. Peter looks back at her and notices she must have been standing there for hours as there is no place to sit. She must have either feet of iron or superb judgment when it comes to footwear.

Mei comes and takes Peter's hand. The F-word seeps from his forehead into his brain. But the F is rapidly displaced by Mei's light fragrance. Lotus blossom. When did she put that on? And he follows the whiffs of olfactory paradise down the hallway and into the elevator, all the way to the videoconference suite.

Suite is a misnomer, Peter finds as he looks at this enormous chamber with neck-craning high screens in 360 degrees around the perimeter. The room is stark and empty. No chairs or anything, so he stands. Mei centers him in the room, straightens out his tie and takes off his cap. She flattens his collar, feeling around the entire perimeter, then pats down his shirt, tucking it deeply into his pants with her fingers.

To his dismay, she runs her fingers inside the entire waistband, tickling Peter in the process. She straightens his pants by patting them down to their full length.

After discreetly tapping something on her MoxWrap, she waves her hand and Alexander Murometz appears on the far screens. Peter can see him more clearly than on the MoxWrap last night. He has a long face and long ears, with dark eyes that appear very observant, even piercing at moments. He's wearing a black Mandarin-collar shirt with an open neck trimmed in coral, and a simple but elegant gold chain with some sort of pendant Peter cannot clearly discern. A bull's head?

"Mr. Peter Gollinger, so glad you made it to the interview. I apologize for not being there in person. But accept my good intentions. I sent my closest personal representative, Mei, who flew on my jet all night to be there at eight thirty to greet you personally. I trust you find her acceptable."

Peter glances at Mei, standing only a foot and a half to his left. She, of course, gives him another one of her disarming smiles. Peter replies, "She is superb. Simply superb."

"Excellent. She will serve you well, as you will know well shortly. How did you find Mr. Chapwell? Utterly charming, no? He makes Mei look stilted," he says with a laugh. Mei gives a demure snicker as well. "As I said last night, don't worry about those tests. I flunked them too. So if he tells you later that you did, rest assured, you are in good company." He laughs again.

"Peter—may I call you Peter?"

"Of course, Mr. Murometz."

"And, Peter, you may call me Alexander."

"Thank you, Mr. Muro—Alexander. I'm so honored by the privilege."

"Peter, I'm going to ask you a few very candid and personal questions. For the two of us to succeed, you will need to be frank and direct with me. Can you do that for me, Peter?"

"Why, of course, Alexander. My strengths are truth and doing what is right," Peter replies, using his rehearsed interview answers.

"So I heard," Alexander says. "Peter, how did you sleep last night? How did you feel when you awoke? Did you dream about anything special?"

Peter's brain freezes. His hands shiver. How did he know? Peter's fear overcomes him as he replies, "Great. Never better. Fabulous dream about…about…about world peace." Gone is the trepidatious master of words; only a scared, shaking, separation-anxiety-suffering child remains, calmed only by clinging onto his mother's perspiring hand as they watch his father leave this Earth. Forever.

In a conciliatory tone, Alexander confesses, "Peter, I awoke this morning with a profound inkling that I dreamt something of great importance. Something that could change the world. My bed was ruined by my tossing and turning throughout the night, and I agonized as I could not remember what was so important. These lines on my face reflect a lifetime of mornings no different from this one."

He pauses, letting his eyes pierce Peter's eyes as best as a video conference can allow, and then asks, "And how was your morning?"

Peter is astonished at this revelation, feeling as if he has stepped into an episode of the latest *X-Files* revival. He is speechless. Mei moves next to him. She takes his hand into her soft palm and strokes it ever so lovingly with her other hand. A sensation arises. It is very different from any he felt with Sarah, as a calm descends on Peter, enough for him to think about speaking.

Finally, he blurts out, "Lots of crying. Lots of crying and something so heinous. I don't know. I don't quite remember. It hurts so much." And his eyes well up as he thinks about it.

A fleeting feminine face and form taunt his amnesiac afflicted neurons as he senses love—the love between two souls saved from something terrible. He glances at the dark-haired Mei as he becomes more and more convinced she might be the good woman his mother and Pappy described, which would explain why he suddenly has these vague dream inklings. Unclear inklings, but still clearer than he has ever had before.

As if she were in his mind, he feels Mei lift her soft, delicate hand and clear his tears from his cheek. She places his arm between hers and her warm body. His nostrils flare, wanting to imbibe as much of her essence as his sinuses could hold.

"Good response," Alexander praises him. "Courage, my boy. Be courageous and tell me about your grandfather. What about his nights and mornings?"

Peter is astonished again, unsure of what to say. "My grandfather. His grandfather. My mother's uncle. His grandfather. For as many generations back as any of them can remember, all have these dreams of torment," he murmurs, only comforted by Mei's seemingly loving caresses of his arm.

"Good, Peter. You're doing well. Exceptionally well. Peter, listen to me carefully and be candid. What did your grandfather ask you to memorize?"

Fear now overcomes Peter. He stiffens. He squirms. Not even Mei's comforting gestures can calm him. With no sense at all, he blurts, "The stars, the stars are your friends. The winds are their friends. And water will flood all unless it is dry. Only the dove will bring peace once the reindeer are fed. Stand on the tallest mountain and whisper to the sun. And forgiveness will shine down on us once again."

Deep lines run across Alexander's forehead as his face grimaces. "Peter, you dishonor me. I am being candid with you. I had hoped we had established the deepest level of trust where you could be equally candid with me."

Peter realizes Alexander is reading his body language in 360 degrees. But he is so overwhelmed he cannot think straight, much less remember his family's oral tradition. To his continued surprise, Mei, as if one with Peter's brain, leans down to his ear and whispers, "You are courageous and brave. You are so strong. Breathe through your nose slowly. Smell my fragrance you so loved earlier. Smell me. Sense me."

Losing all control, Peter leans into her and smells her. The fragrances sweep into his nostrils and fill his sinuses and lungs. He feels as if they flow into his body, creating the warmest, most wondrous sense of peace. An inner calm and clarity that no woman's scent, save that of his mother, has ever instilled in him. With his momentarily clear mind, he recites the family tradition, word for word, just as his grandfather corrected yesterday morning.

Alexander is pleased, smiling first at Mei, nodding his approval, then at Peter. "Peter, my boy, your recital was perfect. You did well. I am proud of you. Finding the object is of the utmost importance for the two of us."

He pauses while Peter regains his senses. Peter glances at Mei, who gives him a smile of approval and hugs his arm tighter, as Alexander asks, "And is there anything more that either side of the family has passed on to you?"

Another wave of reluctance sweeps through Peter's brain, not wanting to reveal what the parchment means. Mei peers into Peter's eyes, kisses his forehead, and strokes his cheek. Nothing. She looks at Alexander with eyes that say, "Nothing."

Sensing he needs more motivation, Alexander says, "Peter. Rest assured, my interests are your interests. I want to solve the story of the stars, the object, our path to resolution. I want to finally sleep in peace as much as you do."

Alexander follows Peter's body movements and adds, "Peter, think about it. How many generations have wasted how many years, searching for what you and I want to search for? With my resources, the global power and knowledge of MoxWorld, and your special insights, we together have the best chance of anyone in history of solving this mystery."

Peter purses his lips. Mei gazes into his eyes, nibbling her lips ever so subtly. But no response. Peter is close, but not quite ready to bite on Alexander's proposition.

To Peter's surprise, Alexander offers, "Aliens. They brought the object to Earth. It is their way of communicating to us. Think about it. We find the object together, and on behalf of mankind, we will talk with them."

Now alive and chomping to engage, Peter says, "A parchment. A parchment in an airtight tube. A four-thousand-year-old parchment."

"Good, Peter. And what is on this parchment, my boy?"

"Aliens, Alexander. Aliens pointing the way to the object. And obscure dialectic Akkadian writing."

Alexander appears pleased as he says, "Peter, that is perfect. I am proud of you. We will find our aliens and the object and talk with them about anything they want to talk about." He smiles at Peter.

But the white-haired man pauses to look at something offscreen. His face emanates annoyance, or is that angst? But only for a moment, and then he smiles again at Peter.

"My dear boy, I want to hire you. Mei will bring you back to Mr. Chapwell, who has drawn up an employment contract for you to sign."

Peter's dreams have come true, even the ones he can't remember. Though he has to ask, "Getting a job with you is the greatest honor I could ever have, but what job am I getting? The editorial one?"

"Peter, better than an editor. You will get the most important job any human has had in the last twelve thousand years. One of my planes is scheduled to take you to meet me in person within the hour. Mei will get you prepared for the flight and brief you en route."

"Now? Right now?" cries a panicked Peter.

Simply smiling at his new hire, Alexander signs off.

After glancing at her MoxWrap, Mei takes Peter's hand, which she softly fondles as she leads him to the back of the videoconferencing suite, where Mr. Chapwell waits. The screens around the room now show MoxMedia's breaking coverage of the AC's invasion of southern Turkey. But Peter is too distracted to process the importance of this event as he lightly squeezes Mei's hand back. Something about her grasp, her touch, her warmth is so familiar, so comforting and calming.

He looks at Mr. Chapwell's dour face. Has he been there the entire time? Did Peter so definitively and clearly fail the tests that he didn't have to grade them? Chapwell hands Peter a MoxPad with digital contracts to sign—with his finger and not in blood, as Michaela had warned.

Shaking his head, Harlan is disheartened as he mutters, "Why am I here if any old hack off the street can get a prime job with Mr. Murometz? Banana slugs indeed!"

"Peter, we must hurry. We have a car waiting for us, and the plane is on the tarmac, ready for our departure," Mei informs Peter.

"But what about my passport, luggage, my clothes? Can we stop by my place first?" Peter blurts.

Mei gives another one of her mesmerizing smiles, takes both his hands softly in hers, and says in a most sensual voice, "You won't need clothes where we're going."

CHAPTER 8

A person is not just their facial expression, as a small mind
cannot fathom a great mind. Study the middle finger
to tell fortunes by physiognomy. You cannot only look at
the look. What is more important, one must inspect the
personal character conduct, namely heart and morals.

—Mai Youlang, exclusive courtesan
From the Ming dynasty novel, *Awaken the Common Saying*

6:00 p.m. GMT–6, May 7, 2022
Over the Continental United States

"Who are you, Peter Gollinger?" she says back to him.

"Dunno," Peter mumbles with his mouth full of delicious Umbrian strangozzi and black truffle. He is famished as he has not eaten since breakfast. "My mother says I'm more suited to be a librarian than an adventurer."

Mei laughs at him, taking her napkin to wipe an errant piece of truffle escaping down his chin. They sit face-to-face across a table in the front galley, one of five in this custom-built jet. "You are so much more than a cube rat, Mr. Gollinger. There is something lurking within you that begs to come out. Trust me, and I will help you let it out."

Between his first limo ride to the airport, his first private jet flight, and the best food, Italy's best, Peter soaks up the finest of living life on the other side of the tracks. In this case, the other side of the world.

Sipping some twenty-year-old Amarone della Valpolicella, Peter glances to the right and then says, "When I had asked you that same question, I only meant it rhetorically, to say you are someone other than what you project. Or what Alexander wants you to project."

A turn of her head to glance at him shyly, with a seductive smile, and she bounces her leg to rub her foot along his calf, slipping off her lace-and-suede sling-back. "Do you not like what you see? What you feel right now? Is that other side of Peter ready to come on out?"

Eyes wide open. Deer-in-the-headlights open. Peter gulps the swish of Amarone he was trying to sip elegantly, pretending he belonged in a plane like this. "Mei, please believe me. You are the most beautiful woman I have ever met."

She retracts her foot a little as she slips off the other shoe. "Then we agree who I am."

Wiping his mouth with the fanciest lace napkin he has ever felt, he replies, "No. That's not what I meant. I'm trying to figure you out. Clearly you want me to respond to your beauty, but nothing more. Like how you introduced yourself…simply beautiful."

"But that is what my name means. My parents chose wisely."

"I'm sure they did. But there's a different kind of beauty behind the image you project. I can't put my finger on it. Like the beauty surrounding a certain kind of genius."

Pursing her lips, she gazes down at her bare feet, soft, smooth and exquisitely pedicured, her toes bouncing up and down as she ponders his words. She then leans into him, eye to eye. "Then tell me who you think I am."

Nostrils flared again, his breath quickens. "Mei, your fragrance. I can't think. It's killing me. I can only…only." And then his eyes close.

Breathing through his nose, rapidly at first, then slower and slower, and then more calmly, he finally opens his eyes, directly into hers. "You are very valuable to Alexander. Not just because he built this jet for you. Not because you two have some unspoken dialogue. But you know the things he needs. And he trusts you."

She bites her lip. "And what would you say if you knew that what he entrusts me to do is drag you back to my bedroom to seduce you into total submission to my will, and his?"

His eyes widen again. Not deer in the headlights this time, but affronted. "That would be so demeaning to you. How could he expect that? I mean, any man would have to be crazy not to want to be with you that way. You're very attractive. But you're so much more than what you just said."

And a smile emerges again, but not that of a sultry Asian femme noire. Instead in a manner much softer, much more sublime than any she has shown yet. She gets up to take the empty plates in front of them away, but Peter insists on helping. She smiles in that sublime way again and slips into a rear cabin while he cleans up.

On the cabin screen, Rhonda describes how, earlier this morning, while the AC crossed the Turkish border near the Euphrates River, the Russians bombed three of Turkey's airbases in retaliation for the recent downing of their fighter jets over New Kurdistan. Russia has also mobilized multiple squadrons of their most advanced stealth fighters, the Sukhoi T-50, which outclass, outfly, and outshoot the Turk F-16s, to be based in the Crimea. Only moments ago, Turkey condemned the Russian retaliation, claiming they had every right to hunt the Turkish separatist Kurds hiding in the bordering mountains in New Kurdistan. They called for immediate NATO support, but the weakened EU members of NATO are unwilling to back Turkey and risk a war with Russia without the full commitment of Washington and London.

A tap on his shoulder, and he turns around to see huge round glasses. Bigger than his.

"Do you like?" she asks with a laugh. "These are my ugly glasses, when I need time to myself to read," she says as she tries to put on a model's pose.

She leans down to get her shoes and takes his hand. "Come with me."

But he is like dragging a dead fish in her hand. "Peter, come on. We're going to my video galley. What did you think? My bedroom? That will come only when you ask me politely," she says with a giggle and a wink.

They pass through a storage area, with the luggage of the two pilots and three wardrobe racks, and into another lounge with an L-shaped divan on one side and a relaxation divan on the other. Mei points around and says, "This is our onboard entertainment lounge, which doubles as my briefing lounge.

"Please take a seat and make yourself at home. If you would excuse me for a few minutes, I would like to change into something much more comfortable."

Still failing to understand his hostess and her intentions, Peter sits and frets that "more comfortable" means she's going to be coming out shortly in a see-through something. What was that "who am I?" game about if not revealing their innermost selves? Then who is she?

He watches the MoxMedia World News broadcast to divert his anxious mind. Sahir, dressed in a light grey pinstripe blazer with open-necked white shirt, annotates scenes of a meeting between the military ministers of Russia and Georgia, where the former has asked for permission to base armed forces in Georgia. Shots of the Georgian parliament in highly heated discussion are shown. The MoxMedia analysts predict a near-term Russian invasion of Georgia if an accord is not reached. And to what end? In preparation for a land invasion of Anatolia, eastern Turkey?

Peter slumps in his chair, remembering the earlier headlines questioning if the world is on the brink of World War Three. Will the US president break the previous administration's accord with Russia and come to NATO's defense?

Crack. Peter holds his breath as the bedroom door slowly opens. Out comes Mei with her hair tied back in a ponytail, dressed in a loose-fitting V-neck black sweatshirt with elegant mauve trim and a mauve MoxWorld logo, matching black yoga pants with mauve trim at the ankles, and matching silk slippers. Mei says, "And you were expecting… what?"

She sits down right next to him, points to her silver earrings and asks if he likes them. In awe, Peter says, "They're banana slugs! Where did you get banana slug earrings? I never saw those in the college bookstore."

Mei gives him another one of her smiles and replies, "I had them made at my jeweler, while my tailors were making your clothes. They are in honor of your Sammy the Slug, Mr. Gollinger."

She folds her legs up onto the divan with her knees touching Peter's legs. She pokes her glasses so they ride up the bridge of her nose better, then she does the same to his.

"And who are you, Peter Gollinger?" she asks again. "Isn't that where we started?"

"I'm a simple man, just like all the men in my family. A simple man trying to solve the mystery of the oral tradition you heard me recite earlier today," Peter states humbly.

She smiles, but it's the type of smile that is suppressing a laugh. "You know what I think, Mr. Banana Slug? You're a sweet man who plays down those stereotypical Western male hero attributes, in part because of how your mother raised you. So you've convinced yourself you cannot be a hero, what you think women want in a man. But you still try in your own ways to be one, no matter the consequences to your own self, psychological or physical. When you say your motivation is solely to find what your grandfather and his ancestors seek, it is only a means for you to express your desires for the heroic."

To his continued surprise, she puts her index finger on his lips. "But what is it that you truly want, Mr. Peter? You will only succeed working for Alexander if you truly know. Because if you do not, you may get hurt, abused, maybe worse. Maybe ones you love will be hurt."

His mind is afire, not from the hormones he has successfully thus far suppressed, but at how close to home this woman has come to his inner self. What is not true of what she has just espoused? He squirms ever so slightly. His family's talk about the right good woman is all he can think about in this moment. How embarrassing would it be if he let that slip? How inappropriate if he said that? She's the one, isn't she? How will he know for certain?

Resting back on the divan, she says, "Okay. Cat got your tongue? Tell me who you think I was before I worked for Alexander, and I'll show you me. And then it will be your turn."

He looks at those big-rimmed round glasses, her Cheshire cat grin, her intuitive, inquisitive eyes. "You were a teacher. A professor. Not a boring one. But a really inspired one, looking for a way to make a difference in the world."

Mouth wide open, Mei has turned from a vamp into a gapping goldfish. "How? How did you know? You cheated, didn't you? You looked at your MoxWrap while I was changing."

He shakes his head with his mouth open at her response and peers at her with those innocent eyes of his.

Nodding, she touches her MoxWrap, and images appear on the screens around her. "This is me. Assistant Professor of Medical Genetics on cross appointment between the Medical and History departments at Shanghai University."

Fuzzier hair, big black plastic glasses, clodhopper shoes, goofy smile. Peter's eyes are ablaze again. "But how?"

She slaps him. Lightly. "I'm not that ugly. Different, maybe." She runs her finger along his upper thigh very lightly and smiles.

Peter refocuses directly into her eyes behind those glasses and says, "I don't mean how you look, but how you got from there to where you are now. And what does medical genetics have to do with your job now, and me?"

"Like you, he recruited me through a MoxWrap message after he had read my PhD thesis. During my interview, he explained about the dreams, the restless nights, the oral traditions, and the fog that clouds the minds of men like you two. He explained that for some reason, a woman's touch, the right touch, in the right way, helps settle whatever is unsettling you. I voluntarily undertook this mission to find you and bring you on board."

"I can't believe an accomplished woman like you would touch me in such ways only because Alexander says so. There's more to the story than that."

And that same smile returns to her MoxFashion-correct visage. Her hands caress his face, right where his adorable dimple shines through as he grins. "You got me. You know, only one other man has ever challenged me on who I really am."

"Your father?" Peter posits, treading on dangerous territory if she asks him in return about his.

She shakes her head, thinking. "No. Not my baba. A Jesuit father. Well, he says former priest. You'll meet him when we land. A couple of years ago, Alexander found and hired a Jesuit priest who had independently stumbled upon the oral traditions. He had already been combing the Vatican Archives for clues to these traditions for a number of years. This priest had also reached out and contacted those he could find who had lineage connected with these traditions.

"Prior to meeting Alexander, in his interviews with women, he found they were not symptomatic like the men were. It was unclear to him whether or not they were affected, or were simply carriers."

She puts her palm to his chest and slowly rubs. "But he did put together a full pattern of what they did to help their spouses or mates deal with this affliction."

Mei puts her fingers to his forehead and rubs there as well. He closes his eyes. Only his mother has evoked what he senses as she touches him. She has to be the one.

"Like what he did with you and me, Alexander sent a message to this priest, asking him to interview. He made him an offer he couldn't refuse. Alexander showed him the power of combining their efforts and sources, which would hasten their ability to decipher the traditions, find the object, and understand what it means."

"Do his records have more of the tradition than what I've been taught?" Peter interrupts. "Is there more?"

"Volumes more. Volumes in every language known across the globe and in many extinct languages. But much is indecipherable, maybe due to mistranslations over the millennia. And maybe we simply do not have enough analyzed to truly know what it means. And maybe, we were never meant to truly understand."

Peter looks at her in a different way than he did only minutes ago. "I understand now how you were a professor, a highly accomplished one. Very much like a doctor I edit papers and books for. But she dresses differently from you."

"Does she smell like I do?" Mei asks as she pulls his head into her hair.

"Oh my," Peter cries, feeling like he's the fly caught in the spider's web.

He pulls back. "Please, please. I'm having a hard enough time taming the hormones."

She laughs. "And is that really only a hormonal response bursting about in you?" She pulls his head into her neck so her hair can drape over him as her fingers search for something at the base of his neck. "I think not. There's more to what you are feeling than temporal chemicals. There's something more ancient, more genetic."

Back to sitting lotus style, she continues, "Alexander recognized the ancient importance of the five-sense algorithm Jean-Paul amalgamated from his interviews with afflicted couples and the historical texts he found. The female partners used this algorithm throughout the millennia to help their afflicted men not only cope with, but come to understand the messages their minds were struggling to process."

Peter slumps back into the divan as a deep realization begins to unveil itself. He blurts out, "The interview. The hours of tests. You. How you were fashioned to appeal to me. Your actions. Your use of my senses. These were all merely ways for Alexander to screen people for the affliction. One massive worldwide screening tool that only a company the size of MoxWorld Holdings could implement." A mist of eeriness descends and envelops him.

"Good. You will need to have complete trust in me once we get to Luxembourg," Mei says. "As Jean-Paul and Alexander kept interviewing potentially afflicted people, they found they needed someone who would have complete mastery of the five-sense algorithm. Jean-Paul's tests found me to be, in his vernacular, a strong level-ten sensate. I have the highest tested level of senses, the highest levels of compassion and empathy, needed to read the candidate's dispositions, their inner workings, and their senses, through all five senses."

"And your fragrance, the one I felt entering me, that was your use of that sense?"

"Yes, it was designed by Jean-Paul and me with a nasal receptor psychopharmacologist," she says, tossing her ponytail in front of her chest and stroking her hair.

"But there is more," she says. "Fifteen years ago, a geneticist from the

National Cancer Institute proposed the God Gene. He found a correlation between spirituality and a gene that modified brain neurotransmitter transport. Recent studies have shown a larger cluster of genes are found in people with deep religious belief and spirituality. Researchers believe a change in mankind's DNA structure occurred, possibly as early as the last ice age, which led our pre-Neolithic ancestors to be open to notions of mysticism, spiritual concepts, the belief in supreme beings."

She takes his hand and places it behind her head on a specific spot. "Right here lies the brainstem, at the juncture of the brain and the spinal cord, where five years ago, a team of Harvard neurologists discovered our consciousness is located. A joint team between Harvard and my team at Shanghai University recently discovered that spiritual consciousness arises near this same area and that the God Gene complexes are expressed here as well. All funded by Alexander."

Pulling his head into her chest, she touches his neck. "Right here. In fact, you have the same interesting bump at the exact right spot."

A chill runs down Peter's spine again as she continues to rub his neck with his nose buried somewhere very intimate. His eyes start rolling back into his head as he utters, "Please, Mei. I don't want to be one of those monstrous men who attack women. I'm going to lose control if you keep rubbing me like this."

As she holds him even tighter against her softness, his body tightens and he mumbles, "Illyana. Illyana. I can't."

Lifting his head, she peers into his eyes and grabs his cheeks with those dimples.

"What happened?" asks Peter.

"Just as Jean-Paul predicted," says Mei. "Just what my research suggested you would do. You will be the proof that my hypothesis is correct."

She leans Peter back, and he stretches his shoulders and back, then touches that bump behind his neck. "So, we both have a funny bump. I'm an atheist—well, at least according to my mother, who is very Catholic. Although I'm not completely atheist. I follow my father's belief that God is merely a creation of the aliens who have influenced the development of mankind, and maybe all life on Earth. Maybe on other planets. I believe in them."

"You are a funny man, Mr. Banana Slug. I didn't say those with the God Gene complex believe in God, but you are more open to belief because of a genetic predisposition. With that door open, you still need to have a life catalyst to get you to enter the door and believe in God. Or your alien friends."

Peter rubs the back of his neck. "But how does this relate to our finding the object?"

"The dissertation I wrote, which attracted Alexander's attention, posited a genetic history of the God Gene complex that dates back to 10,000 BCE. To the same places that our Jesuit priest colleague traces back your oral tradition, as he will explain tomorrow.

"Enough getting acquainted." Mei touches her MoxWrap, and slides appear. "Here's what we need to cover tonight. I will advise you on all things Alexander—who he is, how he got there, your conduct around him, and most importantly, why your utter obedience is your best strategy. Then you'll need to get some sleep to be fresh for a taxing and demanding orientation tomorrow. We'll start the meeting with him first thing after we land.

"Alexander Murometz. Western-educated. Very well versed in politics, diplomacy, and hardball negotiations. Very smart. Hyper-smart is what Jean-Paul has labeled him. He suffers from the dreams, like you. But he appears to have harnessed them to some degree."

She studies Peter's eyes and continues. "Never underestimate him. Never read too little into what he asks or says. No word is idle. Nothing is a coincidence. If in doubt, ask and clarify when you are in front of him. Never assume. It may be much deeper than you think. Ask for clarification in the moment. He has little tolerance for those who do not use his time wisely. Do not mislead him, and do not hide things from him. He seems to know before you know, and he knows if what you're passing to him isn't quite right. Are we good on this?"

Still feeling that bump, Peter nods.

Her voice deepens as she continues. "Pay attention, Peter. Focus.

Alexander made his initial fortune expanding upon his father's successes in the oil and banking industries, where a number of Russian billionaires also made their fortunes in the late eighties. But unlike some of his peers, he diversified out of Russia in the nineties. Incredibly astute, he avoided Putin's dispersal of the oligarchs, and his banking operation became totally global before the Russian financial crisis in ninety-eight. Likewise, he diversified out of oil before 2010's oil price plunge. He appears to be one, two, and at times three steps ahead of everyone, no matter how great or smart they may be."

"My mother called him a Russian crook," Peter remarks. "Clearly, I don't agree, as I'm here. Everything you've told me simply confirms my supposition that I can learn from his greatness."

Mei just smiles at Peter's naiveté, but crosses her fingers nevertheless. "When you work for Alexander, you must be wary of the jealousy others have of his success. Many have accused him of illegitimate, illegal, ill-gotten practices. When someone or some organization is so successful so fast, critics always come up with these stories, these myths of some conspiracy. His holdings are truly global, knowing no borders. He has fostered connections in all places, financial, industrial, governmental. Governments have tried to curb him, but somehow, they ultimately become his friends. His reach and influence might very well be unparalleled in human history."

Peter smiles. "Somebody said something like jealousy is the root of something. Something bad. But how did his corporate empire expand so quickly?"

"Your country's immigration and economic policies and the botched British exit from the European Union created a financial catastrophe and political turmoil perfect for his meteoric rise in the past four years. His MoxWorld Holdings is only one of many diversified financial institutions and instruments he owns. Leveraging the capital that he had secured in other holding companies, he made bold moves with his MoxWorld organization."

Hand around his MoxWrap, Peter says, "How did these get so popular so fast? Did he bribe some politicians?"

"No, he did not. First, he introduced new consumer technology that quickly altered the status quo in the non-Western world. He gave away

MoxPads and MoxPhones for free to gain instant market share. He was able to provide low-cost data to these users through his revolution in microsatellite communications. People suddenly became truly global, with no dependency on cell towers and networks, sacrificing only some bandwidth. You could be sitting at the South Pole and playing chess on a satellite conference line with someone on Mount Everest for the equivalent of five of your dollars per month."

Peter rolls his MoxWrap around his wrist. "This thing has changed my life and become an integral part of the lives of everyone I know who has one."

He pauses in a moment of clarity, a realization about how abruptly Sarah changed after he gave her one. His mind makes the connection with how his mother began badgering him even more about grandchildren after she got hers. And his ability to remember a small fraction of his dreams only started after this upgraded MoxWrap arrived, unsolicited by him.

Now very unnerved, he blurts, "But I wonder, given how invasive this device has become, how secure is our personal information?"

With her professorial look, Mei replies, "Not an issue for you, or more importantly government customers. The encryption defies the term state-of-the-art. Neither governments, nor other companies, nor hackers can break or replicate MoxWorld's encryption methods, which are multimodal, in part through his proprietary satellites, his networks, and his billions of processors. Some people speculate that the special favors he gets from others in power comes from his affording them special access to the data his systems track. Because Alexander will share important defense security data with nations who work with him, the Mox devices have nearly universal usage in these governments. Ironically, the main holdouts still using the old smartphone technology are criminal and terrorist organizations."

Monologue finished, Mei stretches her legs and then folds them up on the divan again, but this time rubbing her feet.

"When you work for Alexander, you do what you need to do to succeed in your mission. There can be no doubt about this priority, or you will not be working for him long, as you will soon find out. As we will discuss, there are many things you should know and do while in his employ, and the first lesson is to follow his instructions to the letter and not deviate."

Mei grimaces for but a fraction of a second, then gives Peter another one of her delightful smiles as she bemoans, "My sling-backs are about as comfortable as high-heeled shoes get, but a woman's feet can only take so much."

Mei winks at Peter and says, "If it's not too forward of me to ask, would you mind rubbing my feet?"

Without so much as a blink, she puts her feet into Peter's lap. And as his mother had taught, as his grandmother had taught her to teach, Peter is superb. Simply superb at the massage, given the moans Mei lets loose.

He warms her calves with a fast rub and proceeds to address each muscle fiber one by one, in just the right progression from soft, to medium, to pinpoint hard. Then the ankles, the soles, and each toe, one by one. She moans in relief, rubbing his hands back as if to ask for more and higher. And her moans become more and more intense.

Squeezing her knees together, she pulls his hands away with one last deeply satisfying, deeply releasing moan. "I never knew a woman could have an orgasm from her feet."

Shocked, Peter takes his hands away. And she smiles again. "You are who we thought you would be."

As she closes her eyes, Peter imagines the expression on her face must mean she is experiencing the same sensations he did when she first touched him. Is she the one? What did Pappy say again about how one tells if she is a "good woman"?

Mei glances at the clock. "Time for bed." Peter stiffens. Mei retorts, "No, silly, not that type of going to bed! Your pajamas are laid out on the bed. You take the bedroom while I sleep out here."

Peter insists he cannot take her bed. He will sleep on the couch.

Mei replies, "No, silly, you're the key person in tomorrow's meeting, and you need to be fully fresh, awake, and functional. You need to sleep in the bed. I apologize—as I'm sure you can appreciate, I've been so busy today I was unable to get the sheets changed."

With the importance of his sleep clarified, she shows him into the bedroom, takes some things she will need for the night, and is about to turn to the door.

Peter picks up the black silk pajamas laid out on the bed, with teal trim and embroidery and the MoxWorld logo, hallmarks of something Mei would have had custom-made.

She points to boxers in the bathroom. "Made especially for you. A little more special MoxFashion tech. You're just going to have to put them on and tell me about it tomorrow morning." And with a mysterious air, she closes the door.

Alone for the first time since 8:30 that morning, he puts on the boxers and pajamas so neatly laid out for him, brushes his teeth with the toothbrush she has given him, and climbs into her bed. He lies there staring at the ceiling, reflecting upon this amazing day. Slowly but surely, he starts feeling subtly different. He ponders why.

And it dawns on him. Pheromones. Her sheets are full of her pheromones. He imagines the fibers in these pajamas wicking her oils and her pheromones across his full body. Not having time to change the sheets, indeed. This was all planned. Oh, what a night this is going to be. He puts his nose into the pillow and smells, breathing in deeply. Oh, how wondrous this is. He falls asleep in the most peaceful manner of his life.

If only this could last forever.

CHAPTER 9

Try to keep your soul always in peace and quiet, always
ready for whatever our Lord may wish to work in
you. It is certainly a higher virtue of the soul, and a
greater grace, to be able to enjoy the Lord in different
times and different places than in only one.

—Saint Ignatius of Loyola

Late Spring 2018
Vatican City

Nine eighteen p.m. The air cool, the night sky clear, the Vatican is quiet, devoid of the tourists that swarm the piazzas during the day. A priest dressed in his black cassock steps out of the Domus Sanctae Marthae, where a Swiss Guard takes him down the small road between the Palazzo della Canonica and the Campo Santo Teutonico. From afar, it would seem he is being escorted for his security, but up close, the two are jovial, seemingly old friends. But this simple priest could roam the most dangerous streets of Rome and be safe, for he is no small man at 195 centimeters of height. Under his cassock are substantial muscles, and if one looked close enough, maybe a scar or two.

The two enter the office of the Swiss Guard, where the priest partakes in a seemingly informal evening drink with his escort, Captain Buchli, and the Head of the Swiss Guard. At 10:25 p.m., two more junior Swiss Guards escort the priest more formally to the exit gate, and he proceeds alone down Via Paolo VI, along the colonnades forming the south side of the Piazza San Pietro.

A right turn onto Borgo Santo Spirito, where he passes by a well-placed ecclesiastical clothing store. He pauses for just a moment as he notes he will need to cancel his recent order for a new black cassock. But time is short and he keeps walking, passing a series of similar four-story beige buildings. When he reaches a taller one on the corner with five stories, he enters to meet the Superior General of the Society of Jesus.

Father General Antoine Lemoine, SJ, stares out his window, patiently waiting for the tardy priest. He had expected Father Jean-Paul Sobiros, SJ, to return from his private audience with His Holiness the Pontiff an hour ago. What could have detained him?

The Father General is the thirty-first to hold the office of the Superior General of the Society of Jesus, as well as the one who made history as the first Father General of French descent, a heritage he shares with the wayward priest he's awaiting.

Ironically, the Society of Jesus was founded in Paris in 1534 by Ignatius Loyola, who, along with six of his fellow students at the University of Paris, took vows of poverty and chastity. They intended to travel to the Holy Lands and convert the Muslims. However, the Ottoman Wars impeded their professed mission. Instead, they traveled to Rome to seek formal approval for their society from Pope Paul III, and in 1540, the Society of Jesus became an official Order of the Catholic Church.

The Jesuits quickly became an influential force across the New and Old Worlds, spreading the Catholic faith through missions and educational institutions. As with any organization that finds rapid success, the Jesuits became subjects of considerable controversy, accused of engaging in secretive and subversive activities to counter the growing Protestant movements, up to and including infiltrating leading positions in Protestant organizations and national governments. A hundred and twenty years after the Society's formation, the fear of their vast political and financial influence led Pope Clement XIV to issue a papal bull that abolished and suppressed the Society entirely.

It was from this low that successive Father Generals rebuilt the Society of Jesus. Father General Lemoine carried on the good work of his successor in fostering the Order, which still fought the cloud of suspicion propagated by detractors who accused the Order of being truly the "Soldiers of the Pope," the secret military arm of the Vatican. Nonetheless, under his direction, the Jesuits had a historic turn. After many decades of decline, the number of novitiates grew, in part due to the good work and reputation of priests like Father Sobiros, albeit tardy, which helped rejuvenate the interest and reputation of the Jesuits.

Now, only an hour and six minutes late, Father Sobiros finally arrives at the door of the residence of the Father General. Very nonplussed, Jean-Paul Sobiros asks the Father General's forgiveness for his tardiness and is ceremoniously forgiven.

"Jean-Paul, we are behind closed doors. We can now speak candidly. What did His Holiness discuss with you?" the Father General asks. "I will need to reflect upon this matter tonight before I take breakfast with His Holiness tomorrow morning, for surely he will ask my opinion and advice."

"Father General—"

"Please, Jean-Paul, let us drop the formalities. We've known each other for a long time, and we speak in private," the Father General replies.

"Antoine," says Jean-Paul with a little trepidation, "as you had expected, His Holiness heard my request, but expressed his sorrow at the Order possibly losing me."

"Which is the same as I said to you, Jean-Paul. You grew to be one of the most promising and aspiring of our younger Fathers—aspirations which can lead to many more acts of inspirational faith and kindness on behalf of the Order."

Jean-Paul nods. "He asked me to reconsider my requests. He was very gracious and spoke well of my work on the Pontifical Commission for Sacred Archeology, which he encouraged me to continue. He also offered that I act as second chair for his little-known working group on extraterrestrial affairs."

The Father General raises his eyebrow. "Jean-Paul, as you know, his offer is a highly prized honor for a priest of your years, as have been his many personal meetings with you over the past two years. He is trying to tell you how important you are to the Order, as I have said for the past two months, since your first request."

"Antoine, I do appreciate your faith in me. But I believe that it may be misplaced. As I also explained to His Holiness, up until now I have endeavored with deep faith to fulfill the missions and goals of the Church, the Society, and most importantly, the Pontiff. But I find now what I must do would not be consistent with the vows I solemnly took. Simply the fact that I feel that there are actions and pursuits I must personally take, my prioritizing my needs over the greater good, bespeaks to my unfaithfulness to the Order, to my vows."

"Jean-Paul, we can be extremely candid now, can we not? Who is she? I understand how difficult it is for our young priests to fulfill their vows of chastity. We lose too many who rescind their vows so that they may fulfill their marital or sexual needs."

Jean-Paul remains silent on the subject for the moment as the Father General continues, "Jean-Paul, what I am about to offer is not well known, but the Superior General has the blessing of the Pontiff to issue extraordinary, but highly discreet, dispensations for certain priests, those of the greatest promise and potential, to take a leave of absence, so that they may determine with certainty that the pursuit of marriage is truly their calling in life."

Jean-Paul looks out the window into the lights in the night sky. "I could only wish it were as simple as a woman, one who would love me and I her." A quick blink, then he stares directly back into his old mentor's eyes. "Antoine, I will forever be grateful for the space that you, as my mentor and my current Father General, the previous Father General, and above all, His Holiness have afforded me for my unique condition. You, above all, have seen most recently what my affliction can do to me, each night and every morning. I had thought by entering the Society, the spiritual exercises would solve the issue, and for these many years now, they have helped. But my condition continues to worsen, and I find now that to truly address what aches deep in my soul, I must do things that would not be in the best interest of the Order, nor would they allow me to fulfill, to the completeness required, the wishes of the Pontiff."

Jean-Paul looks down in sorrow. "And thus I have requested special permission to revoke my fourth vow, where I further promised an extra obedience to the sovereign Pontiff in regard to his missions. To fulfill my inner mission, I can still remain chaste, still remain in poverty, and still remain obedient in my spirit of faith and love in the following of Christ. And thus I have asked that the Church allow me to retain my ordination, which I believe will be important for me in fulfilling my personal quest, but release me from the special vow to the Pontiff."

The Father General reflects while rubbing his fingers, and then thoughtfully replies, "Jean-Paul, after two months of reflection, do you really believe that forsaking all of your good work in the name of Christ, in the name of our Lord, to enter the employ of Alexander Murometz is truly God's calling to you?"

He pauses, studying Jean-Paul's face. "A rhetorical question, which you have recognized with your silence."

With a voice that echoes the spirit of the Superior General, Antoine Lemoine adds, "Please, with all due respect to your humility, let me remind you of your lifetime of deeds, which have saved souls, lives, and in some cases, prevented needless deaths. Even in your Regency, you and Brother Petrus turned around the violence that local boys perpetrated upon your students. Your academic excellence in biblical archeology and geo-archeology have made you a leading expert in the claims of human-alien interaction in the scriptures. And from this, the Pontiff has found your distinguished value towards his key commission and working group on these subjects."

Flushing slightly at the accolades, Jean-Paul replies, "But a man, a sole man, can never be indispensable. He can be replaced."

The Father General takes a different tack with his young mentee. "And let us not forget the work you have done to save lives. A sole man who saves a life is not indispensable. What you did in Nigeria, the Congo, and in Egypt—

can you tell yourself that those children, those students, those members of our parishes would say you were replaceable? And your relief work after the great quake in Van, Turkey, or with the refugees from Northern Mali—would those survivors say you were replaceable?"

Jean-Paul gets up, stretches, goes to the window and gazes upon the Milky Way. He turns and says, "It fills my soul, your kind words of recognition. Especially as my friend, but notwithstanding as my Father General. Mr. Murometz has shown me a pathway, a solution postulate to a problem that afflicts not only myself but, as I have discovered, many others. My special talents with his resources and access can help save the souls of many who are unaware that their souls could be saved. But to do this, I may need to act in ways that seem superficially to be inconsistent with my vow to His Holiness, the Pontiff. My actions may look questionable for the reputation of the Order, especially to our detractors. Mr. Murometz has indicated that part of his family traces its lineage back to the Jesuit Order in Russia, during the time of Catherine the Great, and thus, he has the utmost regard for what I have vowed to the Order. I trust that you will trust me when I say that I intend to uphold my other three vows in what I will do."

And with that, the Father General gets up, shakes his black cassock and in a deep voice requests, "Father Sobiros, I ask that you meditate on the wishes of the Pontiff for two more weeks. I will take your request under advisement in my conversation with His Holiness tomorrow morning. You are dismissed."

"Father General, thank you for your audience. *Ad majorem Dei gloriam.* For the greater glory of God."

And so the humbled Father Sobiros, perhaps soon to be simply Jean-Paul, leaves the Jesuit Curia. As he slowly walks back towards his residence, Jean-Paul stares at the Milky Way again, deep in contemplation.

Then his MoxWrap taps his wrist. The message reads, "Did he accept our story?"

Jean-Paul taps back, "Yes, Your Holiness."

A few seconds pass, and then the reply comes. "Then may the Lord be with you on your mission."

CHAPTER 10

He who gives away shall have real gain. He who subdues
himself shall be free; he shall cease to be a slave of passions.
The righteous man casts off evil, and by rooting out
lust, bitterness, and illusion do we reach Nirvana.

—Buddha

8:30 a.m. GMT+1, May 8, 2022
MoxWorld EU Headquarters, Luxembourg

"So, I hear you are a Jesuit."

Zara sits on the edge of an exam table while a physician takes her wrist pulse, her poor new bayramlık looking much less crisp after the ordeal she has suffered at the hands of a monstrous man. Or perhaps her holiday dress was fine, but she looked worse for having met "him" again. Against her will. At gunpoint.

"A former Jesuit," replies a tall man a number of centimeters taller than she, with a slight French accent. He is dressed in a black turtleneck vicuna sweater with raspberry trim and black dress pants. "My work with Alexander required I renounce my vows and leave my order."

She stares at his crucifix hanging below his neck over his clavicle. Silver, a little tarnished. Much like she feels at the moment.

"So which kind of Jesuit were you?" she asks with a hint of a grin at the edges of her mouth. "The great educators who taught the world's eager minds in the hope of converting them, or the secret soldiers of the Pope who clandestinely infiltrated and manipulated the greatest institutions and nations on Earth?"

Staidly and calmly, the former priest continues his manipulation of a number of medical instruments, seemingly making some concoction. The physician now standing with him took a cotton swab of her cheeks upon her arrival not long ago after a tortuous nine-hour affair, from helicopter abduction to an airport in Georgia where she was forced to board "his" jet. His very private one with the special bedroom, Jacuzzi, and another galley with tools of his deviancy.

Upon landing, "he" insisted she be given a pelvic exam. That OB/GYN is now nursing two or more broken fingers. Why on earth would "he" insist she be checked down there? He should know well enough. First, that he should have hired a female physician, and, second, that nothing has changed down there since he last saw her.

Fighting her fatigue, as Sasha kept her up all night, she says, "I am still waiting for your response. You must be a Jesuit as you are contemplating the different answers you might offer, deciding whether to mislead me or not. Aren't you?"

He turns to her, and she blinks as the one shiny spot on his crucifix catches the bright white exam lights and sparkles in her eye for a microsecond. He slowly blinks back and states, "I was neither. I was but a humble priest carrying out the Lord's work. And now I am but a humble man carrying out the same work."

As he turns back to those mysterious medical instruments that hum and blink multicolored lights, she asks, "And why would such a humble man work for the less-than-humble Alexander Murometz?"

He glances back at her with a smile. "The Lord works in mysterious ways." He checks her dark eyes, which only stare at him, piercing into him. He chuckles. "That is a priest joke. We have simple humor, we ex-priests."

He holds up a vial of clear liquid and hands it to the physician next to him, who prepares an injection. Very nervously, this male internist approaches the woman with a less-than-pleased look. "Please, madam, could you roll up your sleeve?"

With a smirk and narrowly squinted very dark eyes, she says, "Aren't you the one who splinted the fingers of that other doctor who tried to violate my modesty? You look like you would find my bare limb very stimulating, wouldn't you?"

Scared and shaking, the doctor hands the syringe back to the former priest and hastily exits the room. The man formerly known as Father Jean-Paul peers into her eyes, no smile, no emotion, only asking, "So, where does that leave us?"

"Well, first, you can explain what is in that syringe," she says, flexing her fingers. She grimaces. Her right pinky still hurts as that monster made her remove her splint on the plane ride. How perverse can a human being get?

"It is a genetic vaccine based on DNA sequencing we made from your cheek cells," he says. "It is designed to activate dormant sections of your DNA. Alexander said you had significant reconstruction and therapy after a major traumatic incident several years ago. This vaccine will help repair what they could not back then."

"And you expect me to believe that?" she replies as she scoots up on the edge of the exam table, readying herself for a myriad of physical responses, options formulating in her head. She sizes him up. A dozen plus centimeters taller than she. Likely very muscular, but the black turtleneck does not let her fully discern how sculpted. Not what she would have expected in a priest. She studies his hands, then stares at the scabs on her own knuckles. He has vestiges of scars on the same knuckles. What kind of priest was he?

"How do I know you are not going to sedate me? Maybe that's a date rape drug," she posits, looking for him to drop his calm demeanor. "But you are French. Of course you would want to seduce me and do the unspeakable to me."

And that got the priest to change his expression. His face lightens with a smile and a flash of his glistening white teeth. "*Mais oui, ma chérie.* You know us Frenchmen, we like to wine and dine our women and read sonnets of love before we seduce them. Not drug them," he mocks with an exaggeratedly thick French accent.

One eyebrow up, the other eye squinting, she retorts, "Oh, I know you French too well. You strip innocent Muslim women of their headscarves and force them to show you their legs by banning long skirts and dresses in schools. And you demand women remove their burkinis at the beach because you lust to see our bare bodies. Oh, I know you all too well."

Smiling at her, he looks around the room for something. And he finds a long, thin towel on a rack, which he drapes on his head like a hood. "Monks, Armenian and Syrian priests cover their heads like this. I did too during a yearlong retreat in a monastery. In fact, early Christian women all covered their heads in public and at services. Nuns and Sisters still do today. Our faiths are not so dissimilar."

She's now the lioness ready to pounce at a gazelle. "Yes, while we're at it—what about those women of your early churches? The ones who helped spread Christianity in home churches out of the eyes of the Romans. Where did that get them, by the time your bishops met at Nicaea and banned women from priesthood?" She had him now.

"I admire your theological education. You are right, it is commonly believed that the Council of Nicaea impeded women's ability to serve in the clergy," he says, still with a smile. Not the kind that mocks, but the kind that admires.

"But scholars today read the Nicaean records as saying the female deacons of those days were nonordained," he adds. "No official statement stated whether they could be later ordained or not. However, the Council of Laodicea fifteen years later stated that women may not go to the altar, and the Councils of Orange one hundred years later finally forbade the ordination of deaconesses."

"And do you expect me to believe what is in that syringe will reverse the injustice of what the Daesh did to me, to my family?" the Kurdish woman half-jests. "Just because Alexander wants me injected does not mean I must follow him. I stopped believing in him years ago." She rubs her eyes, suppresses a yawn, and glances down with a tired, dour aura.

The tall Frenchman puts down the syringe and turns to address her. "I am like you. I do not follow Alexander blindly. I do so because what he asks of me is consistent with what I believe is my mission on this Earth," he says before a pause.

"I understand you have been brought here against your will," he adds. "I offer my condolences for your situation. In your anger, you have acted out against a few poor souls who only wanted to help. Something deeply agitates you. More than your flight. So I offer this question. What is it that you seek? The desire, the want, the need that keeps you here in this building. I sense you are more than capable of walking out of here by your own will and force."

She breathes in deeply as this Jesuit, as his Order usually does, has pinned her on the core issue. Exhaling slowly, she then says, "Because he said he would help my people achieve their millennia-old goal of independence."

A glow emanates from the eyes of this former priest as he peers into hers. "Good. And is that the same desire you would tell God?"

She shifts and rocks on that exam table, wanting to hop off and run. Anywhere but here, where she feels he is compelling her to answer this question. One that makes her deeply uncomfortable. Maybe as unsettling as her great-grandmother's discussion with her about Rabi'a al-Adawiyya. Is it God's will that everyone around her should nudge her in the same direction?

"Please, I do not mean to cause you any more discomfort than you have already suffered," he says. "From your trying flight here with Alexander. From your arduous life journey that has led you here, to this moment. As to what is in that syringe, I ask that you trust in God. I can only offer that I believe it will help you in your journey towards what you seek."

Not sure whether to smile, put on her challenging face, or cry, she simply asks, "Which one? My commitment to my people? Or to God?"

And this man, who says he is no longer a Jesuit priest, gives the frustrating answer only a Jesuit could give. "Which one would you want this vaccine to give you?"

As she reflects, now more still and calm on that table's edge, she realizes that is the type of question her mother's grandfather, the Sufi imam, would have asked her. Or maybe he did, but so long ago she no longer remembers.

She nods, for this priest has held his ground, allowing both of them to maintain dignity and respect. Not what she would have expected from a Jesuit lackey of Alexander. Perhaps there's more under that turtleneck than just muscles and blind obedience. She rolls up her left sleeve and jests, "Priest, you may touch my arm. I trust you will not find my limb enticing."

Sides of his mouth uplifted, he says, "Madame Khatum, you are a very beautiful, deep woman. Outside and inside. I would be only so fortunate if I were to be that man with whom you selected to share your innermost wishes. But alas, I am but a humble man, who would simply welcome sharing prayer time with you."

She smiles, a much more genuine one, as she holds out her bare upper left arm for his puncture. He swabs an area with alcohol near what looks like a bullet wound, which he gently touches and avoids injecting near there.

As he puts a Band-Aid on her arm, she says, "*C'est mademoiselle, Prêtre.* And I would be honored if you would pray with me."

"*Bon*, good," he says, and gives her the very oddest of smiles as he stares at her arm. She glances at her arm and finds out why. He put a Hello Kitty Band-Aid on her. She crumples her lips and nods her head at him. Touché.

"Father," she says with a more demure inflection. "If it would not be an imposition, I would like to know how your relationship with God has been since you renounced your vows. I only ask because I had once left my faith. But as God was willing, I have come back to his submission."

He blinks methodically and reassuringly. "I wondered the same as I was asking for my Father General's permission to leave the Order. His Holy Pontiff only agreed because he knew in my heart, in my soul, I would remain faithful to my vows, even if no longer ordained. Just as Christian women did without ordination after Nicaea."

Zara purses her lips ever so slightly as she nods in reflection. And then she peers into his eyes. "Did you ever have the feeling of emptiness, even though you prayed, even though you remained faithful to your vows?"

And he steps up to her, very close and in a way that she thinks he might kiss her. Or maybe that is what she wants.

But he stops at arm's length, takes her hand, and holds up a splint. "I saw you nursing that finger. Would this help?"

And she sighs in relief. He is a man of God. Truly, as she allows him to put the splint around her finger and tape it. He turns her hand over to expose her scabs and puts his knuckles next to hers.

"There was a time," he says, "when I felt such an emptiness. I thought running away with the woman I loved would fill that emptiness."

She is hooked by his words and asks, "And what happened? Was she why you became a priest?"

He smiles and rubs the back of her hand with his thumb. "She let me know that love was truly the way to fill that emptiness. The love of the Lord."

She inhales, nodding her head. "My great-grandmother would love you."

"Thank you," he says humbly. "And you?"

She slyly smiles and replies, "I'm still thinking about it."

A few moments pass, then her YPJ officer face comes forth. "But seriously, I cannot fathom you. One does not truly leave the Catholic Church, much less the Jesuit Order. Not if what Alexander tells me is true. You were close to the Holy Pontiff, were you not?"

He methodically blinks, humbly nods, and smiles.

"Then for me to believe you did leave, it would be like believing a good-looking, well-built, intelligent, charming US State Department agent in Iraq when he says he has left the CIA." She pauses, watching his reaction.

But there is none, other than a rapid blink. Moments pass as they watch each other, and then he glances at the clock behind her.

"Please, if you could excuse me, I must get material ready for the arrival of the Chinese researcher who led the development of the vaccine you so kindly allowed me to administer. I ask that you rest here for another half hour and please let that very terrified physician come in to monitor you for any reactions you may have to the vaccine."

As he is leaving the infirmary, he turns to say, "Oh, yes, I asked the staff here to prepare a prayer room for you. It is down this hallway to the right, across from the men's room. I have placed a nice soft prayer mat in your room."

She hops off the table and walks over to him, taking his scarred-knuckled hand into her own. "You are still a priest, are you not? You never left the Order, did you, Father?"

And he only blinks rapidly and smiles. "I am only Jean-Paul. Simply Jean-Paul."

CHAPTER 11

May these vows and this marriage be blessed. May it be sweet milk, this marriage, like wine and halvah. May this marriage offer fruit and shade like the date palm. May this marriage be full of laughter, our every day a day in paradise. May this marriage be a sign of compassion, a seal of happiness here and hereafter. May this marriage have a fair face and a good name, an omen as welcome as the moon in a clear blue sky. I am out of words to describe how spirit mingles in this marriage.

—Jalāl ad-Dīn Muḥammad Rūmī,
thirteenth-century Persian Sufi mystic

9600 BCE
Northern shores of the Black Sea

A slightly overcast morning with a little sun peeking through. Cool temperatures, but Nanshe is always warm from the love of her family, she thinks as she bundles the tall grass she and her sister-in-law, Zamana, gathered earlier this morning. Like many of the women whom the graces of providence allowed to escape the unspeakable acts and the undignified dress forced on them by their giant captors, they started to cover themselves more completely, allowing them modesty, dignity, and respect.

And they began teaching their daughters, who are now of the age that shows their femininity, to dress in this new manner. As Nanshe explained to her husband and older brother, Namu, this new style will not only preserve their dignity but, more importantly, make their beautiful daughters less attractive to the Reindeer warriors.

Ki and her cousin Taja, younger than Ki by a sun cycle, work today in the nursery, an area set aside for the care of the young animals in the manner of Taja's mother, who taught them how to domesticate. Cycles and cycles of the sun ago, Taja's great-great-grandmother first found and raised the babies of a wild female aurochs that the males of her family had killed in the hunt. And so, generations later, her great-great-granddaughters play with these cute animals, which, when they grow up, weigh as much as twenty men and are as high as Ki's forehead. Although their meat is prized, their skins needed for clothing and simple ropes, and their horns valued for many purposes, it is the milk that comes from the females that is most important to the family. Today, Nanshe calls for them to bring the milk they obtained this morning into the house.

In the clearing in the forest near Namu and Zamana's house, Orzu is helping his brother-in-law defoliate more forest to enlarge the crop-growing area. Fortune smiled on Namu to pair him with Zamana, as she inherited the domestication and farming knowledge of her ancestors. To that end, Namu owed his eternal gratitude to his younger sister, Nanshe, whose brilliance in negotiation made for the fateful opportunity to free Zamana.

Eleven years ago, she and his new brother-in-law met by chance with Other Siders on the big lake and began the trade in this black stone they called obsidian. In the early negotiations with a young Reindeer warrior to protect their families, Nanshe saw hiding in the shadows behind the warrior a teen girl in rags, barely covered, beaten so that her beauty was taken, and in deep, deep sadness. She knew what this meant.

She nudged Orzu and said they should trade all the obsidian they had in reserve for this girl. The warrior, having seen his slave's resistance to learning the ways of pleasing him and his fellow warriors, had planned to slaughter her anyway, so he thought this trade to be a bargain.

Ki and Taja bring the milk into the house and give it to Nanshe and Zamana, who are preparing lunch for the family. During lunch, Namu profusely thanks his sister and her husband for their help in relocating their farm closer to the big lake. The Reindeer warriors get closer and closer each sun cycle.

He and Zamana sheltered many who were fleeing their tyranny, their debauchery. They heard the familiar stories of women taken into sexual servitude, but now also of the young men, as there are fewer and fewer girls for them to abduct. In fear for his sons and daughter, Namu listened to the oral traditions his brother-in-law required his siblings to recite once a day, every day, and so he moved his family away from the tail of the bird star.

Ki and Taja eat at the children's table with their male cousins. Anxiously, the boys arise, saying, "We must practice shooting arrows now." Ki's brother An is not so keen on shooting arrows, for his passion is fashioning them. He has become expert at making obsidian arrowheads and spearheads that are superior in cutting power to those of the Reindeer People. So good is his work that Nanshe asked Orzu to use these to barter with the Reindeer warriors as a way of meeting the increasing price of their safety. Despite Nanshe's expertise at negotiating with Other Siders and villagers, the Reindeer People will not negotiate with her directly as they believe women to be inferior. And so she stays in the background, knowing full well she is always the leader of the family.

Ki comes out to run with the boys to the shooting range after having changed her clothes to something more suitable to the task. Seeing her daughter's dress, or lack thereof, Nanshe yells, "Ki! Come back here right now, young lady."

"What's wrong, Mama?" Ki asks impatiently.

"What did we say about how proper girls dress?"

"Mamaaa, my breasts are fully covered, as are my loins. The boys can see nothing," the disheartened Ki pleads.

"Ki, how many times do your father and I have to remind you of what the Reindeer men will do to you if they find you attractive? Although your father will never speak to you of his sister, remember well what I have told you of her and me. We will not permit the same to happen to you. You must remember that your exposed limbs can be considered desirable, as well as your shoulders and your calves. All can incite the lust of the uncivilized male."

"But how can I shoot well if my arms and shoulders are so draped? Can I at least wrap them tightly in cloth?" Ki begs of her mother.

"You are one of the most lovely and attractive young women of all these lands. And if, perchance, the Reindeer warriors come unexpectedly? Your uncovered beauty may incite them to break our agreement. My soul would shrivel, burn, and die if what happened to me happened to you," Nanshe replies with finality. Ki reluctantly goes back to her side of the house and changes.

Out on the long clearing made for the children to practice their hunting skills, Ki's cousins are missing the targets over and over again, with only a couple arrows even hitting one of the trees in question. Ki holds a mighty bow that clears her head, stout and heavy. After studying Illyana's bow, which her husband kept as a penance for his perceived failure, her mother had her brother An fashion a much stronger one. Ki had to develop great upper-body muscularity to handle such a bow, which she did as she helped with the nets and sails on the fishing boat. Her mother trained her to do all that which the men could do.

Ki, late to the games, takes the range. She draws one of An's special arrows, aims, waits, waits, then releases. The arrow hits the small tree she targeted and shatters the trunk. Not only do An's arrows feature the sharpest, hardest arrowheads, but the shafts are longer and thicker, made from oak trees in this new area. She shoots again and shatters another tree.

In her mind, and more importantly, in her soul, she remembers what her mother drilled into her in secret—the horror her dead aunt faced when three arrows to the heart did not kill that Reindeer warrior. Ki shoots again. Third arrow to shatter a tree. If needed, she will stop a Reindeer warrior. By will and by force.

Orzu left for the fields with Namu before this shooting contest, as Ki with her bow and arrow reminds him so much of his beloved Illyana that he cannot bear to watch. Namu thanks him again for his help. Orzu replies that on the days when Narn is repairing the nets, he and Nanshe are happy to come and help her family.

As they clear a new section of land, with the tamed giant male aurochs pulling out trees, stumps, and rocks, Orzu laments that he is fearful that the trade-for-safety agreement he and Namu's sister made years ago will not last for much longer. The fact that Reindeer warriors are now using young men for their perversions means daughters like theirs are becoming rare.

Namu concurs, shaking his head over the heinous things the Reindeer People are doing to others. He asks the sky, "Is this why we were put on this earth, to be slaves, to be sacrificed, and to be objects of the most egregious forms of abuse for these beasts?"

His brother-in-law's pleas remind Orzu of his beloved Nanshe, who prays every night for the safety of her precious family, Orzu included.

As they clear a dense group of trees and rocks, they spot the tip of a strange boulder, unlike any that cover it, unlike any from all the lands nearby, unlike any sitting beneath the shores of the vast lake. They dig around the giant stone to expose more of the base. Black and somewhat smooth, with some round pitting. They get enough exposed to secure ropes and hooks around it, such that the aurochs can pull it out of the ground. With the power of four of the giant beasts, the stone eventually budges, and with levers and planks, the men roll it onto the open ground. A large black-and-grey fusion of rocks unlike anything on earth they have seen or heard of.

Overhead, the skies rapidly darken with the type of clouds one would not want to encounter when fishing on the big lake. And then come the blinding flashes, with the sound of multiple lightning strikes rapidly coming closer and closer. Orzu grabs his brother-in-law to flee into the forest, seeking some modicum of safety. They reach only the edge of the trees when they are blinded by more than twenty flashes in succession. And the instantaneous booms deafen them. Scared for his life, for the first time, Orzu tries praying to Nanshe's god while assuming the fetal position on the ground. For minutes after the cacophony ends, which to them seems like hours, Orzu looks up and finds his brother-in-law in the same position. He yells, "Namu, you okay?"

Namu looks up and around to ascertain if it's safe and yells back, "What did you say?"

"What did you say? Speak up, you are whispering," Orzu replies. Realizing the comedy of their deafness, Orzu arises and gazes back into their newly cleared field.

There are billows of steam and broken ground. And the stone is glowing, colors of yellow to orange to red. Orzu pulls Namu up and they slowly approach the stone as if it were a wounded wild animal and they wanted to ascertain if it were safely dead. They stare at the object. Its black-and-grey tones have transformed into warm hues. In the areas that are cooling first, the darker tones begin to return. On closer examination, they observe that the lightning strikes have created a fissure between the two rock types.

Inspecting the area, Namu finds a few large splinters of this stone, which are already cool enough to touch. He picks up one that is the length of his arm and weighs like a timber of wood. He tells Orzu he wants to use this to open the fissure in the stones further. He takes a large stone-head club as a hammer and drives the splinter into the crack.

Flash-boom. They are thrown backwards several paces.

Stunned, Namu raises himself into a sitting position on the ground and says, "What? What did you say? Please repeat for me again?"

"Are you still deaf from the thunder?" Orzu yells. "I didn't say anything!"

Namu shushes him as he listens. He says to the air, "A boat? How big? Right here? Angry? How angry? That angry, huh?"

Namu rises and goes to Orzu to help him up. Namu explains the phenomenon to Orzu. "At the risk of you thinking me touched in the head, I was told to build a boat. Big enough to take my farm and my family."

Looking at him as if he has lost his mind, Orzu says, "Maybe we should have Nanshe look at you. Your sister is highly skilled at comforting the madness that we may succumb to in our moments of duress."

"No, no. You don't understand. The voice said to build a boat. I don't know how to build a boat. Will you and Narn help me?"

Humoring his brother-in-law, Orzu kindly replies, "Why, of course. Let's go to see your sister Nanshe, and after her soothing teas, we can go to my house to build your boat."

"No, no, no. The voice said to build the boat here. We need to use the strongest wood from these oak trees."

Orzu is sure now that something is seriously wrong with Namu. Nanshe will need to prepare her strongest herbal remedy for him.

In a rare moment of humor, Orzu quips, "But, Namu, if you build a boat here, how will it float on the lake, which is more than a couple thousand paces from here?"

"The water. The water will be angry," mutters the dazed Namu. "The angry water will float my family away in my boat."

Later that night, Nanshe assures her husband that her double-strength herbal potion should help her older brother recover. As they prepare for bed, she strokes her husband's head and asks if he is sure that he too is not so stricken. After his affirmative response, she says her prayers and they bed down for the night.

That night, the first ever night of the affliction, Nanshe is terrified by the yelling and physical duress of her beloved. So terrified she must awaken him. Their bedding in shambles, he trembles in shock. She asks if it was the dream of Illyana again. In great fright, he says he doesn't know. He can't remember. She tries to comfort him as best she can. He finally falls asleep again, with her in apprehension of the next bout of terror.

This same scene occurs night after night for the next several days. Orzu is getting more and more tired. And one day, he falls out of the fishing boat into the waves of the big lake. Nanshe strips off her outer garments and dives into cold waters to save her husband. Narn, Ki, and An help them back into the boat, and Ki covers her father with the only blanket they have with them.

That night, Nanshe has resolved she must find a cure for her husband. She has talked discreetly with her sister-in-law and determined her older brother does not suffer this affliction, nor does he hear that voice anymore. She concludes that her extra-strong herbal potion needs to be brewed again, for her husband this time. Giving him a bowl of this steaming brew before bed, she prays, and they retire for the night.

And after observing him for a long spell, she is thankful when he appears to rest peacefully. She falls asleep next to him. Then it happens again, no different from all the times before. Nanshe tries to physically comfort him. At her wits' end, Nanshe decides to talk to him. She tells him how much she loves him. How much she needs him. How much his heart speaks to her. How much his thoughts, which he freely shares with her, mean to her.

In a moment of inspiration, she says it again, but this time she rubs his chest and talks about his heart and love. She rubs his sweat-laden forehead with her fingers and talks about his thoughts and how he shows his love through his ideas. He appears to calm more. As she feels the warmth of her loins growing, she strokes his member, saying how he makes her feel so loved in this way. His mind now clear with a modicum of peace, he hugs her, telling her in tears how much he loves her. They kiss over and over again, and with intimate lovemaking, they settle into a blissful sleep.

The next night, Nanshe thinks she is onto something. She begins to try different things to help calm him and clear his head. Hugs and making love are not enough on their own. And she finds over the course of several moon cycles that rubbing the chest, forehead, and loins is a mainstay of all combinations she has tried. But by involving all five senses, whispering to him, licking him, letting him taste and smell her, and touching his chest, forehead, and then lower down, she settles him such that they both rest clearly, calmly, and with love.

Over the next sun cycle, on days when they cannot fish, when the nets or boat need repair by An and Narn, they go to Zamana and Namu's house. Nanshe has found a simply delightful village girl and negotiated with her father to allow her to be the bride for her younger brother. She and Zamana have tried to school her in the proper attire for ladies. At first they are met with resistance, but as her new young sister-in-law realizes, it may very well save her someday from the Reindeer warriors she so dreads, and so she begins to adopt some of the new style.

And during that sun cycle, as they endeavor to complete this seemingly silly big boat, they work late into the evening to finish tasks that are best not left to the morning. Nanshe and Orzu bed down at her sister-in-law's house. She has described to Zamana in private what she has to do to calm her husband, so her sister-in-law prepares the most private area of their home for them to sleep for the night. Much to Nanshe's surprise, her husband rests more calmly that night, not needing even a brief moment of her calming methods.

The next day, they go back to their home, newly extended for her younger brother's privacy. Narn and his bride, Sama, welcome them back. After dinner, Nanshe puts her children to bed, says her prayers, and beds her husband, knowing his affliction is finding a cure. She will not miss his bouts of nightly torment, but she would be sad if the intimacies she has developed as therapy were to end. But that last part is fully in her control, she thinks to herself secretly. And much to both of their dismay, the affliction strikes that night, no less tormented, no less violent, no less unforgiving than all the other nights.

The next day, she begs forgiveness of Narn because they need to stay over at their sister-in-law's home. And sure enough, Nanshe sees that her afflicted life partner is much less troubled, even without her therapeutic comforting. She concludes this stone, this object, must be connected to the affliction.

Morning comes, and Nanshe says to her older brother to take her to this object. Around and around, she circles the black-and-grey stone fusion, which she deems an object, as it looks and behaves as no stone they know of. As her husband and her brother watch, she goes to touch it. Cold. She feels nothing. But she knows what it means to her and her husband, with his cursed affliction.

As she always did, she commands like the older sister she is as she says she will take part of the object back to their house. Orzu shrugs his shoulders at his brother-in-law, who knows that tone of voice full well from their mother and knows that the only thing to do is get it done.

So Namu and Orzu collect the giant aurochs, six of them this time—three for each side. They place hooks and harnesses around different parts of whatever this substance is, and the aurochs begin to pull in opposite directions. They strain and grunt, to no avail, over and over again. So focused are the three, they do not notice the clouds gathering, grey and angry.

Nanshe, not one for suffering fools, people and objects included, ignores the pleas of her menfolk. She takes her brother's club and says to them, "Wood can only be split with a wedge that is cut from its own tree." And she whacks the sliver of the object that had remained embedded all this time, for she is going to take this object home for her husband no matter what, or so she prays.

Flash. Boom.

They are knocked back several paces. The aurochs break loose and bolt. And before they can raise themselves from the earth, simultaneous flashes and booms overwhelm their senses. More than they can count. More than the last time. They are temporarily blinded, deafened, singed. Their nostrils fill with the essence of this energy discharge.

As she calls out to Orzu, Nanshe crawls on the ground, feeling her way to him. She stops, thinking she heard a voice, but clearly not that of her beloved husband. And she yells to the voice to talk louder as she has been deafened. And the voice is beautiful. The voice is harmony. The voice is love. She looks for where it is coming from, but her eyes are blurry from the lightning flashes. And into her nostrils come the most wondrous smells. Peace.

And then she feels the warm arms of her husband come around her with his kisses to her forehead as he places his palms over her stricken eyes. She asks Orzu, did he hear the voice? The voice was a voice of love. Trying to comfort his wife, he says no, he did not. She now understands what her brother has been through.

After much time recovering on the ground, their sight and hearing begins to return. Namu comes to them, saying he heard the voice again. It said the time is near. The end of the defilement is near. The voice said to finish the boat with thick layers of tar and start putting their house, animals, plants, and family into the boat.

Nanshe explains that she heard something entirely different. Beauty. Harmony. Love. Warmth. And she hears a whisper. She looks at Orzu, who shrugs as he heard nothing, obviously the odd man out. She listens very intently and says, "I understand what I need to do. I understand that too." She turns to her menfolk and tells them to round up the aurochs to finish splitting the object. They look at her, still afraid after what just happened, and she gives them the mother look. They shrivel, cower, and chase the aurochs.

But the lightning did the job they started to do. That which six aurochs could not. That which the wedge could not. The object has been split into two. Nanshe's prayers have been answered.

Making a sled with planks, they use three of the aurochs to take their part of this object to their home. That night, Nanshe puts her children to bed and says her prayers, which include the modest suggestion that the object outside cure her husband. She puts her husband to bed and kisses him goodnight. She awakens later to find her husband tossing and turning, but not with the violence or physicality of before.

And as she has been told to do early that day, she takes her husband in her arms, lightly strokes his arm. She opens his tunic to expose his chest and rubs it with her palms, expressing her love of his heart. Then she places her fingers to his forehead, expressing her love of his mind. She continues for minutes, as she licks and blows into his ear and whispers for him to smell her neck and hair. And following her therapeutic regimen, she kisses his lips lightly and whispers for him to taste her. They kiss open-mouthed for minutes as she strokes him lower beneath his nightclothes.

As the voice told her to do earlier, she opens up her nightclothes, brings his head down into her bare breasts and says to him, "See my breasts, smell my breasts, feel my breasts." As he does so with gentle, loving movements, she whispers, "Hear them," as she moves his head against her left breast. And likewise, she says to taste them, which he does as a baby does to its mother. It is working. The voice of beauty, of harmony, of love was right. Her beloved's affliction is linked to his nightmares about his sister. Illyana's heart between her breasts.

What she does as she followed the voice's guidance so comforts her beloved that he pulls back and speaks clearly and calmly. "It was so clear. My dream, it was so clear. We need to go to the other side of the lake. The Reindeer People are coming tomorrow to renege on their agreement." And thinking about what would happen, he begins to shake.

In deep embrace, first in fear, then in deep caress as peace returns into their being, Nanshe takes his head to her breast and strokes his warm, firm member beneath his nightclothes. "It's that time of the month, my love."

He looks at her, puzzled. Why, then, is she stroking him so in the way that leads to the craze of lust and then love?

Nanshe shakes her head and smiles invitingly. "No, silly, not that 'time of the month.' But the other time. The night to make a new baby."

CHAPTER 12

He who climbs never stops going from beginning to
beginning, through beginnings that have no end.
He never stops desiring what he already knows.

—Saint Gregory of Nissa

9:00 a.m. GMT, May 9, 2022
Approaching Belgium in Mei's personal jet

Awakening, he tries to remember where he is. The pillow is nicely placed under his head, the same as it was when he fell asleep. It's not bunched up or thrown around, and the sheets are not all over the place like a war zone. This is not normal. Less fog in his mind. Less ache in his head.

Suddenly, Peter stiffens with apprehension. He looks to his left, where Mei sits atop the bedcovers, stroking his arm. Seeing he has awakened, she smiles at him and then strokes his forehead with her fingers in that way that's just right.

"But I thought you slept outside?" asks a groggy-brained Peter.

Mei pulls her head up onto his pillow. "You were having a very rough night. Very rough. I came in and fixed things. How are you feeling?"

"Fixed things? What things? What did you fix?" Peter yelps.

"You certainly are not the Western romantic hero type. The kind who wakes up in the morning next to his lady love and hugs her with poetic musings about how much last night meant to him," she says with a giggle as she sits up in bed.

Sitting up with her, he rubs his eyes, his temples, and replies, "That's part of this curse of our nights. We don't remember anything."

"Really? Not even great sex? The throes of the most ardent flames igniting the innermost desires of eternal bliss?" she jests as she strokes his cheek.

Confused, fogbound, and very frightened, Peter pauses as he scans her. Her pajama buttons are open at the top, showing beautiful pale skin above her bust with no sign of flush. "You're playing the femme fatale with me again, aren't you?"

She giggles again. "I will as long as you keep reverting back to that boy who does not think he is heroic enough to wake in the morning with a woman he called the most beautiful he ever met." She reaches over and rubs his forehead in that special way.

He closes his eyes and savors the moment. She knows. How does she know to do this? And then he feels her hand opening and slithering through the buttons of his pajama top, then the warmth of her palm on his chest, over his heart as she rubs in a way he has only felt once before—yesterday with her.

And his respiration slows, the fog of his night begins to clear. Palm still on his heart, his head is guided by her other hand into her neck, her hair, and the scents of her, still with that touch of jasmine, fill his nostrils. And time slows.

Minutes pass, and he finally mumbles, "Illyana, I cannot."

Somewhat perplexed, Mei shakes her head. Grimaces. Then puts his head to her chest and says, "Gaze upon me. Listen to my heart." His breath quickens and she says, "Illyana. You can. You can."

He mumbles, "No, I cannot. I cannot kill."

Mei pauses. Shaking her head, lips pursed, she looks to the ceiling. She inhales deeply and then gently brings his head up to hers and open-mouth kisses him.

Peter's body goes limp in her arms. And he mutters, "Nanshe. Nanshe. I love you so much."

Taking the cue, Mei says back, "I am Nanshe and I love you too."

And Peter replies, "Not that time of the month. But the other time. Time to make a new baby."

She hugs him, lightly. His lifts his head up higher as if to see if it is safe to emerge. She musses his hair and smiles, giving him the reassurance he needs. "What were you seeing? I am very flattered you would like to start a family with me. Usually it takes a guy several years before he is willing to take that step, if ever," she muses, hugging him again.

His eyes roll right, then left, then down as he angsts. *What do I tell her? I saw her in my dream. She asked me to make a baby with her. She's the one.*

Mei sits next to him as she says, "You have proven my point that afflicted men need only be touched in a certain way to activate their residual memories. As you will soon find out, Alexander adamantly believes otherwise. He believes that I needed to have had sex with you last night in order for you to have your visions, your primordial flashbacks."

Remembering what Pappy said, Peter nods in agreement with Mei. *She has to be the one I dreamt of. She has to be who Pappy said I'd meet.*

Dazed, Peter stares at the end of the bed, shaking his head. He turns to Mei, who gazes into his eyes, then says, "You still owe me what you can recall of that dream. You know. That baby-making one."

He turns to her, his eyes fixed on hers. "Only if you explain what's really happening here."

She takes his hand into hers and shakes. "Deal. Now, what was going on in your head? What did you see?"

He nods and then feels her hand with his thumb, rubbing in circles. "A man and woman. Together. In the way that my grandfather described. And she with him in the ways in which you just touched me."

A pause as he gazes back into her eyes.

Snap. Snap. Snap. Mei clicks her fingers in front of his face. "Don't go there. We're not those lovers."

"But we are," Peter pleads. "You're the one in my dream. You're the one my grandfather described. You're the good woman my mother described."

She puts on her disarming smile, which sags into a flat line. "My mother would be in heaven hearing you say that. But we need to stay focused here. We have a mission to complete."

Peter gazes down again. "And your turn—what is this mission really about?"

With a rub on the back of his neck, in that special spot, she replies, "In your head, in your dreams, are the images and emotions of what happened a long, long time ago. Somehow, in your DNA, hidden in the ninety-eight percent of your genes that are normally dormant, that knowledge was coded and passed down from one person to another, just as the oral tradition was passed."

"Why me? Why am I seeing things now?" laments a confused Peter, gently touching the spot on his head that the Neanderthal hit two days before.

"We think—that is, I think...my hypothesis is that the five-sense algorithm I used on you helps activate the expression of those dormant genes," Mei replies in a very professorial tone. She then glances to a syringe resting on her dresser. "And if you could forgive me, I injected a genetic vaccine into you last night. One which would activate those genes."

Eyebrows raised, Peter feels both his shoulders, searching for any sign of being injected. "What am I? Your guinea pig? They eat guinea pigs in South America."

Mei rolls up her left sleeve to show a minute red spot. "Silly, I vaccinated myself as well in San Francisco. We both have activated dormant genes. Do you think just any man could make me moan from my feet? We are both genetically special, and now genetically enhanced such that the five-sense algorithm can have maximum effect.

"That is why Alexander made me vice chairman of his prized MoxBioGenetics unit. With the power of his amassed scientific talent, I have access to the resources needed to fully activate what is repressed in your head."

"Your hypothesis? What other hypotheses are there?" asks a pondering Peter.

"Alexander fervently believes the afflicted man and woman must have intimate sex with fluid exchange. Fortunately, the former Jesuit priest you will meet this morning has a much more moderated point of view. One of us is correct," Mei, the professor, the scientist, and the executive, states simply.

"I'm still not comforted by all of this. I feel like a lab rat. All of this, last night, is all about you finding out if you're right, isn't it?"

She buttons up his pajama top. "Last night was all about a very special man who adeptly stepped around the outer persona I was asked to wear. About an even more special man who may have stepped around my outer persona protecting me from the brutality of a man's world."

She takes his hand into hers, very warm and soft, and then touches his left dimple. "A man who might meet the definition of what my mother told me a good man was, who I let have his way with my beloved feet and calves."

Peter finally smiles. "And what did happen between us last night?"

A giggle, a smile, and soft eyes. She answers, "I'll tell you after you meet my mother and pass her 'good man' test."

She laughs again, and that persona she spoke of reemerges. "But in all seriousness, I personally believe in Alexander, his goals, and what the results might mean to all of us. Not only you and me, but a lot of people. He has my complete and utter obedience in this matter. So if Alexander tells me it is essential to our mission for me to be close to you, to nurture you, then I will."

She pauses, looking out the window at the morning skies as they pass over the English countryside. "There are limits, though. He has asked me to go beyond my limits. He will do the same to you too. Every person has to decide when they have reached their limit and weigh their limit against the importance, the value of what is challenging that limit. Sometimes limits change. You may find yourself in this very situation very shortly. You will have to decide on the spot what you will and will not do. You may have microseconds to decide. And the consequences of not deciding may be dire."

Peter stares out the same window, reflecting deeply on what she has said.

"We're an hour out," says Mei, looking out the window with Peter.

"We need to get ready for your big day."

She gets out of bed and tells him to use the shower and bathroom while she goes up to the galley to fix their breakfast. Peter finds a new set of clothes laid out for him—a long-sleeved button-down black dress shirt in a cotton-silk blend, with the softest thread count, the MoxWorld logo embroidered in raspberry on the pocket, matching raspberry cuff buttons, and much looser silk blend boxers and black dress pants. As he dresses, he frets about what is going to happen in Luxembourg.

He comes up to the forward dining galley, where Mei has laid out breakfast. She tells him to start without her as a lady needs a reasonable amount of time to get ready in the morning. So Peter catches the morning edition of MoxWorld News AM while eating. Rhonda is wearing an eye-catching low-cut coral cowl top, which brings back memories of his last moments with Sarah. She has neutral brown smoky eye shadow and coral lip gloss.

Rhonda annotates a video of Turkish bombers being fueled and readied. What is their destination? Sanliurfa, where the AC forces are heading, or the newly declared Anatolian Kurdish State?

The news flashes to the Georgian parliament, where their prime minister is shown giving his agreement for Russia to station several armored divisions, several squadrons of fighters and bombers, and assorted landing ships and frigates within their borders. The screen cuts to footage of Russian T-50 fighters in the Crimea, taking off for their transfer to Georgia.

Sahir comes on screen, describing how the US president is reversing his country's previous stances, committing the US to honoring NATO agreements and defending Turkey. Stock footage shows F-35 fighters as Sahir explains that three squadrons of America's top fighters are in transit to Incrilek airbase in southern Turkey.

Peter is astonished at how quickly the world has descended to the brink of world war as the news moves to the ongoing issues in the South China Sea. However, the object of his astonishment changes as his eyes bug out when Mei enters the cabin.

Matching Rhonda perfectly as if they had talked this morning, on top of a coral silk blouse, appropriately buttoned up to her clavicle, she wears a black suit jacket made of the finest vicuna, with raspberry buttons and trim, and a matching pleated skirt that extends down nearly two inches below her knees. Black silk stockings down to black patent shoes with a one-inch heel and a raspberry accented bow. And behind her sleek black-framed glasses, wireless around the bottoms of the lenses, her eyes peek out from under lids adorned with neutral brown smoky eye shadow. Her hair up in a tight professional bun, she asks, "Do you like, Mr. Gollinger?"

He smiles. "I think that's you. The woman who you want to be and who you are."

"Why, thank you, Peter," she says as she touches her earlobes. "But I meant how do you like my earrings?"

His eyes instantly dilate. His breathing slows as he sees on her ears, of all things, little yellow banana slug earrings with bright raspberry spots and eyes. Peter grows weak in the knees at seeing his mascot adorning her ears.

He stands in awe of the MoxWorld EU HQ campus, surrounded by much greater acreage than the US office, a clearing in the forest. This time, the dark monolith stands outside the front entrance, surrounded by a pool and fountain. But this monolith, a fourth larger than the one in San Francisco, dominates the senses. Is this how the man he is to meet dominates the world, by dominating the senses with something greater than all of them?

Mei leads him inside. As before, Peter sees no guards, no reception desk, only screens showing the different news anchors of MoxMedia broadcasting their stories from across the globe. The US Sixth Fleet is being readied in Naples to sail towards the conflict in the Black Sea. Peter looks at all the female news anchors, worldwide, who all dress in the same color schemes as do Mei and Rhonda.

Well, no one else has the good taste to wear banana slugs, except his dear Mei, whose gesture was so special to him. The first onset of eeriness for today sends him into shivers. He asks himself again what kind of man this Alexander is that he coerces, objectifies his female employees all over the world, forcing them to dress in color coordination as if they were his minions.

Mei touches her MoxWrap. A door opens, and she instructs Peter, "Remember, do exactly what I ask. Trust in me. Trust in what I am about to do. You are here to learn today. Only ask germane questions and not the flippant ones you did with Mr. Chapwell the Third, as doing so will only get you deep into trouble. Not only with Mr. Murometz, but with his beloved Kurdish woman."

Body rigid. Eyes wide. Seeing this, she takes his hand into hers and plants a moist kiss where his right dimple should be. "Above all, remember to be the bold man who courageously challenged my outer persona, seeking the real me. Can you do that for me?"

He nods, and she says, "Now, wait on the other side of the door as I get Mr. Murometz."

And with those instructions, they enter the room. It is round like the conference room in San Francisco, with several doors around the perimeter. But unlike San Francisco, in the middle, five white high-back chairs surround a low round clear glass table, two on one side and three on the other, set up so the participants can see each other clearly. The room is lit all around the edges with a royal blue fading into a sky blue lining the ceilings. A floral scent covers a slight chlorine tinge.

On the other side of the room is an awe-inspiring, towering man, dressed in black, watching the news play on the screens around the room. His height dominates the room as the monolith dominated the outside. More than two heads taller than Peter, over seven and a half feet in height, he turns and faces them with his long face, long ears, and dark piercing eyes that seem as if they look straight through you.

Mei goes up to this giant, and she hugs him. Not quite the typical French two-cheek kiss. To Peter, it seems more intimate, but what does he know? He grew up in California.

"Is he ready?" Peter overhears, to which Mei nods, glancing towards Peter.

The giant glances over at the telltale mark on Peter's right cheek, smiles, kisses the top of her head and says, "That's why I love you so." And Mei leaves through a door opposite Peter.

Alone with the gargantuan giant who turns towards him, Peter's nerves start to get the best of him. Something very primeval quakes inside him as he stares upwards at the towering monstrous man. Should he be scared? Or very scared?

CHAPTER 13

*Obviously one must hold oneself responsible for the evil
impulses of one's dreams. In what other way can one deal
with them? Unless the content of the dream rightly understood
is inspired by alien spirits, it is part of my own being.*

—Sigmund Freud

*12:40 p.m. GMT+1, May 9, 2022
MoxWorld EU Headquarters, Luxembourg*

His long legs only need a few strides to cross the room, and then Alexander Murometz looms over Peter, who strains his neck to look up at the man who is his new boss. At his eye level, he beholds a platinum pendant around the giant neck. A bull's head again? A gigantic hand extends out to shake, interrupting Peter's inquisitive thoughts, and Peter puts his own hand out meekly.

"Welcome, Peter," the monstrous man says. "I'm so pleased you could meet me in person. Please. Sit down."

"It is my honor to meet you in person, Mr. Muro…Alexander. And it is so nice we can talk sitting down this time."

Taking the seat directly opposite Peter's, Alexander asks, "Did you find Mei to be beautiful?"

Peter is thinking all sorts of things; how she appears to be his destined love is not so appropriate for the moment, so instead he says, "I found her to be the perfect tutor. The perfect host."

"Excellent. I trust she briefed you on the work Jean-Paul and I have done over the past few years."

"Yes."

"Excellent. Then I will introduce you to the project for which you will be a team member. You've already met Mei. You'll be meeting the other team members shortly."

Alexander pauses, glances aside and then back at Peter. "First let me ask you, how many people do you know of who experience the dreams you and I suffer?"

Remembering Mei's instruction, Peter pauses to think. He decides to answer conservatively and replies, "Other than you and me, my father, his father, and my mother's uncle. That's five in total."

"Excellent. And why do you think, in a world of nearly eight billion, only five are afflicted?"

Peter thinks again. What did Mei say yesterday? Never underestimate him. Never read too little into what he asks or says. So Peter asks, "Could the answer be that I have yet to meet enough people and ask the right questions of them?"

"Exactly, my boy. There must be more. Finding the true answer is merely a question of reaching a large enough population and screening for the behavioral and genetic markers of the affliction."

Peter sees the same smile on this giant's face that he saw on his father's face when he answered his questions sitting atop his lap with the archeology journals.

"The dreams—the affliction, as Jean-Paul calls it—run in my family as in yours. These dreams dominated our upbringings. And from childhood, I was resolved to finally solve the meaning of the dreams, resolve the affliction itself, decipher the meaning of the ancient traditions, determining what the object means and how to harness it for world peace."

Alexander pauses, gauging his young protégé's response. "And you, Peter, what did you agree with your grandfather to do?"

Peter does not hesitate in this answer. "The same. To finally decode the oral tradition and find the object. I guess I can add world peace too, but in all honesty, that wasn't part of my discussion with my grandfather."

"Excellent. I'm pleased you feel you can be candid with me. Let us seek world peace as a goal you and I will share. Our special bond. My boy, on your journey you will find many ups and downs, many confusing new concepts, many new people whose trustworthiness you will need to ascertain. The one thing that will be certain, the one thing you will find over time to be the one constant, is the bond between us. You and I, we are more alike than different at a very deep level."

Peter's brain pauses. *Alike? Who is he kidding? I have a neck ache staring up at him with those piercing eyes of his. Don't underread him, she said. I don't read him at all, and I'm too petrified to ask.*

Pausing a moment, Alexander then describes why he built up his empire as he did. Fortunate to have access to his father's wealth, he expanded that fortune step by step, not for the money, not for power, but in order to gain access to what was needed to solve the puzzle of the affliction and the traditions. He needed to find a way to screen billions of people in every remote corner of the earth. New technologies needed to be created and put into as many hands as possible. He needed to gain access to historical archives in libraries across the world. Jean-Paul and Mei helped him gain insights into hidden information in the Vatican and China, but he needed the advocacy of bureaucrats worldwide as well. So his reach extended deep into key organizations around the globe.

Seeing the giant pause and stare into his eyes, Peter realizes he needs to acknowledge him. "A very well laid-out plan. Very ingenious. You have so many critics. If they only knew the truth of what you have done for mankind."

"You are very astute, young man. You can go far in my organization," the giant compliments him. "I have my critics. I let them speak, for history is rife with critics of the successful. Driven by ignorance, by jealousy, by impotence, critics do little to build the world. They accuse me of influence peddling. They accuse me of behind-closed-door deals at the highest levels of social, political, financial, and religious institutions. They accuse me of making critics, opponents, suddenly turn favorable or disappear."

Alexander chuckles lightly. "Ironically, the last organization accused of such global influence was the Society of Jesus, and here I have a Jesuit working with me. But a Jesuit who works not for power, or money, or worldly goods, or the charms of a thousand virgins, but to solve the traditions, find the object, and discover what it means, or what it does. And maybe for world peace."

Peter is enamored with this man and his vision. And his grandfather would be so proud of him; he is finally going to solve the mystery of what has ailed their family since the beginning of known time. But Peter refrains from letting Alexander know his true purpose in joining this endeavor. World peace is nice, but helping his grandfather finally to find his peace is what Peter seeks here.

Leaning forward in his chair, Alexander stares into Peter's eyes with his own piercing dark ones and says, "Peter, I trust Mei has reviewed with you the terms of working with me? Are you on board? If so, you must trust me implicitly. Only if you fully trust me and trust your team can this mission be successful." To which Peter agrees fully.

Again with those dark piercing eyes, Alexander stares straight into Peter's soul as he says, "And there's the confidentiality agreement you signed yesterday. If, after hearing what the mission is in totality today, you find you're uncomfortable with it, with what you may need to do for it, then you can leave. But you must keep what you hear, your mere presence here, in utter confidentiality. I want your personal agreement, eye to eye on this." Peter agrees.

"You should know, as well, there is no one alive who can tell you what happens when you break a personal agreement with me," Alexander says ominously, and Peter shivers again.

With these terms made perfectly clear, Alexander raises his hand and a door opens. Another tall man, shorter than Alexander but still much taller than Peter, walks through, dressed in a black vicuna turtleneck sweater with raspberry trim and black dress pants, matching Peter's. On his chest is the flash of silver from a cross.

"Peter, may I have the honor of introducing you to Father Jean-Paul Sobiros?" says Alexander.

Peter stands and shakes this priest's hands, and he says, "Welcome, Peter. It's merely humble Jean-Paul. I have so awaited your arrival."

"Humble, huh?" says Alexander. "This priest's academic pursuits led to his appointment to the Pontifical Commission for Sacred Archeology, which is where he first found the traditions and history of the afflicted. Even more interesting, my sources in the Vatican indicate he was a member of a hush-hush group working on the Vatican's strategic plan if contact were to be made with extraterrestrials, something Jean-Paul will neither confirm nor deny." Peter looks for a reaction from the good Father, who simply stands by with his serene smile.

"My sources also indicate he had a special relationship with His Eminence and became his point person for certain difficult subjects and situations." Alexander looks at Jean-Paul. "I am told you and His Eminence would regularly meet behind closed doors in his private residence, discussing topics to which no one but you and the Pontiff are privy. Other than you, I could not find or develop a source for further clarification. And so I offered Jean-Paul a position he could not refuse. My sources say your renouncement of your vows was very controversial, very disconcerting among the highest levels of the Church. You have my deepest respect for your sacrifice in leaving the Church. And the results of your work thus far have justified your decision."

The former Jesuit simply nods with a rapid blink. Peter looks around to see what flashed into his eyes. Nothing.

Alexander looks at him. "Jean-Paul. You may say you left the Order, but a source says you may still be Father Sobiros. But only one source. The others say the pope fully accepted your renouncement of your vows. I guess some things can be kept secret for the sake of your own privacy."

Before Jean-Paul can contest Alexander's words, Alexander glances at his MoxWrap and excuses himself. And Peter is alone with the former priest.

Jean-Paul, in his serene way, assuages Peter's apprehensions. He informs Peter he remotely watched Peter's entire interview and testing in San Francisco. He asks Peter if he truly understands how special he is. Like

Alexander, he is a direct descendant of many afflicted ancestors, and thus he possesses the most genetic concentration of the affliction markers they have found to date, other than Alexander.

Peter stiffens and interrupts, "How do you know what my genetic structure is? Only three people in my near family are afflicted, and only two in a direct lineage."

Jean-Paul blinks in a measured manner. "Your mother is afflicted. Her parents are as well. Your grandmothers and grandfathers on both sides as well."

Stunned for the first time today, but sure more is yet to come, Peter asks, "And my sister?"

"Michaela possesses almost as close a DNA match with the hypothetical originator cluster as you do."

He explains his hypothesis of an epicenter for this affliction—only a few people. Over the millennia, these genes were diluted. But if clusters of afflicted people interbred, the genetic markers became more concentrated, and their DNA makeup more closely resembled that of the originators.

Scratching his head, Peter asks, "But how? How did you collect and analyze people's DNA?"

"A miracle performed by Alexander's several holding companies, which all provided information and resources in different incremental and additive ways. I joined with Alexander because he had developed the ability to screen billions and billions. You see, each and every one of those free MoxPhones and MoxPads contain a rudimentary one-use genetic sequencer built in. This data, along with their searches, their communications, and their notes are all screened in Alexander's central processing facilities, which are the largest of their kind, orders of magnitude larger than those of any other company or any governmental agency. From this, we garner lists every day of possible new afflicted individuals."

He pauses, closely watching Peter. "Peter, may I ask, how did you get your MoxWrap?"

"That's a good question. I won one for each member of my family and my girlfriend, Sarah, in a contest. Just a few months before Sarah and I moved to New York," Peter adds sadly.

"As in your case, we send free MoxWraps to everyone who tests as a possible high positive on the MoxPhone and MoxPad initial screenings. The MoxWrap is a much more sophisticated piece of technology. It features full gene-sequencing capabilities, multiple methods, and multiple samplings. The MoxPhone only takes finger secretions through the screen membrane. The MoxWrap allows much more skin contact around your wrist as well as a greater array of biometrics. Along with the multitude of other uses of the device, we can get an extremely accurate picture of an afflicted person's behavioral markers and family tree, a list of people we may send a free MoxPhone to if they do not already own one."

The civil liberties gene in Peter erupts. "But what about data privacy? That's illegal, isn't it?"

"Why, Peter, did you not read the user agreement required to activate your devices, and the user agreements of certain apps? Certainly you are not one of those people who simply pushes the 'accept' button, are you?"

Peter, wearing his editor hat, retorts, "You mean line four thousand out of ten thousand?"

Jean-Paul rapidly blinks and replies, "You are close, Peter. Actually, on your unit, it was line 3278 to line 3321, with an addendum on line 8734."

Jean-Paul lets him absorb this information, however true or untrue it is. "The high-probability candidates worldwide are invited to interview at no cost with a MoxWorld company. And then we confirm our test algorithms and gene sequencing with fuller biological samples obtained during the interview process, and we confirm our behavioral and ancestral algorithm findings in that five-hour test you took."

Peter squints, trying to remember at what point they could have gotten his biological samples. Mei on the airplane? Did she take samples from him? Is that what she did when he slept?

"I have personally conducted final screenings with a couple hundred around the world. And you and Alexander are the most exceptional among billions around the globe."

Peter rubs his chin in deep contemplation. He asks, "And Mei?"

Jean-Paul blinks measuredly again and replies, "She is a positive. Not as high as you and your sister, though."

"Does she know?"

"She knows she's a high moderate positive, but not the full extent of the DNA match and where. Sometimes, the DNA match means physical manifestations, including morphology, and sometimes it can mean behavioral, and sometimes it means both."

Morphology? Peter rubs Mei's God Gene bump behind his neck as he sits forward. "But the women—my mother, my sister, Mei—they don't have the dreams, and yet they're afflicted. How can that be?"

A slow blink and Jean-Paul clarifies, "Another very astute question. I have wrestled with this question for many years. I cannot find instances of symptomatic women in the billions we have screened today. In my survey of the historical archives, including the Vatican's, there might exist isolated behavioral cases, but we cannot confirm as we do not have their DNA samples.

"Most of the afflicted males have the dreams, the disturbing restless nights. I would not call it sleep as it does not feel that way. You see, I too am afflicted," the good Father confesses with a quick blink. "But as we look at the oral traditions, in women, and a very, very small percentage of afflicted men, the affliction may manifest itself as voices."

"Joan of Arc," Peter blurts, remembering a discussion he had with Dr. Fontaine.

"Yes, Peter. The historical records of her trial list statements and incidents consistent with the affliction. But the restless dreams are the most consistent marker."

"The oral traditions, like the one your grandfather insisted you know by heart—we have literally tens of thousands of pages of these now transcribed and cataloged," says Jean-Paul. "Interpreting them is another story. A highly complex issue. Much of what has been captured in writing and by oral transmission over hundreds and hundreds of generations may be distorted or entirely inaccurate due to transfer inaccuracies."

Hand on his chin, Peter remembers the sharp chastising Pappy has given him over the years for making the simplest of mistakes.

"Further exacerbating the situation, afflicted siblings of the afflicted parents may transfer a different story to their children than their siblings do.

Most often, something is added to reflect the world of that distinct family arm. Thus, no two sibling lines of oral tradition are exactly alike."

Jean-Paul asks Peter if he would recite his family's oral tradition. After seeing he can do so perfectly, Jean-Paul says his is the oldest in chronological order and is from the original afflicted persons. Peter smiles. And then Jean-Paul recites the fuller, more complete tradition from the originators he has assembled through Alexander's empire's resources:

"Part one: Tens upon tens upon tens of cycles of the stars ago, the long-tailed star came from the sky and our lands became ice, and winter became forever. Only the giants of the reindeer prospered because of power from this star. Thus, the forefathers of our forefathers' forefathers moved away from the land of the ice. We prosper as we move farther away each generation. Keep looking for lands rich in animals to hunt, water to fish, grass to harvest, and settle there. Make alliances with neighbors for safety. And be wary of the Reindeer People, for when they arrive, you must move away from the direction of ice to seek safety. The bright star, the tail of the bird, will be your guide. Watch for the long-tailed star, which came from the direction of the bird. For when it returns, lands will again become winter, and the lands and animals and even man will change again.

"Part two: And be wary of the giants, the Reindeer People, for when they arrive, you must flee and seek the mountains past the hill of obsidian rocks that overlook a land rich in animals, water, grasses, and your new safety. Follow the vision and words of the black object, for this will guide you as you seek your new land.

"Part three: Remember your father's words. But equally remember your mother's words. Only with the two together can you find peace. The object. You might see in sleep, might hear. But only as man and woman. The object can destroy. The object can save. But only with the man and woman together may you guide the salvation of others."

Peter slumps back in his chair. Part of him is disappointed that his ancestors didn't transmit the tradition completely right, even with Pappy replicating the same chastising his great-grandfather had given him and so on up the family tree. The other part of him is entering nirvana. Aliens did indeed come and guide human history. These Reindeer Giants prospered through the power of a star.

But Jean-Paul interrupts Peter's moment of thought. "And, Peter, can you see now why it is so vital we work together to find this object? It can save. It can destroy. It can guide the salvation of mankind. It may somehow be linked to this long-tailed star, which one day could bring another catastrophic change to our environment, and to us."

The former priest adds, "As you may have noted, I broke this earliest part of the oral traditions into three parts. I believe they are temporally different and come from different originators over that time. The last one I believe comes from the matriarch. She is vitally important as one examines the history of the later traditions. I believe she is the one who originated the five senses algorithm."

Peter snaps back to reality and says, "My grandfather said I must find a 'good woman,' one who can talk with me as we work out what this all means together. Only with a man and woman working together can there be salvation."

Peter slumps in his chair again and then thinks about Mei. *She's like me.* And a little smile warms his face.

Astutely watching Peter's every movement, Jean-Paul adds, "And although I said earlier that Mei was only a moderate match to the originators' DNA cluster, I think she may exhibit a higher match to the matriarch's. Under the assumption that I was correct, I trained her in my best reconstruction of the matriarch's algorithms, which I believe she used to address the patriarch's symptomatic affliction."

Nirvana. Peter is near as the image lovely visage of the dark-haired Mei dominates his senses. He has finally found his destiny with the woman of his dreams.

CHAPTER 14

Run from what's comfortable. Forget safety. Live where you
fear to live. Destroy your reputation. Be notorious. I have
tried prudent planning long enough. From now on I'll be mad.
                    —Jalāl ad-Dīn Muḥammad Rūmī,
                    thirteenth-century Persian Sufi mystic

1:20 p.m. GMT+1, May 9, 2022
MoxWorld EU Headquarters, Luxembourg

Only moments after the towering magnate reentered the room did he let the proverbial "other shoe" drop on Peter's head.

Stunned, Peter stares at the giant man. Did he just say Pappy was a Nazi?

"I am only telling you this for your own safety," says Alexander. "According to my sources, your great-grandfather worked in Himmler's Ahnenerbe unit, created to provide the archeological and historical evidence for the superiority of the Aryan race. But Himmler's deep interest in the occult added a different dimension to their work. Your great-grandfather enlisted the help of his teen son, your grandfather, when he served with the Ahnenerbe unit, assigned to investigate the Ukraine and Crimea. We share a common past, Peter. Your great-grandfather saved the life of my father when he was first stationed there. My father was studying the same things your grandfather was. They worked together until the Russians forced the Germans into retreat. I would not put it past the Ahnenerbe to have tasked both of our relatives with exploring ancient alien origins in this region."

Jean-Paul leans over to Alexander, shows him his MoxPad+, and whispers something. Alexander subsequently asks, "And so you do not know how your great-grandfather died?"

Peter, so disturbed he cannot speak, shakes his head no.

"He killed himself before having to face the Nuremburg trials for war crimes," the giant man states, staring into Peter's eyes.

Jean-Paul mercifully takes over. "Peter, my research would suggest your great-grandfather killed himself not because he committed or participated in any war crime per se. I believe he killed himself to protect what he found and took from Crimea. And this is why Alexander asked if there are any other documents or items your grandfather may have."

Peter shakes his head no. Jean-Paul leans over again with the MoxPad+, showing it to Alexander, who says, "Excellent. Then that concludes this discussion. Do you have any questions, Peter, any concerns?"

Thinking hard about Mei's wisdom about not wasting Alexander's time with frivolities, he meekly asks, "But why am I here? Why am I so important to you? What do you want from me?"

Jean-Paul confers with Alexander and answers, "We believe you have the answer to a dichotomous pivotal question presenting an impasse to our search. We believe that in your subconscious, deep, deep inside, lies the answer."

Alexander takes over, stating, "Peter, in your head lies the image of the object as well as how to access its power. I think our object is a monolith of sorts, which is why you have seen my facilities all have a monolith at the entrance. But Jean-Paul here thinks we should be very open to other forms, given his research."

Peter shivers and stutters, "Honestly, I have no idea. Not even the hint from a dream. No vision. No voices. No little drawings that I've made since I was a kid."

In a reassuring voice, Jean-Paul says, "Peter, we believe the answer is buried deeply in your subconscious. Only you and Alexander show a close enough DNA match with the originators to exhibit what Jung might have called an ancient repressed memory, handed down through time in your genes. These ancient memories drive your response to the collective unconscious, the afflicted dreams you wrestle with each night. We believe we may be able to activate this repressed memory or image. Our Mei was tasked to work with you to allow your subconscious to be expressed. I believe…Mei believes with me that a specific algorithm of five senses, which may have come from the originators, will reveal your repressed image, bring it out of your subconscious and into your conscious. As you noted, the tradition says, 'But only the man and woman together will guide the salvation of others.'"

Alexander adds, "My boy, do you understand now why Mei has asked you to trust her implicitly? You can do that, can't you?"

Freeing his head from its temporary paralysis, Peter ekes out a nod. He is definitely in fear of what they have asked Mei to do, what line she has been asked to bend, break, cross, or simply run over to meet this end.

Jean-Paul proceeds, discussing their conclusion that the object is buried either in Crimea or, in his expert opinion, more likely in a prehistoric temple called Göbekli Tepe, in the middle of the battle between Turkey, the new Anatolian Kurdish State, and the Arabic Confederation armed forces. Although there is currently a demilitarized zone agreement that encompasses the area around this temple, getting a team, however small, inserted in there will be tricky. Even trickier will be trying to conduct an archeological excavation in the midst of war.

Alexander further explains, "Over the past years, I took steps to secure the areas around Crimea as well as select areas of Eastern Ukraine, thanks to my Russian friends. However, this area around Göbekli Tepe is much more difficult to control with the many different factions in play. Hence I summoned an intimately personal, dear friend of mine, a Kurd who is expert in the region, to join this team."

Again, Alexander gets up and exits.

Peter, having crossed his legs for the better part of a half hour, pleads with the good priest, "Please, could you excuse me? And could you point the way to the men's room?"

Walking down the blue-lit hallway, he repeats Jean-Paul's words. "Out that door, down the hallway, past the infirmary, and two doors to the…right. Or was that left?"

❦

Zara sighs as she looks around the prayer room the priest had prepared for her. There is a soft yellow-peach tone to the walls, with a blue glow atop each wall. Very peaceful. And the mat he selected will do; however, the room is small. Perhaps a converted closet of some sort. And the priest even thought of a washbasin, where she cleanses her hands.

She slips off her mother's navy flats. Oh, what a wise choice that was not to wear those pumps. These have been on her feet for nearly a day without stop, and still her feet, her calves, are burning. Instead of napping this morning after the infirmary, she opted to continue studying all of MoxDefense Industries' newest tech, especially those involved in air defense. She stares at her feet, once as nice as Peri's, until they destroyed them. Destroyed her. Outside, and deep within.

As she walks onto the prayer mat, her feet sink into the spongy padding. He was quite considerate, that priest. And that warm glow inside her comes back. A feeling she cannot quite fathom, but that she enjoys. Only a day after her family discussed finding the right man, she hears the first non-mahram man ever, a good-looking one at that, tell her he would rather pray with her than seduce her. She takes a slow, deep breath and savors the thought.

She looks again at her feet. How could any man ever think of praying with her with feet like these? In the soles of her feet, she sees the torn shreds of what was once her soul. How could any man pray with her, knowing what is inside her? She sighs, for God's will has been clear on this subject. And she lowers herself onto the mat. The room is too warm, with little ventilation. She lifts her lovely jelli eidi holiday skirt, now wrinkled, up her calves, and loosens her headscarf.

Halfway through her prayer, she prostrates for a second time. And her heart rushes when the room fills with the blue tint from the hallway. Someone has opened the door. And he is looking up her skirt. Her first instinct is to protect herself, not knowing if this stranger is friend or foe. She wraps her skirt tightly around her legs and does the same with her light outer coat. She quickly scans her immediate vicinity for anything which could be used as a defensive weapon. Perhaps she should have visited the armory before praying, but too late now.

"I'm so sorry. I'm so sorry," this strange man with round glasses pleads as he puts his hands over his eyes.

Realizing this man is no threat, she quickly stands, keeping her long skirt and coat around her and then adjusting the scarf around her head. "It's the room across the hallway," she says, annoyed. "Now leave, before you offend God any more than you already have."

She spots the distinctive coral mark on his cheek from the lips of the last victim of this womanizer. That vestige of warmth and glow over having met a man who was divinely different has just been washed from her soul by this voyeur.

If she ever sees this voyeur again, he will not live to tell what he saw.

CHAPTER 15

Love, to be real, must cost—it must
hurt—it must empty us of self.
—Saint Teresa of Calcutta

1:48 p.m. GMT+1, May 9, 2022
MoxWorld EU Headquarters, Luxembourg

"I'm a nice guy. Really, I am."

He stands there shaking, quivering, and certainly not boldly so, with his hands over his eyes as he tries to politely back out of the room. But he trips on something and falls, and something bangs his head. Something not so soft.

Thinking that the woman clobbered him with something ferociously hard, he puts his hands around his head, hoping she will stop hitting him.

"Get up," she yells as she softly kicks him with her foot.

And like an armadillo, he holds his hands to his head even tighter, rigid and cold.

She kicks him again in a different spot. No good. She'll have to coax him out. And she kneels down, carefully draping the pleated skirt to achieve more modesty than she had shown before. In a way, perhaps it was her fault. She let her guard down, assuming the room was secure and didn't need to be locked. The old Zara would never have made that mistake, for errors in the field cost lives. Errors in faith costs souls. And she had lost neither on her watch as unit commander.

His quivering is driving her crazy. What kind of peeping Casanova is this? And then she sees the blood clotting in his hair. She looks around for something to put on his head wound and finds a drying cloth near the wash bowl, which she compresses on his head.

"Put your hand on this tightly and you'll stop the bleeding."

And the man puts his hand upon hers and presses.

"*Dînê*. Fool. Not my hand, this cloth. Press that on your wound."

He slowly comes out of the curled ball into a sitting position, holding her hand still on his head. Without his glasses, he tries to focus to see who this woman is. One moment on the attack, the next peaceable.

He's dizzy, but her image becomes clearer. And he says, "Nanshe."

"No, *dînê*. My name is Zara. And I would appreciate it if you would give me my hand back."

Letting her hand go and reapplying pressure, he realizes lightning did strike twice as he was hit in the same place Randall had clobbered him. Still foggy and not fully himself, he says again, "I am so sorry. I didn't mean to intrude. I was only looking for the men's room."

She realizes he cannot see well as she spots and reaches for his glasses. This time, she makes sure her body is fully covered before she puts them on his nose and adjusts them across his ears.

As she brushes his temples with her fingers, he feels it. The same feeling as when his mother rubs his temples. He tries to focus, and he sees a woman of great presence who is taller than he, even sitting.

Her body stiffened, she says sternly, "You should be ashamed, walking in on a woman in her private moment. You have offended God with your actions. And if you are not afraid of offending God, you should be afraid of offending me."

"I am so embarrassed," he says. "My mother raised me better than to treat a woman with such disrespect. And she would be even more appalled if I offended God as I inadvertently disrespected a woman." He tries to focus through his fog but only sees that dark-haired woman from his dream, the one who said it was baby night.

"I suppose you did not mean to look up my dress." She shakes her head again, making sure her attire fully covers her. "But you should act with greater respect for a woman's modesty."

Taking her hands away from his temples, she puts her headscarf over her right cheek scar, for as close as he is sitting, one could count all the ridges. One more visible sign of what was done to her. Outside and inside.

"I would appreciate it if you would not stare at me so. I know I am hideous. You do not need to remind me." And she stares down and sighs.

"I am so sorry again. I didn't mean to stare. It's just you remind me of someone. A woman of great warmth, compassion, and faith." He takes the cloth from his head and feels to see if his wound is still bleeding.

She hears his words, but does not know what to make of him. She stares back at him. And his eyes—she realizes she has seen eyes like these before. Four of them, to be exact. He has eyes like her baby lambs. So innocent. Could he be telling her the truth?

She softens her defensive stance towards this intruder and puts her hand back on his to continue the pressure on the wound. "We better get you to the infirmary and put an ice pack on that spot." And she helps him stand up while carefully ensuring her skirt falls across the right places.

Sitting in the infirmary where she had been earlier today, Peter holds the ice pack she prepared. It must be an unlucky spot on his head. A spot of embarrassment. A spot to remind him that he cannot take care of a woman in need.

"You didn't get that wound today, it looks like. Did you get injured there recently?" she asks as she sees if she can wash his blood out of the cloth.

He wiggles on the table's edge as he hems and haws again. "It's nothing I'm proud of."

She turns and with her eyes darkened, she stares into his. Still innocent as before. And she offers, "I have had a few of those myself."

"Oh, I couldn't imagine that," he says. "You have the air of a person who is very capable of taking care of herself in any situation. I wish I could do that."

She drops the red-soaked cloth in the sink to soak and walks back to him, standing square in front of him. "I believe it is better if you are not able to take care of things as I have. Tell me. What happened to you?"

He stares down, but realizes he is focused on her skirt, so he stares to one side. "It's embarrassing. My neighbor's ex-husband was dragging her to her bedroom against her will, and I tried to intervene. Not so successfully."

The edges of her mouth have the slightest of uplifts at hearing his story. Maybe she misjudged this fool. And that spot on his cheek.

"Your cheek. That spot. How do you explain that?" she asks somewhat tersely.

His eyes light up. "Oh, my dimples. I usually only get those when I'm smiling or happy."

"No, it is a mark that a woman makes on a man when she is trying to signal others she is involved with him," she asserts, shaking her head.

Looking confused for a second, he says, "Oh. Oh, she must have left a...I'm so embarrassed again. You must think the worst of me. It was just Mei's good luck kiss before I met with Alexander. I guess she was a little aggressive with it."

She shakes her head again, but hearing that man's name, she asks, "Are you the man Alexander has flown here to search for the object? Are you the reason why I was rushed out here?"

"I'm so sorry. I should have introduced myself before. I'm Peter Gollinger, from San Francisco, California. New copyeditor in MoxMedia's Middle East correspondent unit. Well, that's where I hope he's going to put me." He holds his hand out to shake. "And, yes, I wish to help find the object—the dying wish of my grandfather."

She stares at his hand. California? No, it cannot be. How could Sara know? She pictures the two one-hundred-dollar bills her great-grandmother had given her just before she was kidnapped by that monster.

"Peter. I found you, finally," cries Mei as she enters the infirmary. "I have been looking all over for you. Alexander is waiting. How did you get here?"

And Mei gives Peter a huge hug. Which does not escape Zara's notice.

Maybe her intuition was correct all along.

To Zara, she gives a quick greeting and turns to retrieve a filled syringe in the refrigerator. "This is perfect, we had a booster vaccine ready to give you."

Eyes wide open, Peter hedges. "Uh. Didn't you already administer a vaccine on the plane?"

As Mei returns with an alcohol swab for his shoulder, she says, "What did I say, Peter? Once we are in Luxembourg, you need to trust me. Explicitly."

She jabs him as he lets loose an ouch. "Remember the God Genes we discussed? I had a sample of your body fluids processed by the lab here to engineer even better viral vectors containing DNA-altering enzymes that will activate the dormant areas in your genes related to the God Genes. Both Jean-Paul and I believe these God Genes came from those who originated the oral traditions of your family, of the families of the afflicted."

Mei turns to Zara. "Jean-Paul tells me you had your vaccine earlier today."

Eyes very dark, watching Mei's and Peter's every move, Zara nods in acknowledgment but stays quiet. She retrieves a new ice pack from the freezer and replaces the now watery one Peter holds.

"Oh, Peter, what happened?" Mei asks with a modicum of surprise. "I was so engrossed in what we have to do. How could I have missed what happened to your head?"

As Peter tries to find the words to explain his indiscretion, Zara steps in. "He had a little accident. We should be careful of that area of head as he has a previous wound there. I hope he did not injure your God Genes by accident."

Wiggling and writhing on the table's edge, Peter blurts out, "If you two could excuse me, I really need to go to the men's room."

Pointing the way right out the door, Mei says, "Of course, Peter. It's two doors down the hallway to the left."

He looks at Zara apologetically as he gets up to leave. "Oh, left. That's where I got it wrong last time."

Now the two women are alone together, both having had very different interactions with Peter. Mei says, "Zara, isn't it? We met a few years ago, did we not?"

"Yes, we did. It was at Alexander's birthday party. He briefly introduced us. He introduced you as his new find, his new girl," Zara says with a raised eyebrow. "I am impressed that he allows you to dress with such modesty and professionalism."

Mei squints at Zara with head turned slightly to the side. "I don't know what you mean by that comment. I know you have a long history with him, and what you imply must be significant."

Zara smiles, but not the nice kind. "Sasha has only two uses for women. If you have not found that out yet, then your time will come quickly. He starts by making sure you are obedient. You are very attractive and charming. I am sure Sasha must have noticed as well."

And before Mei can ask her to clarify her veiled comment, a booming voice calls out, "Ladies, we are late. You need to get dressed. Now."

Still angry about her abduction and his conduct on the flight here, Zara launches into him. "I am appropriately dressed already. You even complimented my bayramlık as you ripped me away from home."

"Mei, take my dear little Zara to the dressing room," he commands. "I will be down there shortly."

The walls of the dressing room are lined with racks of dresses. Some Mei recognizes, and many she does not, as she would not have designed or ordered such articles of nothingness.

Zara, on the other hand, simply nods her head, pointing to certain garments and saying, "As I said, only two uses for women. He has not changed."

The giant man returns, screaming, "Ladies, why are you still dressed? Quickly now, strip down."

This time Mei pushes back. "Alexander, I agree with Zara. My outfit is fine for what we need to do. Peter likes it."

"We're not going to a board meeting, Mei," he says with frightening piercing eyes, which makes Mei cower. "Here, I took the liberty of having your favorite tailor Giancarlo make this for you two."

One of the two gasps. And that one says, "Sasha, those clothes—they are not appropriate. They are not the clothes a respectable woman wears in public."

Mei takes the dress in her size and stretches it out in front of her. Clearly Giancarlo's signature. A deep V-cut coral midi sleeveless shirtdress with black trim and raspberry accent buttons down the entire front. Poking her finger into the soft, stretchy vicuna fabric, it is clear it hides nothing of the wearer's form, top or bottom. But with the right bra and panties, at least her intimate parts would be hidden.

Zara, on the other hand, is not willing to be so accommodating as she continues to rip into her Sasha. "You can see yourself. It shows too much flesh above and around the bust. And it shows my arms, my thighs. You, more than anyone else in this building, should understand our faith's modesty guidelines. Anything that could create sexual interest should be covered. Neck to ankles."

Siding with Zara, but from her scientist persona, Mei pleads, "Alexander, we discussed this with Jean-Paul before I left Shanghai. With the God Gene–enhancing vaccine and the five-sense algorithm, we should be able to get what you need out of Peter. You saw yourself the evidence on his cheek. He's smitten with me. I already got him to visualize the originators."

The monstrous man only flashes a dark grin back at her. "But you had to sleep with him to get that information. Tell me I'm wrong?"

Zara's jaw vibrates as she stares first at him, then at this Chinese woman. Is she his mistress, or is she a victim? Either way, Zara was right. He has only two uses for women.

Mei is silent, staring at the vacant floor between her and her boss. Silently shivering.

Towering over both of them, the world's most powerful man, at least in this room, commands, "You two know better than not to trust me, especially on affairs of the dreams, the affliction. I know better than anyone what an afflicted man wants from a woman. And these clothes are designed to do just that. I need to tend to other affairs. Ten minutes. When I get back, you two better be dressed in the right clothing."

Zara just seethes at him, clenching her fists. Mei closes her eyes, exhales, and then goes to the undergarment rack and pulls out a selection that might cover her enough.

And from the door, Alexander turns and yells, "And no underwear."

In near tears, Mei puts back the undergarments she had picked.

In total defiance, Zara grabs a rack of clothes, the most offending ones, and tosses them across the room, screaming all sorts of things in Kurdish. Not satisfied yet, she repeats this again and again and only stops at seeing Mei disrobing.

"You're not going to dress in that immoral garment, are you?" she asks.

Mei meekly nods, not stopping her actions. "You've known him longer than I. But I know you do not disobey him. People disappear. Especially those who fail him. I value my family. They are everything to me." And she removes her bra and panties, slipping the soft vicuna dress around her shoulders and buttoning up.

As Zara stares at her in defiance, Mei says, "Zara, I completely understand your situation. If I comply, perhaps he will allow you to make an exception. He seems to favor you. I am not so fortunate, I guess."

Softening her stance, Zara replies, "I apologize for what I was thinking. I was thinking you had slept with him. But that was rash of me, and I ask for your forgiveness." And Zara blanches, seeing Mei's body in vivid detail through that dress, Alexander's instrument of their submission to him.

Catching herself from falling victim to Sasha's will, Zara stiffens her back. She will not cower in that man's presence. Nor let this unfortunate woman cower either—a poor woman who did not know what she was getting herself into when she signed up with him.

"Mei, I don't know you. But I think you are not the type of woman Alexander normally subjugates and objectifies. We will dress in a way that befits us. I will stand up to him. He knows I can and will. We both can stand up to him. But you know what our choice of garments are in this room. Find something else that will cover us, but still be attractive—our one concession to him."

At first, Mei stares at her in disbelief. In her four years working with

Alexander, no woman, no man, even, has stood up to him without terminal penalty. She has heard of Zara, incredulous stories of the confidence Alexander had in her. Should she place her life in her hands as well? Will her family forever suffer the penalty of her trust in this woman?

Nodding her head, Mei answers back, "I know just the things."

A series of undergarments and a long black vicuna sweater coat later, Zara smiles at how she is covered. Mei puts on four-inch black-and-coral suede ankle-strap stilettos. She brings a pair for Zara, who turns white again. No, no, and no. She shows Mei the scars on the soles of her feet, at which Mei gasps. They match the scars along her calves and inner thighs. Mei pets her feet compassionately and finds another solution.

And to Zara's delight, to her feet's joy, Mei holds up a pair of black suede ankle-wrap flat sandals. Mei leans down to help her tie the bows around her ankles. Zara, elated, lifts her heels to admire her new best friends.

Out of a small black box, she pulls out a pair of yellow banana slug earrings, with the most adorable ruby eyes. Zara shakes her head no. And Mei simply gives her the "come on now" look. Zara points to her ears, which are unpierced, and Mei turns the banana slugs over to show they are clip-on. Zara complies.

Mei has one more surprise in a box she brought from China. Zara opens the box and pulls out a beautiful black scarf with red-and-gold embroidery. Super-silky soft lamb's wool. She holds it to her cheek, near tears. "How did you know?"

"Alexander told me about your grandmother's headscarf, the one you lost when those boys tried to attack you in London," Mei replies. "He really does love you, from what I can tell. I sourced the finest Persian lamb's wool on the market and had my tailors in Shanghai replicate it based on Alexander's recollection of her headscarf."

As Zara begins to cry, Mei offers, "Zara, thank you so much for allowing me to dress you for today. In your holiday dress, I agree, you are more radiant, more exquisite, and more elegant."

Zara smiles. "Kind words will unlock an iron door." She kisses Mei on the cheek. "Beauty passes; wisdom remains." She kisses Mei on the cheek again. "And may your wisdom last you an eternity."

And the two hug.

Hearing his monstrous footsteps, Zara pulls back from Mei. "I know him, all too well. What he will ask today, be prepared. Someone may die today."

CHAPTER 16

Yesterday I was clever, so I wanted to change the
world. Today I am wise, so I am changing myself.
—Jalāl ad-Dīn Muḥammad Rūmī,
thirteenth-century Persian Sufi mystic

9:35 p.m. GMT+3, March 18, 2018
Yacht anchored three kilometers off the Crimean Peninsula

"Barren," she laments as she gazes upon the stars. "I am barren. Not from what was taken from me. Not the void within my womb. But the emptiness of my heart, of my soul."

She stands tall upon her Sasha's yacht. A vessel designed for pleasure. But not tonight. She searches the sky for the North Star, for the legend told to her by her great-grandmother is very clear on what she must do now.

As the damp, darkening fog rolls in off the Black Sea, she shivers, hands shaking. What's wrong with her? She's never shaken before with gun in hand. The cold steel made colder by the iciness of her hands, her heart, her soul.

"I know he sent you, Zara. I know it's you under that mask," says the man about to receive a bullet to the chest. Clad in a white t-shirt becoming wetter with the fog mixed with his dripping perspiration and clinging to his sculptured muscles. His back against the railing of the rear deck of this luxurious yacht, he holds the gift he had made for her. One that she rejected earlier today when she was not masked. A scarf. Black lamb's wool with red embroidery. "Sasha said you would love this. That it would have special meaning for you."

Staring into her dark, angry eyes, the only part of her face exposed by the black mask covering her face, her head, her essence, he says, "I guess not." He drops his hand holding the scarf. "You need to decide. Are you going to kill me? Or join me? But whichever you choose, show me the respect of letting me see your face. Your whole face and hair."

He knows her. Too well for her comfort. She glances down in reflection, then gazes back up to the stars. But they no longer shine. Only the darkness of the fog surrounding her. Dark as she is inside.

"I know you've killed dozens, maybe more. All without remorse," he says, standing taller than she without a shiver, without fear. "Why would Sasha sanction my death? Because you refuse my offer that we partner in finding that which we must seek? What we both know needs to be found, needs to be touched? Because I have fallen in love with you?"

Pop.

Wrong words, she thinks, now no longer lost or indecisive.

That beautiful chest, the defined pecs, now tarnished by red. He looks at his right upper chest, at the growing crimson spot on his once white shirt. "But why, Zara? Why?" he asks as he applies pressure to the bullet wound with his right palm.

He is right. Why? How could she miss at this range? What is wrong with her? She could take out his heart at fifty meters with this handgun. Why is it different this time?

"My little Zara," booms a deep voice from behind her. "You are losing your touch."

Her Sasha stands a full head and a half taller than her. Her Sasha places his monstrous hand on her shoulder.

Dressed in black as is she, he has a long crimson sash tied around his waist, accenting his black turtleneck and black slacks. His cold, dark piercing eyes beam into those of the now terrified bleeding man. He points at the younger man, half a head shorter than he, and says, "The little Zara I know and love would not have missed. Either accept his offer to be yours, forever yours, or kill him."

Zara pulls the monstrous hand off her shoulder and peers into her Sasha's unforgiving eyes. No one betrays his love, his trust, his will. Not her, not the man she shot, not the hundred others, either. She drops her hand holding the gun to her side as she pulls off the black mask hiding her face, hiding her hair, hiding her soul, hiding her emptiness.

Staring at the cloth of the mask in her hand, she laments to herself again, *This is not the head covering I should be wearing. This is not the modesty of the woman I want to be.*

After a moment of reflection, she turns to her Sasha and puts the mask and gun into his monstrous hand. "Kill me and not him. I am the one who has failed you the most, who has failed herself the most."

She takes the red sash from her Sasha's waist and wraps it around her oval head. With great care, she tucks her shoulder-length dark hair under the crimson cloth and covers the disfiguring scar on her cheek—the curse of her mistake, the reason Sasha should kill her and not the man she shot. For she will no longer be barren. With the tail of the red sash now wrapped securely around her neck and draped along her right shoulder, she says, "This is how I wish to be remembered."

The giant man beside her places the cold steel against her head. She feels the chill now as she has regained her warmth. She closes her eyes, ready to meet her destiny. Ready to surrender. Ready to fully submit.

Pop. Splash.

And she smells the sulfur from the gunpowder. Obviously she's still alive. She opens her eyes to see the gun still pointing where the man she shot once stood. She runs to the deck railing and sees him still alive but near drowning as his twice-shot upper torso no longer retains the strength to swim. Hurriedly, she finds a life preserver and tosses it near the drowning man. "Abram," she yells. "Grab on to this."

She slips her shoes off, preparing to jump in to save Abram, the man she was about to kill. But Sasha holds her back, pointing the gun at the doomed drowning man.

"But why, Father? Why? I am your son," Abram pleads. "I did everything you asked of me."

"Zara made her choice. And you are not her destiny," the giant man coldly replies.

Pop. Pop. Pop.

Zara closes her eyes, for there are tears forming. The first since he saved her two years prior. She owes everything to this man who just killed his son. Because of her.

Looking at the waters bubbling with the expired air from the lungs of Abram, the black lamb's wool scarf he held floats next to the life preserver. The only sign left of what he felt for her. She turns to her savior, her Sasha, and cries, "Why? He was your son. Why didn't you tell me?"

Putting his monstrous hand on her shoulder again, he replies, "My little Zara. If he wasn't worthy enough for you, then he is not worthy enough for me."

She forcibly removes his hand from her body as she spits out, "You can no longer touch me. I am no longer your little Zara."

"Is it not said, the male was born to be slaughtered?" the giant man asks sagely. Around his neck hangs a chain and a peculiar pendant. Something ancient, he told her. A bullhead cranium. With the hand once again on her shoulder, he clasps the bullhead.

"I do not expect you to understand at this moment," he says. "But one day you will. That which is our past reaches into our beings today, guiding us to our tomorrow. Your tomorrow, your compassion will one day save us all. But not alone. What you yearn for, the emptiness you seek to fill, there is a man who will fill it. And if that man at your side was not to be the father of your children, then he could not live, so that others could not take from him the secrets you and I share."

"I don't know who is sicker, you or me." She straightens out her makeshift headscarf, tucking in errant strands of hair, and her dark piercing eyes meets his dark piercing eyes. "But what I know now, this is who I am. This is my faith. Take me back to port and we are done. My debt to you is paid in full. Forever."

The monstrous hands held out, he replies, "I will, if you give your Sasha a hug."

Shaking her head, looking for the stars hidden behind the fog, she says, "I am no longer that woman. I am not that kind of woman. If you don't take me back, I will swim home. Newroz started today. I can be back home before the end of the festival. I have New Year's resolutions, amends, to fulfill." She looks out over the railing again at the black scarf and life preserver bobbing on the intensely black Black Sea.

"My little Zara, Sebastopol is on the other side of the boat. You'll die trying to swim there."

She turns to her once favored Sasha and says, "And is it not said according to your legends, '*Be wary of the giant Reindeer People; when they arrive, move away from the direction of ice to seek safety. The bright star, the tail of the bird, will be your guide*'?"

Pointing over the railing she leans upon, she says, "And that is the direction away from the tail of the bird star. The direction of my home. Of my people. Of my Kurdistan."

She turns back to the giant man staring at her in bewilderment. "And is it not said that the wolf only repents in death? If my destiny is to die, then I die in repentance, trying to return home. Trying to return to who I once was."

He reaches out to her. "No matter where you go, your destiny follows you. And your destiny is to be with him. As the legend says, only man and woman together. You will be with him, no matter where you flee to."

"Then he will have to swim," she replies before diving into the black waters.

Splash.

Upon the dark, black seas, the crimson sash floats up and mingles next to the black lamb's wool scarf. And only bubbles are to be seen where Zara entered the water to meet her destiny. Only silent, empty, and dark.

CHAPTER 17

*There are three degrees of filial piety. The highest is being
a credit to our parents, the second is not disgracing them;
the lowest is being able simply to support them.*

—Confucius

*3:15 p.m. GMT+1, May 9, 2022
MoxWorld EU Headquarters, Luxembourg*

"I am going to put a hole in your head. If there is a gun in that box, that is what I will do," says Zara, in a staring contest with the big man, her dark piercing eyes boring into his. He does not flinch. A mahogany box sits open in front of her.

Having just returned from having taken a tour of the headquarters with Jean-Paul, Peter, on the other hand, shakes. Not in apprehension of what Zara will do to Mr. Murometz, but because Mei, holding another mahogany box in her lap, is in total tears.

Peter stands with eyes wide open at the entrance of the main conference room, with Alexander, Mei, and Zara already seated around the clear round center table. Mei is jittery, no longer the confident woman she had been on the flight over. Zara's face appears heavily lined, but taut. And Alexander's grimacing face breaks from glaring back at Zara and then shakes back and forth as he watches what is transpiring on the wall.

Screens all around the circular room blaze MoxMedia WorldNews broadcasts from around the world. But the one of most interest to Alexander and Zara is the live video feed of the Turkish army sending half of their advanced Leopard 2B2 main battle tanks, equipped with Alexander's latest tech, away from the defensive line with the Arabic Confederation forces around Sanliurfa towards the capital of the Anatolian Kurdish State, Diyarbakır. MoxMedia analysts predict that from there, they will roll eastward towards Batman and Siirt.

On another screen, videos show the Russian land, naval, and air forces moving to take positions in Georgia near the Turkish border. MoxMedia analysts predict Turkish forces will be too stretched to fight on three fronts if the Americans and British do not commit more military support soon. Alexander smirks as he nods.

As Peter enters, the room felt more sterile, nothing but the screens, five high-back chairs, an agitating accent lighting in deep red to light orange, and that very light bleach-like smell, as if something had been sanitized a day or two ago.

The lower center circular table has two boxes, slightly larger than shoe boxes, made of mahogany. One is carved with a five-legged dragon, the other with a falcon, the kind that flies in the mountains of Zara's father. And Mei only focused on the box with the dragon, not blinking, not meeting Peter's eyes as he enters.

But Peter's eyes focus on her dress, or the change in dress. Fully covered from shoulders to ankles, the same as Zara next to her. And yet, the ever-so-confident Mei appears clearly distressed in what she wears now. Arms crossed defensively across her chest, avoiding eye contact with anyone. Visibly shaking. And the room is not cold.

He takes the empty seat between the two women, with Zara eyeing him as if she were a falcon stalking prey. He turns towards Mei, then Zara, then back to Mei. And moves his chair next to Mei to console her.

Amidst the tension, the great Alexander Murometz rises. From his altitude, he could command any room, but as Peter looks around, no one engages with him, each staying in their own corner of the world. That smell in the room, chlorine? Where has he smelled that before? He racks his brain, sensing an impending doom. The troops are battle worn before the war even has even begun. And the commander wears a face so much less friendly, so much less fatherly than the man who welcomed him only hours before. His sister was right. He should have reread Faust.

And the giant's booming voice says, "As you see, the war situation has quickly taken a grave turn. The key areas where we believe the object of Peter and my oral traditions lies are in the midst of impending mortal conflicts."

He turns to Zara and adds a tinge of a smile. "And my condolences to your family for what might happen to them if the Anatolian Kurdish forces are not successful."

The monstrous man turns to Jean-Paul. "If you would, please brief the team on exactly what we need Mr. Gollinger's dream imagery to decide for us."

With a wave of his hand, Jean-Paul puts up a 3-D map of the world, projecting from the center glass table. "Here are mapped the identified high-probability afflicted people from around the world. The lines represent the ancestral paths from their previous generations."

"And with much thanks to you, Jean-Paul. The Vatican records were invaluable to this mapping of the ancestral lines," Alexander says. "I want to draw your attention to the highlighted area around the Black Sea, Caucuses, Anatolia, and the Levant. It would appear from Jean-Paul's work that the origins of the traditions emanate from this area."

Jean-Paul points at a new spot illuminated in red on the map. "This is the location of Göbekli Tepe, the oldest temple known to us today. Carbon dating suggests it is over twelve thousand years old, possibly built around 9500 BCE. Note its location is central in our triangulated origin of the traditions."

He then overlays a bumpy roundish area highlighted in light blue around the Black Sea. "In this area, we have found a very slight pattern of electromagnetic disturbance representing several different possible epicenters. Crimea is a notable epicenter, perhaps the strongest. Keep in mind, these are minute low-level EM signatures, only made detectable recently by Alexander's newest satellite EM sensors."

Jean-Paul overlays another set of lines. "These are the pathway of proto-Indo-European, or PIE, language development. The Kurgan hypothesis suggests that PIE first started in the Pontic-Caspian steppes here above the Black Sea. Alternatively, the Anatolian hypothesis suggests it started within our oral tradition origination area." He then overlaid the two target sites and dates with the first pre-Neolithic sites where agriculture has been found, which fell within the same zone.

The good Father further summarizes, "And this is why we believe the originators of the tradition may have spread their language, farming, and the oral traditions from Crimea to Anatolia."

He highlights the dot for Göbekli Tepe. "And most importantly, they may have started the first large-scale organized religion. This site may very well be where mankind first truly communed with God. Our object could have allowed them to communicate with God. Mei has tracked the genetic mutations that have led to the God Gene complex, which possibly originated during these times."

Alexander smiles at Jean-Paul and merely says, "And QED, *quod erat demonstrandum*."

Communicating with God reminds Peter of something. First feeling the bump behind his neck, Peter gently touches behind Mei's neck and rubs. The worry lines around her face subside as she begins to relax and smiles at him. As she puts her fingers on his, he closes his eyes; he has found a woman like his mother, a woman with a God Gene bump. He opens his eyes and sees her in a different light, as his heart opens in the way his mother would want.

Zara rocks back and forth in her seat, watching them. She then rationalizes out loud, "According to the People of the Book, Yaqub ibn Isḥāq ibn Ibrāhīm, Jacob son of Abraham, laid his head on a stone pillow and had a dream of a ladder to heaven. And there Xwedê spoke to him. My grandfather told me the Torah's account of Jacob's dream of the ladder was allegorically similar to the Prophet's ascendancy to heaven in the Mi'raj journey, where he spoke with Xwedê."

Mei's fingers on his special bump also having settled his nerves, Peter snaps back into action. "Let's not discount the possibility that this object is a device for communication with the aliens who profoundly influenced human history. I agree with Alexander about the monolith hypothesis. It's like *2001: A Space Odyssey*, where the monoliths were technology from aliens sent to influence the development of humankind. They somehow changed our DNA and changed our evolution. My DNA aberrations, they were caused by this alien object, which zapped my prehistoric forefathers."

Peter smiles proudly as he continues lightly rubbing Mei's petite node of DNA aberrations. Mei, on the other hand, began to flush and well up at his touch to this spot on her neck. Something that did not escape the eyes of Alexander. Nor Zara.

Jean-Paul smiles serenely at both Zara and Peter, blinks slowly, and says, "All possible interpretations. But let us not jump to conclusions just yet."

Peter eagerly jumps right back, asking, "And if we find it is the aliens the object communicates with, and they have been the voice of God all these millennia, what will happen for you and your faith?"

"We will see," Jean-Paul replies in his contemplative manner. He blinks methodically again. "That is a bridge to be crossed if we get there. As I'm sure Mei has passed on to you, Alexander's philosophy is that we all must examine our limits, because one day, something may come along that will challenge that limit. And either we adapt or, if not, someone may die. Simple as that."

Alexander raises his hand. "Ladies, gentlemen. We need to focus on the core point we need to resolve immediately. Do we focus our search on Crimea? Or do we search Göbekli Tepe?"

In response, Jean-Paul outlines the simple logic for both locations. "Mei's genetic mapping leads to both areas. The PIE language origins and faint electromagnetic epicenter favors Crimea. Furthermore, there is the question of several unexcavated ancient pyramids all along Crimea, forty-five meters high and seventy meters in length. The proposed date of construction is much earlier than Göbekli Tepe, suggesting there once was an highly advanced ancient civilization there. Peter's oral tradition best matches this area.

"On the other hand," he adds, "most of the oral traditions uncovered to date point to southern Anatolia, now the Anatolian Kurdish State. These, matched with Göbekli Tepe, also situated near a possible EM epicenter, say we should go there. Hence the choice we need to make today."

Fiddling in her chair with arms folded in front of her chest, Zara pipes up. "This is very simple. Go to Crimea. The three of you can go without me. You won't need me there, and I can go back to Siirt and help my family evacuate into the safety of our mountains."

Alexander scans the room. Zara's shoulders tense up toward her neck. As Peter has stopped rubbing her neck, Mei's face has become more pallid, her hands trying to straighten out her hemline. Jean-Paul has his face buried in his MoxPad+, monitoring readings. And Peter's eyes look up to the left, processing. That is, until he notices the big man staring right at him.

"Peter, my boy, in your genes, in your head, lies the answer. What say you?" asks Alexander.

Panic now sets in. What should he answer? He only began recalling bits of his dreams two weeks ago, that morning when Pappy revealed the parchment. He glances at Mei, who glances back with eyes that beg for his help. With what? Then over to Zara, whose eyebrows are set to fierce, yelling for him not to screw this up. Maybe his mother was right. He should see a priest for confession, but the only one in the room isn't making eye contact with anyone.

What should he do? One more look over to Zara and back to Mei as he spies his beloved banana slugs on their ears. And he gets it. Tell the truth.

"Love and babies," he blurts out.

That gets the former priest's attention as he joins everyone else in the room in a collective incredulous stare at Peter.

"There were a woman and a man who shared a deep and profound love. And she wanted to make a baby," says Peter, who then glances over at Mei. "I could only hope to fulfill what our oral tradition said. Man and woman. Only as the two together can you find peace. The object can save. You might see in sleep, might hear."

"My boy. Perfect," says Alexander with a smile. "And what can you tell us of the object?"

Shaking his head, he replies, "Alexander, you must believe me. That is all I know. All I can remember."

And the monstrous man looks over to Jean-Paul and then to Mei. "It appears your strategy on the flight failed. Perhaps you now will follow the plan I recommended to begin with."

And finally, the priest speaks. "Alexander. It would be prudent for us to consider Mei's work a success. She did get Peter to confirm our hypothesis of two primary originators. A couple." He glances at a nervous Mei, who gives a smile back at him. "Remember, you accelerated the timetables. We only were able to administer the God Gene vaccine to Peter last night, with a booster an hour ago. Let Mei have another chance."

"Priest," Alexander replies, looking at the screens showing the latest on the confrontations around the Black Sea. "I'll give you and Mei one more chance. But we are quickly running out of time. If she fails, we do things my way."

Mei takes the cue and scoots closer to Peter. "Remember what I said— you must trust me and not stop me from doing what I am about to do. Can you do that, Peter? For sure?"

Peter nods, although he too has his shoulders tightened.

Mei kisses his cheek, but he shivers and his arms tense. Sensing this, she starts the algorithm. Petting his arms first for a few minutes, she unbuttons his shirt to fully expose his chest and puts her hands to his heart, rubbing for minutes, then fingers to forehead.

She brings his head into her neck. "Breathe through your nose slowly. Smell my fragrance that you so loved earlier. Sense me."

That unique jasmine fragrance beckons Peter to release control of his senses as he leans further into her and smells her. Once again, the bewitching aroma sweeps into his nostrils and fills his sinuses. He senses its flow into his body, creating the warmest, most wondrous sense of peace.

He feels the warmth of her hand, which places his fingers upon her cheeks as she says, "Feel me." And his fingers run along her face, softer and smoother than any woman he has touched or who has touched him.

His head lifted to eye level, she says, "See me." And they gaze into each other's eyes. And Peter begins to lose himself in the pools of chestnut bliss surrounding her pupils.

With her coral-glossed lips, she plants a wet kiss upon his lips, then pulls back, smiles, and says, "Taste me." At which Peter pulls her close to him and kisses her back.

Her hands guide his head to her chest, ears to her heart and the rapid beats in her chest. She says, "Hear me."

Stroking his hair, she asks, "My dear Peter, what do you see?"

Looking in front of his nose, he replies, "Soft, delectable, wondrous. So perfectly formed." He licks his lips, salivating.

"Enough," Alexander yells, standing up. "He's salivating over your breasts, Mei." Looking to Jean-Paul, he says, "You two have failed. Billions of euros in research wasted."

Staring back at a distraught Mei, he yells, "And you, what was that? It was so clinical. We are not in a research lab. There was no passion, no love, no intimacy in what you did. Is that how you act with your boyfriends? What did you think the originator wife did to her husband? I told you from the beginning, the afflicted men needed sex from their afflicted female partners."

As Mei trembles, lips trying to say something, Zara shakes her head, frowning, glaring at the big man. She yells out, "Don't you do this to her. She's too good of a woman for the likes of you."

He walks over, standing in front of her, his towering figure casting a veritable shadow over her. "Then maybe you could do better, my little Zara."

She sneers. "You know I am not that kind of woman, Sasha."

Tapping his MoxWrap, he then points to the screen opposite her. "There. See for yourself. Live satellite intel. The Turkish tanks have taken position twenty-five kilometers outside Diyarbakır. See the northern force? This one is poised to strike deeper towards your Maryam, your Roza, your beloved Sara."

She bolts up, standing toe to toe, looking at him, "Let me go home. Now. There is nothing I can do here. If a woman as beautiful as Mei cannot induce your Peter to tell you what you need, how do you expect me to do any better?"

Tapping his MoxWrap again, he points to another screen. "There. Forty cargo helicopters ready to fly from Georgia, carrying the beta models of my latest antitank weapons. My Russian friends are ready to declare their support for your newly formed nation."

He touches her on her chin, then trails his finger downwards along her neck, clavicle, to between her breasts. "You and I know you will do whatever is needed to save your family, your people."

As Zara glares at him, he walks over to Mei, lifting her out of her chair by her hair. His monstrous free hand clasped around her face, squeezing the blood from her cheeks, now a blanched white, he says, "And you, it is time you pay me back for the twenty billion euros I spent on your fruitless genetic research."

Zara stands to intervene, but to her surprise, Peter beats her to it. Nostrils flaring, but not from the want of Mei's sensual fragrance, Peter rises up, grabbing those hands off Mei's face and hair and pushing himself between the two.

Staring upwards as if trying to see the top of Mount Ararat, Peter asserts, "Zara's right. Mei is a good woman and doesn't deserve how you are treating her. And if you have to know, she slept with me on the plane exactly as you asked of her. And it was more than just sex. It was the passionate bonding you wanted to see here on public display. And I should have told you earlier, but I was afraid. But I'm not afraid now. I saw the object. They had it."

"Of course you did, my boy," Alexander replies, with his dark piercing eyes beaming into Peter's. "And where is the object?"

He tries to be brave. He tries to look bold. But he cannot stop his lower jaw from quivering.

"That is what I thought," concludes Alexander, who puts his hand across Peter's head and squeezes. He turns and points to the two boxes on the table. "Pick which box goes to which of your two new lady friends. They will know from the content what they will need to do with you next. Love and death. That is all we have. Love and death."

Slowly, apprehensively, Peter approaches the table. It is obvious which one was intended for whom. The dragon for Mei. The falcon for Zara. But what if it's a trick? What did Mei say? Never read too little into him. Never underestimate him.

That smell. Bleach. Like they used in the urgent care clinic to clean up blood. Whose blood was spilled in here? Or should that be, whose blood will be spilled in here?

What should he do? What should he do? That ancient question forever to haunt his mind, his soul, his destiny.

CHAPTER 18

Now the works of the flesh are evident: sexual immorality,
impurity, sensuality, idolatry, sorcery, enmity, strife,
jealousy, fits of anger, rivalries, dissensions, divisions,
envy, drunkenness, orgies, and things like these. I
warn you, as I warned you before, that those who do
such things will not inherit the kingdom of God.

Galatians 5:19-21

9600 BCE
Northern shores of the Black Sea

I lie watching the stars. Their beauty. Their harmony. Their love. And even though the grasses covering the roof of our house stand between me and the night sky, I lie here next to my precious husband, Orzu, watching these stars. From these stars came our object. The object that has pained my husband. The object that leads to peace in my husband, and myself. I Iis Nanshe.

My hands on my womb, I feel the peace inside like a warm fire on a winter night. And from my womb, the warmth spreads slowly into my body. It is different this time than thirteen cycles ago, when we conceived Ki, and five cycles later, when we conceived An. Not better, as I love them with all my heart, but different.

Eight cycles have passed since I gave birth to An, and no child since. I should be so thankful for having two wonderful children, but after several baby bumps gone wrong since An, I came to a peace that I am now barren.

But this voice. This voice of beauty. This voice of harmony. This voice of love. I heard this voice say that I should have more children. That tonight I must take Orzu into me and conceive now. And so we made love with the same passion he had taken me that first night I crawled into his bed, much to his surprise. And now, as the voice had asked, I lie here with my legs elevated as my dear beloved sleeps in deep peace at my side.

And I lie here under the stars, feeling such a state of bliss that I must push all other thoughts and worries aside. And I could have wished for the voice or my beloved's dreams to be more explicit on the time of day the Reindeer warriors would arrive tomorrow. But I must allow this peace to spread through my body and throughout my mind tonight. I will awaken before dawn to prepare. For now, my eyes say good night to the stars and slowly close.

Peace. Beauty. Harmony. Love.

My eyes open. It is very bright. Oh my, I overslept. And there may be Reindeer warriors outside our home. "Wake up, Orzu. Wake up, we overslept. We must dress for the lake and get our essentials onto the boat with as much haste as we can," I say to my sleepy-eyed savior.

And in my robe, covering my nakedness, I go to my brother's chamber. Newlyweds, oh my. Clothes tossed to the sides and sheets to the wind, they lie in their nakedness after another wild nuptial party. My brother, so embarrassed, grabs the sheets to cover himself. I assure him there is nothing that his big sister has not already seen of him. And Sama, she has no modesty. She arises, flaunting her body not only to her new husband, but to me as well. She has such pride in her beauty, but sometimes it is misplaced. Such is youth.

As she combs her hair, in priority over finding a robe to cover herself, I discuss with my brother the dream Orzu had and how we need to leave. I ask him to run to our brother Namu and warn him. Sama cries and comes to my brother, and says she is scared and he must stay to defend her. With the look of no contest, my brother shrugs his shoulders at me and says a man must do what he must do. Well, my definition of a man is different, but we do not have the time to argue. I say to him then to help Orzu load the heaviest items we need for life on the other side of the lake onto the boat.

And now to the children's room. Ki is just awakening. Orzu is right, she has the beauty and innocence of his sister. Well, maybe some of mine as well. An is cowering under his bedsheets, hoping the sun will decide it was a mistake to come out today.

"Up, you two. We must load the boat. Gather your things that you will need on the other side of the lake." Nothing I say is a surprise to them, as we have talked about this possibility for many sun cycles and they have been drilled on what they must do. I say to them, "We must take all the arrows, spears, weapon heads, and all the obsidian we have." They dress in their boat clothes and start implementing our plans to move.

So that I do not prance around in my bareness like my sister-in-law, I go back to my sleep room, take the robe off, wash, and put on my boat clothes. It may be a very long time across that lake to get to where the Other Siders told us to go, the land of the obsidian mountain. Dressed appropriately, I then find the plainest head cloth I have and put it over my head. I should look as unappealing as possible to the Reindeer giants.

Outside, I go to check on my menfolk. And what are they doing? The two men are playing around with that object, hooking it up to the aurochs. I tell Orzu in no uncertain terms that there are more important things than this black thing, which was not in our long-discussed departure plans. We must put the things most vital to our survival onto the boat. He's still touched with madness. He is arguing with me that the object is the most vital thing to our survival. I remind myself to teach Ki how to get her husband to do exactly what she says and not something so frivolous.

Good—Ki and An have packed the weapons and obsidian onto the boat. Ki has kept her bow and arrows just in case. I tell both of them what a good job they have done. "Ki, help Sama with the food, seeds, and cooking items. An, get two mating pairs of chickens and a mating pair of goats onto the boat." He wants to bring more, but I explain we only have so much room on this fishing vessel.

Inside the house to help with the packing, and I see my sister-in-law. What is she thinking? We have the same stupid argument over her immodesty. She, having been an abductee like me, should know what will happen if they capture us again. She spits back at me, saying I am only her sister-in-law, not her mother. And then she criticizes me, says that I play mother to her husband, and that must stop now that she is here. He is hers, not mine. I wish Ki was not here to witness this inane conversation. Otherwise, I might beat this silly woman myself. I take some black grease and put it on my face, and go over and do the same for Ki, who has listened well to her mother and has an ugly, really ugly, scarf around her head.

An has returned from the boat, and I ask that he take watch outside. Easier said than done, as the warmth and beauty of the sun has been replaced by rapidly moving black and angry clouds. We make two trips back and forth to the boat, the four of us, with Ki armed with bow and arrows. The silly menfolk have moved the object to within twenty paces of the boat as they prepare planks and ropes to pull this beast up into the boat.

Final tour of the house. I am nearly in tears as we are leaving so many memories around our home that we cannot take with us. My last moment of tears is interrupted by An screaming as he runs into the house. Reindeer warriors. Two, maybe more. We grab whatever we can and run to the boat.

The angry black clouds cry on us as if to mourn our impending deaths, or worse than death for the women. We run by the menfolk, still fiddling with that stupid stone, and yell that they are coming. On the boat, I hide my children as they ready themselves with bow, arrows, and spear, not that An is very good at any of these tools of the hunt.

To the front of the boat, Orzu is going back to the object with spears in hand. I hold him back. The touched fool, he says he must take care of what he failed to do before. He has seen the giant, and he needs to avenge Illyana. Avenge Parcza. He needs to redeem his failure, his sense of being a loser when he failed to kill when he needed to. Even with my tears, my embrace, my declarations of love, he is still intent on going to his death. I say to him that if he truly loves me, truly loves his children, he will stay with us. We need him.

He points with his spear to the tides around the boat and with all logic says they are not high enough yet to float the boat. Someone needs to stall the Reindeer warriors long enough so we can escape. And with revenge and love in mind, my husband leaves, heading to his death.

I watch him march towards the giants. Fearless, or just plain stubborn? For fifteen cycles, he has dreamed of this day, prepared for this day, sparred spears with Ki when she was old enough. And now this day has arrived.

The anger of the clouds is in full bloom as the rain falls, pelting our garments, pelting our faces. And through the darkness, I can just see the outline of his face. A face that I could not forget, not even with the love of my beloved savior, I could not forget. For this face has haunted me in my nightmares as he taunted me. The face of the man who violated me. Who defiled Illyana. Tureal.

And there Orzu stands, defiantly in the way of the giant killer who killed his grandfather, destroyed his sister, and enslaved his wife. He is no longer the boy who could not kill the rabbit. He is a man who has trained and trained to one day kill a giant as he did the boar. He stands without fear, no fear of death.

But inside, he has the dread of fifteen cycles of living with his moment of failure. That microsecond where he could not overcome his ethical limit. That microsecond where his failure led to the death of Parcza, his revered grandfather who taught him all. That microsecond where his failure led to his sister's life in torment. And he has sworn never to have that microsecond again as he visualized, every day of his life since then, the mortal goring of Tureal. And the anger of the black clouds reflects this blackness, this inner anger that has now found its moment. The moment he is no longer a loser, a failure.

He stands as he did fifteen sun cycles ago, long limbs and giant hands protruding from under his feathered cape, and dark piercing eyes peering out from under the large bird headdress. In a deep, booming voice, Tureal speaks.

"I know you, boy. You killed my favorite slave, the girl you had not the courage to kill before I had my pleasure with her. And now I have come to take your daughter. Your penance for killing my slave. An eye for an eye. A girl for a girl."

And to the giant's left is a boy, a boy giant still much larger and taller than Orzu, dressed in the same bird clothing of his father. The boy speaks. "So you are the killer of my mother. You killed her as she weaned me. How savage are you slaves that you would kill a boy's mother while she still weans him? How angry the gods are with you for violating the moral ethics that bind us all. Including you slaves." He scans behind Orzu, looking for the flesh of the slave who will soon become his own.

On the boat, the children have come forward to see what is happening, much to Nanshe's angst. She pushes their heads below the forward strake of their boat. The giant boy points to Sama, who is standing with the wind blowing her hair and meager clothes, exposing her bare face, arms, upper chest. Her husband, Narn, seeing the imminent threat to his bride, leaps down the planks with spear in hand, ready to defend his family.

Tureal, seeing these little animals futilely charging, says to his son, "It is time to show you are a man. To take what is yours by right of the stars. Secure these males and take their women as you see fit."

And with his father's challenge to prove his worthiness, Doroda moves forward, towards the two puny males bandying their sticks as if he could even be touched. They poke at him in vain as he swats their spears aside as if they were mere thorny branches of a sapling tree. Tiring of this game, he butts with the blunt end of his spear at the one called Narn, striking him in his thigh with enough force to make him crumple. Part of being a warrior is not to kill the males, so they can be taken back as slaves for building the pyramids. He approaches the other, who vainly tries to defend the one on the ground, and grabs his spear out of his hands, throwing it back towards their boat. He picks this puny animal up and tosses him towards the boat like a small stone.

Nanshe closes her eyes in prayer. She is watching her dearest two men losing a fight that cannot be won. Tureal picks up Narn and carries him towards Orzu like a dead animal as his son comes forward to collect his female prizes. She prays, as this is the only path to salvation. And before she can react, Sama is running down the ramp to get Orzu's spear and defend her husband.

Sama tries to throw the spear at Tureal, but it only tumbles feebly in the air and falls, not even reaching his feet. Tureal drops her husband as he recognizes her. "You. You are my family's property. You escaped from my cousin. I will take my pleasures with you here and now."

In horror, Sama realizes the numerous errors she has made today, but too late, as this giant, who she now remembers in deep anguish, picks her up and strips off her lower garments.

But suddenly, she tumbles to the ground as her giant assailant falls. Orzu, having thrust his spear into the center of the giant's loins, yells, "That is for Illyana. That is what she would have wanted to do to you herself."

And then Orzu crumples to the ground as Tureal's son, Illyana's son, Orzu's nephew, slices his back.

Doroda lifts the bleeding Orzu over his head and tosses him towards the boat, towards the object, where he lands with a dead man's thud. Helping his bleeding father stand, Tureal limps to finish off the stricken Orzu, while Doroda grabs the near-naked Sama woman to have his pleasure in front of her husband.

Towering over him, the giant who killed his closest relatives holds a spear to the heavens as Orzu can only see the angry rain pummeling his eyes. And as Orzu tries to roll, the giant spear comes down, piercing his thigh next to his groin. An eye for an eye. A groin for a groin, missed. Enraged, with the blood running down from the deep cut, Tureal steps on the puny man and raises his spear again, not to miss this time, as Nanshe closes her eyes and prays, for she cannot watch her savior's horrible death.

Flash-boom.

Stunned and blinded, Tureal is thrown off balance from the lightning strike on the object and staggers back.

Whoosh. Whoosh. Two arrows from Ki's bow strike his head, one a direct hit in the eye, and his facial bones crack. *Whoosh.* A third arrow hits him in the gut and he falls to his knees in front of Orzu. If it is to be this giant's last act on this earth, he is going to kill this puny man, the man who killed his slave. Still blinded, he feels for where the puny corpse-to-be is, takes his knife, and raises it over his head to plunge into the destitute animal's chest.

Crunch. Through his neck crashes Nanshe's harpoon as she drives it with all of her might and twists it. She is consumed with blackness and anger, as if the black clouds and angry sky were created from deep within that dark place in her soul. She has not had the time or the mind to reflect upon the significance of the distinct change in her essence, where not long before she basked in the peaceful existence of beauty, harmony, and love. For she is the epitome of dark and cold anger. She pulls the harpoon out of his neck, with the red essence of his mortal life covering her garments and running down to her feet.

As her former tormentor, the grotesque hulk who haunts her precious husband's dreams, the evil one who stole her virgin innocence, that essence she wanted to save for her husband, rolls to the ground, she raises her harpoon and drives it into him over and over again, until nothing is recognizable.

Covered in his blood, she yells, "That is for me. That is for me," as she falls to her knees, crying into her bloody hands. And Nanshe becomes the first woman, the first human, to kill one of these monstrous heathens who descended from the abominable violation of her female ancestors by the denizens of the stars, sons of gods.

Having been perversely occupied by Sama, Doroda finally notices the death of his father and runs to avenge it. He picks up the woman who has ruthlessly mutilated his patriarch and tosses her as hard and as far as he can. She lands twisted and crumpled, screaming in agony. And then there is the prick of the point of a weapon at his throat.

Seeing what his beloved mate has done to avenge herself, Orzu has found the inner strength to stand despite his wounds and take her harpoon to this giant boy's jugular, pressing hard enough to ensure that the boy's slightest move will rip his artery open and send his vital fluids spurting into the dark, cold rain.

Nanshe sits up on the ground, unable to stand on her mangled ankle. "Kill him, Orzu. Kill him," she shouts. "You must. Save Ki. Kill him."

And as Orzu puts a little more pressure on the harpoon, slicing just a bit of the boy's throat, he sees Illyana's face in this boy. He cannot kill him. He is Illyana's son. He has her face. He cannot kill the son of his beloved sister.

And he yells, "Nanshe. I love you. You must leave now."

Doroda stares into his uncle's eyes with the eyes of Illyana. No fear, no terror, just the look of her son. And as Orzu tries to find the courage to rip out the throat of this giant, the evil one who lusted for his daughter Ki, his mind echoes, "You cannot. You cannot kill Illyana's son. Your nephew."

As Nanshe yells for him to kill the giant boy, Orzu puts down the harpoon and kneels in front of the image of Illyana.

This makes no sense to Doroda, but he seizes this opportunity and draws his knife, holding it to the throat of this puny man, the frail, failed brother of his mother, the slayer of his mother, the father of his new slave. And as he starts to slice, three piercing blows hammer his left pecs. He doubles over and sees the girl he came to possess running at him, dropping her bow.

Ki, having learned from her mother of Illyana's inability to fell her tormentor, leaped from the boat and shot the boy who was about to kill her father, with three shots made in rapid succession as she was running. She picks up her mother's harpoon, takes the scarf off her head to show her face to this boy, the last face this boy will ever see, and stabs him repeatedly as he rolls to try to dodge her assaults. "That is for my mother. That is for my aunt. That is for my grandmother. And that is for my great-grandmother." And as he tries to scoot back away from her, she runs the harpoon into his shoulder, through and through, pinning him to the long, large piece of driftwood he has backed himself up against.

She leans down to her father and holds him tightly. Covered in his own crimson fluid and the splatters of the giant boy, she says to him, "Father, I love you. You have taught me well. You have nothing to fear for my life. I will be no giant's slave, ever."

The dead and the wounded litter the beach. Brimming with the blackness and anger, as does the darkness within Nanshe, the skies continue to cry on the casualties, the stricken and the cursed from old blood spilled, blood that can never be brought back. And as the dark and angry waves sweep over her, Nanshe finds she cannot find redemption in the abyss, the blackness, the blindness, the malignance of her actions. She prays to her god for forgiveness as she comes to understand the lack of restitution, the lack of fulfillment of her acts.

The angry waves start to lick Orzu's legs as his dearest daughter holds him. As a battered, lame Narn helps his assailed and crying Sama to the boat, An has his mother's arm around him, supporting her as she limps in great pain across the beach.

And the dying Orzu looks into his daughter's eyes, sees the soul of his Illyana, and says, "Leave me. You must take the object away from here, away from the tail of the bird star, or all is doomed."

CHAPTER 19

Love knows no reason, no boundaries, no distance. It has a sole intention of bringing people together to a time called forever.

—Unknown

4:30 p.m. GMT+1, May 9, 2022
MoxWorld EU Headquarters, Luxembourg

She gasps. Looking back up to Peter, Mei violently shakes her head, and then stares vacantly at Alexander and shakes all over. Inside her box? A tube of personal lubricant. Scented, of course. He has degraded her from one of his leading executives into a mere piece of flesh to be used at his whim—the monster who had only two uses for women.

Zara, on the other hand, hisses, staring at what is in her box. The pistol from that night on his yacht. A MoxDefense Industries upgrade of the Russian silenced version of the Makarov, the PB—standard issue for the famed KGB. Next to it lies the crimson sash he wore, she wore. How perverse, how bent is this man. She has not used a gun, nor any deadly weapon, since that night. She has been the woman of peace she had sought to be ever since.

She holds the neatly folded crimson cloth, once around her head, her inspiration to seek herself, to change, to go back home, to be herself once again. If only she had been more moderated and replied that she cared about him, maybe Abram might be alive today. She killed him, her arrogance killed him. Sasha may have pulled the trigger, but his heart was mortally pierced by the way she rejected him. And why did he put these in front of her now? To torment her with her past? To show her she has not changed substantially since then? And now, what does he expect her to do?

A wave overcomes her, hot, heavy, and dark. She glares at her Sasha, slapping a magazine into the PB and taking aim. "I am going to put that hole in your head." And they stare at each other until... *pop.*

And Alexander stands firm, not yielding, not flinching, not even blinking. And there is no crimson either. He laughs and says, "Welcome back, Zara. I knew you could not hide in your sorrows forever. What was that? All of a few seconds for your true self to reemerge and take your best shot at your dear old Sasha? I knew you could not tame the Zara I love so much. That is why that magazine is full of blanks."

That monster. He baited her. Fooled her. And the evil djinn was let out of the deepest, darkest prison within her soul. There would be no hope for her now. Her babies would become orphans again before this was over.

"In the bottom of the box, there is another magazine," says Sasha. "Those are neurotoxin-dipped hollow points. Made to inflect mortal wounds of the worst kind. Excruciating pain from eviscerated flesh, accompanied by a loss of one's ability to breathe. This time, you cannot just wing him and he lives."

Already traumatized by the sight of a gun, Peter's heart rate jumps beyond three hundred. *And that man called me son earlier today?* Who was the *he* Alexander was referring to? Peter wouldn't wish such a death on anyone, but he hoped he was not that *he.*

"Jean-Paul, would you join me?" asks Alexander as he rises to exit the room. "I will leave you three to discuss your options."

The giant man glances at the disheartened Mei. "Trust me, my dear. To get what you have asked of me, to save your family's honor, you must perform what the ancients did to find the truth of the object. As I have said from the beginning, I know what Peter needs. You must disrobe." And they leave.

After moments of silence, Peter says, "I'm so sorry. I fell into his trap. I was sure that the dragon box was supposed to be for Mei, so I gave it to Zara."

"And so, you would rather have me use that tube? How kind of you," Zara admonishes, taking the second magazine out of the box.

"No, no. I mean, you are a very alluring woman. Hauntingly so. But a very alluring woman who seems to know what to do with a gun. Perhaps we would fare better if Mei had the gun. She doesn't look like the kind of person who can shoot," says a petrified Peter, staring at the stark black steel in her hand. The same color as that in his father's hand. Was it always his destiny to die like his father, but at the hands of that dark-haired woman in his dreams?

Seeing Mei sniffle, Zara puts the gun down. "Perhaps this is for the best anyway. Mei already had sex with you on the plane. Alexander is only asking for you to repeat what you have already done. Only in public. Then no one will have to be shot today."

Mei finally crumples, a raging stream of tears soaking her all-but-too-revealing vicuna dress. Peter comes to her side and hugs her. "It'll be all right, Mei. I won't look."

"You don't understand. Neither of you," she cries. "Nothing happened that night, Peter. Nothing. I mean, I did obtain genetic material from you, but nothing else happened between us."

"Genetic material?" he exclaims. "What does that mean?"

"It means that if you two don't consummate a man-and-woman relationship and cough up the location of the object, Alexander is going to conclude that Peter is of no use to him," Zara states. "Mei, he will kill Peter to ensure none of his adversaries can access his genetic material."

Wrapping the crimson scarf around her hand, she adds, "This is not the first time he has done this."

He leans into Mei's ear and says softly, "Remember your moans when I rubbed your feet?"

Confused, she nods. "Good," he says. Then he whispers into her ear.

Mei nods, rips open Peter's shirt, and plants deep crimson kiss marks all over his chest, neck, then mouth. Zara concludes Alexander has won again. Two more poor souls he has coerced into breaking their ethical boundaries.

"Zara, could you please give us some privacy?" says Mei, "And Peter, this is what I need you to do. First, we need some water…"

❧

"Oh, Peter, you are the best. Truly, truly the best," exclaims Mei as she lets out a moan, mounted atop Peter sitting in his chair when Alexander and Jean-Paul return to the room. Zara is turned away from them, shaking her head. Peter is drenched, as is Mei, as he buttons up her blouse while she still straddles him. The tube of lubricant lies at their feet, emptied. And they embrace one more time.

Zara turns and watches the two forced lovers melt into each other's arms. Glaring at Alexander with her eyebrows set to fierce, her mouth ablaze, she yells, "Are you satisfied, Sasha? It is over. Let us all go."

Alexander is watching on Jean-Paul's MoxPad+ and moments later he stands and applauds. "Fabulous. I've never seen better," he decries. "Better acting, that is. But tell me please, how do two lovers not have flushed skins, not have deep respiration? Do not think you can fool me. Such a pity."

Nervous like criminals caught in the act, Mei and Peter zip and button themselves up as Alexander turns to Zara and says, "My little Zara. You know the drill. Either do what Mei failed to do or take care of business. You reject him and Peter is of no use to us anymore."

Zara stares at the PB gun in the box. Once guns were her next best friend after Peri. But no longer. If she picks it up, she will forever be lost. Forever into the darkness, the abyss, with no hope for light. With no hope of return.

A very loud snap of fingers focuses her back to Alexander, who is pointing to a screen. "There, those blue dots. Zara, those are the Turks' F-16 fighter-bombers fueling preparing to bomb your new capital and your family's city. One call and I can have the Russians declare the Anatolian Kurdish State a no-fly zone, just as they did New Kurdistan. And those helicopters in Georgia will supply your friend Peri's military colleagues with everything they need to repel tank and air attacks."

And before Zara can blink, he says, "But this offer is good for twelve minutes. The time it will take before my Russian friends' T-50 fighters will not be able to intercept Turkey's fighter-bombers. The fate of your people, your family, rests in your hands."

Zara looks to Jean-Paul. "Please, priest, you must intervene. This is not the path that God would want, is it?"

The former priest stands and looks at Alexander, who only shakes his head in disagreement back at the former member of the Vatican inner circles. In resignation, Jean-Paul lowers his head, hands together in front of him, lips moving as if saying a prayer.

His eyes, once reddened, are now dark black. Not even his pupils showing. The giant man yells, "Zara, you know what you need to do. You know what happens to all who fail me, who deceive me. Kill Mei first, but make it a thigh wound so Peter can see her die in neurotoxic agony in front of him. He needs to learn the price for deceit."

Aghast, Peter quivers. His lips want to cry out, but nothing comes out of his vocal chords. He looks to Jean-Paul. Another tall, imposing male who has the best chance of standing up to this monster he has signed a contract with. But the former priest still has his eyes closed, seemingly in prayer. And from Peter's point of view, these are his last rites the priest is administering.

He looks to Zara. A woman distraught, in hesitation, indecision, in deep agony over the choices in front of her, seemingly in fear of the gun in her hand. He lifts Mei's head and peers into her tear-ridden eyes. A deep, loving kiss on her forehead. And he says, "I would have loved to meet your mother."

To her surprise, he rises, helping hold her dress down as he buttons the last open buttons. To Zara's surprise, he steps over, respiration rate at max, and takes the gun from the box. Hands shaking, he hands it to her. "I love my family as much as you do. But I cannot be the reason for the suffering of your people." And he stands in front of her, shaking, sniffling, eyes closed, waiting for the inevitable. He opens his eyes and says, "Pray for me. In case I'm wrong about our alien origins, then I'll need someone to vouch for me with God."

Zara stares at the gun in her hand. She aims it between his eyes as he shakes uncontrollably. Those eyes. Those eyes. Her babies.

Sasha will not get the satisfaction this time. This innocent boy from California is not the one who should die today. No more than Abram needed to die on Sasha's yacht. It is time to make amends.

Lowering her aim, she places the gun in his palm and wraps his fingers around it. As he stares at the instrument in his hand, she lifts the barrel to her heart and says, "Even, smooth trigger pull. It will be quick. I won't suffer."

And there, Peter is frozen. As if he had been there for all of time. He quivers not. Only frozen. But he stares down the barrel at Zara's well-covered breast. He mutters incomprehensibly.

"Illyana."

Mei nods to Zara and then mouths something. Zara gets it and says to Peter, "Illyana. I am your Illyana."

And Peter begins to mumble again. "Illyana. I can't. I can't kill you."

Mei nods her head to Zara and mouths a kiss. To which Zara shakes her head no. And Mei gives her that "come on now" look. What she is asking is nothing more than what she had done before. If it will save the three of them, then maybe God will forgive her for this. And Zara leans into the gun and lightly dry-kisses Peter on the lips. She leans into his ear and whispers, "I am Illyana. I love you."

And all Peter can mumble is, "I'm so sorry, Illyana, but I couldn't kill you. I couldn't." He stares into Zara's eyes with his look of utter helpless innocence. And Zara remembers what he muttered to her in the prayer room.

She takes the gun out of his hand and gives the first moist kiss she has initiated in nearly a decade. Eyes closed, her lips feel the wet warmth and gentleness of his. And she feels something so very different from any kisses before. A warm, open white light, a peace emanating up and down through her inner being. She is losing herself. The old self and the new self both melting away, into something different.

Fearful she will become lost in this unknown, she pulls back enough to utter, "Nanshe. I am Nanshe. I love you."

And Peter pulls his head into her headscarf and whispers, "Nanshe, Nanshe."

Sensing his nose pushing on her head covering, Zara pulls her headscarf back, letting him smell her hair. And he inhales. "Nanshe, I will love you forever. But you must leave me to die. You must take the object away from here, away from the tail of the bird star, or all is doomed."

He collapses into her arms muttering, "I will love you forever."

CHAPTER 20

*Goodbyes are only for those who love with their
eyes. Because for those who love with heart and
soul there is no such thing as separation.*
—Jalāl ad-Dīn Muḥammad Rūmī,
thirteenth-century Persian Sufi mystic

5:55 p.m. GMT+1, May 9, 2022
MoxWorld EU Headquarters, Luxembourg

Finishing her Asr prayer, Zara straightens out her dress. She hopes she has Xwedê's forgiveness for her transgressions with this man she has only known for a few hours. For what is worse, that she kissed a strange man, or her straying interest in how she felt as she was doing so? Either way, she hopes, she believes that her prayers will help her move on from this moment as they have saved her from the atrocities of her past, like prayers did for her mother, her grandmother. But will God one day talk with her and tell her so? Then she could be sure. Until then, she continues to pray faithfully, as did her family before her.

She gazes at the black lamb's wool headscarf as she re-wraps it around her head and thinks about Roza's words to her. About modesty, self-respect, desire, and men.

Those words, "I will love you forever," however sweet, like dewdrops on a budding spring flower, make her quiver inside. That feeling he made her have inside. Peace as she has not felt since she was… And then she catches herself. Promises. Just as they all said. Even her father. Words, only to be broken when she needed them the most. She cannot and will not allow the hurt to come back.

She will tell Mei that Peter is hers to do with as she pleases. As the Kurdish saying goes, "Whoever is fond of cream should take the cow around with him." He won't mind, for Mei is very beautiful, and she not so much so, anymore.

It doesn't matter anyhow. For she has by choice opted for celibacy. Her life is dedicated to her family and her renewed faith in Xwedê. He would of course be happier in the soft, smooth, lithe arms of Mei rather than in the roughness and wretchedness of herself. Not her skin, but what hides within her. He does not appear as a man of prayer, for only such a man might forgive what is within her.

But she is satisfied, as she received her reward, shortly after Peter's revelation in her arms—MoxMedia's breaking news announced that the president of Russia declared both Kurdish nations no-fly zones under the protectorate of mother Russia. One tap from Alexander. The world changes.

Exiting the men's room, Peter is relieved he could clean up and change. Even though those black slacks hid the stains well, having poured that lubricant all over left him sticky and messy. But that was nothing compared to the trauma of holding a gun to Zara's chest. He had thought staring down that barrel on 157th and Broadway was terrifying. But that was nothing compared to holding a gun on someone. One false twitch of the finger and it is permanent. One can never recall a bullet after the hammer strikes.

Now that they know the object had been moved, all evidence points to Jean-Paul's main hypothesis of Göbekli Tepe. They are preparing their gear to fly there immediately, before the Arabic Confederation forces overrun Sanliurfa, closest airport to the world's oldest temple. Peter is ready to move on and leave the horrors of this building as he moves down the hallway in deep reflection.

Smoosh. Once he opens his eyes again, he looks up to see Zara with her hands up against his chest and his around her. "It seems, Mr. Gollinger, you cannot keep your hands off me. Alexander's gambit is over. You won. We don't need to keep practicing his absurd notions of what you perverse afflicted men need."

"I'm so sorry, Zara. I didn't mean to accost you again. I mean…"

She laughs and says, "Normally, men who touch me inappropriately suffer at least broken body parts. But because in your heart, you had the best in mind for me, and for Mei, I will spare you."

Peter notices she is still wearing the banana slug earrings. He peers into her eyes. He can't tell if she's jesting or telling him the truth.

"You had me fooled back there, Peter. I thought you were only taking advantage of the situation so you could have gratuitous sex with Mei, with Alexander's blessing. You should know, no one tries to fool Alexander and lives. I misread you. It won't happen again."

She removes his arms from around her and turns down the hallway. The warmth of him again solidified her resolve. Never again will she be left vulnerable. And she says, "I am sure you and Mei will have a chance to develop a truly meaningful and deep relationship during our mission. If I were her, I would be emotionally, and perhaps physically, very open to you. We Kurds have a saying. 'Whoever is fond of cream should take the cow with him.'"

Unsure of why she has said this, especially the part about him being a cow, or was it cream, Peter turns into the infirmary as Zara continues down the hallway. Mei is there, focused on sorting through vials in the refrigerator.

"Oh, Peter. I'm glad you are here. You can help me pack more vaccines for the trip." She turns to him and kisses him on the cheek. "I didn't get a chance to thank you properly earlier. I just wanted to get out of that dress right away. I mean, you and I were so sticky."

She kisses his other cheek. "You are a clever man, Mr. Banana Slug. I owe you my deepest gratitude for your gallantry, standing up to Alexander." And she hugs him.

She shakes her head, though. "But I don't understand it. The vaccine should have worked. The five algorithms should have worked."

"But it did, Mei. Your work succeeded. We now know that the originators moved the object."

"That's so sweet of you," she says, giving him another peck on the cheek. "But I'm not so sure how and why it came out of you. It makes the selection of which vaccine formulation to bring very daunting."

Dimples ablaze, Peter places a very warm hand on her cheek. "Mei, I almost couldn't come up with a solution back there. For a moment, the only way I thought I could save us was if I told Alexander I would marry you."

Her anxious look melts as she tilts her head, peering at him, into those innocent eyes of his. "That is so sweet, Peter. A little rash, maybe. Not too logical for sure. But I appreciate, truly I do, what you did for me.

You are so delightful, Peter," she says before kissing him on the nose. "But this isn't over yet. We haven't found the object. And who knows what I will have to do to you to coax those memories out of your brain? But I'm afraid that dress he wanted us to wear won't do out in the middle of the wilderness."

His face starts flushing as he gazes upon her stylish version of khaki expedition wear. "That is so lovely, what you have on. You're even coordinated with Rhonda's evening broadcast. And how could I not love your banana slug earrings?"

"I'll let you in on a secret," she says. "I design Rhonda's outfits. Well, my team at the Shanghai-Paris Fashion Institute does, under my direction. I'm also vice chairman of MoxFashion. Would you believe that there is a genetic component to what we find fashionable?"

His eyes light up. Another coincidence? Maybe she truly is the dark-haired woman of the dreams, of his pappy, of Michaela's suggestion. And like the good big bro that he is, he says, "My sister would love to meet you. She's been agonizing over how to get into that place. She's doing her doctorate in material design at Shanghai University."

Another peck on his nose and she says, "Then, my banana slug man, we'll just have to fly to Shanghai to meet your sister. And if you are nice, maybe my mother as well."

☙

Out in the lobby, Alexander and Jean-Paul are having their last face-to-face briefing before the mission team takes off. Jean-Paul is shaking his head. "Alexander, I still don't know what came over you, pulling Mei from the mission. We should reconsider and put her back on the team."

Alexander shakes his head too. "No, I have arranged too many other elements that are now in motion. Intel shows we have competitors to worry about. My enemies, my customers. We have a limited window to go in and get the object before others grab it first. Time is running out. We can't afford the risk of Peter being confused by two women on this trip. And you witnessed the results of my test back there. Peter was willing to save both women. But who rose to the occasion to save Peter? Not your precious Mei, who could not compromise her illusion of bodily honor. But my little Zara, she was willing to make the ultimate sacrifice. Her life. Isn't that what your translations of the afflicted's traditions said about who would find the object?"

Alexander beams with pride. "Let me talk with Zara in private about what she needs to do on this mission. She will come through. She is my little Zara, after all."

Jean-Paul, still shaking his head, implores, "You should tell her. You haven't yet. She should know about her DNA cluster."

With a stern look from his piercing eyes, Alexander commands, "Under no circumstance will you tell her. Nor my Peter either. Do you understand, Father Sobiros?" Jean-Paul nods. "If my little Zara were to know, it might change her outlook forever, perhaps in ways detrimental to our end objectives. Father Sobiros, you and your pope have your theories of what will happen when they encounter the object, and I have mine. Let me handle Zara."

"One more thing, Alexander. You were right, Peter needed Zara's DNA to stimulate the object dream vision we needed. But you were wrong that they needed to have sex. In fact, Zara never had sexual contact with him. Either you or I should clarify this finding with Zara."

"Priest, you do not know that for a fact, only mere speculation. We cannot endanger our timelines by you acting on your so-called morality and falsely assuring my Zara that diluted physical contact will get what we need from Peter during this mission. She is a big girl, and do not let her fool you—she is no virgin. She knows well how to handle a man adeptly in these regards. Better than Mei, as we saw." And the giant smiles lasciviously as he says, "Trust me. I know exactly how bad she really can be."

As Jean-Paul exits the building, with fist tightened, he turns and with a rapid blink says, "And, Alexander, for the record, the Vatican's official record, for you, I rescinded my vows. As with everyone close to you, I crossed my ethical lines for you. It should have been me, not Peter, who intervened on Mei's behalf earlier today. So, it's just Jean-Paul. Simple Jean-Paul, who failed someone when she needed him the most." He frowns and leaves, taking his gear, out to the private car that waits for him.

As Zara exits the building carrying two packs, her battle-ready combat face comes back as she sees Alexander. How could he take Mei off the mission team at the last second? He will soon find out she will not take care of him. She can't. She won't. She'll make that boy's life so miserable, he'll shrivel up at her touch.

As if nothing had happened earlier, Alexander opens his arms for a goodbye hug. But Zara only says, "Not happening, Sasha. You burned up all your hug credits when you put that specific gun and sash in the box. You are a sick man. It's over between us. And I'm not taking care of your boy in Mei's absence."

Every sheep is hung by his own leg, say the Kurds. And Alexander hangs this sheep by her leg. "My little Zara, you can fool everyone but me. I am the only one in your life who knows your whole life history. I know you are intimately capable of doing what Mei was tasked with, and much, much more."

Biting her lip, she tries to restrain her welling emotions, which this monstrous man has unleashed with his cruel intimations of the past she has worked so hard to suppress. "Sasha, it is bad enough you sent your Russian goon squad to rip me away from my family, deprived me of my treasured Sugar Festival, and forced me to renege on my promise to put down arms."

The giant with the dark, piercing eyes smiles smugly. "I am proud of you. Be honest with yourself. You were waiting at home, bored, hoping I would pull you out of your silly retirement. A woman like you cannot sit back and not take action when the world needs her compassion, her wisdom, her leadership."

As much as anyone, Zara likes being complimented, even by a man she so despises, who knows her buttons all too well. She will never again let a man get so close to her, to know how to woo her, to move her, to manipulate her. Neither him, ever again, nor the priest, and especially that Peter. If she has to let loose that old Zara again, she will to protect herself.

Knowing his real-life chess game all too well, she pushes her pawns into play. "When you asked me, as a hostage trapped in your jet, to help you, I said under protest, under duress, that I would take them there safely and find what you wanted. Did I not? And there was nothing in my promise about taking care of them after getting them there."

She pauses, folds her arms across her chest and moves her queen into position. "Nor bringing them back alive. Only finding and retrieving the object. And for that, you promised—you swore to meet my two requests. We said nothing about mating with your precious Peter. You know all too well the strength of my renewed faith and what I will and will not do."

At first with an annoyed face, he smiles and strokes her cheek. "My little Zara, is it not said, 'If you are an anvil, be patient; if you are a hammer, be strong'? You have been a hammer for the last six years since coming back from your miraculous escape. Who but me has been your greatest supporter during these difficult times? Now it is time for you to be an anvil again, with Peter. Be patient with him. Be someone solid he can lean on. He needs your support. He needs to know you will be there for him, as I have been there for you. I ask nothing but this. Can you do this for me?"

Striking the giant in the lower gut with her fist, she says, "I am not the woman you once loved, Sasha. She is dead. You killed her." She pulls back away from him, with a stern matron look beyond her years. "And don't give me that family talk. We are so beyond family now. I do this last thing for you because I love my great-grandmother Sara, and then it will be over between us. Forever."

He grabs her arm with such force she cringes. She strikes his arm with a fierce blow, trying to dislodge her limb, but to no avail. He is a monster who will use any leverage to get what he wants. Even crushing her arm.

"My little Zara. You know there may come a moment when you are at the temple grounds, when those who broke our security yesterday have sent their extraction team, when you are faced with your death, when you will concede to what nature has fated for you. You will need to be intimate with Peter. For whether or not you know it now, you have already chosen him."

He lets go of her arm which she rubs to regain blood flow to her pale hand. "There is nothing you can do to force me to do anything. Not anymore. I have chosen, all right. I have chosen celibacy. And that is that." She takes her packs and rams them into his gut as she leaves.

As she walks to her private car, Alexander waits for Peter as he checks the time on his MoxWrap. Tapping his foot, he too is challenged to be the patient anvil with this boy. The door to the lobby crashes open as Peter tumbles through it. He is carrying only one gear bag with difficulty, lifting it only a few meters at a time and then dropping to the floor. Out of breath, he says to Alexander, "I'm so sorry. This is heavy. What's in here? I've backpacked the Sierras, the Andes, and my packs didn't weigh this much."

"It weighs so much only because so much weighs on your mind," Alexander says as he helps the hapless Peter by picking up the bag using only three of his giant fingers. "You did well, my boy. Those were very astute and decisive ploys you pulled. And how you manipulated those women to do what you wanted. How you tried to manipulate me. Fabulous. We are more alike than not."

Blank-faced and panting, Peter stares into his dark, piercing eyes, incredulous at what this man is implying.

"You and Mei seemed to connect well," Alexander posits. "You like her, don't you? Maybe you could love her, no? And you are dismayed that she cannot join you?" Peter nods yes. Yes, with an anxious smile.

"Know that Zara is stronger than Mei," says Alexander. "You can lean on her, depend on her even more. If you give her room, her compassion will overwhelm you in some surprisingly positive ways. She is the most compassionate woman I know. But do not expect her to be Mei. Or Sarah, Or Ciara. Or Tara." Peter is stunned Alexander knows his past three girlfriends' names. But he is Mr. Murometz, isn't he? Peter stares into those piercing dark eyes and nods his agreement.

To Peter's surprise, this gigantic man puts his arm around him like his father used to. Didn't he just ask Zara to shoot him with some worst-way-to-die bullets?

"My son, in time you will know what I do. You, me, Zara, we are family. One day, not too long from now, you will know exactly what I mean. On that day, please remember, we are family."

With these mysterious words said, Alexander, the world's richest bag porter, takes Peter's bag in hand, or fingers as the case may be, and like a proud father keeps his arm around Peter, walking him to his private car. Peter is taken aback at what he sees. It is one of those armored SUVs that ferry around presidents of countries. There are three armed men with submachine guns waiting with several more on the lookout around the property. Outside the gates, there are two more SUVs with more armed personal guards. Peter cannot resist saying, "Expecting company?"

Alexander hugs him, perhaps a little too hard as this one hurts, and says, "Peter, there are many people who would also want this object. There are spies everywhere, and I fear, despite my best security measures, which as you know are the world's best, information on our project, and possibly about you, has leaked. These people will stop at nothing to beat you, Jean-Paul, and my Zara to the object. They may even try to kidnap the goose that lays the golden eggs—you. As you see, there are three separate convoys taking you three along different routes, all to help confuse anyone seeking to capture you before you reach the airport."

Peter's knees go weak. This is for real. Can he turn around and dive into the warm, comforting and, most importantly, safe arms of Mei now? Two helicopters launch from behind the MoxWorld Europe building and take hovering positions over the roadway to the airport. The buzz further unnerves Peter.

He is helped into the car by one of these submachine gun toters. Alexander leans his head in for last words. "As my grandmother would say, 'Both the hunted and the hunter rely on God.' Remember Mei's guidance about your limits. What you are going to find out there, my son, will test your limits, test your faith, and you will have to decide what you truly believe and don't believe."

With this odd form of love expressed, the giant closes the door, and Peter shrivels into his seat, in searing fear of what he has gotten himself into.

Surprisingly, Alexander knocks on the window. Peter rolls it down. "Peter, my son. You are good at pattern recognition. Tara. Ciara. Sarah. Ever thought you have some subconscious thing going with your choice in girlfriends? Sarah, Tara, Ciara…Zara. A little something I thought you might want to ponder as you test your faith." And the SUV rolls off.

Mei reveals herself from behind the giant black monolith outside the lobby, dressed in a plain navy cashmere pantsuit with a white silk blouse, fully buttoned up. Her face is devoid of makeup, hair in a rough ponytail. But on her ears still hang the yellow banana slugs. Clearing a tear from her face, she approaches the man she once called boss.

"He's doomed, you know. You've doomed him by pulling me off the mission," she says.

The giant stares down at her. "He was doomed the day he was conceived. As was I. He and I have only two missions in life. Find it, or create children who will find it."

Straightening her skirt, she replies, "You could have at least left a condom in that box. You made me into a piece of flesh. I can't believe it." And with her two-inch patent navy pumps, she forcefully kicks this monster in the groin.

Smiling through the whole act, the giant man merely says, "Feel better now?"

Lifting her injured toes, she massages them. "I'm not going to be an object for you. That's why I tendered my resignation. Let me out of my contract."

He only smiles and points to her MoxWrap.

"What? Are you going to show me the gory reminders of those who broke their contracts with you? Those you have disposed of?" cries a distraught Mei.

But instead she watches a video of her father's brother being released from his seven painful and humiliating years in prison.

"Isn't that what you wanted?" her big boss asks nicely.

She nods, starting to smile again, and tears form for a different reason. Her boss has listened and decisively acted in appreciation and respect, albeit in his own way. And most importantly, she smiles because she won't be the victim of an unexplained disappearance for trying to deceive him.

"Your plane is fueled and ready to return to Shanghai, where you will pick up a passenger and go to San Francisco. You may visit your home only to refresh your wardrobe and pick up any other equipment you may need, as you are required in San Francisco as soon as possible. Your uncle will be sent over in another one of my planes, and you can help him settle into his new country."

He puts his giant hands around her cheeks and lightly kisses her forehead. "Never say that I do not honor my commitments, especially to my most favored and dutiful employee."

Alexander looks up at the sky and says in a philosophical voice, "San Francisco, Mei. San Francisco. No matter where you go, your destiny follows you."

He turns back to Mei and affirms her recent suspicions. "It was never your destiny to go with Peter. It was always Zara's."

PART II

*I am neither of the East nor of the West, no
boundaries exist within my breast.*
—Jalāl ad-Dīn Muḥammad Rūmī,
thirteenth-century Persian Sufi mystic

CHAPTER 21

I have loved Thee with two loves,
a selfish love and a love that is worthy (of Thee).
—Rabi'a al-Adawiyya,
eighth-century Persian philosopher and mystic

7:20 p.m. GMT+1, May 9, 2022
Infirmary, MoxWorld EU Headquarters, Luxembourg

Pureness. The purity of silver. Swinging on a chain above his heart. Zara fixates on the former Father's cross.

I know these Jesuits. All too well. The good and the bad. Which one is he? Need I ask? He's with Sasha. And how did I let him talk me into this? But a milk run, he said as he kidnapped me. And I have not slept in two days as I madly caught up with his newest land and avionics security systems.

Sitting diagonally from the good priest in the four-passenger section in Alexander's custom armored security jet, Zara stares at the priest, confidant of the man who once dominated her life, who she thought for a moment, when they first met, that she could trust. But now, she has reasonable doubts as he failed to stop Alexander's denigrating that poor Mei. It was not this priest who stood up for her defense, but a lesser man. Peter. It was incomprehensible that a man of God would be party to his protégé being bullied into sex with a complete stranger at the mere command of that giant.

But a part of her remembers his kindness, his sageness, his words of love for God. And if things were different, she might have fallen for him in that moment. Further proof of her impaired mindset in this moment. She cannot, will not, must not, give her intimate trust to any man ever again. But maybe he is different. A man who would forego physical intimacy with a woman because he valued prayer with her more. If only such a man existed.

Decisively, she devises a plan to test him and the nature of his inner convictions. She says, "*Ad majorem Dei gloriam.* Isn't it?"

He looks up and smiles. "For the greater glory of God. You know Saint Ignatius, do you?"

With terse eyes staring into his, she replies, "No, I do not. I only know you sacrificed your mentee, an honorable woman who looked up to you. Sacrificed for the greater glory of God. In this case, you have traded your God for Alexander."

As his forehead lines deepen and his mouth frowns, she can see the shame as it sweeps across his face. Transparent and clear.

At first staring at the floor, the good Father looks up at her and calmly says, "I had a moment of indiscretion, of weakness. I hope you will trust me that this will not happen again. I will have your back on this mission." He offers his hand out to shake, and she reciprocates.

As he extends his arm out, his tunic sleeve rises up and she spies the scar on his forearm. As she thinks about her own scars, he squeezes her hand in such a way that she fully comprehends his strength, after which he says, "I will not be a hindrance. I am quite capable, in many ways."

Zara nods and says, "Understood, priest."

Jean-Paul rapidly blinks, smiles, and adds somberly, "It's just Jean-Paul. As Alexander may have let you know, I rescinded my vows. I rescinded them for him, for this mission." She stares at him, processing the implications of what he said and his eyes as he said it.

❧

After a fear-filled twenty minutes, ten more than what the direct route needed, Peter arrives at the plane, the same size as the one Mei has. Zara must be as important as Mei to have her own plane like this. But this one is different. It has camouflage paint. Four cylinders hang underneath the front fuselage, and what look like doors are mounted in the rear fuselage. He is escorted up to the ramp by many men with heavy guns.

He peeks inside, and to his surprise, it is not luxurious like Mei's plane. After the boarding door is the galley, of course, albeit much smaller than Mei's, but after the galley is a sole four-seat cabin, two seats on each side, facing each other, and what appears to be the lavatory behind it, large enough to be a changing room as well. Jean-Paul points him to the seat across from Zara as he spreads his documents across the table on his side of the plane. Peter sits down in front of her meekly, as she has glared at him since his late entrance. She taps her MoxWrap, and the flight crews prepare the jet for takeoff.

Peter knows he is seriously out of his element, and Zara's silent stare is not helping any. He avoids her eyes and stares down at her feet. For a few moments, in and outside the prayer room, in the main conference room, he thought they had a connection. But she can turn in a second from a warm and compassionate being into a cold, distant, even threatening entity. She is such a complicated person, for Peter, that is.

Watching him watching her, Zara ascertains she will certainly make sure he gets the message that she is not Mei. She is fully capable of keeping him distant. This one scares so easily. But somehow, he figured out how to get the best of Alexander. By accident? She can take no chance that he gets the best of her.

With the determination that won many battles, Zara goes on the attack, taking her first offensive swing at him. "Staring at my feet like you stared up my dress?"

Physically smaller than her and, he surmises, younger than her too, Peter is petrified, stiff like a statue, and can do no more than stare motionlessly at her, still wearing his beloved banana slugs on her ears. Who is she? The woman who kissed him while he had a gun at her chest? Or the woman who would have put a bullet between Alexander's eyes?

Knowing Alexander's boy will need to quickly adapt to her land, her people, her culture, she flings her second volley. Pulling her headscarf across her face so only her eyes show, she yells, "What's wrong? Do I look like a terrorist to you? Are you in sheer terror of me?"

On the other side of the table from her, Peter's brain wrestles with Alexander's advice: "Be open to her." How? He avoids confrontation and changes the subject. "Not quite the same in here as Mei's plane, is it?"

Zara takes the opportunity to scare the naivety out of this silly man and replies, "There is no room for luxuries. All the space back there is taken up with defensive systems, including Alexander's latest state-of-the-art electronic countermeasure system. There are several different chafe systems for evading missiles, as well as the four drones mounted below for misleading the most advanced missiles known from NATO, Russia, and China. And we are heavily armored to be able to take direct 12.7mm hits as well as to absorb shrapnel. Where we are going, we will be lucky if all of this allows us to land safely and not be blown out of the skies."

Lifting off from the runway, Alexander's flying tank pretending to be a private jet takes off. Peter cowers in his seat, pinned there both by this woman with her evil stare and from the combat takeoff the pilots made to evade, as Zara described, any MANPAD missiles.

Everything is so surreal for Peter. It's Luxembourg, for God's sake. Who fires MANPADs in Luxembourg?

To avoid that stare, Peter gazes down as he reflects upon how he got himself into this situation.

Suddenly his thoughts are interrupted by Zara yelling at him. She clicks her fingers and points to her eyes. "My eyes are up here, not down there." He suddenly realizes he has been staring at her chest.

As he gazes aside to his beloved slugs on her ears, she remembers she forgot to take them off. And so she does, throwing them on the table at him as she says with great disdain, "Insects."

That puts Peter over the edge as he interjects, "They're not insects! They're mollusks! And they're very sensitive creatures, who don't take criticism very well."

Oh, he should have listened to Mei, for Zara gives him the scariest, meanest, angriest face. "I do not care. Bugs. Slugs. God meant for them to live on the land, and not my ears."

Very deterred, Alexander's boy stares out the window to avoid having any more transgressions. And from behind a cloud he sees them. He yells to Jean-Paul, "Look, we're being attacked by F-35s! Tell the pilot to use that chafe stuff!" And a pair of F-35s come up and take positions behind their jet.

Looking out the window as well, Jean-Paul verifies they are American. Must be from a German airbase. He taps his MoxPad+, waits and says to Peter, "They are not hostile. They're our escort."

Staring at these jets, Jean-Paul mumbles Alexander's last words to him: "He's arranged too many other elements that are now in motion."

And for Peter, those F-35s are certainly in motion. He's never seen a real one before. Only the ones on MoxWorld News and pictures in the article he edited on the world's most advanced fighters. The authors concluded that, between the American F-35 and the Russian T-50, it was a close call, with the slight edge to the latter, in the model that was introduced only last year at a third the cost of its American rival. Now having met the man in person, Peter has to wonder what Alexander's role has been in all of this. Selling upgrades to each side year after year? Why else would the Americans send him two of their precious weapons to escort them?

His deep thought is broken by Zara talking into her MoxWrap. She speaks quietly, first with a smile and then a look of consternation. They must be speaking in Kurdish. Peter hears the word *dayik* used very often early in the conversation and then *mama* much more later on. She ends the call with pursed lips, tapping her sandal below the table, and gazes out the window.

Peter decides to try and dive into the deep end of the pool again. He figures as long as this table sits between them, she can't attack him if she gets mad. At least not right away. "Everything all right? That was your mother, wasn't it? I recognize those types of calls."

"Thank you for asking, Mr. Peter. It was my mother. You are perceptive. And it is none of your business, as you Americans would say," she says, glaring back at him.

He cowers back into his chair. He'd like to call his mama too. He so needs to be comforted by someone female and nurturing. And the woman glaring at him certainly is not the nurturing type, regardless of what Alexander may think.

Okay, I'm already in the deep end of the pool, drowning. I might as well ask. You can't get if you don't ask, Peter thinks.

He takes his MoxWrap and says to Zara, "Can I call my mother too? The last she knew, I was in Luxembourg."

Whack. Zara slaps his wrist to the table. "What part of secret, confidential, do you not understand? If you compromise our target location, you will get yourself killed. And I do not really care if you live or die. But I do care if you get me killed too."

Peter cowers even deeper into his chair, muttering, "But you talked with your mother."

She just glares even more intently at his insolence.

Looking out the window again, Zara says, "It has been a day and a half since Alexander panicked and shanghaied me against my will because of his fear of a security leak. Yes, he did wait until Ramadan finished, but just. He sent a helicopter to track me down at my mother's village. As it hovered and set down, blocking my vehicle from going to my treasured Sugar Fest, my family, my panicked mother, screamed in terror, thinking they were being attacked again as they helplessly watched the armed soldiers escort me away."

Turning back to meet Peter's eyes, she says, "We Kurds, we have no friends but the mountains. We have been attacked again and again throughout history. And when police or soldiers come to your house and take someone away, they are going to be tortured. And if they are fortunate, they will be killed quickly."

She stares at Peter with a face mixed with anger and terror as she puts her hands between her inner thighs, rubbing them. "And if I talk to my mother, it is because she has been in anguish thinking I had been abducted. Been tortured. Been mercilessly raped by dozens and dozens of soldiers for days on end. What would you even know about what it means, in the context of where we are from and where we came from, for a woman to be abducted and what those captors would do to a woman? Death would be better."

Peter realizes that was not the deep end of the pool he dived into; he dived headfirst into a pile of manure as high as Mount Ararat. Frightened about what he has heard from Alexander, he mutters, "But my grandfather, my mother, my sister. They're in danger. Alexander told me whoever these people are, they would stop at nothing. Nothing to stop us. Not even kidnapping me."

Head shaking side to side, her eyes roll as Zara snaps back, "Don't worry your little head. Alexander dispatched a team to secure them. One who Alexander trusts."

The air has thickened so much in this little cabin flying at ten thousand meters high. Jean-Paul plays diplomat and asks, "Zara, Peter, can I call your attention to the diagram I have set out on the table here?" He moves it over to their table, partly for them to see, partly as a neutral zone between two militant camps.

The history teacher in Jean-Paul points and explains, "In 1994 a German archeologist, Professor Klaus, uncovered what is now considered to be the world's confirmed oldest religious site, which we know as Göbekli Tepe in Turkish, or Potbelly Hill."

Jean-Paul points to ovals drawn on the diagram. "There, his team uncovered four large ovaloid areas with as many as twelve pillars around two massive central T-shaped pillars up to five point five meters high, or eighteen feet, and a weight of fifteen metric tons. Ones vaguely similar to the black monolith you, Peter, and Alexander remembered from *2001: A Space Odyssey*. Over time they found fifty of these monolithic pillars of various sizes in the areas they had excavated. And hence, thinking like you, with your fantasies of a *Space Odyssey* type object, Alexander thinks our object might be a monolithic pillar somewhere at this site."

Zara fixates on the diagram with amazement. She has heard of this site, living only hours by truck from here with her mother, but she has never had the time to learn more. She thinks proudly, *Once again, more evidence the Kurds started civilization.*

On the other side of the table, Peter, having edited a number of articles about this temple for his favorite alien nation journals, points. "These pillars here, they're aligned with an astronomical point. As you go to from older to newer enclosures, the alignment changes, reflecting the change over time in that astronomical point."

Zara stares at him, a different kind of stare. Maybe Alexander is right—there is more to Sasha's boy than meets the eye.

"Good, Peter," says a pleased Jean-Paul. "Think about the oral tradition from your family. The bright star, the tail of the bird. If you can believe this is the star Deneb in the constellation of Cygnus, the diving swan, then your alignment hypothesis links the traditions to Göbekli Tepe."

Bing, it finally dawns upon Peter. The MoxWorld logo. The constellation Cygnus.

"And Jean-Paul, what about the phrase, 'the long-tailed star came from the sky,' from the oral tradition? What do you think that was? A falling star?" asks Peter.

"Unsure," answers the good priest. "But I believe it was a comet or small asteroid that came down at the end of the Younger Dryas Period, otherwise known as the last ice age, around 10,000 BCE. As you edited in the paper that got you fired from your last job, you were probably right that some event around 9500 to 10,000 BCE caused the Caspian and Black Seas to rise. My research suggests that, although rapidly melting glaciers might have been the cause, it is possible a more cataclysmic event happened in the Black Sea that washed away the civilizations all around its shores. Those pyramids in Crimea, they were likely well away from the current Black Sea shoreline. Something massive washed up and buried them in sand and mud."

"Aliens. It's aliens," Peter affirms, at the risk of Zara's ire. And of course, she glares at him with piercing dark eyes. Her pupils certainly are not dilated, but are as tiny as pinheads.

He frets at what that means, but courageously being true to himself, he needs to say his piece. "Aliens landed with the long-tailed star, which was their spaceship descending through the atmosphere. The oral tradition said, 'Only the giants of the reindeers prospered, because of power from this star.' The giants were descendants of the aliens. They had extraordinary powers and advanced technologies. They built all these monolithic buildings, which we don't understand how our prehistoric ancestors could have built. Your Crimean pyramids, the temples at Göbekli Tepe."

Jean-Paul smiles serenely and simply replies, "Peter, a well-reasoned hypothesis. But we have no proof, only the archeological evidence and what we know from the oral traditions."

Undeterred, Peter taps his MoxWrap a few times and says, "Jean-Paul, is it not true that Genesis said, 'The Nephilim were also in earth in those days, and also after that, when the sons of God came in unto the daughters of men, and they bore children to them'? And who were these Nephilim? Passages earlier in Genesis say they were sons of God who saw the beautiful daughters of men, and they took them. It says, 'whomsoever they choose,' which to me sounds like these daughters were abducted and forced to bear children."

Zara pulls back in her chair and flinches. She puts one hand between her legs while the other touches the scarring on her cheek as she turns to look out the window and exhales.

On a roll, Peter taps a couple more times on his MoxWrap. "Furthermore, the Book of Enoch clarifies how these Nephilim forced these daughters of man to bear them giant children. I quote, 'It happened after the sons of men had multiplied in those days, that daughters were born to them, elegant and beautiful. And when the angels, the sons of heaven, beheld them, they became enamored of them, saying to each other, 'Come, let us select for ourselves wives from the progeny of men, and let us beget children.'"

Peter goes on to annotate the verses on how the Nephilim taught the women they abducted how to paint their eyebrows, how to do sorcery with potions, and committed upon them acts of defilement. He quotes again, "'Impiety increased; fornication multiplied; and they transgressed and corrupted all their ways. They have gone together to the daughters of men; have lain with them; have become polluted; and have discovered crimes to them. The women likewise have brought forth giants.'"

Chest out, proud of his thesis, Peter concludes, "These Nephilim were the aliens who came down in that long-tailed star and took our beautiful women they found on Earth, and their alien-human hybrid children are the Reindeer People of my oral tradition!"

"Enough of this. Enough of this nonsense!" Zara screams at Peter. "You know nothing of life, only that from your books, written by the profane. You know nothing of the suffering of others," she says with some tears forming.

She murmurs under her tears, "You know nothing of rape." She hides her face in her shoulder next to the window and cries.

Jean-Paul, the former Father Sobiros, gets up to put a reassuring hand on her shoulder. Zara counters him, throwing his hand away and yelling, "Don't touch me. Don't you ever touch me like that."

Turning back to Peter with a glare from her piercing dark eyes, she warns, "And you. Keep your words from touching me." She huddles over a little at the table, grimacing with hands below her navel as she takes deep breaths.

Forever the broker of peace, if possible, Jean-Paul softly intervenes. "Zara, he didn't mean anything. He is naïve. We knew that when we found him. And it may very well be that his naiveté is part of why his inner makeup is so valuable to our mission."

Mr. Naïve himself puts his hands out palm down on the table between them and offers, "I'm so, so sorry. I just get carried away sometimes, especially talking about extraterrestrials."

With lips pursed, she stares at him with anger. Dark and overwhelming anger. In a deep, even voice, she asks, "Your sister, has she been raped? Your mother, has she been raped? Have you been raped?"

In sheer terror, Peter shakes his head no in the tiniest way his frozen neck and facial muscles will allow. He certainly will not tell her about his little sister. Not now.

And the torment within her wells up and out with great duress. "My sisters, they were abducted by those infidels who profane the words of the Prophet, calling themselves righteous under their so-called Caliphate. They perverted the words of the Qur'an and deemed it was their right to take women they had captured. They passed my sisters around for months on end as if they were their chattel. No better than animals. Cattle prods and all."

Clearing a tear, she glances at Jean-Paul and back at Peter. She subtly shakes her head as what she feared about this mission has already happened. In her game to shut down Peter to drive him away, she has opened herself up to much, much worse. The scabs over her deepest wounds came off as Alexander's boy countered her with his idiotic debates. Has she become that weak in the last four years? Any fighter knows when you overextend a punch, you open yourself for a counterpunch. And whether he knew it or not, Peter reached her in her most sensitive spots.

She decides to let it bleed out as she quietly says, "One of my sisters, she killed herself. She would rather have been dead than to continue living as their slave. In my world, in my culture, a woman who is defiled has no place in life. Even if she were to have returned home, she feared she would live her life in a state of shame, even with my assurances, her mother's assurances that she had nothing to be ashamed of. Her family would have lost honor. In some families, the male members would kill her. It's called honor killing. And the police and courts overlook these murders as, in their male-oriented hearts, they believe the woman deserved it. And what is a woman to do? She kills herself to end the shame. End the dishonor."

And an eerie silence descends from the heavens and engulfs the jet. Each one does not look at each other, only out their window or, in Jean-Paul's case, at his MoxPad+.

Jean-Paul retrieves a pill bottle from the lavatory and puts a pill with a cup of water in front of Zara. "Alexander would like you to take this."

Very suspicious of anything linked to that beast, she reads the label. Doxycline. Why? The Peshmerga doctors gave her this when that betraying Zengo gave her chlamydia. But more importantly, Alexander had her take a daily dose for the three years she paid back her debt to him after her rescue.

She slams the bottle in front of Peter. "I think there's a mistake. He meant this for you, as you are the one who had unprotected sex recently."

Peter looks at the bottle. Hmm. Yes, it is often used for bacterial and fungal infections. But in the last few years, psychiatrists, like his Dr. Beverly, have been prescribing it for prevention and amelioration of PTSD. He takes two pills out, takes one and puts the other in front of Zara. "We both take it. Remember? You're the one who kissed me."

Zara's MoxWrap taps her wrist. She takes the pill and rises up to go to the lavatory area. She glances back at Peter. "This time, some privacy please."

And with that, they listen to the muffled crying emanating from the lavatory. Ten minutes pass and Jean-Paul spends some time on his MoxPad+, at different times seeming like he is having a chat session. Or perhaps he is playing a video game, muses the overactive mind of Peter. Jean-Paul puts in earbuds, closes his eyes, and smiles again.

Remembering one of Dr. Fontaine's discussions of PTSD among survivors of war atrocities, Peter searches on his MoxWrap for guidance on how he can be more sensitive and appropriate with his obviously tormented tablemate.

A few articles later, he finds Beverly's dissertation on Joan of Arc. At first, he thinks Joan of Arc's description of her first vision of Saint Michael resembled an extraterrestrial interaction. He reads experts' speculations that she suffered migraines, bipolar disorder, or brain lesions. To the latter, he rubs that spot at the base of his cranium. Then the paragraph describing Joan's short fuse rings true to Peter, who wonders what happened to the dark-haired, dark-eyed woman who just throttled him. A past that piques his curiosity, but he has learned in the past quarter hour that with her, curiosity could be lethal.

After a half hour, first with muffled cries, then minutes of silence, and again the muffled cries, the door of the lavatory slowly opens. Zara is somewhat disheveled. Her eyes are reddened. Her sleeves are wet with her tears. And her headscarf only half covers her head.

Jean-Paul stands, reaches his hand out to her head and softly says, "May I?" She nods. And he straightens out her headscarf. He lightly touches her hair and tucks it in where strands have tried to escape. He smiles at her. Zara nods in gratitude for his favor. Jean-Paul, very carefully reading her, holds his open palms out to her sides, but not touching her.

"I am sorry about before. I was not appropriate, hitting your hand away so violently. You may touch me. But only because you are a priest. One that Alexander deeply trusts," Zara responds apologetically as her body stiffens, readying her for his touch.

Assuredly gentle and measured, Jean-Paul puts his hands on the outside of her upper arms. He looks at her as if reaching for her soul. She looks down, trying to hold back her tears. He slowly moves his hands to the back of her shoulder blades. And to his surprise, she leans into him, vigorously grabs him from the back, and hugs tightly.

And Jean-Paul reciprocates, hugging her back strongly. They hug for what seems like a blissful eternity. A deep hug. A warm hug. And not the kind of hug a man and woman have when they initiate their passions, but a deep familial hug. For Jean-Paul was once a Father. And she misses her father so much and cries into his shoulders.

As the tears subside, Zara slowly lets go, with her head still leaning into his upper chest. She straightens, peers into his eyes and says, "Thank you. You are so kind."

She takes her seat and faces Peter. "You. You are not allowed to hug me." She pauses, glances out the window. "But I accept your apologies.

"I apologize for my outburst," she calmly says as she watches the stars. "As you can understand, I worry for my family. And I miss my babies."

And that comment gets a distinct rise from Peter. This poor woman. Was she widowed? Her husband killed by terrorists? Or simply a misfortuned unwed mother? PTSD and alone with babies. He should be kinder and gentler to her no matter how much she lashes out at him. For she has suffered so much in her life.

She turns to Jean-Paul, pointing to the diagram on the table, and asks, "What do we need to do when we get to this ancient temple?"

"Two years ago," answers the good Father, "as Alexander and I developed better intelligence around the oral and written traditions, he funded exploratory work at both this site and the Crimean pyramids. As we examined the ovaloids in these sampled sectors here, here, here, and here, we found these figurines."

On his MoxPad+, Jean-Paul shows several expertly sculpted figurines of a woman with a man, all of them showing a different stage of the five senses algorithm. And not escaping Zara's notice, all the matriarchs have bare, modestly ample chests, not too dissimilarly proportioned to hers. Pagan rites. She shakes her head as she once again folds her arms across her chest.

Jean-Paul concludes, "And thus why I suspect what we are looking for is in one of these unexcavated ovaloids across these several hectares.

"In the packs we carried onto the plane are chest-pack devices that will allow us to survey the area for electromagnetic radiation," continues the priest. "With those devices, combined with the EM detectors in his satellites and the power of his vast network of processors, we should have the best chances of pinpointing one or more zones where we should dig."

"But what if we are not able to detect or discern the EM readings? Maybe they're confusing," says Peter.

Jean-Paul smiles and simply replies, "And there you have identified your role."

Zara, now more composed and appreciative of Alexander's interest in the naive man sitting across from her, interjects. "I think I am finally now comprehending. We have a saying, 'When it is springtime, the grass will even grow under a big stone.' You, Sasha's boy. You will grow under the object. Or over it."

She turns to Jean-Paul with a terse eyebrow. "And just how are you expecting to shake loose what's hiding in his head?"

Jean-Paul simply smiles at her.

"No. No. And no. Listen, you two. I am only going to say this once. What happened back in Luxembourg was a one-time deal only. My future forward deal with Alexander is very clear. And nothing stipulates he and I have any interactions. Physical, metaphysical, imaginary. Nothing."

With this briefing done, Jean-Paul returns to his seat and taps away on his MoxPad+. Zara is examining the site diagram and then what appear to be area maps on her MoxWrap. Peter is gazing out the window, wondering what Mei is doing, and hoping, praying, that magically she is actually on her jet, flying to the target, waiting for him with open arms, dressed in her fashion-forward khaki best.

Then Zara starts tapping a lot on her MoxWrap, appearing somewhat agitated. Tap, tap, tap. She shakes her head. Tap, tap, tap, even faster. She shakes her head again. Tapping and shaking again and again. She gazes out the window, wringing her hands, looking very apprehensive. She taps again. Shakes her head again. Wrings her hands over and over again. And then taps once.

She looks up at Peter with her irritated eyes. "Put your hands out on the table."

Remembering the threat she made about his misguided chest gaze, Peter violently shakes his head no. She gets even more irritated and demands, "Fool, put your hands out." No, he wiggles his head, in a state of perpetual terror.

She kicks his shins under the table, as she is getting madder and madder at his foolishness. And then, with her sensual black suede–sandaled foot, she spreads his legs apart and says, "Put your hands on the table or I am going make you sing soprano."

That gets a rise out of even the normally serene good Father. She offers her hands in peace, palms up on the table. Mystified by Alexander's claims of her compassion, Peter closes his eyes, hoping nothing bad is going to happen, and slowly puts his hands out on top of hers. He thought his palms were sweaty from his apprehension, but hers are even more so. She wraps her fingers around his hand, and he wraps his around hers. Peter shivers, waiting for that something bad to happen to his hands. *Maybe she's going to pull my fingernails out*, he frets. He remembers what Mei told him when she calmed him and starts to take slow breaths through his nose.

And then it happens. Like when they kissed earlier, but even more intense now. He senses it first coming from their fingers, and then in their palms— something. A sensation he cannot yet describe, but one he wants to keep having as he gently squeezes her hands. And to his surprise, she gently squeezes back. The feeling slowly permeates up his arms, up into his thorax, into his heart. Like the Pavlovian dog, he opens his legs wider in habitual response from the five-sense routines he has been subjected to. But the inner wave goes not downwards, but upwards to his neck. And then his mind. He feels peace. Utter peace.

And they float in a never-ending zone of lightness for an eternity of blissful peace and harmony until the plane shifts radically. He opens his eyes and sees the woman across from him, eyes closed, with the same expression he felt. She slowly opens her eyes and looks into his, in a way he never thought this lioness could ever do. She slowly takes her hands back, seemingly a little embarrassed, and slowly looks away.

Seeing that it is now okay to talk, having watched what just happened with deep interest, Jean-Paul points out the window and says, "We must be approaching Ukraine. Our fighter escort has changed."

Hesitant to distract from this special moment, Peter peers out and sees the four F-16s have peeled off, wagging their wings as six T-50s come up to take positions in front and to each side of their aircraft.

Zara, also looking at this exchange, peers serenely back at Peter while the corners of her lips lift slightly, and she says, "Alexander does not play around, does he?"

She shifts her position in her chair, sitting with her back to her window, and pulls her legs up to her chest, holding them with her arms, and stares meditatively out the other window. A salve somehow has covered her deepest wounds, a feeling she does not want to dismiss. Peter gazes at her, which sustains that peace.

As Jean-Paul taps away on his MoxPad+, his two companions extend their moments of peace for a while longer. Then Zara slowly gets up and excuses herself while she takes care of some "personal business." Peter stares at the T-50s, which like the F-35s before them are the first ones he has seen live. His serenity is displaced by a growing apprehension as he ponders why Alexander needed to have six of Russia's finest escort them.

Jean-Paul, listening to his earbuds again, gives one to Peter. To his surprise, expecting some medieval prayer chants or something hyper-Catholic like that, Peter hears a woman singing something extraordinarily beautiful in French. He looks at Jean-Paul with a shrug, communicating, "What is this?" Jean-Paul says she is his favorite French singer, Mylène Farmer. Same generation as Alexander. But she is so beautiful—that is, her music and voice, since he as a priest should refrain from enjoying her physical beauty, he says, tongue in cheek. And Peter sees another side to this French priest, or ex-priest, as Jean-Paul just reminded him.

The lavatory door opens slowly, and Zara emerges, straightening her tunic dress and sleeves. "Okay, gentlemen. We need to get a couple hours' sleep before we land. The pilot is going to take the long way around the Black Sea, so we'll have another change of fighter escort as we pass over Crimea and then again as we pass over Georgia. We are going to be escorted across the new Anatolian Kurdish State and land in Sanliurfa. Once we land, our vehicle, land-based equipment, driver, and guards will greet us and take us the fifteen klicks directly to the site."

She sits back in her chair and adds, "That is, God willing, if no one shoots us down before we get there."

CHAPTER 22

Whenever Beauty looks,
Love is also there;
Whenever beauty shows a rosy cheek
Love lights Her fire from that flame.
When beauty dwells in the dark folds of night
Love comes and finds a heart
Entangled in tresses.
Beauty and Love are as body and soul.
Beauty is the mine, Love is the diamond.
—Jalāl ad-Dīn Muḥammad Rūmī,
thirteenth-century Persian Sufi mystic

Friday, March 27, 1998
Northern Iraq near border with Syria

Leaving the mosque after the Jumu'ah are a simple man and woman. Yes, many other man-and-woman pairs leave this special weekly prayer as well. But this man and woman leave with their much cherished and beloved daughter with them, a youngster whose charm and persuasion has both of them holding her hands as they exit the mosque, heading down the road on the long trek to their simple house near the hills.

Dressed in a dark burgundy ankle-length dress with a black scarf over her head, Maryam feels Xwedê's blessing as she holds the tiny hand of her daughter, who joyously sings a song Maryam has taught her, as the two now follow behind her husband.

Normally, a child of this early age does not come to this mosque. But at the exceptional request of her great-grandfather, a Sufi imam of local note, an exception was made for this one time. Her husband, Nawdar, thought it was more the logic of his father, a local mufti, that earned this exception. His father put forth that the Prophet had brought his grandchildren to the Masjid, and they climbed on him. That the Prophet was merciful and kind towards the children. Therefore, it must be permissible to bring young children to the Masjid as long as they behaved correctly. Either way, both sides of the family agreed that Maryam's daughter, Zara, was someone exceptional who would benefit from early exposure to the religious traditions of their family.

But only just having turned two, little Zara's energy and bounce suddenly switches off, and she will need to be carried back home. Maryam looks to her Nawdar for help, as she carries another baby bump—Zara's little sister, hopes Maryam, or brother, hopes her husband. And so Nawdar lifts the limp Zara into his arms. Maryam glances around to check if they are alone and puts her arm through her husband's, walking by his side. She would not want others to think ill of her husband, for she understands that their local tradition of men taking the lead is to allow them to fulfill their role as the protector of their women. It is their duty to clear the way for their women. But her beloved husband is concerned more by the public display of affection that others might find objectionable. As long as no others are around, however, he too enjoys her arm in his as they walk. And for Maryam, sidling up to her Nawdar allows her to be next to her sleeping daughter.

Once in their small but comfortable home, Maryam takes Zara from her father's aching arms and puts her to bed. She takes off her headscarf, one of her favorites, given to her by her grandmother, Sara, black lamb's wool with beautiful gold embroidery around the edges. She changes from her low-heeled black shoes into simple leather sandals and comes back into the kitchen/dining room to prepare afternoon tea for her husband.

With two cups of tea prepared, she puts the steaming brew on the table in front of her Nawdar, who is opening a letter. She sits next to him and puts her head on his shoulder. She says she received a letter from her sister Leyla, who says she has successfully settled into the village of their childhood near Sinopli, Turkey. She laments the sadness of her sister's life, as Leyla's marriage was not one of bliss as is hers with Nawdar.

She hugs her husband and gives him a kiss. She is blessed that Xwedê's plan included him as her husband. She reflects upon how her sister Leyla's life differed. For soon after her marriage, her husband, three decades older than her, showed a different side, and he who beat and abused her. Leyla stayed with him for years, battered and bruised, for she feared her family more than he. In the end, Leyla had to flee to live with their mother in Turkey in hopes of hiding from her male family members.

Maryam kisses her Nawdar again and hugs him so tightly. "Nawdar, you are my blessing. I love you for not blaming her for her actions. I love you because you treat me and your daughter so well. But I must ask of what may not be of our traditions."

Nawdar peers into her eyes and kisses her eyelids. Then her nose. Then her lips. And he says, "Of course, my love, my beloved wife, mother of my beloved Zara."

"The traditional way we Kurds pick husbands for our daughters can be a real game of chance for the woman. It did not go so well for Leyla. My father's friend's son did not respect women at the root of it. I was so lucky. I was blessed by Xwedê that your father, one of the muftis from Duhok district, knew of and loved the Sufi poetry of my imam grandfather. And so I thank my grandfather each time I talk with him for the introduction of your father to my father. And praise be to Xwedê for his blessing of our family." And she leans her head into Nawdar's chest and wraps her arms around his back and hugs him as hard as she possibly can. "Our life is so beautiful. I thank Xwedê every day."

Maryam leans back and looks into Nawdar's eyes. "I can only hope Zara will marry a man as good as you. I ask if at all possible that Zara be given the free choice of who she wishes to marry, with all our support and our love.

And if Xwedê's will does not allow her such a choice, then I ask that we do our best to accept only the offers of a man who can be a good husband as you have been to me A man of dreams. A man of heart. A man with a soul filled with love. A man of the dreams." She takes Nawdar's hand and kisses it, and Nawdar leans down to her baby bump and kisses her there.

The next day, Nawdar plays with his beloved Zara. Playtime ranges from more intellectual pastimes, like having her remember where a certain playing card lies among many spread out on the floor, to more physical activities, like tag or hide and seek. Sometimes Nawdar plays at being Zara's horse to ride, and the game she loves most is the floor game of sheep and wolves, where two black stones represent the wolves and twenty white ones represent the sheep. She loves being the wolves, trying to eat the sheep before they surround her. And the few times her father's white stones surround her black stone, he surrounds her with his large, warm arms.

Zara so loves her father. He can do anything and shares these things with her. She says to him, "Mama says she is so blessed to have you. Zara says Zara is so blessed to have you." And Nawdar puts his warm hands on her cheeks, kisses her softly on her forehead, and gives his little Zara a big, warm bear hug. It is these hugs that Zara will remember with the greatest fondness throughout her life. That is, until one day.

After lunch is Maryam's time to take Zara for a hike into the hills. Because the mountains are the Kurds' only friend, Maryam fears Zara needs to know mountains, know them well enough to save her one life one day. Zara, the happy child that she is, runs, and skips, examines every plant, every butterfly, and sings with each bird. And when her two-year-old engine runs low on oil, they stop and rest.

As she does each and every day, Maryam sits and talks with her precocious Zara. For Zara, with a working vocabulary of maybe eighty to ninety words, is advanced for her age, and she will surprise her mother each day with something new that she says. Zara repeats a simple Sufi poem from her great-grandfather, which her mother has taught her. Maryam then recites some of her own favorite poems from Rūmī, the great thirteenth-century Sufi poet, scholar, and mystic. She whispers to Zara not to tell her great-grandfather that

Mama likes Rūmī's poetry more than his. Zara loves it when her mother plays these "don't tell anyone" games. She senses her special place in her mother's heart.

And though Maryam recognizes that Zara is too young to understand, she is committed to drilling a specific line of thought into her at the earliest possible age. And so she tells Zara of her deepest wish for her happiness, her wish that she will one day find a husband as good and kind as her father. Maryam pledges that, as her mother, she will do everything within a woman's power to ensure that Zara has a compassionate, loving husband. Maybe she will have her own choice. If not, then Maryam will do everything a woman is permitted to see that an arranged marriage is with someone who is caring and loving, and most importantly, someone who respects Zara. And Maryam adds her corollary wish, "I hope you have a child who is as good as you are," after which she kisses Zara and they spin around and around and around like her grandfather and her great-grandfather. She and Zara pray together.

And so every day, every month, every year of Zara's childhood is spent this way. Although she is too young at two to fully comprehend, these moments are what mark the close relationship she will have with her mother by the time Zara becomes a young woman.

After dinner, when Zara is in bed, Nawdar confides in Maryam about a letter he has received from his brother, who lives towards the east. The letter speaks with graphic and violent detail about how the villages around him were attacked and completely destroyed by the Baathists, who first sent airplanes to bomb the villages, then helicopters to shoot what was left, and then the armies to gather, shoot, or take to torture camps any survivors. The leaders of the Kurdish community have heard that this is called the Anfal Campaign, where the Arab majority intend to exterminate the Iraqi Kurds like they were insects. His brother intends to join the Peshmerga, the military arm of the Iraqi Kurds, to fight back.

Maryam, having listened to the part about killing hundreds of women and children, and having heard the horrible, just horrible rumors of what happened to women in those torture camps, expresses how frightened she is for herself, Zara, and their unborn child. But even more, she fears for her

Nawdar, as she knows that the police or soldiers could come at any moment and take him away again on some false charge to be tortured, maimed, and maybe killed. Nawdar takes her into his arms as she cries and cries and cries. His fingers upon the back of her neck her only salve.

When her tears subside a bit, he tells her that tomorrow she should pack two bags with the bare necessities in case they need to flee. He describes where in the nearby mountains they should go for safety, over an hour's fast hike away. He says that tomorrow, as she plays with Zara, he will go into town and search for gas masks, as his brother told him of many villages that were subjected to this barbarity, which was supposed to have been banned after Europe's first Great War. Hearing this, Maryam cries and cries and cries. Nawdar carries her to the bedroom, where she can cry herself to sleep.

The next day, Sunday, Nawdar has a shortened session with Zara, but not without the warm hands on the cheeks, the kiss to the forehead, and the big warm bear hug. Maryam engages in her usual routine with Zara, this time sitting only minutes up the hill near their home. After the terrifying discussion with her beloved husband, she feels compelled to add to her daily teachings with her dear Zara. She says to her today, after the future husband discussion, "You are a very special girl, Zara. In you is a woman of great inner beauty, wisdom, and strength. Never forget this, and never let anyone or anything make you feel or believe otherwise. Say, 'Inside I am strong, beautiful, and wise.'"

Somewhat confused, little Zara replies, "I am wise, strong, and beautiful, Mama. What does this mean, Mama?"

Smiling at her most precious girl, Maryam replies, "For now, say, 'I have beauty within, Mama.'"

In her superbly cute voice, Zara says, "I have beauty within, Mama. I do. I do. I do."

"Zara, if you say that every day of your life, you will always be pretty inside," says an endeared Maryam. "Zara, if you say that every day of your life, you will always be pretty," says an endeared Maryam.

The cutest of little girl smiles, and the precocious Zara tilts her head with eyes looking up to the right. "Mama said to Zara, seek abun-dance. Find Peace. Have we found abun-dance yet?"

"Dear Zara, I hope that your world is one of peace. Zara, I hope that you will be a leader of peace in your time." And she hugs Zara as if it were the last hug she would ever give.

The beauty of their special moment together is broken as they hear yelling in the streets below. And they hear the buzzing of aircraft coming in. Maryam picks Zara up and carries her, running down the hill back to the house. Once there, her heart falls out of her chest. Nawdar is nowhere to be seen. The bombs now explode in the village. She panics and screams, running around the house. Zara follows her, thinking this is the new game for today. Maryam trips over one of the bags she packed this morning and remembers what to do. She grabs one, and in her other arm she carries Zara. As the bombing deafens her, she runs up the mountain to where Nawdar said they should go. She is afraid to turn around and look, but one of the explosions must have been near the house, if it didn't destroy her house. She concentrates on holding her daughter, knowing she must stay focused to save her little Zara.

Never before has she needed to carry so much so far and so high. After an eternity, she reaches the spot where Nawdar said to go and collapses with fatigue, arm cramped and screaming in pain. She looks and looks and looks. No husband to be seen. She calls and calls. No one. She sits and cries and cries. Zara looks at her and decides she should cry with her mother.

So Zara cries too, little cries. But after a minute, Zara stops the game and comes to her mother, saying, "Mama, it will be all right. You will be safe. You will be safe with me, Mama." Her mother looks up at her, wiping her own tears off her cheek, and Zara says, "I have beauty within, Mama. I do. I do. I do." And with that, Maryam smiles at her daughter, picks her up, and hugs her.

Other villagers eventually come by in their flight from the village. They tell of the gas attack and the hundreds that are dead. Many have skin already showing signs of blistering. Others have to be guided along by hand as they cannot see. Maryam asks if any has seen her husband. No. No. No. And Maryam sinks to the ground and cries and cries and cries.

Little Zara comes up to her, kisses her mama's forehead, and says, "It's time to be a brave girl, Mama," mimicking what her father has told her. Zara takes Maryam by surprise, reciting one of Maryam's favorite poems from Rūmī that her mama only once recited to her father in front of her:

A moment of happiness,
You and I sitting on the verandah,
Apparently two, but one in soul, you and I.
Feel the flowing water of life here,
You and I, with the garden's beauty
And the birds singing.
The stars will be watching us,
And we will show them
What it is to be a thin crescent moon.

Maryam hugs Zara and says, "I love you, Zara. You are the prettiest and loveliest daughter a mother could ever have."

CHAPTER 23

*Hidden behind the veil of mystery, Beauty is eternally free from
the slightest stain of imperfection. From the atoms of the world,
He created a multitude of mirrors; into each one of them He
cast the image of His Face; to the awakened eye, anything
that appears beautiful is only a reflection of that Face.*
—Nur ad-Dīn Abd ar-Rahmān Jāmī,
fifteenth-century Sufi mystic and poet

11:30 p.m. GMT+3, May 9, 2022
MoxWorld armored private jet, somewhere over the northeastern Black Sea

Joy. Rapture. Introspection as the peripheral noise within her mind fades and blends into the colors of her inner visions. Zara has not felt this way at any time during the past two decades. Something she lost along the journey of life, along with many other things, including her grandmother's headscarf. Her loss of innocence, back for a brief moment of time.

A short nap, but one that rested her more than any other sleep in her adult life. She stretches her arms and legs out like a cat, with her muscles streaking pulses of ecstasy. And nowhere in her being can be found the consciousness that she is seated in a jet pummeling through the skies above the eastern shores of the Black Sea at nine hundred kilometers an hour.

But across from her, Peter Gollinger has a thousand percent consciousness. Not of his geographic location or air speed; he is solely focused on this woman, who had kissed him in a way no other had, who only hours ago threatened to drive his gonads into his intestines, and who now has one foot pressing into his chest and the other hanging precariously in his lap. In utter fear, perhaps of his personal mortality, he is doing everything he can to focus on her feet and divert all blood flow away from his nether regions, lest something poke into her delicately placed foot.

As Peter tries to distract his blood flow, he thinks, *How did her feet get onto me? And where is the table that separated us as I fell asleep? And what is this scent, this aroma making rapture inside my head? I'd love for this never to end. Well, never end and she doesn't hurt me when she awakes.*

And she slowly opens an eyelid, exposing an eye still basking in the glow of joy. As this eye begins to focus on the external world, Zara pulls her legs back and snipes at Peter, "Ahem, why are you staring at my feet again?"

Aghast with visions of all the horrible things that might befall him, Peter mumbles the last thing he was thinking. "I was smelling them."

"Are you saying my feet smell? I just washed them before boarding the plane," Zara asserts as she pulls her bare feet up onto her chair and rubs them.

Apologetically, Peter replies, "No. No. I'm sorry. I didn't mean they smell bad. They smell nice."

Again, he gets too close to her. She puts on her aghast face, pulls her feet under her to hide them. "Go back to your Mei and whiff the perfumes she and the priest concocted. I do not wear magic potions made by some chemist. My body is all natural and has no fragrance or malodor."

Peter says, "No, I didn't mean fragrance or malodor, but your pheromo—"

Jean-Paul cuts him off with a hand signal across his throat. Peter would gladly have anyone save him from this conversation, which could only go downhill. But that hypercurious gene sparks and commands his mouth to ask, "How did your feet get where they were, anyway?"

As the corner of her mouth quirks up, Zara responds, "We have a saying: 'Stretch your feet according to your blanket.' And I did. Because of your afflicted person's sleep, you were kicking and screaming. Your priest friend here said I could stop your insanity if I just pressed my foot into your chest. And his advice worked. You muffled your cries and your movement subsided."

Needing some space to think about what has happened between them, Peter excuses himself to go to the lavatory to freshen up. Zara glances at Jean-Paul, slips her treasured black ankle-wrap sandals back on, and moves over to him, sitting on the armrest of his chair.

"Priest, what happened back there? Do not play coy. I know you and Alexander conspired to force me to touch that man," Zara asserts, staring right into his eyes.

With his methodical blink, Jean-Paul replies, "Tell me, from your perspective, what did happen?"

Zara turns away and reflects. She says, "I cannot explain it. His palm was so sweaty. But so was mine."

"What did you feel?" probes the good Father.

Zara reflects more and slowly replies, "Nothing. Nothing, but then all was bliss, peace. Only a little moment of it." She pauses again. "A long, long time ago, with my great-grandfather, I felt a similar way. He was a Sufi imam and taught me their whirl, their form of meditation, their way to be closer to God."

Still facing him, she reaches out to his shoulders and massages them, now with her chest at his face level. And the good Father simply smiles serenely. She says, "You are a calm one. No tension in these muscles." She continues her massage and draws her hands to his chest. "What is Alexander not telling me?" And the good Father continues to smile serenely at her and blinks rapidly.

"What is it with your eyes, priest?" she says.

He blinks rapidly again back at her, saying, "The air in these planes is so dry."

Seeing she is getting nowhere with him, she strokes his neck lightly and in circles. He does not flinch and remains his serene self. She says sensually and softly into his ear, "You know, you are a very good-looking man. A woman could easily lose herself to you."

She hugs him and says, "What you did back there with your hug, we felt the chemistry between us. You know it and I know it." And she kneels and lays her head on his chest. She tries to imitate Mei's seductive voice and says, "Is it possible for a man to truly love a woman, not her body, but her spirit? To seek joy in her in prayer, not in bed?"

He nods yes.

"Are you such a man?" she softly asks into his ear as she strokes his crucifix upon his chest.

Nothing. No response from this man. For her, it felt as if she stroked her father. Zara stands up, straightening her tunic and sleeves, and in her commanding voice, she says, "You are still a priest. I knew it. You did not renounce your vows, did you?"

And Jean-Paul simply smiles at her serenely with a quick blink. He says, "Zara, you are the kind of woman who could make a priest think twice about his vows."

"I was not sure about you. Now I know what I needed to know," Zara asserts as she sits back in her chair. She makes eye contact with him and affirms, "This will not happen again. I am sorry if I did anything that offended your faith."

Jean-Paul replies, "Do we have trust now? I will be there when the time comes. I will be there for you. You need not worry about me."

"Priest, after what has happened in my life, trust does not come easily. All whom I have misguidedly given my trust have failed me. Have broken their promises. As you must have to poor Mei." Zara glances away and says, "We have a saying: 'Expect the worst from your enemy so that you won't be disappointed.' And I do not trust, so I will not be disappointed. Or dead."

Zara reflects on the implications of what she has confirmed in her mind about the good Father as she stares out the window. She then rises and knocks on the lavatory door. "Sasha's boy. Be a gentleman. It's that time of the month, and a poor suffering woman needs this room."

A minute later, Peter comes out, still buttoning up.

"Did you leave the lid down?" Zara teases as she peers into the little room. "Good, your mother has raised you well." And she closes the door behind her.

Peter comes over to Jean-Paul, who again is listening to his earbuds, but looking a little more flushed than when Peter last saw him. "Are you okay?" asks Peter. "That French singer. She's making you blush, isn't she?"

Peter taps a few times on his MoxWrap and says, "She's really elegant. Wow, were you watching her videos from the eighties? No wonder you're flushed."

Feigning embarrassment, Jean-Paul says with a grin, "If she had been available and liked younger men, a lot younger, I might not have become a priest. I have made more than a few confessions during my youth that featured my thoughts about her. And others like her."

Looking around to make sure Zara is still in the lavatory, Peter says, "You saw what happened. The sweat. The pheromones. It's not just me. It's her too, isn't it?"

Jean-Paul smiles serenely. "Remember, keep being patient with her. You are starting to do so. Let what must happen unroll slowly at her pace, at the pace of the Lord," he says, ending with a pause to allow Peter to reflect. "There is nothing you can do, Peter, except get in the way of what she needs to have happen and derail her."

Peter says back, "But, the wetness of the palms. Our kiss. Is something transferring with our bodily fluid? And the pheromones. You knew her foot beneath my nose would do something. Is something passing between us?"

Continuing his serene smile, Jean-Paul states, "Simply be patient with her. Do not overthink it. Be patient and open and let what happens come."

The lavatory door opens, not so gently, and Zara comes out freshened up and ready to throw another verbal spar at Peter. "I washed my feet, so you will not need to tell me they smell."

She retakes her seat and taps her MoxWrap, and a map of the region comes up on a screen. "Here is the latest intel on what is happening around our target. When the AC, the Arabic Confederation, united the fragmented elements of Syria and Iraq in late 2019, they agreed to the formation of a Kurdish nation in the northern regions of Syria and Iraq. However, earlier this month, for some reason, they transgressed the Euphrates and took Kobanî, Sarrin, and the mountains surrounding them the same areas my soldiers helped liberate from the Daesh in 2015. As you can see, this position is about sixty kilometers southwest from Sanliurfa, which is the birthplace of the Prophet Ibrahim, a very beautiful city with historic ruins, mosques, and the Balıklıgöl, the legendary Pool of Sacred Fish."

"The prophet Abraham is the unifying originator of Judaism, Christianity, and Islam alike," says Jean-Paul. "Is it coincidence that where we go is near where he is from?"

With a nod acknowledging the priest, Zara then points out areas around the city. "The Turks control the area immediately surrounding the city. The Anatolian Kurds control this mountain range forty kilometers to the east of where Göbekli Tepe sits. As the Turks withdrew half of their main battle tanks to strike the Kurdish capital yesterday morning, the Arabic Confederation launched major attacks here, crossing the Euphrates just west of Nizip, which they took yesterday, and here, crossing the Turkish border from Kobanî."

Scratching his head, Peter asks, "Why is this important to our mission?"

A smile and Zara answers, "Because where we need to go is about to be sandwiched in. MoxWorld News military analysts believe they are planning a pincer movement to cut off the Turkish troops from supplies from the north while they drive their main attack from the south. We have special permission to land right in the middle, directly in Sanliurfa. Given the Arabic Confederation invasion, many evacuations and relief aid flights are coming in and out of this airport. We are carrying a supply of rare antibiotics as part of our relief cover."

"Very clever of MoxWorld," says Peter. "How much time do we have before the war reaches the temple?"

Pointing to the areas southwest of Sanliurfa, Zara explains, "MoxWorld intel predicts the AC should be outside the city within nine to ten days with little resistance from the Turks and Kurds. The new Anatolian Kurdish State controls this mountain range towards the northwest, but like the Turks, they have insufficient forces here as they too moved their limited military north to defend their main cities from Turkish attack."

Peter asks, "Why are the Turks not working with the Kurds and joining to counterattack the AC from both their positions?"

"Peter, you have to understand, everyone is against the Kurds. After several hundred years of Kurdish provincial rule, the Ottomans were the first in a long history to systematically displace or eliminate the Kurds using brutal techniques of scorched earth, massacres, mutilations, torture, and terror. With the dissolution of the Ottoman Empire in World War I, the Western powers promised a Kurdish nation to gain the help of the Kurds in fighting the Turks. And as has happened many times since, the Westerners reneged on their promise, leaving the Kurds to fend for themselves. And then the Turks have suppressed our culture since 1925, likewise Assad in Syria, Saddam Hussein in Iraq, and Khomeini in Iran. Saddam sponsored a systematic genocide of the Kurds. They moved us out of our lands so Iraqi Arabs could resettle into our homes. The Americans promised to help us in 1991 as we made an uprising against Saddam in conjunction with their Gulf War. And they abandoned us."

Peter patriotically interjects, "But we came back in 2003 and removed him."

"Pampered man from California. You sit in your comfortable cities and know nothing of the barbarous acts that were caused by your government," Zara chastises. "I lost my father because the Americans abandoned us in 1991. We have lost most of the males of his generation due to the Americans. Powers wanting our oil, or our help to secure oil, come in and make promises, and then leave us. We Kurds have no friends but the mountains, because when we are betrayed and crushed, we flee to the safety of the mountains, which take care of us."

Peter, digging himself deeper, tries to interject. "But—"

"But nothing. Thousands upon thousands of our people were killed in government attacks. Gassed. Crushed by tanks. Taken away to torture camps they called prisons. With no warning, you could be taken from your home or off the street, and tossed into their prisons with no legitimate claim against you. And for women, the prisons had their government rapists, whose duty was to violate women in front of their husbands, defile daughters in front of their fathers. For some women, they asked their loved ones to ensure they were never captured, meaning they should be killed before ever being taken."

Jean-Paul says, "History is rife with the same horrible stories, full of well-documented cases, such as of the Romans committing the same atrocities against women in their conquests. Husbands would kill their wives and daughters rather than let them be taken as Roman sex slaves."

"The Greeks, the Romans, the Franks, Arabs to non-Arabs, the Japanese to the Koreans and Chinese, the Nazis to the Jews and their military brothels, and the Russians back to the Germans, millions of women mercilessly and helplessly violated," Zara adds.

"And, Peter, these atrocities continue into the modern day," Jean-Paul adds. "Bosnia, twenty thousand raped in a systematic genocide and ethnic cleansing. The same story repeats in Sierra Leone, Rwanda, Liberia, Sudan, Uganda, and the Congo, where reports estimated up to four hundred thousand women were raped in a twelve-month period from 2006 to 2007. And in this decade, the Boko Haram have taken hundreds of girls for 'brides,' and then the abduction of over three thousand Ezidis by the Daesh."

And with cracking voice and emerging tears, Zara asserts, "Enough. Enough. You just do not know. Neither of you. How can you know the horrors?" And the plane goes silent.

The silence is broken with the rocking of the plane to the left. Out the window, they watch another change of fighter escort as nine T-50s from an airbase in Georgia take up positions around the jet. Zara looks at her MoxWrap. "Six more SU-27s, which Russia supplied to the New Kurdistan, are coming to join us in ten minutes." She puts up the MoxWorld security system radar map on the screen.

Peter shivers as she points to two new groups of dots on the screen. Twelve F-35s from the US and nine F-16s from Turkey. The pilot announces that the US fighters are telling them to turn around. The Russian fighters are replying they will defend any attack.

With a look of consternation, Zara taps away on her MoxWrap. The MoxWorld security system announces that both the Russians and the US have radar lock on each other and will be in missile firing range in two minutes. One minute. And then the screens show the US fighters disengaging. Out their window, the trio see the Russian fighters turning back to Georgia. Alexander at work again.

The Turks, though, continue their approach, with the New Kurdistan fighters turning to them to engage. A dogfight ensues as their armored jet dives towards the earth. Two Turkish F-16 evade the Kurdish fighters and follow their jet down. Peter, panicking, says to Zara and Jean-Paul, "Do something."

Zara shushes him and puts up a virtual workboard that ties in with the pilot's. The security system announces radar lock, and the fighters have launched missiles. Zara taps all over the board in front of her as the plane makes nauseating turns and twists, and the missiles pass their jet, falling into the Kurdish landscape below.

"Alexander's electronic countermeasure systems are always one step ahead. Pray that I learned enough in the last day about his newest tech," she states. "The Turks also have his systems, which are recalibrating based on our last evasive moves. Right now, his processors are working on a countermeasure for their next move on us."

The Turkish fighters come around again and launch more missiles. Two thuds from the bottom of the aircraft bump their plane. Zara says a pair of drones have been launched as the plane makes evasive maneuvers. The drones off to one side are detonated by the Turkish missiles.

The Turk fighters swing around and launch their heat-seeking missiles. Their plane makes radical seat-belt-testing turns up and down and around while their infrared countermeasure flare systems launch and lasers activate, both confusing the heat seekers. And their plane is safe again for the moment as the Kurdish fighters return to chase the Turks away. With this moment of calm, their jet dives into the mountains northeast of Bingol and flies nap of the earth to evade detection by more Turk fighters.

Peter's face wears several shades of green as he wishes he was on Mei's jet over the Atlantic, taking her home to meet his mother. Their plane suddenly turns upwards at great speed as the MoxWorld security system announces two Chinese Shenyang J-31 fighters are on a collision course. Zara explains these are the Arabic Confederation's latest-generation fighter jets, which China has supplied. Now they are in the frying pan.

The finest from China make radar lock and fire missiles. Zara initiates their electronic countermeasures and launches their last two drones. And Peter holds his breath as the missiles narrowly miss them as they chase the drones. Zara is now shaking her head. The Chinese have modified Alexander's systems aboard their jet, and the MoxWorld security system is slower to find a new countermeasure. And the Arabic Confederation jets launch their last round of missiles.

As with last time, the plane makes evasive maneuvers with the infrared countermeasures, flare systems, lasers, and old-fashioned chafe. One missile clearly misses. The other one detonates off their left engine, which catches fire as they hear the fragments pelt the armor around their cabin. Zara is on her MoxWrap with the pilots, who say they need to land the jet now. They need to make an emergency landing at either Diyarbakır or Batman airport. Zara says neither are safe. Land at Siirt.

"As they say in your movies, hold on tight, it is going to be a rough landing," Zara says in her best attempt to make a joke of the dire situation as the plane begins to dive in a not-so-comforting way. "Once we land, if we land, we need to get our gear off the jet as fast as possible. More AC jets have been alerted and are coming in after us."

The plane lands, barely. And before the jet stops, Zara is already searching for something. Several flashes with small explosions come from the back. Peter panics. She explains that she detonated the key security chips in the electronic countermeasure systems so no one can get access to Alexander's latest tech. She shows Peter the detonator switch she retrieved, which could detonate the whole plane if needed. Flip this knob this way, it is a press-button detonator. The other way, it becomes a "dead man" switch, one where you need to have your thumb on this switch at all times or it will detonate.

The plane stops, and Jean-Paul and Zara go back to the storage and retrieve the five packs they brought on board from Luxembourg, the ones Peter could not lift to save his life. And much to the anger of not only Zara, but Jean-Paul, they can only carry two packs off the plane before Zara's MoxWrap blares a warning of satellite-guided munitions imminent on their location. With the pilots, they flee as far as possible from the plane, which erupts into sky-high flames as the AC bombs destroy one of Alexander's most secure jets.

The Kurdish military police arrive on the tarmac. Zara shows them her identification and they show deference to her, something which definitely does not escape Peter's attention. And they are taken back to their building at the airport.

In the police building, Jean-Paul checks the equipment in the two packs he prioritized to be taken off the plane first. Peter cowers in a chair in the corner with his head shaking between his knees. After a few MoxWrap calls, Zara returns and asks Jean-Paul, "So what is our situation?"

"Okay. The two chest-pack EM detectors are functional. But we have no other supplies," says Jean-Paul, shaking his head and looking at Peter, who was utterly useless when the pinch happened.

Zara stares at the shaken Peter. How could he have been so courageous to stand in between Mei and Alexander and yet cower here?

She catches herself in a moment of weakness, feeling pity for him as she replies, "I know. I know. He will be the death of us. All of our security and weapon systems are now lost in those packs back there. They are dust and fragments spread across the runway."

She turns to Jean-Paul and jests, "I think this is the last time they are going to let me land here." With that, she helps Jean-Paul carry the two packs outside to a waiting car.

Outside, a midthirties Kurdish woman is standing by an older-model minivan. She comes up to Zara, giving her the hug of an old friend. And she playfully gives her a salute.

Zara introduces Jean-Paul to Peri, who shakes his hand, and then feels his arm muscles, leans down and feels his thighs. She asks Zara if there is anything between them.

Zara drops the bomb on her, saying he is a priest, so Peri is not going to make a husband out of him.

"Priest," says Zara, "if you have a coin, I'll flip you for who has to lift the silly American out of here." And she smiles and goes to retrieve Sasha's boy while Peri helps Jean-Paul load the packs into her minivan.

Peter is near tears still with his head quivering between his knees. He stares at his shoes, certainly not what he was wearing when he got up a couple of days ago in a daze. How much he misses the Pacific. And then he sees the signature black ankle-wrap sandals his lovely Mei gave to Zara tapping with impatience. He peeks up, only to be met by her intense glare at him.

"I can't do this. I literally can't do this. Can't you leave me here and I can take the next flight back to San Francisco?" Peter cries.

"Okay, Little Boy, time to stand up and be a man," says Zara a little more compassionately as she helps him up. "If you're a good boy, I might introduce you to my friend Peri, who is waiting for us outside. She is so crazed to land a husband, if you put your brave face back on, she just might take you home with her and do to you what you fantasize your Mei doing."

Outside, Zara introduces Peter to Peri, who looks him over and says, "Cute, isn't he? He reminds me of someone. Not much on muscles. How are you at milking goats?"

Still cowering, Peter climbs in the back with Jean-Paul, who is taking inventory of the two pistols and rifle Peri brought with her, lying next to elementary school games. Nice to have your own personal supply of weapons in your minivan for those just-in-case moments.

As they drive through the city, Peri and Zara catch up in machine-gun Kurdish. Peter is amazed to see the tall buildings, the tree-lined boulevards lit up with streetlights, the traffic, the latest-model cars, the yellow taxis, the malls and stores. This was not the Turkey he had imagined. Oh, wait, it is now the Anatolian Kurdish State, which he never imagined. They leave the city, heading towards what looked like mountains in the night sky.

Not long after, they pull up to a house featuring an older part with a modern addition. Grey cinderblocks are built on a rock foundation with a flat roof. Peter observes people sleeping on their roofs. Outside, a woman is waiting, dressed in a dark brown outer gown with sequins covering her chest to her feet, with beige underdress and pants, a coarse yellow headscarf, and a gold belt. Zara gives her a big kiss and hug, as does Peri.

Mehhh. Mehhh. Two toddler lambs, one black, one white, come running out of the house and kick their little front feet upon Zara. She picks both up, hugs them, peeks into their adorable eyes, and kisses them.

In horror, Peter watches this. *She kissed me. Open-mouthed. With lips that kiss lambs' lips.* He will never be able to eat lamb again. Or kiss her.

Still hugging her babies, she turns to Peter and Jean-Paul. "Please, may I introduce Maryam, my mother."

"Please, please, enter," says Maryam in not-so-confident meek English. Peri excuses herself, giving Jean-Paul and Peter her goodbye, squeezing the latter's tush. Inside the first building, the *mal* as Zara said, they enter the family sitting area. A multitude of colorful flowers decorate the room. Zara and Maryam have a small disagreement in Kurdish, after which Maryam excuses herself.

"Please excuse my mother. She did not know I was bringing men home with me. She lives here with her sister, who comes here on the weekends, my grandmother, and my great-grandmother," Zara explains.

Maryam returns with a turquoise headscarf with complementary sequins to the ones on her gown. She and Zara have another minor disagreement, but as a good daughter, Zara concedes. "My mother says Jean-Paul can sleep in my aunt's room, and you, Little Boy, you may sleep in my brother's room," says Zara. "It's right over there, next to mine."

She turns to her mother and asks in Kurdish, "Are you happy now, Mama?"

Maryam simply smiles at her beloved daughter and goes to the kitchen. Zara shows them where the washroom is, then shows Jean-Paul to her aunt's room and finally leads Peter to her brother's room.

And before Zara can say no, Maryam has laid out a veritable Kurdish feast on the dining area floor. "Mama, no, no," cries Zara. But to no avail. Her mother has something in mind. One of those mother things a daughter cannot control.

As Peter reenters the room, having washed off some of the torturous terror from the plane flight, Maryam grabs his arm and shows him to a special place on the dining floor, the one that her husband, Nawdar, would favor, much to Zara's objections. She puts some berbesel soup in front of him, a dish of maqluba, a traditional upside-down casserole of lamb, fried vegetables, and rice, and a plate of assorted cheeses. Jean-Paul enters and is bemused. For the priest, nothing.

As for Peter, Zara's mother dotes on him. He smiles at her kindness, wondering if she is really related to Zara.

Not so amused, Zara goes to the washroom, then to her room, and changes into another, more domestic robe. Upon her return, Zara politely offers food to Jean-Paul. After the famished priest has had a bit to eat, she helps Maryam clean up the plates. Tired, she kisses Maryam good night and bids good evening to her two weary travel companions, who retire to their guest rooms.

In the empty mal, Zara takes a seat on the sofa with her little babies coming to nap next to her, the first real rest since her abduction by the malicious Sasha. And oh, how her feet are killing her. Even with those lovely sandals from Mei, her feet hurt so much, and her calves are cramping. So she rubs her aching muscles.

Peter meekly peeks his head in and, as he has done repeatedly since he first met her, he apologizes profusely. "Peter, what do you want?" Zara asks in an extremely tired voice.

"I liked your mother's lamb casserole so much, I thought maybe I could steal another bite," Peter says sheepishly, like the boy who got caught looking for leftovers in the refrigerator. He glances down at her sore feet. "Feet killing you?"

Too tired to keep pounding on this man, to pretend to keep him at bay, she rubs her feet and moans, "Peter, I have been through a lot in my life that has not been kind to me. My feet, my poor feet." She closes her eyes, hoping he does not link the state of her feet to the state of her inner being.

Kneeling down in front of her, Peter risks his life by saying, "I'm really expert at solving the feet problem of women. May I help?"

Zara stares at him cross-eyed, but she is so fatigued she cannot fight him anymore. And besides, she needs help. So she holds her bare foot up and wiggles her toes in front of him, asking him, "Peter, do you think my feet are attractive?"

Peter finds this a conundrum. Her feet, rough, scarred, are very different from the soft, smooth, pedicured ones of Mei. But if he says no, he insults her. Say yes and get yelled at for being a foot fetish pervert. No-win scenarios. What should he do?

"Zara, I need your help in how to answer your question. If I say yes, then you'll think me having inappropriate thoughts for your foot. If I say no, then I dishonor you, for you deserve to have wonderful feet."

For Zara, this is the first logical thing this silly little boy has said to her since they first met earlier today. The teachings of modesty by her grandmother Roza, who is sleeping only meters away in the adjoining building, ring in her ears. "Peter, if you find my feet attractive, do they create desire or temptation in your blood?"

"Not at all. Your feet are a very important part of your happiness, and I merely offer to help give a little relief back to you," replies Peter, who recoils, waiting for the proverbial shoe to drop and for Zara to attack him.

Zara drops her gaze to her ravaged feet. She has suffered so, and a foot rub is so viscerally appealing at this moment. But in her upbringing, one should not let a man touch you so. She has been so faithful to her traditions since she has come back to live here. But what harm would there be in his helping her in this small way?

And to his surprise, she puts her foot into his hand and says, "You may. Only up to the ankle. No higher, or you will lose your fingers."

And Peter proceeds to perform the miracles he did to Sarah's feet after the day-long hikes, to Mei on the plane, with each toe getting released, the sole of her foot rejuvenated. He can only sympathize with this poor woman, for the scars outside her foot are surpassed by the scar tissue inside. What she must have suffered through. And as he finishes one foot, he does the same to the other with much more empathy. Then, he works his miracles around her ankles.

Zara has had her eyes closed. This rub is almost as enrapturing as their sweaty palm touch. *No, Grandmother Roza, there is no sex going on here. Just what a woman should have every day of her life. Someone waiting at home to give her a foot massage.*

Maybe having Peter around is not such a bad idea after all. Certainly, not for what Alexander wanted, but he may have other redeeming values.

Unseen to the two of them, Maryam is peeking out her door, watching the whole interaction between her daughter and this new man. And she smiles. The best smile she has had for her little Zara in over two decades. Finally.

"She has finally found him and let him in. Maybe finally it will happen," she hopes.

CHAPTER 24

*If one dream should fall and break into a thousand pieces...
never be afraid to pick one of those pieces up and begin
again. That's the beauty of being alive... We can always
start all over again. Enjoy God's amazing opportunities
bestowed on us. Have faith in Him always...*
—Saint Bernadette Soubirous

9580 BCE
Northside of juncture of Tigris and Batman Rivers

Twenty-five cycles ago we landed on the other side of the big lake. As my father said to me, his oldest daughter, Ki, we should find lands of great beauty between two great rivers rich in animals, grass, and water past the mountain of obsidian. And now we live there as the traditions said we should.

My mother, Nanshe, has fifty-four sun cycles and continues as our group's spiritual leader. My brother An has thirty-seven cycles; he has two sons and a daughter with his wife, Sorba. I was so fortunate to have finally found a husband worthy of my hunting skills, Mawra, who has thirty-eight cycles, one less than I. We have a son, Parcza, named in honor of my late great-grandfather, nineteen cycles of age, and my daughter-in-law, Serima, with a beautiful little granddaughter, Perima, of two cycles. We also have a daughter, Ramana, seventeen cycles of age, who is pregnant with her first child.

My mother says to me every day, "Ki, you are so fortunate to have such lovely children and such a lovely granddaughter. Pray to God with your thanks."

Our community now has ten families in addition to ours. We have the good fortune that God has led Nanshe to this place, where we have such an abundance of food, game, nuts, fruits, grains, and water. We have more food than our community can ever eat. For the first time in our existence, we have buildings solely dedicated to storing our excess food. The word has spread of our abundance and wealth, so that each week, new people come from afar to trade with us for food. I have said to my uncle Narn and my brother An that we must remain vigilant at each of these visits, for a robber group may come and raid our peaceful village.

My two sisters, Zirbani and Sarpani, twins with twenty-four cycles, were born less than a year after we landed on the other side of the lake, now this side of the lake. I joke with them that they were conceived the night before our great fight with the giant Reindeer warriors, and so they must have the blood of the warrior in their veins. They do not find my joke as amusing as do I.

I tell their sons and daughter, my children, An's children, the oral traditions and drill them every day in repeating them, just as my father did with me. I also tell them the story of how we came here. I remember as if it were yesterday.

The rain fell harder and harder as I held my father after he tried to delay the giant Tureal from taking me as his son Doroda's first slave. I pinned that giant boy to a log with my spear. I will never, ever be any man's slave, I said to him and to the world. After helping Mother to the boat, An helped me fulfill our father's last wish. That cursed dark stone he said was more important than his life, we needed to save it. After pondering how to get that thing onto the boat, it dawned on me we could put a net around it, tie it to our anchor ropes, and drag it with us as we do the anchor. Brilliant, if I do say so myself, for I was never the modest one of Nanshe's children. After Narn had his wife, Sama, secure in the boat after her tragic and vicious violation by the giant boy, he carried his brother-in-law, my father, onto the boat. None too soon, as the rising waves would have drowned Orzu only minutes later.

And the waves began to lift the boat up with the stone, or the object, as Nanshe says. As we floated, An and I set up the sails, catching the winds that fiercely blew out from the direction of the tail of the bird star. I have never seen the wind blow one way and the tide crash in from the opposite direction, but that day was like no other. The winds blew at the strength of four to five winds, harder than any I had ever seen, and I had been on that boat since I had three cycles. And we flew like ducks across that lake.

I remember looking back at the shoreline. The waves began to recede, exposing the beach and lake bottom. When we reached the dark part of the lake, where we could never set anchor, we were lifted up and down on the highest waves I have ever seen. As Nanshe had yelled to do, I was roped in tightly at the rear of the boat, helping Narn with the rudder. And then we saw it behind us. The waves, which were enormous when we crested them, became the size of mountains as they rushed across the exposed lake bed and then demolished the beach in front of it. Nanshe told us later that God had killed the giants, who had defiled God's people. We all prayed that my uncle, Nanshe's brother, Namu, his wife Zamana, and my dear cousin, Taja, were all safe in that giant almond-shaped thing they had built.

It took a little more than half a day to cross the lake with the winds blowing as hard as they did. God must have been looking out for us, as the winds blew constantly and straight. If they had gusted or come at varying angles to us, our little boat would have been ripped into timbers, and I would not be able to tell our story to our grandchildren. Even half a sun cycle was too long for Nanshe as she treated her sister-in-law's lower body injuries. And then she treated my father, who was surely one step away from his death. Nanshe's herbs were the best of any in the villages that had surrounded us. Only she could have saved him. And she did, barely.

Once the worst of the storm had passed, my father, so sure he was going to die, made sure An and I gathered with him to recite the traditions. And he added more: "And be wary of the giants, the Reindeer People, for when they arrive, flee and seek the mountains past the hill of obsidian rocks that overlook land rich in animals, water, grasses, and your new safety. Follow the vision and words of the black object, for this will guide you as you seek your new land." And I obediently memorized this forwards and backwards, just like Aunt Illyana could.

Having reached the other side, Nanshe insisted we turn to the left and sail along the coast until we reached the trading village, which the Other Siders, with whom she had traded that great shark, had indicated as the gateway to the obsidian mountain. As we sailed along the coast, we could see the devastation on this side as well. Houses were underwater, and boats had washed hundreds and hundreds of paces inland and some up onto cliffs. We finally reached the place where that trading village was supposed to be, sailed into the flooded inland area, and dropped the object as our anchor. We exited the boat to scout, while Narn and An rode the boat back out to the new lakefront when the waters began to recede, leaving the object where we had anchored. As the water receded in the days that followed and exposed the land, Nanshe had us kneel with her in front of the object. And we prayed our thanks to God for saving us.

We made our house there. Narn and An continued our fishing traditions. I found an abundance of wild animals in the hills surrounding us. Once the dark clouds that overshadowed her mind dissipated, Sama began to gather fruits, nuts, and grasses.

Within our first day on our new shoreline, we helped a number of Other Sider families survive with our abundance of fish, wild game, and plant foods. Nanshe was generous and asked nothing of these families other than to pray to God with us in thanks for our good fortune. And she led prayers with our community every night at dinner without fail. And in that first cycle, my twin sisters were born, as well as a new boy cousin, Nirra, son to Sama and Narn. And from the wombs of women, we began to repopulate the lands.

My father never fully recovered. His broken bones did not heal correctly, as my mother had told me they had been broken in too many places. My father, her husband, had been prepared to give his life to ensure we escaped. He never talked too much about this one point, but I clearly recall him saying that giant boy was my cousin, the son of my aunt Illyana and that monster Tureal. And my father is permanently crippled, near death, because he could not kill his sister's son, his nephew, my cousin.

I clearly did not have that problem. I would kill him again if I had to. My mother has become the harbinger of peace. Something changed in her after she harpooned Tureal's throat. So now I am the born killer in the family. Someone has to be. My father wanted me never to suffer what his sister did. And I will forever thank him, as I am the family huntress, the family protector, the family giant killer.

And in my seventeenth cycle, three cycles into our new life, I found a young man worthy enough to consider as the father of my children. Many had previously proposed marriage. Who would not? I was the best provider in our new village, man or woman. But a new family came to our village. Their son, Mawra, would go on the hunts with me. He feared nothing and could shoot almost as well as I, the least humble of my mother's children, could. He was the man I was destined to meet. He was at first taken aback by our tradition of covering our womanly features in cloth, but he came to love me for who I was, not my form or skin. And one hunt, we found what I was searching for throughout our first three cycles here—baby aurochs. We killed their mother together, and together we raised the babies as our own.

And in that same cycle of the sun, an ongoing dispute between my uncle Narn and his wife Sama exploded. My cousin, Nirra, had grown at such a tremendous rate that at two cycles he stood to the height of his mother's breasts. He was still breastfeeding and could do so with his mother standing up. Narn and Sama would have shouting bouts into the night for over a year. My mother would intercede, and her brother would leave for the lake, sulking. But this last fight was the final one. He screamed at the top of his lungs at my mother that this boy would grow to be one of the Reindeer Giants and terrorize all the young women in our village.

Narn grabbed a spear and ran into his house, ready to kill this monster in the making. My mother signaled to me to get my bow and arrows. And when Narn chased Sama out of their house with her monster child in hand, I laid an arrow in front of my uncle to let him know in no uncertain terms that it was over. Nanshe told her brother that I would shoot him if he proceeded to chase his wife and child. It was not God's will for a man to kill his son. He relented, only because she was his big sister. And Sama, crazed and incensed, fled the village with her son screaming for his father. I should have killed my cousin and not have shot at my uncle. That would be a debate that I would have with my mother for years to come. Clearly, I was not as close to God as she. Maybe not at all close.

And maybe God punished us for Narn's transgression, or maybe for my failure to fix a sin, as Orzu became worse and worse. My mother used her techniques in the nights and the mornings to comfort him. He would have his dreams, which they would work together to interpret, along with the words from the voice that guided her. And one day he said he was to die soon and we must leave the village and seek our true destination, the fertile lands past the mountain of obsidian.

And four sun cycles after we had arrived, my father passed away in the night in the midst of his dreams. My mother cried for weeks, for she was lost without him. Since the day they had taken their half of the object, she had said Orzu and she were two halves of the same apple. Now she cried she was only half. She gathered me, my brother, and my twin sisters and said we were her reasons for continuing on and we should seek our new lands together. She then had us recite her addition to our family's oral tradition:

"Remember your father's words. But equally remember your mother's words. Only with the two together can you find peace. The object. You might see in sleep, might hear. But only as man and woman. The object can destroy. The object can save. But only for the man and woman together. Together, guide the salvation of others."

We needed each other. We needed the object.

And we packed to leave. My baby aurochs grew into the massive adults we had known and loved on the other side of the lake, and we loaded the object onto a sled and hitched it to my aurochs to drag across the mountains to come.

Following the instruction of local traders, we followed a valley farther and farther into this new land. The lands were green, full of forests, and the tall mountains reached the clouds. We came to the end of the river and creek we had been following, where the mountains split, showing a pass through to the other side. These were the tallest things I had ever seen, but the beauty of the landscape was bewitching. I knew in my heart we belonged in this paradise. Between coaxing the aurochs to climb up, constantly rebuilding the sled carrying the object, and at times lifting the object ourselves, we took a week to cross the pass.

Another two smaller but longer mountain passes and a larger valley later, we found a fertile plain. And we found a crossroad in trails—one back towards the big lake, another leading to the ancient fire mountain where the obsidian was found, and a third one, which Nanshe said would take us to our destined valley. Our group was tired and exhausted, as were my aurochs. We had lost two families, who had opted to stay in the two valleys we'd previously crossed. My sister, Sarpani, lost her husband, who was killed by a wild boar on a hunting trip. And so we opted to make a temporary camp in this valley.

We formed good relations with those who worked in the obsidian fields where An had visited, looking for the best shiny black rocks for our weapons. The twins went hunting with me, and I taught them the art I had learned from our mother and from the inspiration of our late aunt Illyana. And they found baby boars near where we had killed their mother. And they brought these little ones back. If I did not know better, I would have thought these babies thought my sisters were their mother, as they followed my sisters around the camp and even slept next to them.

My sisters had their baby boars, like their foster children. And I had found an empty fox den, which did not turn out so empty as there were a pair of baby foxes left abandoned. They became my foster children to replace my now-grown baby aurochs. So much better than little boars, as my pet foxes went on the hunt with me, chasing down game for their and our dinners.

Nanshe decided we should stay in this paradise to wait out the cold moon cycles. We had again an abundance of smoked game meat, nuts and fruits that could tide us over through the cold and icy moon cycles. Narn had become our maker of stinky aged grain water, which he called beer, something he'd learned from his lost brother, Namu. When the coldest temperatures I could ever have imagined came, his beer supplies froze, separating the water from the stinky fluids. He said this residual liquid was even more potent. He would take these with us to use in the most special ceremonies, which he and his sister would host.

Six more families joined us and followed Nanshe's prayer sessions. And then one prayer session, it happened. The twins heard Nanshe's voice. The same beautiful harmony and peace our mother had been hearing for the past six sun cycles. And the six sun cycles of the greatest peace of my life were to come to an end, or so the voice had warned. Somehow there were giants on this side of the lake. How, I could not fathom. They were killed by the giant killer waves. *Oh, god of my mother, why are you so cruel to torment us again?*

When the temperatures warmed and the tree branches budded, we left our paradise. Only four families were willing to come with us—the two with fathers who were once slaves of the giants, and two more who had many daughters and were fearful of our stories of what these giants would do to our women. We followed a path over the mountains, away from the big lake, away from the tail of the bird star. And we found the valley. The valley. It was larger than any I have ever seen. Hundreds of thousands of paces of grasslands. Game animals all over. This was the true paradise that Orzu had dreamed of, or so we hoped.

And so here we live in paradise today, twenty-five sun cycles after we fled the other side of the lake. We have ten families in our village, with more on the farms surrounding us. My mother has stepped down as the physical leader of our group, turning that onus over to her oldest child, me, but continues as our spiritual leader, training my twin sisters to take on that role someday. And I teach my children, my nephew and nieces, the lore of Illyana, her strength and beauty, the hunt, and the traditions. I am faithful to my father's wishes. I was not blessed as were my twin sisters with the voice, to hear God. I can only pray and have faith. I can only be obedient to what my mother says. And obedience is what I teach our children.

My mother has wrestled with a fundamental problem. It has been very clear that my twin sisters, Zirbani and Sarpani, have been gifted with the voice. But their children have ten or more sun cycles in age and show less of the abilities my parents or their parents have. Nanshe has discussed her moral dilemma with me in private—does she let the ability to touch God, to hear

God, disappear with the twins, or does she advocate that the girls from the twins marry their brothers? We have already learned about selective mating from the animals we have raised. My mother wrestles with this question and says that one day, not too long from now, I might have to make that hard call with my sisters before their children are of the mating age.

And her prayers were answered, as just over two moon cycles ago, a man came to our village alone. He was fatigued from his long journey to find us. He said he was Morda, son of my uncle Namu and aunt Zamana. He was Nanshe's nephew, born a moon cycle after my twin sisters. Nanshe quizzed him about personal facts that only her brother and sister-in-law would know and determined he was indeed her nephew.

Morda explained his mother had sent him out to find our family, and he had wandered the lands, asking for anyone who knew of us. And then he found traders from the obsidian mountain who knew us, and he followed our trail from that mountain. My uncle's funny boat had taken them to another part of the lakeshore, farther along than where we had landed. They had lost their half of the object into the seas when their boat broke up on the rocky shores on this side of the lake. Somehow they had salvaged only part of that object. The voice had guided my uncle to find another mountain than the one we sought, and his family had proceeded to find that mountain with the remnants of their object.

My mother has become smarter and cleverer since she met the voice of the object. Over a moon cycle ago, she talked with Sarpani, who agreed that she would marry Morda. And today, we have a fabulous ceremony arranged, with the largest feast ever. People from the lands all around our village have been invited, as well as the traders who have come to have alliances with us.

My husband, Mawra, our son, our daughter, Zirbani, her son, and I hunted aurochs, gazelle, boar, and female goats for this feast. An and his wife, Sorba, with their children collected the grasses we call barley and wheat to make flatbreads, as well as wild pistachios, almonds, lentils, flax, and chickpeas. We prepared all the great foods our new paradise had to offer.

As I had admired in my husband, Morda was patient with Sarpani, having been well raised by my aunt, Zamana. For Sarpani kept her respect and modesty at all times with him. Morda married her without ever seeing even her full tresses of hair. And his respect of her in their courtship led her to understand he would be a good husband, the same as I felt about Mawra, my mate.

And as the village settled after the festivities, many drunk on the smelly brews of Narn, a late group arrived at the celebrations. I froze for a moment as I tried to discern who they were. And then I bolted to get my weapons. Giants. My twin sisters and my husband were well trained. As they saw me bolt for my weapons, they did the same.

Spears in hand and bow and quiver across my back, I stood forth in front of my family. And he saw me. And I saw him. How? How had he survived? That was impossible. He had drowned and died on that log I had speared him to. He saw my disbelief and stripped off his top clothing to show the wound in his shoulder where I had drilled that spear through. It was Doroda.

He yelled that he had been searching for a woman, the daughter of Orzu, the betrayer of his father Tureal. I was his rightful property, rightful wife, rightful slave, and he had come to collect what was owed to him. Clearly he meant his pleasures at my expense, as I could see his tumescent demon under his fox pelt loincloth hanging from the belt around his waist. I could see behind him his harem of captured slaves and their children. His sons, of age to carry weapons, numbered over a half dozen. They wore the same belt with fox pelt loincloth their father wore.

Doroda came towards me, close enough that I could see the details of his pendant, a circle in stone, with a deep center hole, sitting above a crescent. He pointed to the hole and said it symbolized mine, which belonged to him. If I came willingly, he would spare the drunken village the slaughter and rape that was to come, for this sun cycle. He saw I was covered, like the rest of the women in my family, and ordered that I uncover my head and remove my top clothing so he could see I was truly the one who was to bear him his rightful sons. That was a lie, for twenty-five sun cycles ago, he could see no more than my ashen greased face and hair and my burning eyes.

And as I had done back then on the other side of the lake, I yelled for him and the entire drunken village to hear that I would never be any man's slave, ever. And then my husband, Mawra, with the best of spirit, faith, and intentions, but not so good tactical sense, charged this giant with his spear in defense of his wife's honor. To my horror, Doroda cleaved his head straight off. I cringed as I heard the fabric of my soul being torn in half. I closed my eyes for but a moment as I prayed for his soul.

And the giant, not satisfied with decapitating my dearest husband, lifted his loincloth to show the four scars around his manhood. He said I had not been able to kill him then and I could not do so now, as my body was destined to be his. I momentarily scolded myself. How could I have missed? I would not miss again. And I charged him with spear in hand.

Doroda raised his hand, and his sons began the slaughter of the men in the village. Our men, only born to be slaughtered. With his hand up, I sliced the side of his neck, dodged his spear parry, and cut his side. But even my speed could not overcome his brute giant strength as he ripped the spear from my hands and threw me to the ground, towering over me as he pulled aside his loincloth. I fumbled to get out my second spear when *whoosh, whoosh*.

My twin sisters fired their arrows into the left side of his chest, giving me the opportunity to plunge my second spear into his gut. These giants have extraordinarily tough meat, tougher than aurochs or boars, but he began to bleed from his chest and gut nonetheless.

But that did not stop him as he ripped off his loincloth and bent down to begin his taking of my body and my soul. As full of themselves as the giants were, he had to give a soliloquy that he was invoking his right to my body granted by his race, by his dead father, by their descendancy from the stars. Talk, talk, talk. I found my knife and rammed it into his gut wound and twisted and twisted and twisted. But he covered my body with his mass as he tried to fulfill his rights as given to him by the stars. My pet foxes attacked his arms, but to no avail as he swatted them aside.

Whoosh. Whoosh. My twin sisters fired into his back at point-blank range, standing right above him, and the giant rolled over, screaming in pain. I got my spear and I finished what I had thought I had done back on the other side of the lake—I speared him in the groin again and again. And I did not miss this time and pinned him to the ground with the spear through this precious part of his body.

Seeing the chaos surrounding the village as our men futilely attempted to fight the giant boys, I took Doroda's loincloth and his pendant onto my spear tip and held them towards the moonlit sky. I yelled to the giant boys that their father was dead and the same would happen to them. And the boys, not as versed in the art of war as their father, decided to flee. I signaled to my uncle Narn and my brother An to try to rescue as many of Doroda's slaves as possible.

As we cleaned up from this battle, it was clear that our paradise had been spoiled with the blood of our own villagers and that of the last of the giants from the other side. We could no longer stay here. We needed to pick up the pieces of our lives and move onwards. The giant boys would grow and they would seek revenge for the death of their father as well as seek their right to our daughters. I talked with my mother and said we had clearly failed my great-grandfather's oral tradition, for we had become complacent in our land of peace and plenty. We could not let our guard down again. And so I added to our oral tradition, which I will continue to drill into my extended family.

"Always watch and be vigilant, for the giants, your new enemies, can come when you are lax. Remember that you are only as strong as your numbers, your practice of the hunting arts, and your faith. Practice peace first, but always be ready to defend and kill if needed."

My mother, the holder of peace, love, and harmony, felt my wording could lead our children's children to lead lives of violence and war, fighting among themselves. And so she added more to our tradition.

"God asks us to be people of peace. Find ways to have peace and harmony. Find ways to create bounty to share and create community. For those who are close to God, they can find peace with ease. But for those who are not close to God, they need to have abundance to find peace. For without abundance, there is want, need, jealousy, intolerance, all things that stand in the way of peace. And avoid killing if all possible, but defend people's right to peace."

CHAPTER 25

*Temperance is a disposition that restrains our
desires for things which it is base to desire.*
—Saint Augustine of Hippo

*5:45 a.m. GMT+3, May 10, 2022
Hills outside Siirt, formerly Turkey, now Anatolian Kurdish State*

The crows of a rooster. The bleats of a goat. Her eyelids open slowly. She is back in her room. A simple room, but she is again back with family. She stretches. Her feet have never before felt so wonderful. No desire. No temptation. She stayed within the boundaries of modesty in letting Alexander's boy fix her feet. Ones ravaged by disfigurement from what they did to her. And she slept so well. Maybe she should let him do this again tonight.

Her mother has probably finished morning prayer. Zara is not clean today, still having menses, and thus has not performed prayer with her. She dons a simple dress and headscarf, for there are strangers in the house, and goes to help her mother prepare breakfast. Yawning as she leaves her room and goes into the main family room, she closes her eyes. When her eyes refocus, she is shocked, simply and purely shocked.

"Peter, what are you doing? Get away from my mother," Zara cries, outraged. Her mother is seated on the couch where Zara sat last night, with Peter's head in her hands as she rubs his neck.

Peter, in great confusion, looks at Zara, then at Maryam, and responds, "But your mother asked me to."

"Get away from my mother now," commands Zara.

In her simple English, Maryam says to Peter, "No, no. Stay."

And mother and daughter have a minor disagreement in Kurdish, with Maryam saying to her daughter, "I understand how much stress you have been under. I only hope you do not lose sight of how important this man will be in your life."

Zara is beside herself. Her own mother. "Mama, this man is a stranger. How could you touch a strange man's neck as you did?"

Maryam smiles and says, "I saw you two last night. He must not be such a stranger if you allowed him to take care of your feet."

"He is non-Mahram, and neither of us should have had physical contact with him," Zara retorts.

Maryam puts on her mother-knows-best face and replies, "This man is practically family. He dreamed of our family words. 'God asks us to be people of peace.' Can you not see? This is the man you were meant to marry."

Zara is at the precipice of utter frustration. "Mama, I have chosen to be single and celibate." She glances down and sighs. "And you know why I can never marry. Ever. No man will want me. I cannot fulfill the marriage promise."

A frown overcomes Maryam's face. "Zara, at thirty-six you are no longer young. Here's a good man who looks up to you the same way your little brother Soran looked up to you. You are not getting any younger."

And Maryam puts on the prospective mother-in-law smile, turns to Peter, and says in English, "You are gifted in ways that Zara is. You have the health of youth in your soul. You know that Zara is still very young."

Zara yells, "Peter, get away from her. She's my mother."

Confused, Peter looks at Zara and then at her mother, who holds his head tighter.

Again, Maryam chastises her daughter in Kurdish. "How can you talk with our guest with such a disrespectful tone? We raised you to be better than that. You will not get a good man to marry you if you talk with him with such disregard."

Letting out a huff, Zara replies in Kurdish, "Mama, these two men are business, and that is all. Bringing them here is but a favor for Sasha, and they will be gone tomorrow, never to come back."

Maryam turns back to Peter and says in English, "Please excuse my daughter. She is a very lovely, respectable woman."

Zara, having enough of this nonsense, tells Peter to leave the room and go wash up. In his haste to get up, he startles Zara's lambs, who back into a floor lamp, sending it into a collision course with the ground. Crash. The sound startles not only the little lambs, but Peter equally so. All frozen in fear together, something that does not escape Maryam's attention.

After cleaning up her children's mess, Zara sits down next to her mother on the couch and asks in Kurdish, "Mama, what led you to touch a man who just came here only hours ago?"

Maryam reaches out to touch her daughter's shoulder and replies, "I saw you two last night. I saw you. The 'you' who you have been missing for many years now. I have not seen you in such bliss for nearly twenty years. This man, this Peter, he brings back your youth, brings back the you who you loved so much. The Zara you have wanted to find again."

Zara takes her mother's hand in hers as she replies, "Mama, what you saw was a moment of weakness. I have had too many of those in my life, and nothing good ever came from those moments. It will not happen again."

Petting her daughter's hand, Maryam says, "You should know he is like your father. No, I do not mean he has Nawdar's beautiful curly black hair and dark eyes, but the same sleep. Your Peter was having a very rough sleep, crying out and swinging his limbs all over, the same as your father would do when I met him. I heard the sounds, the same sounds I heard over thirty-five years ago, and I came to look. I woke him and comforted him."

Alarmed at her last sentence, Zara interjects, "Mama, what do you mean you comforted him?"

"Nothing of which Xwedê would not approve, my daughter. I showed him compassion. I took his head in my hands as I did with you and your brother and stroked his temples and his neck, telling him everything was fine, he only had a dream. He calmed down, told me of his dream, and I brought him out here, so we were not in his bed, if you must know."

"Mama, you and Father, you never told me about his dreams before. Why?" asks a bewildered Zara.

Maryam places her warm hands around Zara's straining face. "We were going to tell you when you married, at which time you might have a son who suffered these dreams. Your father had them. My father had them. My grandfather had them. Sara taught Roza how to comfort a man who has these dreams. And Roza taught me. And we can teach you how to comfort this Peter you have brought home so you can be a good wife to him as we have been to our dream-laden men."

Maryam tilts Zara's head down to make eye contact and says, "He is the one. He is who Xwedê has planned for you."

As her daughter shakes her head no in defiance of the idea, Maryam calls over her daughter's black lamb and holds her up. "See her eyes. They are the same as his. Pure innocence in her heart. Pure innocence like his."

Zara takes her mother's hands away from her cheeks and stares at the ground. "No, Mama. You are mistaken. He is only a silly man from California, and he is here for one more night. And then we are gone. He will never be seen again."

Getting up from the couch, Maryam shakes her head. She turns and says to her stubborn daughter, "You should be open. Xwedê's plan is not always for us to see clearly at first. Give it time, you will see."

Jean-Paul enters the front door and excuses himself as he has taken a morning walk to invigorate the soul in the beauty of their neighborhood. As Jean-Paul takes off his jacket, Maryam sees his crucifix. She bows her head and says, "Please, forgive me, we have never had a priest in our home before. I hope you have found our home appropriate."

"Mama, Jean-Paul renounced his priesthood. You need to do nothing more than we always do for our guests."

"I had hoped you had brought a priest with you to marry you and Peter," says Maryam to her agitated daughter. "Please do not worry, I am fine with a mixed marriage. We need to have a private conversation with Roza and your great-grandmother, Sara, though, about a Catholic ceremony. But for you, I believe they will give their blessings. And even that he is not from here, we would still give him our blessings. They have waited so long for this day."

Zara is clearly not amused, but Jean-Paul smiles at this charming Kurdish mother, who is only looking out for her beloved daughter's best interests. Jean-Paul rapidly blinks as he says, "Please, do not stand on ceremony on my behalf. I am no longer a priest. Only a humble man who thanks you for your hospitality and kindness in housing us on such short notice."

Maryam smiles and says, "Once a priest, always a priest. What order are you?"

"Jesuit. I was a Jesuit," Jean-Paul replies humbly.

Maryam gives a pleased glance at her daughter. "Perfect, Zara likes Jesuits."

"Mama, enough of this nonsense. We need to get dressed and leave to run some errands in the mountains, so we need to hurry."

Peter peeks out his door to see if it is safe to come out. Maryam sees him and waves him over. She says she will show him how to set up a Kurdish breakfast. And on the floor in the room near the kitchen, they lay out a floral-patterned cloth. And Peter brings out assorted breads, cheeses, yogurt, goats' milk, and tea, all under the tutelage of Maryam, who increasingly approves of this man her daughter has brought home.

With Zara perturbed about the delay, the four of them have breakfast at her mother's insistence. Maryam asks Jean-Paul about his time as a priest, for she knows the rest of her family will want to focus on Peter at dinner tonight. Grandmother Roza enters the room, fully covered for the guests. Peter and Jean-Paul rise to greet her. Before she can sit down, Zara kisses her hand and says, "We must leave now, as we have business we must attend to."

Roza apologizes to the men for her daughter's abruptness, assuring them she is normally a polite and respectful woman. Zara is about to go out the front door first, but then thinks, and ushers the men out first. Roza goes to Maryam to discuss what her daughter has learned about these men.

As they drive out of the village, Peter watches the beauty of these mountains. Rivers and valleys of many shades of green. The spring wildflowers are still in bloom, drawing lines of red, blue, yellow, and orange along the hillsides.

Many kilometers later, they make a left up a dirt road, heading into a narrow valley. They pass through a small village as they ascend into the hills. Peter sees someone with binoculars watching them. He yells to Zara, "Someone is watching us."

"Of course they are. You should be glad they watch," Zara states simply.

Further up the dirt road, under a tree, a camouflaged truck is stationed with armed guards. Zara taps her MoxWrap, and one of the guards looks at his own. She pulls up to their checkpoint and speaks with them in Kurdish. The guard salutes her and they let her pickup truck pass. Peter is getting that feeling of apprehension again, the same one that kicked in when the F-16s came to escort their jet. He is hoping nothing like the dogfight they had in the sky yesterday is about to transpire.

Next checkpoint, same thing. Zara taps her MoxWrap and the guards tap back. Though this time, the checkpoint is surrounded by heavy machine guns, and further up the road are antiaircraft batteries near an open area large enough for a cargo helicopter. Peter turns to Jean-Paul, who is serene and composed. Peter cannot fathom what type of training this priest has been through that he can be so serene around such military hardware.

Another five hundred meters up the road, Zara takes a left up another dirt road and stops two hundred meters later in front of a cave. Smelling the scent of oak and pine, Peter is anxious to stretch his legs and move around to alleviate his anxiousness. Zara yells at him not to move or he will get them all killed. She takes a zigzag path to a box next to the cave entrance and punches in a code, then scans her fingerprints. She waves them over.

"The entrance to the cave is mined. Only the depot commander and I have the codes to deactivate. This is one of the special weapons caches that Alexander promised," she says as she turns to Peter. "Thanks to what spilled out of your little head, these are the special weapons needed by the Kurds to defend against the Turks or the Arabic Confederation," Zara explains. "I had all of twenty minutes yesterday afternoon to memorize the plan and the codes. So be happy I did not make a mistake."

They enter the cave, which lights up after Zara taps her MoxWrap. Peter's jaw drops. He recognizes the weaponry here from a series of articles he edited for *Future Warfare* magazine. They are surrounded by the latest Russian antitank and antiaircraft missiles with launchers. Zara explains that these are so new, NATO does not have them classified. They have been equipped with Alexander's latest electronic warfare technologies, the same as the advanced weapons of the AC, Turks, Americans, Chinese, Israelis, and of course, the Russians. As he promised yesterday after Zara extracted what was needed from Peter's brain, Alexander had equipped the Kurds with limited supplies of the latest versions of these defensive weapons, which are designed to overcome the AC, Turk, and American weapons systems.

Peter looks at Jean-Paul to see if this finally gets a rise out of him, but no.

Zara takes them over to another area, where communications equipment is stored. She asks Jean-Paul which ones could replace what they lost last night in the packs they were not able to evacuate from their plane. Jean-Paul grins at the equipment, picking a couple of boxes.

Waving them over to the small arms section, Zara tosses Jean-Paul a pistol, which he ably catches. Peter, on the other hand, fumbles with the pistol he is tossed and ultimately, after seconds of juggling, drops it, much to Zara's displeasure. Zara takes the pistol back, shaking her head. Peter recognizes the rifles Zara has selected as the AK-74MX, a digitally upgraded version of the Russian standard field rifle. Upgraded, of course, with Alexander's latest tech. Zara tosses one to Jean-Paul, who catches it like a professional soldier. She looks at Peter and shakes her head, taking one for herself along with several boxes of magazines for both rifles and pistols.

After securing two other packs and food supplies, she takes them outside and reactivates the cave's security systems, and they drive down to a firing range. She loads a magazine in her pistol, cocks it, and lands five out of six rounds into the center of the target twenty-five meters away. Not bad for four years in retirement, she thinks. She asks Jean-Paul if he can shoot. Jean-Paul coolly takes his pistol, cocks it, and then fires two rounds into the middle of

Zara's cluster of shots. He smiles at Zara and puts the pistol down.

Peter says, "Soldier of the pope, huh, Jean-Paul?"

"What about you, Little Boy? How well can you shoot?" asks Zara as she tosses him a holstered pistol.

With a number of and almost drops, Peter ultimate catches it this time, but suddenly freezes as he stares at it. He goes into a glazed stare, shaking, while he mumbles, "I can do this. I can do this. No, I can't. I can't."

After a momentary reflective pause, Jean-Paul comes to his side, takes the pistol from his hands and waves his hands in front of Peter's face. He waves to Zara to come over and says, "Please, give me your hand."

She reluctantly offers a hand, which Jean-Paul clasps around Peter's. "What are you doing, priest? I do not wish to touch this man again."

"Zara, please. It is only touching hands. Remember Luxembourg? Why didn't Peter fumble with your gun yesterday? And now, he is seeing something we need to know about. Please. Please rub his hands, gently."

Zara hesitates, deciding what she should do. Especially after seeing Sasha's boy in her mother's hands this morning, she debates whether to crush them or comply with Jean-Paul's request. And her mother's words this morning, "I showed him compassion," overwhelm her senses, and she gently rubs this odd man's clammy hand.

Peter's sweaty face begins to show signs of life, slowly. He then clasps Zara's hand with his other, looks at her and thanks her.

"Peter, you saw something. What did you see?" Jean-Paul asks him.

"I'm afraid something very hazy and vague. A segment of a dream both my grandfather and I had. The first time we ever had similar dreams within days of each other. I'm holding a gun. There's a woman screaming at me to shoot. That's all I can remember."

Jean-Paul looks at Zara, who says, "No. Hands are it. That's as far as I go."

"Peter, let us try again with you learning to shoot this gun," Jean-Paul suggests, putting the gun back into his hands. "Zara, would you please proceed with your lesson?"

Peter looks at Zara and says, "Please, I'll try harder this time. I'd love to learn to shoot, to use a gun. That and grow pecs and six-pack abs—then the

Sarahs of the world won't be leaving me for some Neanderthal hunk."

Shaking her head, Zara explains the following sequence: load, release safety, pull backwards on the top slide until it clicks, aim with both hands at shoulder level, feet apart, breathe in, and pull. Peter says all the steps, twice. Then practices them himself. He pulls back on the slide and no click. Zara explains he should not force it and tells him to take out the bullet, reload it into the magazine and start again. He asks what happens if he does not. She explains that in rare instances, the gun could explode in his hands. He shivers.

Peter aims down the gun barrel at the target. Slowly pulls the trigger. *Bang.* And he yells, "The gun, it exploded. My hand. It's injured."

Zara takes the gun from his hand, looks at it. Spits on it to wipe away the blood and says, "It's only a slide bite. You held the gun wrong. Put your left thumb next to your right thumb, with your left finger holding the right ones from the front."

Something about her saliva helps calm Peter. He tries again. Load, slide back once, aim, trigger pull. *Bang.* "Ouch. My other hand is injured," yells Peter.

Zara looks at his right hand, spits on it, and says, "Slide bite again. You are not controlling the kickback, and you are letting the gun rise when you shoot. Okay, let's pull the slide back and see where you are gripping the pistol. Hold your hand lower like this, lower on the grip. Try to do it again like this."

"No, not even for Sarah. I'm not doing this again," Peter cries, despite what her saliva might be activating within him.

Zara looks at him in the eye and says, "If Jean-Paul's life depended on it, you would shoot this gun. You need to shoot this gun." She looks at Jean-Paul and then says, "My life will never depend on you, silly Little Boy. I will never put myself in such a situation. But Jean-Paul, you might want to save him."

Eyes closed, Peter takes a deep breath and tries again. This time no bite. No target hit, but no bite. At her request, he continues shooting, emptying the seventeen-round magazine, proud that he hit the target twice, nowhere near center, but just in the outermost circle. Zara shakes her head, happy he did not shoot them by accident, but she worries what would happen if their lives depended on him.

She takes the AK-74MX, loads the magazine, and shoots off several rounds at a fifty-meter target, shredding a hole in it. She gives Jean-Paul the other one, and he does the same. She looks at him and says, "Fancy shooting for a priest. I did not know there was a firing range under the Vatican."

Jean-Paul simply shrugs.

Zara looks at Peter and decides that discretion is truly the better part of valor. She bypasses teaching him how to shoot a rifle and leads them over to a clearing in an adjacent wooded area, nicely padded with fallen leaves. "Okay. Let us see where you are with hand-to-hand combat." She tosses a sheathed combat knife to Jean-Paul and says, "You first. Keep the sheath on."

She pulls out her sheathed knife and positions her arms out in combat position. Much to her surprise, the good Father drops the knife to the ground. She says, "So you can shoot, but are a pacifist with a knife? No matter, let us see what you can do unarmed." She makes a few exploratory strikes at him, and much to her surprise, he has her in an armlock as he disarms and throws her to the side.

Resetting her scarf on her head, she wipes her brow and says, "Where does a priest learn to do that?"

Jean-Paul nods to her, smiles serenely, and says, "I learned Filipino martial arts when I was in my Regency in the Philippines. Such things came in handy to teach the boys in my school how to handle the local boys."

Zara pulls out her pistol, unloads the chambered round and then the magazine, and points it at him. "Priest, can you teach me how to disarm a gun pointed at your chest?"

Jean-Paul slaps his hands hard around her wrist and the gun simultaneously, and the gun goes flying to the side. Zara is impressed. He says this is the Krav Maga style. He picks up the gun and gives it back to Zara to try again. This time, he slaps the gun with both hands and pulls the weapon out of her hands, saying that is the Filipino Kali method. Zara asks him to help her learn. He asks permission to touch her, to which she says, "Of course." And they spend a half hour practicing different techniques. Zara smiles. This priest will come in handy after all.

Now it is Peter's turn. She gives him a sheathed knife and says for him to stab at her. He reluctantly does, and she steps to one side, grabs his arm, and puts it into an elbow lock. He cries in pain. Such a baby, she thinks. She shows him again, more slowly and gently.

Then it is his turn. She takes the knife and thrusts at him. He gets things all twisted up in a panic, and the two of them go falling to the ground. Zara is so infuriated that she tries to put him into a head lock on the ground, but they just go rolling around and around, with Jean-Paul laughing in the background at the comedy of the situation.

Finally, she secures him, sitting atop his chest with his shoulders pinned by her knees. "There, that should teach you, Little Boy, for throwing me to the ground."

Peter looks up and realizes he is seeing too much. "Zara, your dress."

Looking down, she sees her dress has gotten hiked up, and she straightens it. And then it hits her. Little Boy, what she called her brother. A warmth and love runs from her head to her heart as when her brother would try to wrestle her and inevitably lose, the same as this little boy did. She gets up quickly to take her mind off such a thought.

"Enough of playing. We need to go back to my mother's house and get ready for the trip to Göbekli Tepe," she says as she takes her weapons back to the truck. Jean-Paul offers Peter a hand and they collect their weapons as well.

Zara is noticeably silent on the drive past the security checkpoints, where a senior officer jokes with her about her coming back from retirement. Jean-Paul rests in the backseat, meditating. Peter sits across from Zara, nursing his slide bite wounds, and the internal wounds to his pride. He works up the courage to ask her a question. "Zara, may I ask how you are so fast with your fighting skills?"

She appreciates his question, as it shows he was closely observing. Watching with respect. "Peter, when you are in a combat situation and you are totally focused, time slows down."

"You mean like in the movies? It really happens that way?"

She smiles. "Hollywood is Hollywood, and they will do whatever sells the movie. In real life, you may have this microsecond when you must be decisive. It is so trinary. A good thing can happen, or you may always regret your indecision, or worse, you may be dead. And if you are calm and focused, that microsecond will feel much, much longer. It will appear as if everyone else has slowed down. And you must use that time to be decisive. Yes or no. No maybes."

Peter turns to look out the window, reflecting upon whether he can be that focused, that calm, and that decisive when this moment comes.

They pass a sign that says twenty kilometers to Siirt, and Zara says, "Peter, tell me about your Sarah. How long did you know her?"

"About four and a half years. A little bit more than that," Peter replies, wondering where this conversation came from and where it is going. Jean-Paul's ears have awoken from his meditation and are attuned to their conversation as well.

"What did you love about her, your Sarah? Her appearance, or something else?" asks Zara as she glances at Peter.

"Yes, and yes. What I most loved about her was how we could talk. I thought she loved ancient aliens, and we discussed them for hours on end. But maybe I was wrong about her," Peter laments, remembering their last few conversations.

His answer is not what she had expected, and she probes further. "And how did she dress for you?"

"Oh, she dressed quite modestly. Well, not your kind of modest, but for California, she was pragmatic. She dressed for the weather, for the type of sport we did, very pragmatic. Well, that was until she met that Army Ranger sniper Sam." And Peter turns his head as his eyes well up.

Her curiosity gets the best of her as Zara continues. "Why do you think she would leave you for, as you said, gun, pecs and abs? This seems so shallow for such a woman as you had described."

Peter chokes and mumbles, "I couldn't tell you. I thought she said I didn't understand what unconditional love was. But that day I came home early and saw her and him naked in our bed. And he just had to show how big he was all over. I just don't know. I only know I didn't have what she wanted."

Zara asks, "Do you really think coming back to her with your gun and new muscles will win her back? Is there something I am missing?"

Unable to say anything through his tears, Peter shakes his head.

To his surprise, she puts her hand on his shoulder and strokes him. "Not that I am an expert in affairs of the heart, but some advice. You should focus on your superpowers and not someone else's. Maybe your Sarah's muscular gun man's superpower is killing and maiming. But do not let your jealousy overwhelm you and draw you down a path that is not for you. You will win if you focus on what make you special. Your superpower."

She strokes him more and says, "I know this discussion was hard. But you needed to get your emotions out in the open. We cannot take the chance of these unresolved feelings stopping you from what needs to happen."

Jean-Paul is amazed at Zara. She is what Alexander said she was.

Another five minutes in silence as they pull into her mother's village and up in front of her mother's house. She turns to Peter, puts her hand under his chin, and says, "Peter, we are going to have dinner with my family. My mother, my grandmother, my great-grandmother, they are all respectful women. You will behave accordingly, with dignity. None of your nonsense. Especially no aliens. Say the first half of that word, and I will—I will do something distasteful to you. Do we have a clear understanding?" With eyes wide open, Peter nods in agreement.

Zara says to them to leave the weapons in the truck, as her family does not know the full extent of what she once did with and for Alexander, and she drives the truck back to its concrete-and-steel shelter and packs her backup supplies. She asks the two men to go into the house first and freshen up in their rooms. She will get them for dinner.

Emotionally exhausted from reliving all things Sarah in the truck, Peter turns on the MoxWorld News on his MoxWrap, wondering when, if ever, he will go back to being a simple, safe, and secure editor.

Sahir is describing the drama last night as US and Russian advanced fighters squared off for the first time in history over the new Anatolian Kurdish State. Rhonda, in a green dress with blue accessories and bluish eye shadow, provides the latest updates on the Arabic Confederation battles with Turkey around Sanliurfa. The AC has taken the town of Suruc, forty kilometers southwest of the city, and the surrounding plains. Turkish forces have withdrawn to a new line of defense in the mountains surrounding Sanliurfa. A map showing these positions comes on screen, and a third AC attack force is shown coming around the southern flank of these mountains, attempting to bypass the Turkish defenses.

The butterflies in Peter's stomach flutter away rampantly as he frets that Zara is going to drag him into the middle of a full-scale war zone as he continues to watch Sahir describe the latest naval movements in the Black Sea. The US and Britain have deployed a fleet of fifteen destroyers and frigates through the Bosporus to counter a possible sea invasion of Turkey by Russia. The Russian president is shown protesting this movement as a violation of the Montreux Agreement, which limits the number of warships from non-Black Sea countries that can pass through the strait. In response, the Russians have deployed more ships into the Mediterranean to counter the incoming US Sixth Fleet. Peter turns off the news with the sinking feeling he is sitting at the epicenter of World War Three.

Zara knocks on the door and says they are getting ready for dinner. He pops his head out, expecting to see her in green. But evidently, she is not one of "Alexander's girls" as she said, dressed in a long aqua gown, with gold and yellow accents and a matching headscarf. And there on her lips is the hint of some slight color of gloss. Zara catches him staring and snaps, "What are you looking at, Little Boy? My grandmothers insisted I dress up for our guests."

Holding up a freshly pressed cotton shirt and trousers, Zara says, "Please honor us and dress in these. The trousers will be baggy in the Kurdish style. You can hop over rocks, mules, and enemy soldiers alike in these. I have pressed a couple more shirts and trousers, which you may get in my bedroom if these do not fit well." She smiles and closes the door.

Peter is mystified as this is the nicest, most civil, even polite conversation she has had with him yet. Maybe the fact he let her win at wrestling won her over. He tries on the shirt, and it is tight. In this home, too-tight clothing is probably not good, so he goes into Zara's bedroom to try on the other sizes.

Knocks sound on the front door. Hard knocks. In their past, this could be soldiers coming to take someone away, and so out of habit, Zara gets her spare pistol from under the couch and takes a position to the side of the door. She does not load a round so as not to give away her gun just yet. She asks in a deep, firm voice, "Who is there?"

"Rohat Khatum, here to see my cousin Zara Khatum."

CHAPTER 26

Because of the diverse conditions of humans, it
happens that some acts are virtuous to some people, as
appropriate and suitable to them, while the same acts
are immoral for others, as inappropriate to them.

—Saint Thomas Aquinas

Fall 2005
Philippines

Brother Jean-Paul's students have played the first half of the football game valiantly against the top-ranked local public school team. The aspiring Jesuit is starting the last year of his Regency, the third phase of a Jesuit priest's formation, during which he is a teacher of theology, ancient world history, French, Latin, Greek, and astronomy at a Jesuit high school in the Philippines. He also co-coaches the school's football team. Having loved playing football during his lycée military days in France, he is a natural to coach here.

His second-stringers, Manuel and Fermin, artfully move the ball from left to center, down thirty meters towards the goal, with a perfect series of flicks and short passes. With a clear line to the goal, Manuel readies to take the winning shot when a huge center back slides into the ball, taking out Manuel's leg. And Jean-Paul comes running onto the field as Manuel screams in terrifying agony.

As Jean-Paul tries to triage the extent of damage to this boy's ankle, he laments how he has had to put in his second-stringers due to a rash of absences from his starters. Manuel is an aspiring freshman, but certainly is no match for seasoned seniors, especially as aggressive as the ones from this public school. And so, the good Brother carries poor Manuel to the school nurse's office.

There awaits Sister Magali, dressed in a white short-sleeved blouse covered by a blue vest with matching skirt covering to midcalf. Atop her head is a simple blue veil, and on her feet simple black sandals. But most noticeable to Brother Jean-Paul are the wisps of her red hair that have escaped the sides of her blue veil. She caught his attention in their church choir with her wisps of red hair and angelic voice. Although he has seen her at church and in the school, this is the first time the two of them have ever interacted.

As Sister Magali splints the boy's ankle, she asks in French where Brother Jean-Paul is from, for she is French as well. She says she is working in the local Catholic hospital as a nurse and living in a nearby convent while she is in her First Profession, a three-year period where a prospective Catholic Sister makes temporary vows before taking her final Solemn Profession. With such a high need for nurses, her Order has allowed her to serve in the Philippines instead of staying in her convent in France.

After dinner, Brother Jean-Paul meets with Brother Petrus, his co-coach, who is in his first year of his Regency. Both he and Jean-Paul graduated from the same lycée militaire in France. The coincidence of both being assigned to this school for their Regencies, they find quite profound. The Lord works in mysterious ways, is how Brother Jean-Paul sums it up. They discuss the increasing absences on the football team as well the similar phenomenon randomly happening with their nonathletic students. They have found no pattern, other than an increase in tardiness as well. Brother Petrus suspects their boys are getting into altercations with boys from the community, having observed suspicious bruises. Perhaps the boys who are late are taking the long way to get to school to avoid being assaulted.

The next week, Sister Magali revels in delight that her Brother Jean-Paul has dropped by to see her, and not because of some medical emergency, as she had been thinking of him over the last week, and she asks if he knows Sister Marie-Claire, the Sister-in-Charge at Sister Magali's convent in France. Very surprised, Brother Jean-Paul says she is his older sister. Any brother of Sister Marie-Claire would be regarded with the utmost respect by Sister Magali. And as the good Sister coquettishly glances aside, Jean-Paul inquires if she has been seeing any out-of-the-ordinary injuries or bruises among the boys, to which she replies affirmatively. She asks if the physical education program has changed to be more vigorous, more challenging, to which Jean-Paul says no.

Another week passes, and Brother Petrus tells Jean-Paul he has followed their boys after football practice. Many take long routes home. The others suffer encounters with local boys, ranging from hazing to outright shakedowns for anything of value.

Jean-Paul reflects on the recent lessons given to their students, teaching Matthew 5:39: "But I tell you, do not resist an evil person. If anyone slaps you on the right cheek, turn to them the other cheek also." They have taught their team this to avoid fights during the football games. Brother Petrus jests that their students studied that part of Matthew too vigorously, as they clearly practice Matthew 5:40. "If someone wants to sue you and take your tunic, let him have your cloak as well." He proposes that something needs to be done before these boys lose their cheeks and their clothes as well.

That night, Jean-Paul tosses and turns as this dilemma has brought him back to one of the core reasons why he left the French Army seven years ago. He had followed the path of his grandfather, who fought in the French resistance during the Second World War, then went to the prestigious École Spéciale Militaire de Saint-Cyr to become an officer in the French Army. He fought in the French Algerian war and in French Indochina. Jean-Paul's father also went to the École Spéciale Militaire de Saint-Cyr and served in the special ops unit of the French Republican Guard.

When Jean-Paul was sixteen and attending a lycée militaire, his parents were killed in the 1989 terrorist bombing of UTA Flight 772, flying from the Democratic Republic of the Congo to Paris. With deep grief and hatred, the young Jean-Paul swore he would fight terrorists worldwide to prevent other children from experiencing the pain he felt at the undue deaths of his parents. Two years later after his graduation, he joined the army in time to be deployed as part of Opération Daguet, the French invasion force to liberate Kuwait.

Following in his patriarchal footsteps, he enrolled at the École Spéciale Militaire de Saint-Cyr three years later, matriculating as an officer in NATO's Stabilization Force mission to the war-torn Bosnia. Assigned to a special group hunting down war criminals, he employed his special talents at research and at finding people. Although he was not Italian, Jean-Paul was exceptionally Machiavellian, which did not escape the notice of his superiors. At whatever cost, he would get the job done. The army needed officers like this.

As a hunter of war criminals, he truly learned the atrocities of war as he was assigned to find the leaders of the Bosnian Serbian rape camps. He learned of the use of rape as a systematic weapon of genocide and terror. Experts estimated up to fifty thousand women had been raped during the three-and-a-half-year conflict. He interviewed women who had been gang-raped in front of their families, fellow villagers, and neighbors. He listened to accounts of the brutalization of girls as young as twelve. Houses, halls, gymnasiums housed several dozen women suffering continuous rapes over several months, often done publicly, where women would be forced to watch other women being brutalized. The psychological horror and despair of these women took its toll on Jean-Paul as he descended into an even deeper level of hatred than he had felt after the death of his parents.

His team had caught a Serbian officer who had led one of these rape camps and turned him over to the war crimes tribunals. He cringed during the trial of this monster, as the victimized women had to testify and relive the atrocities. This pain weighed heavily on him as he led the search for the senior officer in charge of all the rape camps in that city. He employed the military intelligence techniques taught to him by his father and found this Bosnian Serb colonel, who he had cornered in a house.

Alone while the rest of his team searched other houses, Jean-Paul aimed his rifle at the terrified colonel, who put down his gun, saying he would surrender peacefully. The hatred within Jean-Paul could not accept his offer, and he picked up the colonel's pistol, firing it behind himself. With the darkest of moments tarnishing his soul, he emptied the full magazine of his rifle, riddling the colonel's body with bullets. As his team came to his aid, he explained this colonel was not going to surrender without a fight. So, justice was served.

That night, Jean-Paul dreamed his deeply Catholic mother recited to him Matthew 18:17–21. "Do not repay anyone evil for evil. Carefully consider what is right in the eyes of everybody. If it is possible on your part, live at peace with everyone. Do not avenge yourselves, beloved, but leave room for God's wrath. For it is written: 'Vengeance is Mine, I will repay, says the Lord.' On the contrary, 'If your enemy is hungry, feed him; if he is thirsty, give him a drink. For in so doing, you will heap burning coals on his head.' Do not be overcome by evil, but overcome evil with good."

He tossed and turned all night, wrestling with his actions and the atrocities committed by the predominantly Christian Serbs and Croats against a mostly Muslim female population. As bad as those atrocities were, he had clearly crossed a line. Without a blink, he had crossed that line. How much farther across the next line would it be before he became no better than those monsters? He remembered his grandfather's counsel to him. After seeing the futility of the conflicts in Algeria and French Indochina, his grandfather had wished he had gone back to his Jesuit studies and become a priest instead of carrying on the hatred he had learned during his time in the French resistance.

And tonight, in the Philippines, Jean-Paul turns in his sleep, thinking about his commitment to "turn the other cheek," his resignation of his commission in the French Army, and his joining the Jesuit Order. How can he and Petrus teach these boys to defend themselves? Their boys are simply following the words of Matthew to the letter. Violence leads to more violence. Peace comes from good ethical foundations. Peace comes from showing the other party what it looks like.

The next week, a typhoon leads to the cancellation of the weekly football game and the local Catholic ministries organize missions to the most heavily damaged villages. Once the winds subside, Jean-Paul joins a group of volunteers destined for a coastal village with significant community infrastructure devastation.

The former Lieutenant Sobiros is particularly adept at setting up bivouacs and ad hoc kitchens in his military missions, perfect for his Catholic mission, as he was assigned to set up the communal kitchen and food depot. From a distance, he sees full locks of red hair waving in the wind as the stormy air sweeps the good Sister's veil off her head. Being the good gentleman and good Brother he is, Jean-Paul helps Magali chase down her veil, which blows three to five meters up in the blustery sky.

It is the first time he has seen her laugh, as well as her full face and hair, and it feels good. It's the first time she's had a knight in cassock armor come to her rescue, and it feels good. She has come, of course, with the medical team from her hospital. They will be sleeping and working in the same place for the next week, for which the good Sister thanks the Lord. A week working with Sister Marie-Claire's little brother, serving the needs of the desperate and poor. What more could a good Sister ever ask for?

At dinner, Jean-Paul coordinates the ad hoc chefs and food service personnel serving meals for a couple hundred villagers. The good Sister comes by. Seeing he is busy, she helps with the food service. It is nearly midnight by the time the kitchen closes and Magali walks the good Brother back to his tent. She teases him as she looks inside his one-bed tent, as the big chief is able to get a single, while the little nurses are stacked six to a tent. But she observes he did not get a pillow and uses his towel as a poor substitute. She bids him, "*Bonne nuit. Belles rêves,*" or "good night, sweet dreams" in English.

The next morning, Jean-Paul awakes, and he feels it. A bad night's sleep. He is groggy and achy and not so coherent. He goes to help the early-morning breakfast crew, and there is Sister Magali, holding a mug of steaming hot coffee and waiting for him. She has two-day-old croissants she brought with her to share with her French compatriot. She does not want to tell him she baked these herself, for she is sure that he would think that too forward and personal. As Jean-Paul begins to retrieve his humanity with the coffee and rediscovers his Frenchness with these croissants just like Mama made, she confesses she came by his tent last night. She brought over a spare pillow and witnessed his sleep, which was physically violent and restless with cries, as if he were yelling at someone. The good Brother does not know what to say, as he dreamt again of his execution of that Bosnian Serb monster, a story he does not want to share with her.

Sister Magali explains that her father had the exact same issues she saw Jean-Paul have last night. She recognized the symptoms clearly. The good Brother's eyes pop wide open when the good Sister's hand reaches under her blouse, atop her ample chest. She pulls out a medallion, a replica of one her grandfather gave to her, as the original rests in a safety deposit box in their local bank. He also suffered from the same agonizing dreams at night and said the affliction went back as many generations in their male lineage as anyone could recall. From generation to generation, the medallion has been handed down to the next generation's most afflicted male with the instructions to do the same until someone can answer the question of the medallion's meaning. She hands the replica to her new good Brother.

Jean-Paul's hand shakes as he holds this medallion. During his studies at Saint-Cyr, he took courses in ancient archeology and in the proto-Indo-European languages, both in preparation for military service in the Middle East. He once aspired to be part of the teams assigned to protect ancient monuments, temples, and national museums. Holding this object in his hands, he has realized his wildest hopes and dreams. Authentic Proto-Greek writing, the bridging language between Modern Greek and the first speakers of PIE.

One side has a schematic of the Cygnus constellation with the tail star highlighted. Two humanoid figures stand adjacent, one nearly twice the height of the other. He tries to translate the Proto-Greek writing. "Beware the giants of the star." The good Sister verifies that is what her grandfather told her as well.

The other side shows what looks like a long rectangular object with a woman touching it. In her hands are two halves of an apple, and at her feet is a large worm. While he fumbles with the translation of the Proto-Greek symbols, the good Sister recalls her grandfather saying it was, "She hears the voice of God," which pleased her to no end, as it is a woman who hears the Lord.

Magali says she wears the replica as a good omen for her passage to becoming a Catholic Sister. As she is an only child, her father was agonizingly disappointed she chose this as her path, since he would have no grandsons to pass the medallion on to. She asks the good Brother how old he thinks this might be. She drops her coffee mug as he says Proto-Greek dates back to 4,000 to 5,000 BCE. He then smiles and jokes that, between a Catholic priest and a sister, they can say BC, before Christ. She loves his joke, his humor, as she lightly touches his hand holding her medallion.

Magali puts her hand around his, folding his fingers over the medallion. Sensing the warmth of his hand, she wants this moment to go on forever. She says with big dilated eyes that, as she will not have children, given her lifelong commitment to the Lord, she would ask he keeps the medallion for now so that he might find out what it means. She slowly gets up, as she is expected at the medical tent to begin the morning vaccinations. She smiles at her good Brother and says she expects him to return the medallion after he finds out the hidden story, and expects him to return in person. Then she winks and leaves.

Brother Jean-Paul starts his day a little later than he expected, but nonetheless eminently pleased at why he is delayed. As he leads the team in rebuilding a permanent communal kitchen structure, he cannot help imagining what this medallion was trying to say. Who are these giants? A woman hearing the voice of the Lord, several thousands of years before the prophets of the Old Testament. He has never been so intrigued by anything in his life to date. Maybe this is why the Lord sent him the dream of his mother citing Matthew. So he could bring this message to light the world.

At lunch, he takes a break. He almost had his head lobbed off twice by beams as he daydreamed about giants and the voice of the Lord. He needs to take a walk. As he reaches a nearby clearing, he sees the volunteers and villagers getting ready to play a game of football. He recognizes one of the volunteers from his church, Antonio. His warm-up routine looks highly atypical for a footballer. It looks much more like a fighter's movements and stretches. In fact, a couple of players are doing the same. And then he spies two sparring. He has never seen this form of martial arts. After the game finishes, he approaches Antonio from his church, who is overjoyed that one of the Jesuit teachers wants to talk with him. Antonio explains that the Filipino martial arts encompass the empty-hand techniques, Mano Mano, which he saw there, along with many sophisticated weapon arts.

The afternoon becomes steamy hot as the sun returns to grace the island after the terrible storm. As Jean-Paul's construction crew roasts, taking off their shirts, off goes his black cleric shirt. Even though he left military service seven years prior, Jean-Paul has kept his physique in top condition. His muscles glisten with sweat as he lifts building materials, with his biceps, pecs, and abs all flexing with each motion. A pair of green eyes watches every flex from the medical tent. All afternoon, these eyes are transfixed, saddened when the work is finished and the black cleric shirt is redonned.

Sister Magali waits for her good Brother, the one with muscles like she has never seen before, to come to the food tent. She helps serve food until it seems very unusual he has not shown up. She goes to his tent to find him. He has just awoken from a nap as he was knackered. She asks permission to enter his tent as he groans over the inadequate sleep he had. She explains her father had the same thing happen with his naps.

She gives a little smile, looking to the side as she also reveals her mother had many ways of helping her father deal with his sleep and taught her what to do if her future husband suffered the same. With that, the good Sister puts her fingers to her good Brother's forehead, rubbing it a certain way. Jean-Paul can feel his headache just melt away. After several minutes, Jean-Paul stands to go to the food tent. She touches his arm and asks whether, if he is ever in distress again, it would be okay for her to stop by and help. Her mother taught her much, much more. Jean-Paul is not sure what to make of this interaction, except for one clear dominant thing. He likes her. He nods yes as he leaves for the food tent.

That night, he dreams of his lycée martial arts training—Parisian street savate, the French kick-based martial art. The street version he learned added open-hand blows, palm strikes, and stun slaps. His feet and hands wave in the night as he dreams and grunts through his memories of his adolescent savate matches.

Sister Magali, the good nurse that she is, comes by to see how her "patient" is doing. And no surprise to her, her new Brother is thrashing about again. She comes into the tent, closing the opening. Her mother taught her a special way of approaching the violent stage of the afflicted man's dream phase, which she executes perfectly. Jean-Paul awakens to see an angel on Earth. A redheaded angel with green eyes passionately looking into his. An angel wearing but a light tunic on top and no veil to constrain her voluptuous waves of redness.

Before Jean-Paul can speak, she holds him, whispers in his ears, intimately personal things in French, and then blows on them. She puts her palms on his bare chest and rubs his heart area for several minutes while she holds his head into her neck with her other hand. She lifts his head and rubs his forehead for several minutes as they stare into each other's eyes. She asks if he is feeling better. Of course he is, he thinks as he nods.

She says that there is more, but given they have taken their vows, she will exercise the appropriate constraint. He is absolutely curious what he is missing. He thanks her profusely for her compassion. As she leaves his tent, his guilt overtakes him for his allowing her to do what she did under the pretense that she was fixing her father's affliction.

This guilt remains as he awakens with a bad feeling. Well, actually, he feels incredible. How could someone not, when an angel from heaven showed such physical compassion? But he feels the guilt of his less-than-honest answers. So this morning, he avoids interactions with his angel, making excuses of needing to tend to urgent issues. She is truly his angel as she is always so understanding, further adding to his guilt.

This time at lunch, he goes to the footballers and warms up and stretches with the martial arts crowd. He is impressed with his kicks, and after the game they come over to compare techniques. They explain that the martial arts skills have improved their football game. This statement sticks in Jean-Paul's conscious. The wheels turn and tick. Maybe, just maybe, he can come up with a solution for his boys at school.

That night, he cannot fall asleep, thinking about his possible solution. Then he hears her soft, gentle footsteps as she enters his tent. He groans with his eyes closed and thrashes his arms about. And she performs the same wonderful, simply euphoric compassionate acts she did the night before. This time she adds smelling her neck and putting his head on her chest so he can smell her ample bosom. He is in heaven. And as she leaves, he reckons he is not going to go to heaven the way they are going. And guilt settles back in.

And so, their week passes in the same manner every day. Football and martial arts at noon. Compassion and embrace in the evening. The last night of their mission arrives, and they will board separate buses the next day, never to be so near each other ever again. The good Sister has been somewhat despondent that, despite her best emulation of her mother's compassion techniques, her new Brother is not getting better from night to night. She does not want to tell him about her despondence as she does not want him to think she is incapable of being the life partner a good afflicted man needs. She has already begun to rethink her vows, never having imagined she would ever meet a man like him.

The good nurse Magali is certainly not going to let her new man not get better. So, she dials up the techniques. Tonight, after having him smell her neck, she puts his head directly on her bosom and asks him to inhale deeply. She takes his hand and places it on her breast, helping him stroke it lightly. She has thought about this next part long and hard every night this week. It is probably the missing part that has prevented the afflicted Jean-Paul's full recovery. And as Jean-Paul's head rests on her bosom, she reaches down to stroke his crotch. He flinches but stays put. Much to her delight, he really does love her, down there. Hot and hard love at that. No words pass between them after she crosses the line she set at the beginning of the week. She blows him a kiss as she leaves his tent, and he waits for the cloud of guilt to descend upon him.

The next morning, most of the mission teams are packed and ready to leave on their respective buses. The two, the brother and the sister, meet in the middle between their buses. Neither one speaks of the night before, only of the good acts and services their teams have accomplished this week, and they thank the Lord for the opportunity. Their primordial carnality beats at them to kiss goodbye, but they can only kiss with their eyes, which they do over and over again until the last call to board their buses. And they separate, knowing, but not knowing.

Jean-Paul wastes no time getting with Petrus to discuss his ingenious idea. Jean-Paul's solution is simply elegant and has a plausible deniability factor, which Petrus loves. And so, they meet with Antonio and his Mano Mano master. They will make a fair deal for the exchange of services. Antonio and his master will help develop a series of martial-arts-oriented warm-up routines for their Jesuit school's footballers and come and teach them at practices. In return, Jesuit Brothers Jean-Paul and Petrus will come to their club and teach them French savate techniques. Exceptional deal accepted. Both sides win, of course, as Jean-Paul has received the highest grade in his negotiations class.

For the first week, Antonio and the Mano Mano master come to a few practices a week and show the boys how to warm up in a new way. The next week, they show them a new way of kicking to help them on the field. The third week, they have the boys practice the kicks with blocking moves on each other.

Jean-Paul just smiles as, by the fourth week, he already sees less absenteeism, both on the field and in the classroom. Petrus wants to follow the boys after practice, as he did before, and see if this turnaround is truly due to the boys fighting back. Jean-Paul, who previously quoted Matthew, this time quotes US President Bill Clinton. "Don't ask. Don't tell."

By week five, with Jean-Paul's literal blessings, Antonio begins to integrate hand techniques into the warm-ups as a way to develop their reflexes so they will not touch the ball on the field of play. Week six, throwing techniques as a way of learning to fall correctly during heated football matches. The two Jesuit brothers are ecstatic as attendance and tardiness among their footballers has been one hundred percent fixed.

Jean-Paul brings the attendance problem to the attention of the head of the school, who already noticed the exemplary academic attendance of the footballers. And thus, Jean-Paul gains permission to introduce new stretches and calisthenics into the general physical education program for the whole school. By the middle of winter term, the whole school attendance issue is resolved.

Sister Magali is a patient woman as a good Sister should be. However, her patience is being tested over the winter as her Brother Jean-Paul is always busy after school with his footballers in some new training program. She comes down to some practices and is rewarded by seeing her afflicted man practice with the boys without his cassock. On a number of occasions, they are assigned to missions together, but he shares quarters with others, so what transpired between them in that village on the coast does not happen again.

She is overjoyed when Jean-Paul declares his new training program a total success, for he has time now to see her. On the days she is at his school, after the football practice or after the game is over, they go on walks. Not long, thirty minutes, sometimes forty. And they talk. And they talk. And they talk.

What do they talk about? If you asked her, she would say, "*n'importe quoi*," or whatever or anything, as she does not care. She only cares that she is with him. And if you asked him, he would say they talked about school, the hospital, world affairs, the next steps in their formation, why they decided on the religious life devoted to the Lord.

As spring comes, and the days become longer, she asks for longer walks. She really just wants more time with him, as for her, time is running out.

As they become closer and closer, Magali asks more personal questions. She asks about what he is most afraid of. To her surprise, he talks about the horrors of witnessing soldiers burned alive in combat. He has always had this deep fear of incineration, as he studied the Inquisitions and other religious movements' acts of burning people at the stake. He would rather be shot than be burned. Her answer is very different. Her fear is never truly knowing love. She hopes and prays she will truly know the love of the Lord.

One afternoon later, she pushes him, not for commitment, but for the full reason for his commitment to the Lord. He has never truly described the moment of his epiphany. And he sits her down and tells the story of the war, the rapes, the atrocities, and the monsters. She strokes his arm as he professes his guilt over what he did, the smug vigilante administering his own justice, not the Lord's.

And as he recounts his dream of his mother quoting Matthew and his inner awakening that peace should be his advocacy, she knows he is it. He is to be hers. He is her other half of the apple on the medallion. And the question she has been wrestling with since her First Profession has been answered. The Lord has answered her question through Jean-Paul's final candor and trust of her in telling his most personal story.

Feeling they have come to a major point in their friendship, she decides to test the waters. She asks him if he is a virgin. Jean-Paul stammers, taken fully off guard. He blinks and blinks and blinks in rapid succession as he flushes. And with hands in his lap, he says physically he is, but he had unchaste eyes as a boy and as a soldier.

He quotes Saint Augustine. "Do not say that you have chaste minds if you have unchaste eyes, because an unchaste eye is the messenger of an unchaste heart." And the good Saint's message rattles the good Sister. And Jean-Paul, somewhat taken aback by her question, throws it back to her, asking if she still is a virgin. Magali, with a shy schoolgirl look, simply replies that is a question one does not ask of a good girl.

Sister Magali, the nurse, the compassionate woman, becomes the angsty one as spring passes and the close of the school year creeps closer and closer. Her coworkers in the hospital notice it. The sisters at her guest convent notice it. The Mother Superior notices it and knows what her changing demeanor means, and she lets Magali have the space she needs to make her decision.

But her beloved Jean-Paul, he does not see her angst. For him, she remains his angel from heaven. She represents the melodic voice of the woman on the medallion who conversed with the Lord in Proto-Greek.

In different ways on their walks, she artfully probes him for his intentions when he completes his Regency at the end of the school year. He is so philosophical, with answers ranging and varying as different thoughts pass through his mind. In her angst, she finally just grabs his hand so they can walk hand in hand when they are out of view of others. From then on, she picks paths for their walks that offer much privacy so she will at least have his hand to herself. He certainly does not mind.

One afternoon in the late spring, Jean-Paul is surprised to see the good Sister at his office door. It is not her normal day to come to the school. She asks permission to come in and then closes the door. She takes off her veil, allowing her crimson rose tresses to fall upon her shoulder as she sits on his desk facing him. She takes his hand in hers and says she is going to take the big leap of faith that she has read him correctly.

Sister Magali proceeds to say, "My dearest Brother Jean-Paul, my dear, dear Jean-Paul. Our walks are worlds of wonder for me. You have enlightened me about so many new things, ideas, thoughts, and ways of communing with our Lord. They started as the second most important part of my life after my commitments to the Lord as our time together renewed my life and my faith. I can only hope that you feel the same way when I say I have found that my time with you has become more important than anything else, the Lord included."

She looks for a response from him as she has started to renounce her vows in front of him, the biggest decision in her life to date. "And I look into your eyes, Jean-Paul, and I see you yearn for more, as do I."

And she kisses his hand. He reciprocates and kisses her hand back.

Witnessing this sign that she should go for closure, she says, "It is not too late for the two of us to cancel proceeding to our permanent vows. Can you not imagine the two of us back in France, raising our family? You could become the professor of theology, history, and archeology that your heart yearns for, and I could continue being a nurse. I love you, Jean-Paul. I truly do." She takes his head in her hands and kisses his forehead.

Jean-Paul is very contemplative. He would equally love to express his undying love to her, but he wrestles with the prudence of making rash decisions, perhaps hormonally driven, at least by him. He kisses her hands, then each finger, and responds, "My beloved Sister, my cherished Magali, I cannot hide that I too find a love in you that beckons me to come to you, to come with you wherever you wish to go. You are my angel from heaven. As always, you are right that the time is now for each of us to decide either to go forward with our vows and commitment to the Lord or to go forward with each other, still with the blessings of the Lord."

Kissing her forehead in return, he strategically pauses before continuing. "We should go slowly with this decision, as the implications for us, those around us, and those in the future could be quite profound. We should meditate, reflect, and reach out to the Lord as we finalize our future."

He stands up out of his chair and lifts her off the desk. As his large, warm hands around her waist move to enwrap the soft mounds of her derrière, he kisses her, passionately and slowly. He pulls back and they look into each other's eyes, losing touch with anything other than each other. He brushes her lovely scarlet and cerise tresses back behind her ear and leans in to nibble on her lobes and then lets her go. She blushes as she composes her clothing and her veil and mouths a kiss to him as she leaves.

And as happened each evening at that coastal village, Jean-Paul's guilt overwhelms him that evening as he tries to fall asleep. At first in rapture over having professed his love for his dear Sister, the guilt takes a turn for the worst, for he has not been fully honest with her. If she leaves her Order, if she leaves her life with the Lord, she will be doing so for a priest in training who has not been fully truthful with her. And how could a lifelong relationship be built if not on a bed, a foundation, of honesty and truth? He tosses all night in his angst.

The next week is near condemnation in hell for the two of them, for different reasons. One in angst over possibly losing the only man she would ever love. The other in angst over lie after lie. And who first said that when it rains, it pours? For Jean-Paul, a drenching typhoon of guilt comes in an expected envelope. He receives a letter of commendation from the president of the Jesuit Conference of Provincials for Eastern Asia and Oceania for his work improving the morale and attendance at the school. His euphoria is quickly followed by his guilt.

And the situation only worsens two days later when the school secretary comes running into his classroom to pull him away for a personal phone call from the same regional president of the Jesuit Conference. For ten minutes, they talk as he receives his personal plaudits for his innovation in education and peaceful resolution of the school's attendance issues.

The Machiavellian in Jean-Paul cries out that night, for he is a success, just as he excelled in the military schools. He could do very well in his life by his series of half-truths. He did not lie. He merely was not asked to provide the whole picture. He truly provided honest answers to the questions he was asked. Sort of. He could have the world's most fabulous wife and research the secrets of her medallion. Or he could climb up in the Jesuit Order with a mere minor bending of the spirit of his and their faith. He prays for guidance.

Over the next few weeks, Magali comes over many times each week to take walks with her new professed love. She finds discreet places to stop and kiss him. More than thrice each walk. Often a lot more than thrice. She tells him of her secret fantasies after she lightly rubbed his warm crotch that one night, and how every night of their life could be like that night. And she replicates what she did with him that night. Jean-Paul cannot summon the courage to tell her no, nor does he want to. His Regency ends in a couple weeks, and they need to make their decision soon. Very soon.

As his beloved Magali parts with him that evening, he continues to walk in meditative silence. He thinks about his grandfather's words about becoming a Jesuit rather than being a soldier. And he thinks of the moment when he found the courage to tell his commandant he was resigning his commission to become a priest. Knowing his junior officer's exposure to the atrocities of that war, the commandant understood why he resigned, but he wanted to hear it fully from Jean-Paul.

And Jean-Paul said he wanted to help the world. He wanted to prevent tragedies like the bombing of his parents' flight, the World Trade Center, and so many other acts of terror. He had thought he could best do so as a soldier in the military, but he knew now that being a soldier of the pope would be far more impactful. He would save souls. And they let him out of his commitments to be that different kind of soldier.

The next morning, Jean-Paul wakes up as a man on a mission. A priest on a mission. He calls the president of the regional Jesuit Conference and tells him he does not deserve his commendation. He has not told his superiors the full story about how he fixed the situation. He should have been fully truthful. Much to his surprise, he is not reprimanded. The president commends him for his coming forward with the truth, which he needed to speak to be honest to himself and to the Lord. They already knew exactly how he had fixed the situation.

Then the president adds that there is a place in the Order for priests who are willing to innovate and take positive action as he did. His pathway through the rest of his formation will be followed with great interest. Accordingly, the Father General has personally assigned him a position in Rome, under the Society's watchful eyes, to complete his formal theology studies in preparation for his priestly ordination. A plane has been arranged to take him back to Rome three days after his school year ends.

And as he hangs up the phone, Jean-Paul realizes his true calling. He loves Magali more than any woman in his life, save his mother, and maybe his sister. She is his personal angel from heaven, his intellectual joy, his spiritual companion. But he loves his work with God even more.

He planned to go to her convent and talk with her there, but she shows up at his office door before he can leave to see her. She closes the door, locks it, and comes over to him. Taking off her vest and veil, she removes his cassock, lifts herself up on her tippy toes, and kisses him. He hugs her in return, deep and strong. And she says she is ready to be his wife, to love him, honor him, and worship the Lord with him, forever.

Jean-Paul reciprocates, torn about what he needs to do, desperately torn. He professes his undying love for her, for her spirituality, her intellect, her compassion, her beauty, and kisses her back. He then adds that he most admires and respects her love for the Lord, a love that is his own personal inspiration. He looks her in the eyes, full of passion and desire, and tells the truth, finally, the truth. He loves her so much, he could not bear to take her away from the Lord's love.

And Magali begins to cry hard, beating on his chest as she chokes on her tears, saying that is what a man says when he is trying to graciously dump a woman. She cannot even look at him as she turns away. Jean-Paul pulls her back and holds her tight, letting her cry into his chest. And she cries and cries until she feels her medallion hanging beneath his shirt. She opens up his shirt, exposing his chest and the medallion.

Jean-Paul takes her head in his hands and leans in to blow on her ear and nibbles her lobe as he says, "*Elle entend la voix de Dieu.*" *She hears the voice of God.* He whispers to her that her calling to God is so strong. She is the woman in the medallion, and he cannot stand between her and the Lord. He kisses her again, and hugs her. He professes his love for her, always and forever, and he will be there for her anytime she needs.

Sister Magali gazes at the medallion on his chest and then into his eyes. She realizes his love for the Lord is like hers and is part of why she loves so him so. She sees his trueness and honesty in his profession of his love for her and wanting only the best for her. She steps away from him and looks out the window into the sky. Jean-Paul stays still, letting her find her inner voice.

Still looking out the window, she says, "Both your love and the love of the Lord, how can I say no?"

She turns back to him and touches the medallion on his chest. "But this means we will not have children to pass on this family artifact. My father will have to understand that I give this to you so you can find out what this means, and how we can fulfill the Lord's mission, which is embodied in the partial story told here."

She puts her head to his chest and hugs him, saying, "And we will have children together. They will be the world's children, who will inherit the peaceful earth we create from this medallion."

They kiss. The last one, maybe. Maybe not. She separates from him, walks to the window, pulls down the shades, and turns towards him with an inviting smile.

CHAPTER 27

A seeker went to ask a sage for guidance on the Sufi way.
The sage counseled, "if you have never trodden the path of
love, go away and fall in love; then come back and see us."
— Nur ad-Dīn Abd ar-Rahmān Jāmī,
fifteenth-century Sufi mystic and poet

4:45 p.m. GMT+3, May 10, 2022
Hills outside Siirt, formerly Turkey, now Anatolian Kurdish State

Did she hear correctly? Rohat? Zara leans her back against the door, trying to remember the last time she talked with her ultraorthodox kin. Okay, he tried to marry her when she was seventeen, claiming his right as her oldest male first cousin. And then he led her paternal family to shun her six years ago, for the acts of atrocity committed upon her against her will. Now what does he want?

Zara makes sure the door's safety latches are secure, opens the door ever so slightly, and peeks out. There indeed stands her cousin. A couple of centimeters shorter than her, strong defined bearded chin, broad shoulders, and imposing chest, with a little bit of a belly. He must be living well. What is he doing up here, so far away from their homeland in the former northwestern Iraq?

She says, "Just a minute, cousin Rohat." She puts her gun under one of the couch cushions and goes to open the door.

Rohat greets her with a salaam, a low bow of the head and body with fingers touching the forehead, and Zara reciprocates, swinging her hand to show him into the house. Roza and Maryam have come from the kitchen, and each greets Rohat. Tradition does not allow her to ask the purpose or length of his visit, so she says in Kurdish, "My nephew Rohat, we are pleased to see you. Your journey must have been tiring and long. May I offer you something to drink?"

"The hour of Asr prayer comes upon us. We should pray as a family first," Rohat suggests.

Maryam leads him to their prayer room while Zara stays in the front room. Rohat turns to her and says, "I had understood you had returned to the faith and submission to Xwedê again."

Zara runs her hands outside her uterus and says, "It is that time when I am unclean. Please forgive me."

With a grimace and head down, Rohat goes with Maryam as Roza goes to fetch Sara, and they perform their Asr prayer rituals.

After prayer, Roza returns Sara to her room, then comes to the front room and tells Rohat, "We are honored you have traveled far to share prayer with us. How else may we help you this evening?"

Rohat says to Maryam and Rosa, "Aunt Maryam and my grandmother-to-be Roza, the borders are now open across all of Kurdistan. Now, Kurds can freely travel to see family in each of the four former countries that artificially separated us. Up until this week, these border restrictions prevented me from fulfilling my duties as the most senior male in the Khatum family. I express my sorrow again, Aunt Maryam, that your husband's two brothers, and Grandmother Roza, that your two sons, were tragically killed. Honoring the traditions of our family and people, I am ready to fulfill my duties to ensure your family is taken care of properly."

Not unnoticed, Rohat addressed the two elder women at the exclusion of Zara, which does not please her as she is no longer the child he knew, and he is only three years older than her. Her pride getting the best of her, she steps in front of Rohat, and her grandmother extends her hand, begging her to show respect and move back.

Zara speaks in a firm voice. "Rohat, I now take care of this family, and as you can see they are prosperous, happy, and most important, faithful in their submission to Xwedê."

Rohat pushes Zara aside and addresses her grandmother. "I will forgive my cousin's transgression of her place, for I know she has been weak and feeble in her respect for our faith. I am prepared to forgive the past and take her as my second wife as per our tradition." He looks at the angry Zara and says, "She is still young enough, barely, to bear your family children. And I will be able to take care of you and my aunt Maryam in the traditions of our people."

Outraged and ready to attack her cousin, Zara steps forward into him, but the hand of her grandmother pulls her back. She will not fight her grandmother. That is a line she knows better than to cross.

And Roza states in the voice of a true matriarch, "Rohat, we are sincerely honored by your travels and efforts to fulfill your family tradition and honor. But we four women left the lands of your family to return to our lands, the lands of my grandfather. The Khatum family tradition does not apply to our household. We are thriving here." With a slight bow of her head, she concludes, "We thank you for your kind and respectful gesture."

"Old woman, even though you will be my grandmother by marriage, you are a fool," Rohat yells with a stern face. "I am the oldest male in our patriarchal lineage, and as such there are rights and responsibilities that transcend borders, for we are still Kurdish. I will forgive your transgression as well as those of Zara. Even though she has strayed from her Muslim roots, you have shown your faith well in restoring her to submission to Xwedê again. I thank you for this. As is my right, and more importantly, as is best for her, I will take Zara back home with me to the lands of her birth, the mountains of her childhood, and the proper traditions of the Khatum family."

Incredibly incensed at this display of archaic and obsolete patriarchal patronage, Zara tries again to step in front of Roza to settle this issue, but her wise grandmother holds her back once again. "As your mufti grandfather and your grandmother, my old friend Amina, understand well, our faith, Islam, allows the woman in question to have the final say in any marriage. I am sure Amina's son, your father, raised you better than to act like you are. What has changed to make you act like men did in the days of my grandmother?"

Rohat's face twists as he says, "You dishonor me, the eldest male in the Khatum family. I do not deserve such dressing down by such an old woman." Before he can assert his physical power, Peter comes out of Zara's bedroom, which Rohat can clearly see is hers, buttoning up this shirt, which finally fits him.

Seeing the four of them, with his innocent, polite smile, Peter says, "Oh, please excuse me. I didn't know you had another guest. I was just dressing for dinner."

Rohat pulls out a gun and points it at Peter, who freezes with his best deer-in-the-headlights stare. Rohat says, "You, kafir, are an affront to our family's honor, sleeping with my cousin."

Zara stands between Rohat and Peter and yells in Kurdish, "How dare you bring a gun into our house of peace?"

Rohat sneers at her and says back in Kurdish, "You bitch. You did not change. You are still the donkey slut. You let a kafir horse into your bed. I cannot even think of such acts. You are a woman of no honor, a harlot. You dishonor our family." And he pulls the slide back on his pistol, pointing it at Zara's head.

And before he can shoot, Jean-Paul arrives from outside. Gun in hand and a side shot on this invader, he says in Arabic, "Drop the gun. I cannot miss shooting you first from this distance."

Rohat peers at the tall man with his crucifix and yells in English for all to hear, "You bring a Christian soldier into your household to endorse the defilement of our Kurdish women by kafirs. The honor of our family means you must die, even if it means my death." And he pulls the pistol hammer back with his thumb.

In less than a blink, Zara puts Jean-Paul's lessons to use, disarming Rohat and sending his pistol flying across the hall into her mother's room, where it discharges upon impact. Zara proceeds to kick him with such force that he trips and falls over their couch. She grabs her own pistol from under the couch cushion, pulls her cousin up with the pistol in his gut, and pushes him out the door.

In her most vile Kurdish, she scolds him. "You dishonor us with your shameful actions. You dishonor the Khatum family. No woman should be treated as if she were no more than a sheep to be traded at a man's will. Go back to your little backward village and never come back."

In shock, Rohat stands there looking at the beast of a woman who has taken the soul of his cousin. Zara turns to go back into the house but remembers she owes him one. And she turns, wishing she had steel-toed combat boots on, and kicks his groin as hard as she possibly can in her soft sandals. He doubles over onto the ground with a bloodcurdling scream. And Zara stands over him and says, "That makes us even."

Zara is not done with her cousin. She leans down and puts her pistol straight into his injured groin. He begs for mercy. She shakes her head and pulls the trigger. He nearly faints, but there was no bullet chambered. "Be thankful to Xwedê that I forgot to chamber the bullet. Next time, you will not be so lucky," Zara admonishes as she kicks dirt into his face and takes his belt and shoes. "Stay away from my family or you will not be so lucky again. I will hunt you down and kill you if any of my family is hurt," she says as she returns into the house.

As she locks the door, she sees her family gathered on the floor around Peter. Apparently, he fainted during the best of the action. Jean-Paul comes over and congratulates her on her excellent execution of the disarming move. His best student yet, he thinks as he hugs her from the side.

Zara hugs Jean-Paul back. She turns away to glance at Peter. *Did I just stand between him and a bullet? What must my family be thinking?* And she sees Roza looking back at her, nodding her head and smiling. Then the adrenaline rush disappears as she sighs and sinks for the first time since her Sugar Fest abduction.

Maryam stands up to grab her daughter. She takes her head into her chest and hugs her, and years of repressed emotion unwinds as Zara cries, "I will never be a man's slave. Ever. Ever again." Maryam hugs and comforts her little Zara as she murmurs, "Ever, ever again." Maryam brings her daughter back to her room so she can change out of her sullied clothes.

Roza and Jean-Paul lift Peter off the ground and onto the couch. Roza cannot help but see Jean-Paul's glistening crucifix. She says, "Man of the cloth. Man of arms." She smiles at Jean-Paul. "But I am very glad you came to my granddaughter's defense. You are her friend. She needs friends like you." Jean-Paul simply smiles, in his serene way.

Maryam comes back into the room and invites her guests to be seated in the dining area, where a beautiful floral cloth of roses of all colors lies in the middle of the floor. She shows them the area to remove their shoes and seats them so she and Roza can surround Peter. Zara comes back in a royal-blue dress with yellow-and-black trim, escorting her great-grandmother Sara. Peter gets up and fetches her a chair, but Sara waves no and gracefully sits on the floor with the rest of the family.

Maryam and Roza have worked all afternoon to prepare this feast. Mehir, a cool yogurt soup, curecur, a lamb stew, and kutilk, meat-filled dumplings, along with fresh-baked flatbread, a bowl of mixed local greens and herbs, and chai tea. And for dessert, koliche, a pastry delight.

Zara sits next to her mother and Sara. In Kurdish, she introduces Peter and Jean-Paul to Sara. She acknowledges, apparently having been well briefed about them by her children in Zara's absence. She gives a special smile to Peter.

Sara asks Zara something in Kurdish as she touches the hand of Jean-Paul, who is seated to her side. Zara explains to Jean-Paul, "My great-grandmother would be very honored if you would say grace before we eat."

Jean-Paul smiles at Sara and folds his hands together and says, "*Bismillahi wa 'ala baraka-tillah.*"

Zara's family is very surprised and pleased. And Roza says, "In the name of Xwedê and with the blessings of Xwedê. That was very nice of you, Father Jean-Paul, to honor our faith in Arabic. Please continue with a grace in your faith."

Jean-Paul searches his index of graces for something that would be appropriate for this interfaith gathering and says, "For good food and those who prepare it, for good friends with whom to share it, we thank you, our Lord. Amen." And Sara pats him on his hand and says thank you in Kurdish.

Zara translates again for Sara. "My great-grandmother welcomes you all to her home. As you can see, the part she and my grandmother sleep in, where your room is, Jean-Paul, this is their historic home. The newer additions here—the kitchen, the other bedrooms, the bomb shelter—are all gifts from my great-granddaughter."

Pausing to give thanks to Sara for her acknowledgment, Zara continues translating. "My daughter, Roza, married Zara's grandfather, Baho, who was also a Sufi like my husband. He worked in the oil fields in Batman. Sadly, they needed to move to Baho's hometown, Silopi, twelve years ago, after PKK military actions disrupted the oil industry in this area, and innocent Kurds like him were under investigation. I am thankful my great-granddaughter and my great-grandson moved my daughter back after the Turkish police tragically took Baho into custody. May he return to Xwedê."

Sara asks another question for Zara to translate. "My great-grandmother would like to know if a Catholic priest like you is comfortable in a Muslim country, a Muslim house."

"Please let your grandmother know, I have fulfilled my missions in many Muslim countries. I was near here over a decade ago, working relief services in Van after the great earthquake. I also helped people in Egypt, Mali, and Nigeria. And so, I have learned a few words in Arabic along the way." Zara translates to Sara, who nods her appreciation and approval of her guest's nobility of character.

Roza speaks to Jean-Paul. "Please excuse our poor English. We learned from watching the news on Zara's devices she gave us a few years ago, that MoxRappea thing. It has brought us closer to the rest of the world, even more so than when we first had access to the internet, something we would not have been able to do when we were mere farming people. Zara tells us little of what she really does, other than take care of us as a good daughter and granddaughter. We are familiar with her times in the Peshmerga and met some of the soldiers and officers who served with her in her fighter roles. We are very curious, all three of us, why she would be in the company of nonmilitary men, an ex-priest and an editor."

Zara interrupts quickly in Kurdish. "Grandmother Roza, what I do has kept you, Great-grandmother Sara, and my mother all well taken care of. All your needs are met, and you are safe. And I do so in full respect of the wishes of Xwedê. That is all that needs to be said."

Roza lets her impertinent granddaughter understand that her tone is inappropriate, but concedes her point and redirects her conversation. "We love our Zara so very much. She is our treasure," Roza says to Jean-Paul. "We hope you are able to help her find what she has lost. She is, at heart, a very beautiful girl full of love and joy. And she loved her little brother so much. We are happy she did not join the PKK as he did. May he return to Xwedê."

"And to her sisters too," blurts Peter.

Looking confused, Maryam and Roza are about to respond when Zara explains in Kurdish that he means her cousins Rona and Diyar, who were like her sisters. They nod in agreement.

Roza turns to Peter to her left and serves him more curecur and kutilk. "Peter, young man, what do you know of women of the Islamic faith?"

Scratching his head, Peter needs to think long and hard about that question, as the only woman of Islamic faith he has ever met, he only met a day and a half ago. And he has not been very successful at engaging her in any meaningful discussion of her faith, or anything else for that matter, since then.

He squeezes his brain until it hurts and something comes out of his mouth. A glance at Zara folding her the hem of her dress under her leg, and he remembers that fateful moment when they first met. "Dignity. Respect. And modesty as a sign of self-respect." He looks at Zara and then Roza to see if he is going to be disciplined for his ignorance. Nothing. So, he continues, "A man should respect a woman and allow her to pursue her faith, to pursue her growth of knowledge." He crosses his fingers that he did not make some huge transgression of faith and still gets to finish his dinner.

Sara nods at Roza. Peter catches that, but is unable to discern what is happening other than that he is being grilled for dinner. Maybe he is the dessert. But Roza and Sara are not yet finished with this young man. Maryam leans over to Zara and whispers. She then says to Peter, "You are doing fine.

I thank you, personally, for your dignity in your answers."

Zara looks at her three generations of matriarchy, and then says in Kurdish, "My mothers, we should discontinue this conversation. As I have said to my mother, this man is only here for tonight, and tomorrow we go to complete his mission and he will never return here. There is no deeper interest between us other than helping Sasha with this small favor. Please, let him finish his dinner and we can wish him farewell tomorrow morning, Xwedê willing."

To Zara's surprise, Sara addresses her in Kurdish. "We have already heard from Maryam your statement about this young man. We simply wish to know more about him, even if you have no interest in him. Please be the good girl you are and let us proceed." And Zara, the good daughter, the good granddaughter, the good great-granddaughter, sits back in submission to her elders.

And Sara proceeds to tell an old riddle and asks Zara to translate. "Peter, my great-grandmother wishes to ask you this question. There is a certain piece of flesh in your body, and if that piece of flesh is impure, then all of your body will be impure. What is that piece of flesh?"

Jean-Paul puts his finger up and is about to answer, but Zara intercedes, "Please, Jean-Paul, I know you know. It is for Peter to show he knows."

And poor Peter, he sinks into the ground, if that were even possible on this cement floor. This is worse than the five hours of interview test questions he endured only two days or so ago. He closes his eyes and wishes Mei were here to help him out. He pictures her and how she comforted him in his angst. And then he sees it. Actually, he sees her palm on his chest.

"It is the heart," Peter replies with his eyes open and mouth smiling.

Roza smiles at him for the first time. Now he understands where Zara gets her demeanor from. The apple does not fall far from the tree, even in Kurdistan. "Mr. Peter, for a sheltered young man who has never ventured farther than his safe little town on the Pacific, you have done surprisingly well. We would never have expected this." She takes his hand into hers, wrinkled, having seen the ages, but nonetheless warm.

And much to Peter's surprise, she places her warm hand behind his neck, right on that spot, and she says, "Your dreams, tell me of your dreams."

In shock, unsure whether her hand is there by some strange Kurdish tradition or she is aware of the God Gene cluster, not knowing what to say, he looks at Zara, then at her mother, who is nodding her head. And he gets it—Maryam has told her mother and grandmother about this morning.

With a sigh, he tells of the nights, the fighting with the pillows and sheets, the dreams that cry out to him as if the world depended on him taking action, the mornings with the fog and haze, not being able to pull together their importance, and the tiredness that plagues him. Roza asks him about other family members who experience the same, and he confirms his grandfather and his mother's uncle, strategically leaving out the DNA information Jean-Paul shared with him yesterday about all the women in his family.

Roza rubs his special bump, then takes his hand up to her lips and lightly, but moistly kisses it. And he calms. She lightly kisses his forehead. Roza confesses—a confession that is done only among family, as per her definition of Mahram, "Mr. Peter, your dreams, your angst, runs deep in our family. Maryam's husband, Zara's father, my husband, my father and uncles, Sara's father, her uncles and grandfathers, all suffered what you do."

Zara's eyes betray the shock of this revelation. She looks at the three matriarchs and says to Roza in Kurdish, "Why do you say this now and never before? Why in front of these strangers? Am I not your blood, your daughter, your granddaughter, your great-granddaughter? Why do I not deserve the respect to be told this in privacy?"

Sara tells Roza in Kurdish that this should be explained in the language of their guests. And Roza replies in English, "There was no need to tell you until the day it was needed, the day you brought back home a kind man who had such dreams. It was not important unless you were to marry someone who suffered these nightly torments. And last night, you brought Mr. Peter home with you, and he suffered the dreams in your brother's room, to be discovered by your mother, who, like us, knows very well how to comfort the men who suffer so."

Rocking back and forth, adjusting her legs under her, Zara grimaces, trying to maintain composure with her most important family members. She starts to speak in Kurdish, but Sara admonishes her and Zara continues in English. "As I said, these men are only here on business. I am not here to marry this man. He is an employee of Alexander Murometz, the same as the ex-priest is. They merely must complete something for him. That is all. No marriage. No children. Nothing but business."

Jean-Paul has been literally sitting on his hands this entire time, balancing on the floor in front of his food. With an inquisitive look on his face, he asks, "Then the Sufi traditions were vital for your husbands, to help them manage their conditions. Is this not correct? The meditations and prayers helped them."

"You are a very wise man. You are still a man of God at heart. Yes, my husband, my grandfather, they managed their pains with their closeness to Xwedê. Of course, we as their spouses played our role, actions of which I cannot speak in mixed gender company. But we can teach Zara," says Roza as she looks at her granddaughter, who is still reeling from the shock of tonight's confessions.

"This ailment, it has been known for hundreds and hundreds of years," says Roza. "As Zara may have said to you, I have recited the works of the thirteenth-century Sufi mystic, Rūmī, to her mother and her since they were children.

Listen to this poem of his.
No memory of his past abides with him,
And from his present soul he shall be changed.
Though he is fallen asleep, God will not leave him
In this forgetfulness. Awakened, he
Will laugh to think what troublous dreams he had.
And wonder how his happy state of being
He could forget, and not perceive that all
Those pains and sorrows were the effect of sleep
And guile and vain illusion. So this world
Seems lasting, though 'tis but the sleepers' dream;
Who, when the appointed Day shall dawn, escapes
From dark imaginings that haunted him,

And turns with laughter on his phantom griefs
When he beholds his everlasting home."

Peter identifies very much with this poem, and the editor in him says, "I wish I could have edited a poem about the dreams so eloquently. That is exactly what it is like."

Roza continues, "Those who have the dreams, they are halfway to Xwedê. They just need a little extra help to get the rest of the way. We spouses have been like their other halves, and between the pair, we are closer to Xwedê together. It takes both halves to make an apple."

Seeing the despondence seeping back into her granddaughter, Roza says, "Zara is a special girl, full of love and joy. She may not seem like it now, but that loving girl, she is still in there." She looks at Peter and Jean-Paul and says, "I am happy she has found friends." She looks back at Zara, who refuses to make eye contact, and says, "For she needs true friends. The kind of friends who can help her find her way back."

She looks at Maryam at Zara's side and asks in Kurdish if she and her daughter could recite the last lines of Rūmī's Two Insomnias poem. Maryam whispers to Zara, who shakes her head no. Maryam whispers again, rubbing her shoulders, and Zara sits up straight. And together they recite the poem, Maryam in Arabic and Zara translating into English.

"When I am with you, we stay up all night.
When you're not here, I can't go to sleep.
Praise God for these two insomnias!
And the difference between them.
The minute I heard my first love story
I started looking for you, not knowing
How blind that was.
Lovers don't finally meet somewhere.
They're in each other all along."

Jean-Paul is very impressed how true this poem is to the afflicted he has studied. For Peter, there is another meaning. He looks into Zara's eyes, and for a moment they connect just like the poem, but then she disconnects.

With tears about to form in her eyes, Zara gets up, looks at her mothers, and says, "The day has been long. We have a hard day tomorrow. I must retire." And she heads for the door. She pauses as a butterfly flutters through her stomach. She turns back and peers into Peter's eyes for only a glance. She moistens her lips, and with her head down, she leaves.

CHAPTER 28

Beyond those hills and oak woods,
Beyond those vineyards and gardens,
We passed in health and joy, glory be to God.
We were dry, but we moistened.
We grew wings and became birds,
We married one another and flew,
Glory be to God.

—Yunus Emre,
thirteenth-century Turkish poet and Sufi mystic

9565 BCE
Site of modern-day Göbekli Tepe

Sixty-nine cycles, cries my mother, thinking she is old. My twin, Zirbani, and I, Sarpani, can see into her soul when the three of us pray together. And she is still young. She is still that young woman whom our father, Orzu, saved from a life of the unspeakable. I pray to God that my daughters, my granddaughters, never face the same choices—death or life worse than death.

But Nanshe's body is old, and she says she may not have more days ahead of her as she pushes with her will, her might, her indomitable presence to overcome our band of families' fatigue and desire to settle down. She has let us settle on the side of an ancient mountain of fire for a season while we planted grains and let our animals reproduce. We saw great plains on the horizon, but she said these were still not the right ones. But by the cold months, she willed us into moving, leaving some weary families to continue their farms.

Continue we did until we found this mountain ridge. And from here, we see it finally. The plains of grasses that extend forever. The promised lands. And here, my mother said she can finally die and rejoin her husband, our father, and be buried under the object.

We have left a trail of our farming, our animals, and our language as we wove down this land on the other side of the big lake. A trail that can be traced through the stories we left and the abundance we created. In my communion with God, I can see our descendants will view our work someday long into the future, long, long into the future. Ki, my older sister, my second mother, is always vigilant, afraid the giants, Doroda's boys and even our cousin Nirra, will follow our trail.

Nanshe calms us, saying it is our destiny to be here, for great worlds will be created from our presence here. One night, my dear husband, Morda, suffered through a dream, which, of course, I helped him recall with the methods my mother taught me. He dreamt of a great man arising from the valley below us. A man from whom great religions would arise.

Ki, ever the cynic, the forever loyal, dismissed him, saying our mother is that great person, if only more would listen to her as faithfully as she listens. I feel so bad for Ki. I feel her pain that she cannot hear the voice as do her sisters and mother. She prays with us always, but she is an outsider to the voice who guides us. But her faith, her obedience to our mother, her will to make what is right happen, leads to my utter respect for her. I am proud to be her little sister.

I feel too for my inseparable twin, Zirbani. As girls, we were so alike, but subtly different. Of course our mother could tell us apart, but we loved to play games with the villagers, pretending to be one another. And even though we continue to live in the same household together, we have regrettably grown apart, no fault of hers. My second marriage changed everything. My mother noted this change with great interest. She not only taught me how to comfort my cousin, my husband, each night as he experienced his dreams, but taught him, as well, how to comfort me based on the way my father did with her. She confided in me that, after the battle with the giant Tureal and his son Doroda, my father was critically injured and they could no longer have children. But he found ways of comforting her without the intimate capacity. She said sex was not the key to the maturing of a pair who, as she says, are afflicted with the dreams and visions from the object.

And as Morda and I comforted each other, we grew. We grew in our ability to understand the message of the voice, the meanings of the dreams. So true what she had put into our family oral tradition: "Only with the two together can you find peace. The object. You might see in sleep, might hear. But only as man and woman." For nonbelievers, for nonafflicted, they will not know the bliss of this togetherness, the power of it.

Whereas our mother and her twins form the spiritual leadership of the group, she and Ki form the earthly leadership. Ki, as she always has, continues to fulfill our father's request to teach our children, their children, and their children the oral tradition of our ancestors. But Ki and my mother lament that, despite their best intentions, efforts, and practice, the younger generations are not recalling the traditions well, nor are they as motivated as we. For we have been successful in creating a life of peace, a life where our family, our people, prosper and can explore the world, their minds, and most importantly, our deepening relationship with God.

Ki was so funny. She said if only we could not depend on passing the tradition down by mouth, we could ensure the safety of generations to come. I guess I cannot feel her pain as much on this point, as the voice is our continuity, but poor Ki cannot hear it. She talked with An of carving our story on rocks, stones, anything that will last forever, so the wisdom and warnings of our ancestors would not be lost. And for a woman who neither has a husband who is possessed by the dreams nor can hear the voice herself, she has great vision for the future. She convinced our mother we should build a massive monument that will last forever.

Thus, twelve sun cycles ago, my mother persuaded the community to join together to build this monument. The word of our ways had spread rapidly, and we enjoyed the company of over forty families in our area who came to pray with us and share in the bounties of our food and our methods to plant and harvest grains, to breed and raise animals. She would say, "Activity breeds prosperity."

Whatever happened to my mother with the object on the other side of the lake, it not only allowed her to hear the voice, but gave her an understanding of the nature of things far beyond the comprehension of the rest of us. She showed the community how to carve, lift, and fit stones that even the giants could not lift alone. Of course, my uncle Narn and the two men who had also escaped from the pyramid-building slave camps brought the techniques they had learned from the giants. But it was this extra-special cerebral understanding of my mother that showed how.

After we erected the two massive grand pillars, we placed the object in between them. This became our place of worship. Over Ki's protests, my mother wanted to limit the number of carvings on these main pillars as we should not be distracted from our focus, our communion with God. Ki, just as strong-willed as Mother, asked An to carve a special smaller pillar to be placed on the side, one that would show the tail of the bird constellation. An's sense of humor led him to invert the constellation and place the tail of the bird star at the bird's head. Ki was not so amused. Twice in her life, Ki had the experience of facing an attacking giant with erect member. And so she asked An to carve such an erection-laden figure into this smaller pillar. A warning for all women of the future.

Last moon cycle, my dearest Morda had a torturous dream. Horrors of the giants attacking our village. And horrors worse than that. Of great wars to come. Ki and An were at their wits' end trying to figure out how to communicate the dangers that our descendants would face. She wished they had carved the most dangerous animals we know onto the pillars, but she always followed the will of our mother. She looked at the grand pillars, which were designed to show the way to the tail of the bird star, just as her father made in stones in front of her childhood house. She wished as before they could clearly communicate to our next generations the danger of the giants.

And so they began to make another monument area, right next to the one we created. The central pillars would more clearly show the giants. On the first pillar, Ki instructed for the arms of the giant around a fox to be carved, just as Doroda fended off her pet foxes. But at the top of the side of the pillar, she had An carve the pendant. The one she has worn since she killed Doroda. The one that Nanshe has told us was worn by our aunt Illyana during the moon cycle they had known each other before our father had saved both their souls.

A circle with a crescent below.

CHAPTER 29

Even if the aliens are short, dour, and sexually obsessed—
if they're here, I want to know about them.

—Carl Sagan

8:00 a.m. GMT+3, May 11, 2022
Highway D370 west of Batman, formerly Turkey, now Anatolian Kurdish
State

The hot, dry air outside predicts searing temperatures, deadly for those who did not come prepared. But the silence in the car is far deadlier, as Zara fumes, peeved at her family, the family secret that they withheld from her, and this silly little boy next to her, who charmed them. Putty in his hands, silly little hands.

Peter, sensing the extremely dangerous tension and seething fury in the woman next to him driving the truck, sensibly looks out his window, avoiding her gaze and reflecting on what her family said to him this morning. While Zara and Jean-Paul were loading the truck, Maryam and Roza pulled him aside into Roza's room.

Maryam, meeker than yesterday morning, said, "I must apologize for my actions. In my eagerness to find a good husband for my only daughter, I may have made a number of missteps with you. Clearly, the road to marriage in our culture is very different than in yours." Blushing and looking at the floor, she quietly said, "The Qur'an, much like your Bible, says that the unmarried must have no sex or paths leading to sex as one thing could lead to another. They must avoid everything that may incite one to have sex."

The much-less-timid Roza interceded. "That means no kissing, no sensual touching, no gazing at her sexually. Zara has had a very hard life. She was raised with great faith. She strayed. Fell upon very hard times. Lost her way and balance. Praise Xwedê, she came back to embrace her faith, our faith, and found her balance."

With the deep love of a mother, Maryam added, "Zara returned to being very devout and pious. It is what holds her together. We pray together many times a day each time she is back. You may mistakenly believe your affections are innocent. But if you care for her as a friend, a colleague, then you will do nothing, absolutely nothing that will pit her against her faith."

Roza shook her head again and excused herself; being over seventy, she could only be direct. She pointed to his crotch and said, "Keep that zipped up and tucked away. Do we have a clear understanding, young man?" And of course, a scared Peter nodded yes.

Her finger tapped on his chest as Roza opined, "Where you are going, heed not the temptation."

His lips quivered as he readied himself for more admonishments of improper thoughts about her granddaughter.

"My Zara, your priest, they are exceptional in what they do. You, Peter, are exceptional in ways very different from them. You are what Zara is not. And there may be a moment where your focus on what you are best at will be what she will need the most, what might save her."

Taking Peter's hand, calming him by petting him lightly, Maryam said, "You have learned much about our ways in only a day. But you must understand that Zara's husband will need to fully embrace and practice her ways, all of them. I again apologize for my haste at inviting you to marry her."

A sonly Peter rubbed, then kissed her hand to show his respect for her words. She was different from his mother, but in some ways just the same. And that made him smile.

Roza, watching this young man very carefully, nodded to Maryam, who then put a lambskin sac into his hands. Inside was a pendant, a grey stone with a carved circle with a deep center hole and a crescent below. Clasping her hands around his, she whispered, "I believe in my heart that you are the one. The one who will free my daughter from her chains. You are kind in your heart. Your head, it may need some work, which we can fix. And Zara will need your inner strength on this mission that Sasha has sent you on."

She held the pendant up and said, "This is very ancient, having been handed down through many, many generations. It is for Zara to pass to her children. As she had not been told about her legacy, we never shared this with her. Only show it to her if it is absolutely necessary to save her. It is on loan to you. You will give this back when you return."

"But Zara said I was never coming back, ever," Peter replied.

Maryam nodded. "I know that you will."

❧

Peter's reflecting out the window is jarred by Zara admonishing Jean-Paul. "So, priest, did you have a good time with my family after I left? I heard the singing of poems and my mother's laughter."

Tucked in the backseat, next to the two EM detector packs, Jean-Paul leans forward and says, "We found a lot of commonality, comparing the thinking and words of the Sufi mystics with the Catholic mystics."

With crossed legs, Peter interrupts, asking, "Can we stop for a break? I had too much tea at breakfast."

As Peter is outside the truck taking care of business, Zara turns around with a serious frown, looking at Jean-Paul square in the eyes. "I am disappointed with my family for not telling me about our affliction. I am disappointed with you as well. What have you not told me yet? I know you are conspiring with Alexander about something. Why did I have to find out my family is afflicted at my house in front of guests?"

Jean-Paul remains silent, no serene smile, just blank. And Peter, not knowing the danger he is in by coming back into the truck, closes his door and says, "Ah, I feel so much better."

"Well, I hope you are happy, Little Boy," Zara whips at him. "I am a mutant just like you. I am so happy I have not passed on this accursed disease to children. Even more reason not to have any."

Trying to ease her temperament, Peter jokes back. "Think of it this way—when we find the object, our alien DNA will come in handy as we try to talk with them."

And he has pushed the wrong button again as a disdainful Zara says, "Do not even think of blaspheming the prophets. Those who do will burn in Jahannam, either burned by fire on the skin or by boiling water across their body."

Face shaking, the priest says, "Let us not talk about being burned alive. I would rather be shot than burned alive."

Peter fights back as he is tired of being pushed around and threatened by the Khatum family today. "Talk about blasphemies and heresies, your saintliness lied about her connection to terrorists. Your brother was PKK. You lied to us. What else have you lied to us about?" He crosses his arms indignantly.

"My brother was PKK, the same as he was YPG," Zara affirms. "And he did not die in jail as a terrorist. He died trying to evacuate a village under air and ground attack." Zara pulls her headscarf over her face, only exposing her eyes, and stares at Peter. "You Westerners, you think if a woman has a veil, she is a terrorist. If a man joins an ethnic organization, he must be involved with violent terrorist acts. He was fighting with the YPG in Syria, just as I had been. The line between YPG and PKK is very blurred if not nonexistent. Do you call me a terrorist too?"

She pauses to let Peter absorb her words and then says, "After he saw what happened to our grandfather, what government forces did to our villages, he moved my mother and grandmother out of Silopi, out of harm's way to Siirt to be with Sara. And then he joined the PKK to help others escape attack."

And silence once again falls upon the truck.

The once-again-serene good Father breaks the silence, saying to Zara, "Your cousin Rohat, he is someone we should not take lightly. Honor killings are another tragic part of an ancient tribal patriarchal culture. There are over two hundred per year each in Turkey and Syria. One year in Iraq, more than a thousand. Sometimes, the woman is asked to commit suicide to save the family dishonor. Sometimes it is made to look as if she committed suicide."

Zara adds, "The judges, they are often lenient, sympathizing with the men. I know of women who set themselves on fire to escape their families, their husbands."

Jean-Paul shivers again at the word *fire*, and he says in sympathy, "It is sad and tragic, indeed. Zara, have you considered exactly how Rohat knew where to find you? And on the exact date you would be there?" That gets Zara's attention—that odd coincidence she missed in her anger towards her ultraorthodox cousin.

While her mind chews on this coincidence, she says, "We have a saying, 'It is better to be a male for one day than a female for ten.' The life of rural Kurdish women is difficult. On average, they bear five to six children, in contrast to two for non-Kurdish women. The lack of access to education and good healthcare in their language prevents their empowerment. Their bodies are not their own, but belong to their husband's family."

She looks at Peter and says, "You have not seen the villages further into the mountains. Life is beautiful there. People can live off the land and mountains. They eat well and live well. But when people get displaced from their villages, poverty and hunger set in, followed by despair and depression. It is especially difficult for the women."

Pointing her finger in shame at Peter, Zara says, "Your remarks about the PKK are uninformed. Was your George Washington a patriot or terrorist? It depends on who is writing history. I do not condone the bombings and attacks the PKK did. In fact, in surveys, most Turkish Kurds did not advocate for a separate nation. Their issue is the right to be able to speak their language, to celebrate their culture. But you must understand, the PKK was created as a result of oppression, in the same way Washington's armies were formed. Was it right for the Western world to list them as terrorists? I suppose if you were King George in London, you would have labeled the founders of your country as terrorists. Labels aside, what you do not see, what the rest of the world did not see, is the PKK came into the mountain villages and advocated for the equality of women, for they are equally essential for a strong Kurdistan.

Where they came to visit, conditions got better for women."

Feeling humbled and regretting his terrorist accusations, Peter meekly asks, "What is the solution?"

Zara smiles as she steps up on the soapbox. "Simple, but not so simple. It's a matter of economics and education, which generally follows economics. Rural Kurds need access to top education, in a language they understand and that is accessible from their homes, farms, and villages. The country needs sources of income other than oil."

Peter speaks. "Oil is the world's evil."

If she had a collar, she would be hot under it now. "What do you think these conflicts are truly about? Religion, politics? Oil and energy. Kurdistan sits on some of the best oil fields in the world. The fight for Sanliurfa for Ibrahim's birthplace? Iraq-Turkey crude oil pipelines runs from where I was born in Iraq all the way to Cerhan on the Mediterranean Sea right through this region. The Russians? They want the Iranian gas line and the former Iraqi gas line to be rerouted. The Americans? They see the threat to their gas and oil supplies. And the Chinese? Inscrutable, like your Mei. Can you figure them out? I can. They want the Arabic Confederation oil supplies for themselves."

"In this, we are kindred spirits. Like minds," replies Peter, who begins to relax in her presence.

Surprised by his reply, she glances at him, and her anger subsides a little as a hint of smile peeks through. "Maybe we cannot change the world, but we can change what we can."

An upcoming security checkpoint appears on the horizon and, as before, Zara taps her MoxWrap. When they pull up to the checkpoint, the officer in charge wants to see documentation. Zara explains she transferred her authorizations by MoxWrap, showing them on her device. They look at her device, look all over the vehicle, ask what they are carrying, and peer into their packs. They look at the two rifles and pistols they are carrying and ask if they have any other weapons. With that, the officer waves them though. Jean-Paul watches them make a call on a smartphone.

Looking very peeved, Zara says, "They were not normal Anatolian

Kurdish military. In the Peshmerga, I worked with the Americans, and part of my job was to find and capture Jahsh, the Kurdish traitors who worked as spies and informants for the government. These checkpoint soldiers felt like Jahsh. There was something not right about how they behaved. Jean-Paul, your observation about Rohat was very astute. There is a mole. Who would have known we made an emergency landing in Siirt? The pilots? Anyone from the airport? I had only informed Alexander that we would be one to two days delayed getting to the target. Did either of you communicate with anyone?"

Peter shakes his head no. Jean-Paul rapidly blinks and says no. Zara is suspicious, very suspicious.

"This is a very serious situation," says Zara. "Who could be after us? What did the Americans or Turks or Arabic Confederation have to gain by attacking our plane? Who is paying these new Jahsh?" She looks at Peter and says, "And I don't trust Mei's loyalties. The Chinese have a hand in this somewhere."

She turns back to glance at Jean-Paul and asks, "And, priest, what do you get out of this? You do not look like the type who is doing this for money, nor for any nation. Are you sure you are not here to steal Alexander's object?"

Peter jokes, "Yes, and he will have it stashed a thousand feet below the Vatican in their secret archives." Jean-Paul is not amused with this conversation and keeps quiet.

Another half hour on dirt back roads to avoid detection, and they see lines of smoke on the horizon. The battle for Sanliurfa is near. Zara pulls her truck into Göbekli Tepe's empty visitor center parking lot. The place has been closed for over a year. No guards. Only the fence securing the excavation areas.

And down the hill, they see the enclosures surrounded by coarsely built stone walls surrounding the dry tan limestone monoliths, which appear as if they beg to speak their history, the story of their builders. The excavated areas are accessible by wooden walkways. The rest of the hill looks like any other—peaceful waves of grass around sporadic mulberry trees and clusters of little yellow wildflowers and grazing goats overlooking the Harran Plains, with scattered farms to the left and Sanliurfa on the right.

Zara excuses herself as she pulls out a prayer mat from the truck's cargo bed and performs a Qasr, a quick afternoon prayer. On the other side of the truck, Peter listens to the artillery fire past Sanliurfa and watches the smoke rise from the battered areas of conflict. His knees begin to quiver. This is too real, too lethal for him.

As Jean-Paul unloads the EM detector packs from the cab, she proceeds to get security gear from her truck. After taking packs out of the cargo bed, she erects clear shields that protect the rear of the truck, with a slot for firing a rifle. Peter asks what this is, and she explains these are transparent aluminum armor that can stop a 12.7mm heavy machine-gun round. She laughs and says her whole truck is lined with this material, thanks to Alexander. Peter goes pale as he wonders what they need to be so heavily protected from.

Zara makes a three-hundred-and-sixty-degree scan with her binoculars. She says to Jean-Paul she does not like this situation. They are very exposed. The terrain is not very defensible. Jean-Paul methodically blinks and points out several ways they can set up an effective crossfire defense.

Zara smiles and says, "Your eyes tell me everything I needs to know. We may not have
time to set up a defense." Zara shakes her head and gives Jean-Paul one of the AK-74MXs, taking the other for herself. "Expect the worst from your enemy so that you won't be disappointed."

Peter quips at Jean-Paul, "Soldier of the Pope, eh?" which the good Father ignores.

Zara pulls out Rohat's gun. "Here, Peter, take this. He has ten-millimeter rounds that will stop an auroch, the ancient bull that wandered this area. Watch out, he used repacked rounds, not factory ones. They can be sticky. Slide back once, and only once."

Jean-Paul leads them to an entrance gate and opens the lock. Peter asks how he got the lock code. The good Father shrugs his shoulders, looks up into the sky, and says he has special sources. Zara rolls her eyes as she takes point to ensure the area is clear.

"Peter, in my culture, women follow men. You Westerners say this is a sign of women's submission to men. In my world, the men are merely making sure it was safe for their women. Snakes, scorpions, other nasty lethal animals who live in our wilderness."

And Peter shakes again, as Jean-Paul puts his hand on Zara's shoulder, signaling he will take the lead, because he knows the way. He leads them down planks taking them to the main enclosure, now covered with elaborate tenting to protect the monoliths and stone reliefs. He explains that the enclosures were lettered in the order in which they were found. The biggest is Enclosure D, where he takes them first.

Zara is stunned. She never imagined such wonders existed. Twelve thousand years ago, her ancestors erected these huge temples, six millennia before the Giza Pyramids were built. She stands in awe of the two T-shaped center monoliths towering over five and a half meters high. She sees one with a leaping fox, its teeth bared for attack. Another with what look like three flamingos on top. Did these lovely pink birds once live here? Or was this verification of the story of the Prophet Nuh and the animals of the Ark?

And of course, Peter comes by and tests her faith, saying, "These flamingos, they're proof that aliens were here. How else could these people know what a flamingo looks like?"

Zara puts her hands up, mocks a face of fright at Peter, and says, "Fear an ignorant man more than a lion."

Jean-Paul, truly in his element, points to the animal relief carvings, and the fact each enclosure has different animals as its focus. This one concentrates on reptiles, with thirty-one reliefs, in addition to the seven ducks and geese, a vulture, an ibis, five foxes, and three bulls, actually their ancestors, aurochs. Zara walks among these animals, proud of her heritage.

Pointing to the main T pillars, Jean-Paul explains the line formed by the top of the T points to where Deneb, the tail of the bird star, would have been the polar star around 9,500 to 9,600 BCE. This is why Alexander and he are keen on investigating these temples.

He brings them to a smaller pillar showing a bird holding a round object. Jean-Paul then traces the constellation Cygnus in the bird, saying this was also why they thought the traditions came from this place.

Peter says this could be interpreted as an alien holding a human head, and the background is his spaceship. Jean-Paul counters this could be an

Anunnaki god, the primordial Sumerian gods who often had bird heads. Peter recalls the Book of Enoch, the watchers. This relief shows they were here.

While the two men play with their reliefs and archeology Trivial Pursuit, Zara keeps a constant eye on the satellite surveillance on her MoxWrap, very worried about their situation.

And Peter, looking at one of the central pillars, yells, "I knew it. The watchers were here. These pillars represent the giants. Even Professor Klaus said they were 'beings from another world.'"

He runs over to the side of the western central pillar and points to the side, at a giant with a belt and fox pelt loincloth. On top, he wears a double V-collar and a pendant below. Jean-Paul says that many think this is a bull's head shape on the pendant, given the bull reliefs found elsewhere in the temple.

Peter puts his fingers on his chin. Scratching his head, he says he's seen this before. But for the life of him, he can't remember where.

With Zara following, Jean-Paul leads him to the eastern central pillar to show him another giant with the same belt and fox loincloth standing on a base with seven birds. Peter is speechless. He tries to speak and nothing comes out as his hand points to the top.

Mocking him, Zara says, "Too much alien here for you? Magical alien powers have ripped your tongue out?"

Peter shakes his head and pulls the lambskin sac out of his pocket. He holds the pendant up high in the air, showing it is exactly the same as the pendant atop the giant.

"Peter, where did you get this?" asks Jean-Paul.

Peter looks at him, gagging, and then towards Zara. He mutters, "From her mother."

CHAPTER 30

How easy his task and mine might be in these meetings
that we held if suddenly there was a threat to this
world from some other species from another planet
outside in the universe. We'd forget all the little local
differences that we have between our countries…
——Ronald Reagan

At our meeting in Geneva, the US president said that if
the earth faced an invasion by extraterrestrials, the United
States and the Soviet Union would join forces to repel such
an invasion. I shall not dispute the hypothesis, though I
think it's early yet to worry about such an intrusion…
——Mikhail Gorbachev

2:00 p.m. GMT+3, May 11, 2022
Göbekli Tepe, fifteen kilometers west of Sanliurfa, Turkey

Everything is pardoned the brave, or so says the Kurdish proverb Zara reflects upon as she stares at the pendant Peter is holding up.

She has suffered so much in her life. Suffering she thinks brought upon by herself through her past transgressions, by her straying from the faith of her family, from their traditions. She was bad. In the words of her Catholic classmates at Georgetown, she thought she had atoned for her sins through her suffering. She minored in theology, searching for a deeper sense of world connection, while she majored in economics, searching for a solution for her people.

Her and her cousins' brief Erdil affair with wearing Western clothing a touch too revealing was a trifle of a transgression compared to her following Zengo into the Peshmerga. She bent the lines of her faith, of her grandmother Roza's words of wisdom, only a little, she thought. He did propose marriage. They were practically married.

But as she was to learn more than once, practically is not the same as actually. She gave herself to Zengo, her virginity, her soul, her deepest love, which he enjoyed over and over again, promising they would marry after the next mission. And one mission turned into the next, and the next, and then into never. The passionate love turned into lowly sessions of physical relief on his part. And after the embarrassment, the dishonor, the shame she felt when she was told by the Peshmerga doctor she had a sexually transmitted disease, chlamydia, she beat Zengo silly when he came for his next round of filthy and disingenuous sex.

What was she to do? She could never go home after having eloped, now unmarried and shamed. She would dishonor her family, and she loved them too much to cause them this kind of pain. Worse, how could she in good faith return to practice the faith of her family? She had crossed a line that could never be uncrossed. And she wore that pain on her shoulder so that all would see. "Keep away, all," her pain said to others, "for I am the dishonored. I am a bad girl."

And then she met him. Blue eyes, blond hair, amazing body, just like the magazines she and her "sisters" Rona and Diyar used to ogle. He was an American military advisor, Dan, a civilian working for the military, who romanced her with notions that she could become a Kurdish hero, working for him and hunting down the traitorous Kurds, the Jahsh, who informed on her people to Saddam Hussein's evil Ba'ath monsters, the ones who had killed her father, taken her uncles and grandfather. And she agreed to be trained, to become the invisible assassin in the cause of righting the wrongs done to her family and her people. And in time, she agreed to live in his bed, for unlike Zengo, Dan's passions never ended. She knew love. Finally.

But paradise was never meant to last, at least here on Earth. She cried the day he told her of his transfer to Washington, D.C., to take an assignment at Georgetown University while also working at the State Department. She begged him to take her with him, but he said the conditions with the war limited the number of Iraqis who could immigrate to the US.

She suffered alone in the Peshmerga and took it out on the evil men she hunted, killing indiscriminately. Until one day, the distant relative who had sent her for her high school semester abroad to the UK and France offered her a student visa, airline ticket, tuition, and most importantly, an acceptance to enter Georgetown. Xwedê did hear her prayers.

No more than four hours after checking into her dorm, she set out on her search for Dan. And their affair blossomed to new depths of passion, of intimacy not possible in a war field bed. But no matter how much she hinted, no matter how much she directly asked, the time was not right to be married. She did favors for him, being sent on missions for his job, ones he would not want anyone to know about. She did it for love, hoping that one day he would father her children.

Being so terribly blind in love, it took her three years before she put the tracking skills his people had taught her to use for herself. She tracked him. And the love and trust in her soul evaporated, forever. He had a wife and beautiful children. Little Zara with beauty inside became forever the ugly bad Zara as she went into a dark place and thought about telling this woman about her unfaithful husband. But as she watched the other woman's children, she saw her own childhood, the one she so loved. She could not do that to children, ruin their innocence.

And like the generations of Kurds before her, she learned she had no friends. Only men who had used her. Used her body, not her. She made Dan forever in debt to her, forever afraid of her. For he worked for the State Department. He owed her, and she intended on collecting.

After graduating summa cum laude, she found her people once again embroiled in civil war, this time in Syria. Twice burned, she would not fall in love again, would not let a man touch her again, not her body and for sure not her heart. And a year later, she joined the YPJ, the all-women's fighting arm of the Syrian Kurds, sister unit of the YPG, the men's fighting arm in which her brother Soran now served. Her friends would be women, the faithful mountains, and her weapons.

Eight years ago, she thought God had finally punished her for her misdeeds, her killings, her monumental straying from submission, from modesty, from the words of the Prophet. Although she put those unspeakable months out of her mind, she knew her punishment meant she could never be loved by a man ever again, even if she so wished. God had made sure of that.

And now God is punishing her again. This little boy, this idolizer of yellow mollusks, has been given their family ancestry, their heirloom, their connection to the original Kurds, her legacy. Why did her family do this? Why do they want to punish her? She has been faithful, in submission to Xwedê, ever since her return home four years ago. She is the perfect daughter, other than not marrying and having children. Is this why they told him about her family's legacy of that accursed affliction? Is this why he now holds what is rightfully hers? Because she has no children?

And faster than Jean-Paul can stop her, Zara puts Peter's hand into a wristlock, throws him to the ground, taking the pendant away from him, and plants her foot on the side of his head as he begs for mercy.

"This is mine. And do not ever, ever talk with my family. Ever again. What is theirs is rightfully mine," she asserts as he writhes in complete fear of her. She glares at the priest, whom she increasingly distrusts, and says, "What is their secret is rightfully mine to be told. It is not for you or Alexander to hide from me."

Zara walks away to look at the form of the giant standing five meters high and ponders why her family held back this pendant, which is clearly and exactly engraved on this twelve-thousand-year-old monolith. Jean-Paul helps Peter, who is clearly shaken, to stand. Peter wants to go to her to apologize, but decides being the little boy will win her forgiveness. He puts his hand on the side of the monolith and says, "Kirk to Enterprise. Spock, beam me up immediately. I am under attack by hostile forces. Fire photon torpedoes at this location."

For the first time, Jean-Paul lets out a little snicker. Zara remains unamused, but no longer looks as if she is going to dismember him.

"Jean-Paul, seriously, how are we going to know if anything here is the object in the traditions?" asks Peter. "If the originators had some special relationship to the object, how would one know how it manifests when a descendant is near it?"

He puts his arms around the fox pelt loincloth relief on the monolith and hugs it, saying, "Shouldn't I feel something?"

Zara, annoyed by his silliness, says, "It is easier to make a camel jump a ditch than to make a fool listen to reason. God would not talk through a giant stone to someone as ridiculous as you, Little Boy."

Peter is relieved Zara is back to normal again, for he has come to understand that the term Little Boy is her form of endearment. And he has come to embrace her odd way of showing affection, albeit heavily bruised from it. He walks carefully back over to her and softly says, "Your mother said I should return the pendant to her. You know her much better than I. Will I be in trouble if I will not be able to return it to her?"

Not knowing what to make of her mother's intention other than she did not tell her own daughter anything, she replies, "What did she tell you to do with this?"

"I'm not sure I'm supposed to tell you, but I already violated one of her requests by showing you," Peter replies, putting his hand over his heart. "But she said this was very ancient and had been passed down through generations. It was meant for you to pass to your children."

Zara's face softens as she hears *children*. Her mother must be deeply disheartened knowing her only daughter, her only living child, has failed to find a good husband, twice, and has since said she cannot have children, ever. Maryam must be in a conundrum as to what to do with the family heirlooms and secrets. If this is the case, maybe Zara can forgive her mother. But forgiveness for this little boy? That is yet to be seen.

Peter observes the harsh, angry lines on her face dissolving and finds the courage to say, "She said I shouldn't show this to you unless it was absolutely necessary. And I should give it back to her when I return. I reminded her that you said I was never to return, ever." Peter waits to see if the angry lines return, but Zara only seems puzzled. "She told me she knew I would return."

"Did she say anything else?"

Shuffling his feet, he thinks maybe he should run now while he is ahead. But for sure she is a faster sprinter than he, so he decides to stand his ground and be truthful. "She thinks I can help you."

"Help me? How are you going to help me? You can't even help yourself?" Zara cries in exasperation.

"She thinks I can free you, that my inner strength will be helpful for you," Peter says meekly, unsure if he should duck or offer his hand in friendship.

Zara, unsure if she should feel shunned that her mother did not tell her or confused at what she meant by her words to him, hands the pendant back to Peter. "One can never repay one's debt to one's mother. I love my mother. I trust her implicitly. She meant for you to have this, for now. It is only on loan, as it rightfully belongs to me."

Peter clasps his sweaty hands on hers, and the magic happens again. She senses it. And she does not pull back. They have a special bond, and even more so with this pendant.

While the two hold hands, they are oblivious to two points. First, Jean-Paul has brought down the chest-pack EM detectors, and second, their silhouette perfectly matches the H-shaped reliefs found throughout Göbekli Tepe.

As Zara pulls her hands back, now shivering, scared of what these precious moments of physical contact foretell, she asks Jean-Paul, "What next, priest? Peter finally made a good point. How will we know which of these behemoth stones is the object we search for?"

"We scan these enclosures and let Alexander's tech do the rest," replies the Father. "Logically, we should start with the oldest enclosures first and then span out."

"And if we find nothing in the oldest enclosures, you said there might be at least twenty more," Peter laments, trying to lift the EM detector with little success. "We could spend weeks doing little more than hunting for the proverbial needle in a monolith stack."

That gets Zara's attention, and her fierce freedom fighter face returns. "We do not have that much time. We have a day or two."

And her words rile Peter's "we should be afraid" gene as he says, "But the AC forces are still far away."

Looking at the real-time satellite surveillance on her MoxWrap, Zara replies, "It is not the AC I am worried about. It is the possibility of a radical Daesh offshoot assassin squad that worries me the most."

"A what?" Peter utters, now thinking he should be terribly afraid, as he mounts the EM detector across his chest with Jean-Paul's assistance.

"The Arabic Confederation is a nation now recognized by many countries, following ethics consistent with those of most neighboring countries. But the most radical elements of the former ISIS, the Daesh, did not fully join their national movement. The AC tolerates these radical groups so long as they do not act against the AC. One of these radical group's assassin teams could easily slip through the lines of battle and surgically strike us here. They are exquisitely good at what they do, maybe better than me."

Jean-Paul adjusts the EM detector on Peter and tells him, "You are ready. Touch nothing. Take tiny baby steps very, very slowly around this enclosure, starting on the outside and making a spiral to the inside. This walk should take you two hours and no faster, or we will get a poor read." With that, Jean-Paul takes his pack and goes to Enclosure C while Zara takes a high position and scans the horizon with her binoculars.

Peter is sweltering in the heat, no worse than Death Valley back home, but still death. Zara, who seems to have a built-in air-conditioner under her tunic shirt and headscarf, succumbs to an overwhelming sense of pity for him and brings him a constant supply of cold water. *That is love if he has ever seen it*, Peter muses as a way to distract himself from the pain of carrying this device.

When Peter is finally finished, he gently lets himself sit down in the center of the enclosure and peer up at his T-shaped alien giants. Zara excuses herself for Asr prayer, the afternoon one, and Jean-Paul comes over from Enclosure

C. Much to Peter's chagrin, Jean-Paul says they need to return the EM units to the truck for data processing as well as security in case of an attack, neither of which are popular concepts for Peter.

Sitting under the shade of the truck, Peter asks what he thinks is a safe question. "What are we doing for dinner? Did we bring a microwave?"

"Don't look at me. I don't cook for men," Zara whips back.

"Does that imply you cook for women?" replies Peter.

"In my old unit, we cooked for each other, and yes, we were women. I am not your domestic servant. I am the one who is going to get you to your imaginary object and maybe save your silly life in the process. So you need to cook for me."

And the peacekeeper, Jean-Paul, intercedes lest they starve this night. "I believe it is God's plan we prosper and find this object, so I will cook. But, Zara, unless you want reconstituted freeze-dried gunk, someone needs to hunt and clean some local game. And, if you could be so kind, please show Peter where to find some edible plants."

And three headless rabbits and some local greens later, they sit satiated around their camp. Peter asks Zara why all three rabbits had their heads shot cleanly off. She shrugs her shoulders and says there is something in her that does not find them so cute. And so she shoots them just behind their cute wiggling noses. She points out that her AK-74 is not a hunting weapon, but a blunt instrument of death. And so, their heads are blown off. Peter is seriously not feeling her warm and fuzzy side, if she has one at all.

After evening prayer, Zara offers to take the first watch, with Jean-Paul to relieve her at two a.m. She watches Peter toss, turn, flail his arms, and mouth something unsaid. If the object is talking to him, then they must be close. If the object is supposed to calm him, they are doomed.

And so passes the next day in the same fashion. Zara stands guard as well as attending to her five daily prayers. The men scan six more enclosures, which nearly kills Peter, who is exhausted by dinner. And so they eat reconstituted freeze-dried gunk with a couple more headless rabbits. The night passes, with Zara taking the later watch, again witnessing Peter's nightly distress.

A third day passes, and the men complete only five enclosures as Peter collapses after doing two. Zara comes to Jean-Paul to assess the situation, about which Jean-Paul has no good news. The scans are not interpretable, meaning either they do not have enough data yet to discern the object, or the object is not here.

Zara shakes her head, saying their time is running out. The AC forces have broken through to the southern side of Sanliurfa and are proceeding to the western side, where they are. The air campaign is not favoring the Turks due to the superiority of the AC's Chinese-made advanced fighters. The US has decided not to launch their advanced fighters for fear of Russian intervention defending the Kurds.

Jean-Paul walks Zara away from Peter and says, "I share your apprehension over the situation. We do not have enough time to be sure that this site does or does not have the object." He looks her in the eyes and says, "There is another way that could help us."

And with wide eyes, Zara shakes her head in protest. "No. I told you and Alexander, no. I am not that kind of woman. Fly Mei here."

And the fourth day passes, with the same results. Five more enclosures, a dead-tired Peter, and nothing conclusive. And Zara shakes her head all day, watching the battle through her binoculars and the live satellite surveillance. She has taken the precaution of setting up perimeter sensors to give them some advance notice of any small infiltration teams.

Again, she and Jean-Paul have the same conversation, and she replies, "Priest, I cannot tell you why what you ask is not possible. It just is not. I cannot do what Mei could do. Not only is it against my faith, it is just not possible for me to do." And she walks away to perform her Isha evening prayer before taking the first watch.

In response to Zara's complaint a couple of nights ago, Peter decided to sleep far from the truck so as not to disturb the others. Zara stands watch in sight of him as he undergoes his nightly routine. This time he hits a rock and screams. Her latent motherly instinct tells her she should attend to his pain, lest he attract an assassin team. He sits whimpering with his injured hand next to his chest. She takes it and sees just a little scrape, no wounds, no bone breakage. What a little boy he is, worse than her baby lambs. And she spits on the scrape and rubs it with her palm.

And the magical something between them starts. She feels the peace emanate from her palm. He puts his other hand on hers and rubs. She senses the peace move up her arm, up her neck. She looks at him, a wounded child, and she decides to try what Mei did. She puts her thumb on his forehead, drives it in, and grinds, for her fingers lack the delicate softness of Mei.

"Ow! That hurts," Peter yells. "It's not supposed to hurt."

Zara puts her hand over his mouth to shut him up. He is going to wake up the dead at this ancient temple, or worse, they will be the dead if he alerts an assassin team. Emulating what Mei did, she puts her palm on his shirt over his heart and applies pressure, firmly rubbing it.

He screams again, under her hand cupping his mouth. "I'm not having a heart attack. That's CPR you're doing. The kind that breaks sternums. Ow!"

Peter puts his hands over his crotch, deeply afraid of what she might do next, and whimpers, "Please, I beg of you, not down there. My mother wants me to keep them intact for her grandchildren."

She's had it. She tried. She was not made for this. *Give me someone to kill,* she thinks, as that is all she is good for. She spits at him in her disgust over her own inability. He spits back. As she uses her hand to remove his saliva, she senses it again. She gets it, finally. And with Peter looking at her in fear, imagining what horrible things she is going to do this time, she leans into him, kisses his forehead, and then licks it softly, drawing circle after circle with her soft tongue.

Peter leans his head into her scarf and inhales through his nose. And her pheromones begin their work. The fog that permeates his night brain begins to dissipate, and he ducks as they come roaring out, dozens and dozens of wild boars. From his dream, he remembers fighting one with a spear. And then he remembers a woman wearing the pendant, praying at the object in the middle of the T pillars.

They are both awakened by the shrill of Zara's security systems. She checks her MoxWrap and says, "We have to run. Satellite-guided munitions are coming down on our heads."

They get no more than thirty steps and the bombs strike the grounds around them. Monoliths split and shatter, spitting out shards all around them. In sheer panic, Peter crumples into a sitting fetal position. Zara, unable to get him standing, drags him to the truck, where the priest is kneeling in prayer. She yells, "Priest, this is no time to ask for God's help. Help me get him into the truck."

The blast debris from the temple starts raining down on their heads, pelting the truck as Zara gets into the driver's seat and bolts out of the parking lot, her foot to the floorboard as more munitions explode all around them and throughout the entire complex.

Jean-Paul looks back and sees that Göbekli Tepe is no longer.

CHAPTER 31

Strive to discover the mystery before life is taken from you.
If while living you fail to find yourself, to know yourself,
How will you be able to understand
The secret of your existence when you die?
—Farīd ud-Dīn Attar,
twelfth-century Persian Muslim poet

9540 BCE
Site of modern-day Göbekli Tepe

It has been thirty-five sun cycles that they have known peace at last. The daughters of Nanshe have fulfilled her vision—bountiful food and years of safety lead to the desire to search for higher sense of meaning. The villages in the plains below have blossomed, as have the numerous farms. Hundreds upon hundreds of people now live within a day's walk of the monuments, which serve not only as the storyboard for all time, warning future generations of the dangers of the giants, but, in their magnificence, to inspire the awe that has led the villagers and farmers to come worship with the sacred twins, Sarpani and Zirbani, and their children.

The forever faithful and obedient Ki, still never having heard the voice, never experiencing its peace, beauty, and harmony, honors her mother's wishes, her father's wishes, and teaches the three dozen grandchildren of her, her brother, and her twin sisters. They range from toddlers to her two granddaughters, Iriana, twenty cycles, from her son Parcza, and Vatlana, seventeen cycles, from her daughter Ramana. These two young women have listened to her as she had to her mother, faithful and obedient. And as Ki held a special place in Nanshe's heart, so do these two oldest granddaughters with Ki.

Iriana and Ramana, her dearest and most obedient. Similar to Ki in her youth, they are not married yet, as they have not found men who live up to the standards they have expected of their lives, although many dozens of marriage offers have come and been turned down. Someday, they hope, the right man will come.

Until then, they follow their grandmother Ki's lead—pray with the family, honor the object and those who hear the voice, and go on the hunt. Ki, seventy-three cycles of age, still takes them. She is still young at heart, but age has lessened her strength and agility. No longer with great bow strength or speed of firing, her aim and accuracy remain as sharp as ever.

Sun cycles ago, Ki turned leadership over to her two younger twin sisters, Zirbani and Sarpani, as she focused on teaching this new generation. Clearly there is a split between their children. The ones who suffer the dreams or hear the voice, they are much more attuned to memorizing the family oral tradition from her grandfather Parcza. The ones, like her, who do not dream or hear, can only obediently pray in faithfulness. Aside from Iriana and Vatlana, the other unafflicted grandchildren think their grandmother Ki is being excessive in asking their obedience to some silly words, as only peace has reigned in their lifetime, in their parents' lifetime. None of their villager friends are made to do such things.

Ki teaches the lore of her aunt, Illyana. The strength, the will, the benevolence she embodied—or that is what she was taught by her parents to believe. Deep inside her, as she ages and nears her own death, she trembles with the dilemma her father faced. If a loved one were faced with a life worse than death, would you kill them out of mercy?

She saw how much her father suffered and agonized over his indecision and ultimate decision. And somehow this agony has passed itself on to his descendants who suffer the dreams. And so she teaches them the lore of Illyana so they can come to their own peace through the moral lessons and dilemmas of her life and death.

The lore of Illyana's name has been given to Sarpani's oldest granddaughter, the oldest child from her daughter Tallia. As Ki's mother had said, to preserve the ability to commune with the voice, with the dreams, they would need to make the hard choice of telling the afflicted to marry among their kin. And so, Tallia was married to her cousin, one of the older sons of Zirbani. And the wisdom of Nanshe comes true again as the younger Illyana possesses the strongest touch, the strongest bond with the voice of any in her generation. She will become the successor to her grandmother, Sarpani, as the group's new spiritual leader.

But even though the villagers come to embrace the faith that Nanshe started and Sarpani and Zirbani continue to teach, they are skeptical whether the next generations of children will share the same wisdom. They worry about falsehoods, having seen shamans come and go. They demand to see proof that the children who have the dreams, who hear the voice, are truly procreating together and their children are the rightful heirs to their faith.

After long debates between the daughters of Nanshe, they reached the compromise of having the procreative moments of the twins' daughters be public. Starting with Sarpani's oldest daughter, Tallia, her choice of husband was made public. The demonstration of her ability to comfort him of his dreams was public. His recounting of the dreams was public. And their mating to create Illyana was public.

Ki, the keeper of Nanshe's modesty, ensured they were clothed during these public exhibitions, but today is the day for Illyana to choose her mate among the two oldest grandsons of Sarpani, her cousins. The elder villagers have decreed they must see the touching, the bonding, the flesh to flesh, in order for them to believe. Ki thinks they are simply corrupt and lewd. Old men looking to satisfy their vices, only a touch better than the giants, but without the violence. But Zirbani, knowing the primacy of creating peace among the lands, agrees to allow her granddaughter to publicly expose her top to her prospective husbands, with their garments partially obscuring the view.

And Ki spends time before this ceremony readying her special granddaughter, Illyana, who truly has embraced the wisdom and benevolence of her namesake. As Ki dresses her, she puts around her neck the pendant her aunt Illyana wore when Nanshe met her, the one Ki took back from the giant Doroda. Ki tells Illyana this should be her reminder of both the lore of her great-great-aunt and the dangers of becoming complacent. She will need to lead spiritually with both in mind, for which this pendant will forever be her reminder. The circle and crescent.

And Zirbani and Sarpani come to bring their heiress out for her choosing ceremony. Zirbani whispers to her grandchild, asking if she is comfortable with what she must do in public. Zirbani assures her that if she is not, there is no shame, as they have lived the respect and modesty as taught by Nanshe. Zirbani will push back on the village elders for what Illyana feels is right. Illyana, showing her strength of will and nobility, says she will proceed, as creating long-lasting peace is why they were so gifted. And she is led by the twins to the ceremony.

On this hilltop, where the voice said to Nanshe that this was their final destination, the family and some extra-faithful villagers, who assist with daily worships, have made homes. In the center of the small village is the first monument Nanshe and Ki designed. Next to it is the second, larger one that Ki designed more fully, telling their family's oral traditions as best as can be done in pictures alone.

Illyana emerges from her home, greeted by her mother, Tallia, and they walk to the first monument, where resides the object. Around the pillars on one side are the twins, their husbands, their children and grandchildren. All of the afflicted in one area. On the other side, the elders of the surrounding villages, or the lewd men, according to Ki, have clustered to witness the ceremony. Outside the perimeter stand Ki's and An's families, the unafflicted. And on the hilltop, more than a thousand villagers and farmers have gathered, as following the ceremony will be the biggest feast to happen since the marriage of Tallia decades ago.

The young Illyana takes her place, sitting atop the black object. The older of her two cousins, her prospective husbands, comes forward and takes her hands into his. She takes his shirt off and rubs his chest, then his forehead, and finally his loins, which become visibly aroused. She takes off her headscarf and holds his head into her neck and hair, and he inhales deeply as she strokes his hair. Minutes later, she pulls back and opens her upper garment to him as he rubs her chest, her heart, her forehead, and then her loins. She pulls his head to her breasts and tells him to breathe her essence. And he begins to recount his dream.

As this is happening, the sun is blotted by dark clouds coming overhead. Ki looks up. She has seen this before. And this should not be happening for a wondrous ceremony such as this—only the warmth of the skies, the clearness of air, and the joy of the moment, not dark and angry clouds. She stands up on one of the lower pillars and scans the horizon. And there they are.

Over the top of the hill, giants have silently snuck up on the group, surrounding the crowds. There must be more than a hundred of them. How? Ki ponders in despair. And a dozen of them are slowly making their way through the throngs of villagers to the ceremony area. Ki comes down from the pillar and gathers her and An's sons, telling them to get the weapons and be prepared to take the object away from here. Ki discreetly gets to her twin sisters and lets them know what is happening, that they should ready their children to flee. The afflicted grandchildren who see the visions, who hear the voice, must be protected at all cost.

Ki frets inside for the first time in her life. Her sons return with bows, arrows, and spears just as the giants near the inner ceremony area, and they arm the twins, their sons, her children, and An's family.

Ki says to her family that today is a good day to die. But not for the afflicted children, as they must survive. Her sons understand fully what she is willing to do, and they pledge their allegiance to defending the rest of the family. Her most beloved granddaughters, Iriana and Vatlana, cry, saying to their grandmother that it is not a good day for her to die. Ki, ready for her finest fight, says her time has come, and she is ready to accept it.

One giant steps forward, wearing a pendant that looks like a bull's head on a double-stranded ribbon. Ki recognizes the signature belt and fox pelt loincloth. And then she does a double take, as to the left of this giant is a woman older than her, with breasts and loins exposed. It is Sama, the former wife of Narn, and the mother of Zirra, the lead giant, her cousin.

As the crowd gets agitated, Illyana stops the ceremony, covering her breasts and head. She has only heard her grandmother's stories, but these are the giants. She kneels and prays on the object as the skies darken further, as if the anger and hatred of the giants fuel them with fury.

"I have come for the coward who abandoned me," Zirra decrees. "The weakling who could not face having a son so superior to him." He holds up Sama's hand and says, "My mother did not deserve such a gutless animal to mate with. And so I have sired her children as well as taken my slaves from villages from all corners to sire my children, as is my right from the stars." And he points to the thirty-plus giant men who wait behind them.

And as he speaks, Zirbani and Sarpani instruct their children to lead their grandchildren away from the ceremony area. In the opposite direction, Ki and An's family slowly move away. But Illyana and her two prospective husbands remain at the object as she continues to pray.

Nirra scans the crowd and says, "I will spare these people if my father comes to face his disgrace. To abandon a child is a great evil, even for you slave animals, and justice must be met."

As Narn begins to come forward, Ki quickly leaves her family to intercept him, telling him not to go. They can fight. He tells her he has eighty-six sun cycles of age. He is ready to join his sister, who is buried near the object. She relents to his logic. If his sacrifice will spare the village, then it is the right thing to do. His death will have served a purpose. Ki says then he needs to buy them time to get the grandchildren out of the area to safety.

And Narn comes forward and gives a soliloquy to buy time. And Nirra takes the bait and gives a soliloquy back. As this goes on, An escorts his family, only to be blocked by giants, the same for the twins, and the same for Ki's family. As Ki goes to help her family, Narn kneels in front his wife, Sama, for he never remarried, and professes that his love for her never ended. She sneers, and Nirra raises his axe and cuts his mother's husband in half.

Next to Nirra is another giant who comes forward and speaks, for these giants suffer giant egos and must hear themselves roar in might. He is Arnada, half-brother of Nirra, the oldest son of Doroda, the son of Tureal, the grandson of the King Anneal, great-great-grandson of those who are descendant from the stars. By his right, he has come to fulfill his father's right, the right to have the woman who killed his father. And Ki, stalled with her grandchildren and daughter in front of giants, hears his request. She bows her head, knowing her own sacrifice is perhaps their only salvation, as did her uncle. Her life for the lives of her family, her children, her sisters' children. And she goes back to the ceremony area, weapons in hand.

Ki presents herself. She cries out so all can hear, "I am the great Ki, killer of giants. I killed your father, Doroda. I killed your grandfather Tureal. And I will slaughter all of you unless you leave now."

Arnada remembers this woman from that day, when she held his father's pendant and loincloth high. He was only a boy then, but she is one not to be underestimated. And he decides his half-brother was wrong as he raises his spear in the air and decrees that although Nirra promised not to attack the villagers, he did not. And with that, the carnage ensues.

Ki watches on one side as her twin sisters and their children fight their way through giants to save the afflicted grandchildren. She cringes as her brother An, who never could fight, dies defending his family. And she watches with pride her son, Parcza, her daughter Ramana, and her precious granddaughters, Iriana and Vatlana, shoot down giant after giant, clearing the way for her other grandchildren. But they are fighting the tide. There are just too many giants to kill. And to Ki's dismay, her niece Tallia, mother of Illyana, is taken by Nirra, too far away for Ki to stop his inevitable violation of her.

As Ki goes to save her family, she sees in the center of all this the sacred Illyana continuing to pray on the object, her cousins vainly trying to defend her. She hesitates, torn between her own family and her obedience to her mother and father to defend the object and those who are closest to it.

And as happened to her father, in that moment of hesitation, her son and daughter are killed, leaving Iriana and Vatlana alone to defend their siblings. In that moment near the object, Arnada throws one of Illyana's cousins a dozen paces and pins the other cousin to the ground with his spear to witness what he will do to the girl atop the stone.

Ki is torn. She prays for mercy on all their souls, helpless as she watches her granddaughters fight the fight she has taught them, then closes her eyes and points her arrow at Arnada. Two shots into each leg and he falls to the ground, releasing Illyana. Ki runs to her grandniece and implores her to flee with her cousin; for the future of all those who need her vision, her wisdom, she needs to procreate in safety. She takes the spear out of her grandnephew and escorts them through the chaos, clearing a path for them to escape.

And then she hears her most beloved granddaughters scream out for help, scream in terror of what is about to happen to them, for they have heard the stories of what these monsters do to women. She turns and sees Iriana and Vatlana being held by giants, about to take their star-given rights to them. Her heart snaps. She has failed to protect her family. Images of her aunt Illyana appear in front of her, the ones her father was tormented by. "Kill me. If you love me, kill me." With tears in her eyes, she aims, fires, aims, fires. As always, her arrows pierce their targets. She prays that God will show mercy on their souls. And hers.

Bash. She is knocked to the ground. She turns and struggles to see what is happening. Arnada has grabbed her feet, and she is being held upside down, just as Doroda did to her sister-in-law, Sama, on the other side of the lake. She is not so old he cannot take his pleasure with her before he kills her, he says to her. Ki looks up and sees the skies have become even darker. She now knows what Illyana was doing on the object.

Using her best femininity, she suggests to Arnada he should desecrate their object of worship by taking her atop it. He carries her as if she were dead game to the object, where she points to the intoxicating brews of her dead uncle, which surround the object in vats. They should drink some as well as splash it around the object, as this will enhance his pleasure and her ability to perform for him. He falls for it as he drinks and breaks vats over the object, then throws her atop and proceeds to mount her. As Ki prays, she senses the flashes of light begin in the skies. She finds her knife, and before he can stop her, she slices through her neck.

Flash. Boom. Flash. Boom. Over and over again. Twenty times and more.

And she sees blue light. Bright, beautiful, full of peace. Nanshe comes forth and welcomes her, saying that she has been so faithful and obedient all her life. It is time for her to know the voice. And Iriana and Vatlana are there, thanking her for showing them her mercy, her compassion as they take her hands to lead her onwards.

The energy from the angry skies strikes the object over two dozen times. Lightning can strike more than twice in the same spot when the right person prays for it. The flash fire from the brew and the power of these energy bolts sends shock waves out, ripping the tops off the two great pillars around the object and flattening all around for a hundred paces.

And the giants, having heard Ki's decrees of being able to kill all giants, turn in fear of the black magic these people must practice around this black object of great evil. The remaining giants flee with their new slaves in tow.

The next day, the twins return with their surviving sons. They bury Ki, An, and Narn next to their mother Nanshe, and they load the object, still steaming from the anger the day before, onto an aurochs sled. Sarpani has said they must honor the voice and her mother, both of whom guided them to be near the fertile plains below, and they would find a new resting place for the object on the mountains across the valley.

She prays over the graves of her family, Ki, An, Narn, Nanshe, and says that one day, if they cannot create peace in these lands, their descendants' grandchildren of many times over may need to bury the object until an age arrives where peace may reign and mankind is ready to hear the voice again.

CHAPTER 32

Consult not your fears but your hopes and your dreams.
Think not about your frustrations, but about your unfulfilled
potential. Concern yourself not with what you tried and
failed in, but with what it is still possible for you to do.

—Pope John XXIII

5:00 a.m. GMT+3, May 22, 2022
Mountain ridge, forty kilometers northwest of the former Göbekli Tepe

Jean-Paul, the archeologist, a man with a love of historical religious sites, watches as Göbekli Tepe smolders on the horizon. One of the few monuments to have withstood twelve thousand years of mankind's checkered history intact, destroyed in a matter of minutes. He prays for forgiveness from the Lord for his transgressions. His pride led him to help Alexander find the object here. His pride led whoever it was to obliterate the oldest religious site in the world. He prays more.

Peter sits on his hands in the backseat of the truck, too petrified to look where they were, too ashamed to show his face. For the second time in a few days, he crumbled under pressure, frozen, paralyzed, petrified. He tries to rationalize that his reaction was what most normal people would have had done given the circumstances, but another thought becomes crystal-clear. He wants out. The temple is gone. The object destroyed. He is of no use here in the middle of the next world war gone crazy.

And Zara, furious at the world, parks her truck and walks around it as the priest opens his door. Her beautiful truck, custom-painted her favorite shade of red, scraped, dented, torn, and shattered, all because she lost her mind, her attention, her focus, playing mama to that waste of a human being cowering in the backseat. Kicking him would be useless, so she walks over to the priest and kicks him instead.

"Priest, what were you praying for back there at the temple? Did you pray for two dozen one-thousand-pound munitions to crater that temple of yours?" Zara yells.

"Certainly not. I was praying for your souls."

"Could you not have prayed faster and gotten my truck started so it would not have suffered so?"

He gingerly exits her truck. And Zara softens, "I am so sorry, Jean-Paul. I did not know you had been hit. Are you bleeding? Anything broken? Can you stand?"

Jean-Paul limps around and looks at her. Not the serene good Father any more. His face is wrinkled and haggard. "Thank you, Zara. The only thing broken is my integrity. I have sinned in this mission and let my pride, my arrogance, my ego negate a cardinal rule to do no harm to mankind's sites of historic faith. We have lost too many important religious sites in this region. The former ISIS destroyed over two dozen important religious sites. They destroyed Mosul's libraries' non-Islamic books dating back to 5000 BCE. Our heritage, our culture, the origins of our beliefs all destroyed. And I am no better than they."

Realizing her venting over her truck was only her surrogate for her frustrations over this whole mission, her desire not to die in vain over some fool's errand to find a rock that talks to aliens, and deep inside, her fear of what is happening between her and Peter, she calms down. "You must understand, Jean-Paul, those who destroyed those treasures, the Salafi, were an ultraconservative movement who strictly interpreted and enforced *tawhid*, monotheism, and sought to rid our world of *shirk*, polytheism. My jests with you on these subjects reflected their reality, one that destroyed so much of our world's finest heritage, including those of my faith."

She shakes her head, thinking about something else, a question she has asked for so long. "I do not think we worship the same God, you, me, or them. I only know that Peter worships no god, and he is lost. How can the same God lead to so many different, disparate, and conflicting outcomes?"

And Jean-Paul gently and carefully kneels and prays for her lost soul.

In the truck, Peter is fishing on his MoxWrap for buses, taxis, trains, and planes that could take him home from this desolate place of bombs, scorpions, and wild boars. No luck—he is stuck here. He searches for his photos of Sarah. Had he just shown her the type of love she was looking for, maybe he would not have been in this situation, alone and soon to be dead. As he searches his photo archives, he spots it. The answer.

"Jean-Paul. Jean-Paul, the parchment. It's the answer," Peter yells, leaping out of Zara's poor battered truck. "Look again. The Hs, they're the same ones we saw all over Göbekli Tepe. An H just like the one above the giant with Zara's pendant, two people holding hands. I saw this woman in my dream last night. She prayed at the object, surrounded by wild boar."

Jean-Paul looks again on his MoxWrap at the same parchment pictures and says, "That would be Enclosure C, populated by dozens of boar reliefs." He ponders the third figure, pointing at a sixty-degree angle away from the tail of the bird star.

"You may have something, Peter," says Jean-Paul, who puts a reassuring arm around him. "Peter, you must remember your strengths. You are not here because of your behavior under fire. Most people would have reacted like you with bombs exploding all around them. Your reactions were normal. You are here because of your ability to do things like this, pulling together many disparate ideas, thoughts, and your dreams. In this, you are rare and valuable. You must always tell yourself this."

And the warmth Peter needed to regain his inner spirit is sprinkled on his soul like a refreshing rain in the desert.

"Jean-Paul, what does the parchment's cuneiform say?" Peter asks.

"It is a very ancient form of Akkadian dialect. We could not translate it. It may be coded."

"What do you mean, coded?" asks Peter.

"The characters may have been scrambled. If it is, it is not a simple scramble, as our computing power could not discern the pattern," answers Jean-Paul.

"Priest, your EM unit has been damaged," Zara yells from the back of her truck.

"Yes, I saw the damage. The other one is still functional."

She walks over and says, "I have lost our perimeter sensors, and my security base unit is damaged as well. We are not in a good situation here." She stares into his eyes and says, "Let us be blunt here, the mission is a failure. Those thousand-pound munitions could penetrate three to four meters into the ground, maybe more in soft soil. If there was an object, it is now destroyed."

Jean-Paul looks at his MoxPad+ and replies, "I am not so sure. If Peter's dream was right, the object was in Enclosure C. If it was, I can verify how its presence there manifested on the EM signatures. His parchment might suggest the object was moved. That third figure is pointing for a reason. Perhaps the cuneiform contains the answer. *Mais hélas*, we cannot translate it. *Merde*." And the good priest, swearing in French, belies the depths of his frustrations.

"Then we are lost," says Zara. "We should abandon the search, as this ridge we are on will soon become the battle line between the Kurds and the AC. Jean-Paul, who do you think bombed us? Twice now, once at Siirt airport and again here. I looked at Alexander's historical satellite records, and five different nations had aircraft in the region at the time of the temple's destruction."

"Given our conversation before, one might think the AC has been influenced by their ultraorthodox factions to destroy it as a non-Islamic religious site. But I do not think so. Someone does not want us to find the object."

Zara turns to look at the horizon, towards the smoking ruins of Göbekli Tepe. "Do you think it was Alexander?"

Jean-Paul was going to give a reflexive answer, but stopped to ponder her proposition. "If he did, why would he send us all the way here, only to bomb us?"

With eyes squinted, Zara replies, "Maybe he has already processed your information and knew the object was there. Think about it—who would be able to decipher exactly where we are at any time? He could have easily fielded a second or third team analyzing our data and your EM feeds. He could easily call up the Americans, the Russians, and have them both bomb us."

"Yours is a special relationship with him. Why would you distrust him?" asks the good Father.

"I learned the hard way to trust no one. And so have my people," says Zara. "And for the record, I do not trust you either. Why would the pope let you leave the Order? I can easily see that your interest here is to remove the object from world's access and secure it for the Vatican. Know I have my eyes on your eyes."

Trying to make light of the situation, Jean-Paul blinks slowly and jests, "I am deeply relieved you do not think His Eminence ordered the bombing of an important religious site."

"But I do think we need to be very careful in our use of any connective tech," says Zara. "I will give you until tomorrow to examine your data. Only pull the satellite EM data you need, and do not allow your devices to interact with Alexander's fuller system. We can trust no one."

Zara looks at Peter, who is fixated on his MoxWrap and says, "If I had to bet, the Chinese used the AC to bomb us both times. If it's not Alexander, then the person who would have the most access to his systems, other than the two of us, is Mei."

Jean-Paul raises his hand, ready to defend his Chinese protégée, but Zara stops his interjection. "I know you think the world of her, for more noble reasons than does our silly Peter. But let us be objective. How do we exclude her from being the mole? And if she is the mole, is not Peter's family in danger?"

Respecting her logic, Jean-Paul reflects and says, "You did not tell Peter, did you, that she was assigned the security detail for her family?"

"No, I thought knowing so might have distracted him. He has the most difficult time staying focused to begin with."

"Then we should contact her," says Jean-Paul. "She may possess more information on the parchment, which would help us determine if the object was moved from Göbekli Tepe. And we can scan her to determine if she is any threat to his family."

Zara smiles at the good priest. She likes how his mind works. Same as hers. She calls for Peter to come over.

"Remember when I told you a trusted team had been dispatched to ensure your family's security?" asks Zara.

Peter nods yes, so anxious to end this mission, he would say yes to anything.

"Mei is leading this team. Someone who you trust implicitly. I am going to contact her to assess the situation there. Jean-Paul will ask her about the parchment. And you can briefly talk with your family. Here are the strict operating rules. No discussion of the object, other than that we are searching for it. No discussion of our location at Göbekli Tepe or otherwise. I have activated location obfuscation tech so they will not be able to find us. Violate any of these and you will lead us to our deaths. Bombs could fall again within a matter of minutes of you slipping up. Can you follow these guidelines to the letter, Little Boy?"

Peter looks to Jean-Paul, then back to Zara. He takes a deep breath and nods yes.

"Okay, here we go. Jean-Paul, ready on scanning her responses," Zara commands.

Using her MoxWrap, Zara connects with Mei, only showing her a headshot with a view of the sky above to hide their location. "Mei, are you in a secure place to talk?"

With no makeup or earrings, simply in a black t-shirt and ponytail braided with a metallic design, Mei answers, "We are very secure here."

Zara asks, "How is the op going there? Peter was fretting about his family."

"I was worried about you three. I saw the bombings near the target. Are you intact? Is the temple intact?"

With her mission face on, Zara replies, "Mei, we believe we have been compromised. As such, I cannot discuss our details, other than that the three of us are very much alive." She looks at Jean-Paul, who is monitoring Mei's biometrics, voice, and body movements against her norms in his database. He gives a thumbs-up.

Zara asks, "Is there anything abnormal on your end? Is there any reason to believe we have been compromised from yours and Peter's time in San Francisco? From his family?"

With an equally serious face, Mei responds, "Negative. Only Harlan, myself, Alexander, and Jean-Paul had access to Peter's interview. Harlan is on a special assignment. His job interviewing possible affliction candidates came to an abrupt halt when we verified Peter. Have only talked to Alexander once, confirming our security details here were in place. I'm with Peter's grandfather and his sister. I've checked out the doctor who was overly interested in Peter as well. She may be legit. However, she is not to be found, so I'm not completely sure of her. Something about her going to Boston for her book. She had access to the parchment. I have a team in Cambridge following her every move. My other security detail is with his mother. Everyone's fine."

Without a flinch, Zara goes for the jugular. "Mei, who did you talk to in China? What is it they want from us?"

Her eyes squinting and mouth grimacing, Mei responds, "You do not trust me, do you?"

"I do not trust anyone right now. Only Peter. He is too silly, innocently so, to be up to anything," says Zara, putting her hand up to shush Peter's objections. She looks at Jean-Paul, who gives another thumbs-up. "Answer my question, who did you talk with?"

"My mother, about her dress my tailor is making. My father, about fixing the car I bought him. And my doorman, about holding my mail," Mei replies. "Are you happy now?"

Jean-Paul gives another thumbs-up and taps his MoxWrap to switch the screen to him. "Hello, Mei. Were you able to interview the grandfather?"

"Hi, Jean-Paul. I miss you. Yes, I have. He won't talk to anyone except Peter. Not even to his granddaughter. Patriarchal bigotry at its finest. All he wants is for me to demonstrate my command of the algorithms on him." Peter's eyes bug out when he hears that.

"Did he allow you to examine the parchment?" Jean-Paul asks.

"Yes, I did a scan of both sides as you asked. I found inscriptions hidden on the back side. Likely wine vinegar ink to make the writing invisible to the normal spectrum," Mei replies, putting the inscriptions up on her MoxWrap screen. "As you requested, I didn't send them, out of concern about the security breach."

"Perfect. It's a shift code key, as we suspected. A very complex and sophisticated one for that era. Good work, Mei, as always," the good Father affirms. "I will switch you to Peter, who is anxiously waiting to talk with you again."

Zara holds Peter's MoxWrap to show only his head and the sky and taps his device to show Mei, who has put her beautiful shining smile back on for Peter.

"Oh, Mei," exclaims Peter, who is near teary-eyed. "How I've missed you. I wish so terribly you were here…" And Zara steps on his foot before he can say where. Bathing in warmth at seeing Mei again, Peter confesses, "I'm ready to come back and sit next to you, editing your genetics history papers."

"Peter, my special, special banana slug man. I miss you too. I'm heading back to your grandfather's room. I have a surprise for you waiting with him." Mei winks with that disarming smile of hers, which melts Peter's heart.

Now very curious, Peter says, "Surprise? Who could it be? My mother?" And then he imagines Sarah. Oh, how awkward would that be? And on the screen comes Michaela next to Mei, dressed in the same black t-shirt and braided ponytail. He notices his sister's mark, though. They both feature metallic designs interwoven in their hair. So very Michaela.

"Hi there, big bro. Your friend here is a real pip. How did you meet someone who's so connected with the Shanghai-Paris Fashion Institute? She got the university to give me credit interning with her tailors here in Chinatown. She brought me here in that fancy jet of hers." And Peter is relieved to see his little sister is doing so well and seemingly taken care of by his Mei.

"Why such a long face, big bro?" asks Michaela.

At first glancing at Zara, then back at the ground, Peter says, "I missed another opportunity to be heroic. To be brave."

"You're being too humble again. You were my hero and always will be," says Michaela with a beaming face. "You should know your Mrs. Harrison dropped by. She says she is doing fine. Her husband agreed to amend their divorce papers so she doesn't need to pay alimony to him. Funny what being charged with attempted rape does to a man's perspective. You are her hero. Oh, yes. Her daughter decided to accept UC Santa Cruz's offer. Personally, I can't see why, but she was so impressed by what that school did for you, her hero, she said it was an obvious choice for her."

Peter asks, "Mei, our mother, she's safe too?"

"Yes, and she is so delicious," says Mei. "Just like you and your wonderful sister here. I'm more concerned about my security detail than her. She's been trying to coax them into giving her leg massages, and they are scared. Not that your mother isn't attractive. They're worried about being worn out by her."

Zara finally snickers. She is starting to get the picture about this Gollinger family.

And then Peter hears his pappy in the background. He asks Mei, "Would it be possible for me to have a private conversation with my grandfather?"

And Mei, still hurting from having so much fun, says, "Of course, Mr. Peter Gollinger. I have not had so much fun in my life until I met you and your gorgeous little banana slugs. Your sister and I will leave the room. I would like to say goodbye to you after you finish with Pappy. What a cute name you and your sister gave him." And with that, she transfers him to Pappy's MoxWrap.

"Peter, my boy," says Pappy, taking his oxygen mask off. "Your little friend is perfect."

"Pappy, you look good. Mei said you've been asking for her to demonstrate her command of her comforting skills. What exactly did you ask her to do?"

"My boy, nothing she has not done for you," Pappy answers slyly.

"That's terrible, Pappy. She's young enough to be your granddaughter. You should be ashamed of yourself."

"Peter, my boy, when you get to be my age, you must get your little pleasures in life any way, anytime you can. The end could come, and before you know it, you missed out," his grandfather answers sagely.

Zara is just smiling now. The apple doesn't fall far from the tree in this family either. And Peter is more assured now that she is smiling.

"Pappy, listen to me. This is very serious. Did you tell Mei anything you haven't told me?" Peter asks with a concerned face. Zara nods that is the right question, as she still does not trust her, despite Jean-Paul's high science metrics.

"No, my boy. Those things are between the men in our family who suffer the dreams."

"Good, Pappy. Good. Remember when you told me about what you and your father did during the war?"

"Yes, my boy. Why do you ask?" Pappy answers with apprehension in his voice.

Peter peers at Zara, and with shame in his eyes, he asks, "Your father, my great-grandfather, he was a Nazi, wasn't he?"

Very surprised, his grandfather meekly answers, "Yes, he was, Peter. And not proud of it. Nor am I. How did you find out? You can understand why we don't talk about this."

"How I found out isn't important, Pappy. He worked in Himmler's archeology and occult unit, the Ahnenerbe. He committed suicide so he wouldn't face prosecution for war crimes. Am I not right?" asks Peter with the most serious face that Zara has seen on him yet, no longer the little boy.

Pappy glances down and nods.

"What did he do that would have made him a war criminal, Pappy? I deserve to know."

Pappy stares at Peter with a grim face and says, "Peter, listen to me. He did nothing but be an archeologist studying our affliction. But his unit was not so noble. They committed heinous experiments on Ukrainians and Crimeans, looking for their so-called alien genes. My father even tried to save some of them. Please do not judge him, Peter. I can only hope that you can clear his name. Our family name." And Pappy cries for the first time in Peter's life.

Pappy is clearly in distress and puts back on his oxygen mask, which he talks through. "Peter, please, you must find the object. Even if I die first, you must find it and show the world we were not criminals."

Realizing the truth and depth of what Alexander told him, Peter asks, "But, Pappy, you have his secrets, don't you?"

Taking his mask off, his grandfather replies, "When I die, Peter. When I die. Then you will know." He puts his mask back on and asks Mei and Michaela to come back.

Michaela screams when she sees her pappy. "Peter, what have you done to him? He's dying. I've got to get a nurse." And she runs out of the room.

Mei comes on the screen. "Peter, he isn't in good shape, but it wasn't your conversation. He's been deteriorating more quickly this week. He asked me to tell you he would die in peace if he knew you had found the object. I know you cannot tell me what the situation is, but I thought you should know that." She pauses as Peter internalizes that information.

Zara squeezes his hand, the first act of true compassion he has felt from her since she first mended his head wound in that prayer room in Luxembourg.

"Don't worry, Peter. Your sister and I will take care of your pappy. Concentrate on what you and Zara need to do to find the object." She gives him an air-kiss and signs off.

Tears have welled up in Peter's eyes. He looks at Zara's hand in his and squeezes her back. She has seen a very different side of this little boy, this man who is hiding his own deep hurts behind his silliness. She hugs him. A big hug. And he hugs back.

She whispers in his ear, "Every person is a hero in their own special way. And the hero in you has not disappeared. I see him now."

He leans his head into her headscarf, breathes deeply, and whispers, "Thank you." His shoulders relax as he pulls back to prevent the drop coming down his cheek from hitting her scarf.

Jean-Paul signals them over. "I think I have the answer. The cuneiform translates to: *In honor of my great-grandmother Nanshe, we built a new monument. In respect for Ki's sacrifice, we saved the object. Three days from the old monument. May the voice always be with us and we always faithful in return.*

May peace and tolerance return to our lands."

He adds, "Peter, this text and the sixty-degree angle on the parchment, they point to another pre-Neolithic temple, Karahan Tepe. I used the EM traces we got from Enclosure C and looked for any matching signatures in a zone around a sixty-degree line from the temple's ancient true south alignment. I was first thrown by the three days' walk, as Karahan Tepe is only forty kilometers south-southeast of Göbekli Tepe. But I realized for a group relocating, they might have taken three days to find this new location. This site is almost as old as Göbekli Tepe and features two hundred and sixty-six T pillars as well. But the grounds are mostly unexcavated, and it may be a much bigger site than Göbekli Tepe."

Zara studies the GPS location. "If God closes one door, He opens a thousand others. With only one chest EM detector left, we might as well build a house there so we can live on site," Zara jests, shaking her head at the next fool's errand that will get them killed. "I have a very bad feeling about this one, priest."

They arrive at Jean-Paul's derived GPS location in the Tektek Mountains. Not much of anything but sheep and grass. The hill overlooks the Harran Plain, the same as Göbekli Tepe did. Jean-Paul explains that Alexander had commissioned a preliminary excavation of this Tepe and a few others in the area, thinking they might uncover more clues about the object hidden on the pillars at different sites. He grabs the chest EM pack and his AK-74XM and limps to one of the few enclosures opened up.

Peter takes shelter from the heat in the shade behind the truck. As he plays with his MoxWrap, he surprisingly finds he can access its communication functions. Not wanting to be heard, he texts someone very important. Someone who holds the key to what he needs to know to manage what concerns him most.

And the good doctor texts him back. "So good to hear from you. I thought you disappeared. Here's a link to a site that will help you with your friend with PTSD. Remember to be patient, don't pressure them for past memories or push their triggers. And gain their trust as a friend and listen."

Now he regrets that he has already violated the advice many times with

Zara, with viperous results. Peter texts back his thanks.

Nervous about how even more exposed this hillside is, Zara scans the flashes of artillery fire from the AC forces on the other side of the Harran Plains through her binoculars. She doesn't want to die here either. Not until Alexander has delivered what he promised. Then she can die. And until then, she has to help these two find that object.

Since last night, she has chastised herself for her own silliness in refusing to rub that silly man days ago. If she had, they would not have been bombed. Maybe that important monument of Turkish and Kurdish history would still be standing today. She wrestles with herself about what she needed to overcome in herself at this new site. And then images come back. The horror of what they did to her. And she shakes her head, knowing she cannot do it. Cannot.

Four more days pass with Jean-Paul and Peter taking turns sweeping the enormous acreage of possible temples. Zara passes time jamming the snooping drones. Who would be using drones in this area when Alexander's tech makes them inoperable? Maybe that is what they are looking for. Dead zones for drones as a signal for where they must be. She hopes not, but their time is rapidly running out.

When not scanning for drones, she watches Peter with an interest she cannot fathom. This man, knowing he cannot lift that EM pack for extended times, insists on doing his fair share of the work as she watches him wobble around, groaning with one muscle cramp to the next. She heard his grandfather. Wise, as is hers. There is more to this silly man than what she gave him credit for. But what?

Night after night, Jean-Paul is not encouraged by his EM readings. The place is simply too large. Even if they had two chest EM packs operational, even if they had a dozen, the site is simply too large. After dinner, the last of their freeze-dried gunk, Jean-Paul asks Zara to come walk with him.

"Zara, there are two hundred and sixty-six pillars here. Only eight of them have been unearthed. Everything tells me the object is here. But my EM technology is not going to find it."

Zara stares down and shakes her head. "I tried the other night, Jean-Paul.

I really tried. I am not the gentle, loving mother-to-be. I am just not. He needs someone who is more compassionate. Someone who he feels could love him."

Jean-Paul lifts her head and looks her in the eyes, and serenely says, "Zara, you are one of the most compassionate of the many I have met. It seeps throughout your soul. Something in you, something that hurts so much, locks up your compassion. I respect your need to keep your sanity by locking this part of yourself up. We all have our limits. Please let me share this one thing with you."

And with that, the good Father undoes the buttons of his tunic, exposing his chest. Zara wonders what this is about. He was nonresponsive to her advances on the plane. He pulls out a medallion hanging next to his crucifix and shows her the side with the Cygnus constellation.

"Zara, someone I loved very much, and truth be told, I still do love very much, loaned this to me. It was in her family for generations, much like your pendant. This medallion is why I search for the object. No mysterious agenda from the Vatican. Merely this medallion."

He pauses while she looks at it, and then he says, "The writing is six to seven thousand years old. This is the tail of the bird constellation, Cygnus, same as the oral tradition states. The giant is Peter's watcher or alien or merely a giant. The text says, 'Beware of the giants of the star.'"

Taking it off over his head, he places the artifact in her hands. He says, "Zara, what you are going to see will change your life. Forgive me if this change was not what you had wanted, but we are on the verge of losing the object if we do not address this moment in time urgently."

Zara braces herself, for she understands this priest does not talk idly about such things. He turns the medallion over, and she beholds the long rectangular object with a woman touching it. And she remembers what her grandmother Roza said: "We spouses have been like their other half, and between the pair, we are closer to Xwedê together. It takes both halves to make an apple." The woman on the medallion had two halves of an apple. How did Roza know this?

"Zara, the text says, 'She hears the voice of God,'" the good priest states.

As did her Jesuit professors at Georgetown, Jean-Paul is trying to enlighten her with inquisitive interactions. He points to the worm and asks, "Why do you think this creature is here? It seems so out of place."

She looks at it and agrees it does seem out of place. "It is just a worm, Jean-Paul. A simple worm."

She pauses to reflect more deeply, having previously experienced how Jesuits never accept simple answers. "The woman has purified her relationship with God by cleansing the apple of the worm."

Jean-Paul smiles and says, "Look closely. It has spots."

She looks more closely. It does have spots! How?

Jean-Paul pulls the logic string tighter, going for closure. "Remember Mei's yellow earrings, the ones you tossed at Peter on the plane? The yellow bugs with red spots."

Zara, the woman who is fully coherent and functional during a rainstorm of thousand-pound bombs, freezes with this thought. It could not be. It simply could not be. Peter's silly banana slug. How could someone seven thousand years ago envision a banana slug would be next to a woman who speaks with Xwedê? Is this idolatry that she should ignore, burn, destroy? Or is this truly the sign from Xwedê?

Jean-Paul pulls his arms around her to comfort her as the very foundations of her faith are being challenged. "I cannot tell you what you should do knowing this. You asked me what Alexander and I are hiding from you. You should know your Alexander gave me strict instructions not to tell you, for he fears that knowledge will change you. I believe he values his private and intimate relationship with you. He does not want that to change. At risk of my life, and you know this is a true statement, I confirm your notion you are afflicted, as is Peter. You, Peter, and Alexander are the most afflicted of all I have studied."

He stops short of saying what Peter and she are. He gives her credit for her intelligence, intuitiveness, and closeness to God to come to this understanding herself.

And he is right. She begins to piece the puzzle together. Alexander asked her four years ago to do what he demanded of Mei—unabashed sex with a stranger on her plane and again in front of everyone. He begged her, insisted that she was the best person in the world for the task at hand. For all the reasons she has held since her escape seven years ago, she turned him down repeatedly.

And then he found the priest and Mei, who completed his task and found Peter. Why was she the best person in the whole world in his mind? And where did love fit in his scheme? Of all the males in the universe, how could her other half of the apple be this bespectacled man, the opposite of everything she is?

She nods at Jean-Paul. He nods back and leaves to give her privacy.

Peter wonders where Jean-Paul is going and then freezes in apprehension as Zara sits down next to him. What body part is going to be crushed now?

"Peter," she says, "I am not Mei. I cannot do what she does. I simply cannot." She takes his hand in hers. "I have come to understand you are a very special person. Someone who is beyond my comprehension, but unique in this universe, nonetheless."

And she closes her eyes and searches for the strength to confront her demons, test her limits, and still believe she has been faithful. She touches his cheek and says, "I cannot do what Alexander expects a woman to do with you. It is more than an issue with my faith. It is about my choice. With what I have lived through, I must follow the path I have chosen."

She closes her eyes again, still unsuccessful in finding that courage. She killed dozens and dozens, in cold blood, face-to-face, and watched their eyes as they died. And yet she cannot find the courage for this. She breathes deeply, licks her palm, and takes his hand into hers. She feels it. That same feeling on the plane when they first touched. That same sensation little Zara had as she twirled with her Sufi great-grandfather.

And the clutter in her mind begins to empty. Peace and bliss come in. Peter touches her neck affectionately, and the peace evacuates. She freezes in horror as the image of that monster invades her empty mind. The grotesque hands that touched her, forced her to touch him, and that ripped her apart, bit by bit.

She pulls back from Peter and cries, "I cannot. I just cannot."

CHAPTER 33

The difficulty is not so great to die for a friend,
as to find a friend worth dying for.

—Henry Home,
Scottish judge and philosopher

Late July, 2014
Sinopli, Turkey

"Mama, remember this?" Zara asks playfully, holding up a garment half her size.

Her mother beams as she runs her hand along its fabric. "Your ninth birthday. I remember this dress, the one you picked out with Roza." She laughs. "That is, after the dozen others she told you were not appropriate."

Grinning right back, Zara reaches into her closet pulling out another dress. "And remember what Roza said about this one I bought with my aunt Birca in Erdil?"

Hand in front of her mouth, Maryam says, "Oh my. You nearly gave my mother a stroke when she saw you wearing that one."

Holding the lithe dress in front of her, Zara grimaces, seeing the hemline more north than south of midthigh. "What was I thinking?"

Taking the frock from her daughter, Maryam holds it front of her and shivers even though it would cover more of her than Zara. "You were being a normal young girl looking to explore her world," she says as she hands the dress back. "Zara, exploring and trying are part of who we are. And so are mistakes. We need only to forgive ourselves and move on."

Laying the garment of lessons learned on her single bed along with the other clothes of her childhood she is packing, Zara stares down, shaking her head. "There is so much I need to move on from."

Her mother hugs her and whispers in her ear, "We both do."

Eleven years ago, she left her mother, soon to be followed by her little boy brother, to join the Peshmerga. Four years ago, her "mama" moved out of Iraq to be with her mother in the home where she had grown up in Sinopli, Turkey, only an hour and half across the border away from where Zara grew up.

Four weeks ago, Mama called Zara, very ruffled. Her brother-in-law, Uncle Talan, the senior officer in the Peshmerga who had looked after Zara and her brother, told her their intelligence suggested that a major northern attack by the Daesh could occur in the next couple months. Thus he suggested that, if at all possible, they should move even farther north for fear the Daesh would not stop at the Iraqi border and would go into Turkey.

But Zara lamented that she could not come help her and Roza move any earlier than two days ago, as her YPJ unit was heavily engaged fighting the Daesh in the villages surrounding the city of Kobanî, five hundred kilometers away, having just repelled a major Daesh offensive. She had been fighting the Daesh nonstop for over two years: in the defense of Kurdish villages around Aleppo in 2012; in the battle for and ultimate capture of Ras al-Ayn on the border of Turkey and Syria in 2013; and in the offensive against Daesh bases around Tell Abyad, another Turkish-Syrian border town, earlier this year. And at the moment her mother called, Zara had spent weeks defending Kobanî.

Many of the Daesh feared the YPJ's female fighters, like her command, for they believed if a woman killed them, they would not go to heaven. And as Zara could not tell her mother, she had ensured many, very many, did not go to heaven.

But after six years of fighting, of faithfully and obediently championing Kurdish independence, half with the Peshmerga, the other half with the YPJ, Zara's mother's call gave an honorable way to pack away her uniforms and resign her commission. Even though Zara had saved many more lives than she had taken, she became increasingly irritated that the political powers who directed our forces had more than Kurdish independence in mind.

Maryam picks up some of her daughter's textbooks to pack. Some in English; others in Russian. "You spent so much time studying economics. After we move you can look for a job in business in Turkey," she says as she packs Zara's masters in international business diploma from the National Research University, Moscow.

But Zara envisions something very different as she stares at that diploma. Anatoly. The Spetsnaz officer, who wooed her for her love and other things. The latter fell into the same state secret category as what she did for Dan. But with Anatoly, she was much the wiser and protected her heart. For no man would touch that part of her anatomy again.

Zara relives her own childhood memories, sorting through her boxes. She finds the other crazy provocative dresses, tops, and short shorts she bought with her "sisters," Rona and Diyar, that summer in Erdil—the ones that got the Sunni orthodox side of her family, Grandmother Amina and her cousin Rohat, all bent out of shape. Now having lived abroad, she sees that these clothes are hardly provocative compared to what she saw in Washington, D.C.

She finds her photo album with memories of the many years of visits and outings with Rona and Diyar, her best friends, always and forever. Up until she left for the Peshmerga, they saw each other at least every week since they were toddlers, shared each and every family event, and were the keepers of each other's girl secrets.

Their father, Avan, Maryam's older brother and Roza's oldest child, had also been abducted by Saddam's police, never to be heard from again. After a number of years, their Ezidi mother, Ezna, moved with them back to her family's home in Sinjar province, home for most of the Ezidis in Iraq. Zara had made it a point to make the three-hour trip to visit them there at least twice a year each time she came home.

Her silly little boy brother, Soran, interrupts her virtual bonding with her sisters, barging into her room and showing pictures of them with Grandfather Baho, Roza's husband, learning to do the Sufi dervish whirling, the spinning meditation dance. She probably forgot her Sufi roots with all those Americans she partied with or those Russians she downed vodka with, he says, challenging her. And so they spin and spin, knocking down everything in the room as they lose balance.

As she tries to remember how to spin correctly, how to articulate the prayers while spinning, she touches the peace she once knew. She wishes she could be with that peace again, forever. And they collapse in each other's arms, Soran giving her the big bear hug that characterized their close childhood together.

They reminisce about how he always followed her around until she finally followed him to Syria. Maybe it was possible, he said, that he was no longer a silly little boy standing up on tippy toes even though she still was taller than he. She says that would never be possible. Once silly, always silly. And she gives him a big bear hug back.

Much to Roza's relief, most of the house is essentially packed when a phone call from Iraq is received. It's Aunt Ezna, calling her mother-in-law, Roza, to see if her grandchildren can help them flee Sinjar. She is afraid of the Daesh forces expanding out after their capture of Mosul, and she wants to join Roza's family in Turkey. And of course Zara is ready to go get them. But she needs Soran to come as well, as he knows the Syrian officer in charge of the border crossing to that part of Iraq.

As she packs her travel kit, Zara looks through her collection of headscarves. She has not worn one since leaving for the Peshmerga eleven years ago. She certainly was not going to walk a Jesuit college in the middle of Washington, D.C. with one, no matter what her two grandmothers had counseled her. And she has done very well in life without one. Nothing bad has happened because she did not cover her head. But not knowing who they will meet on this trip, she finds the blue headscarf with the pretty pink roses that Rona and Diyar gave her for her sixteenth birthday. She sees the little dress that she bought in Hewler and throws it in the bag as well. It will be a girl's fashion day with Rona and Diyar.

Zara drives with her not-so-little, but still silly, brother south to the Iraqi border to cross into Sinjar, allowed to pass by the Syrian soldiers, but stopped by the Iraqi soldiers. For four days, they wait at the border while the Iraqi soldiers, knowing they have both fought for the Kurds, the Peshmerga, deny them access. Finally, after Soran contacts Uncle Talan, who uses his seniority in the Peshmerga to pull strings with Baghdad, the Iraqi soldiers allow them to pass, but without any weapons, knives excluded.

As Zara watches the different Ezidi villages pass, she sees the poverty these people endure. Granted, her own childhood was that of a simple peasant family living off the land, but many of these people make hers and Soran's lives look simply rich. Their religion is very old; some say it extends back twelve thousand years to the ancient Turkish site, Göbekli Tepe. They influenced the development of the Assyrian, Babylonian and Jewish cultures and beliefs. The Ezidi faith also incorporated elements of Zoroastrianism, one of the world's oldest religions, dating back to prehistoric Indo-Iranian times, and of Sufism, guided by the great eleventh Sufi master, Sheik Adi. Some say the Kurds were originally Ezidi who converted to Islam centuries ago.

And like other Kurds, the Ezidi have suffered much persecution over the millennia, with claims of tens of millions having been murdered over the past seven hundred years alone as Islam expanded through the regions. One of the most notable recent acts of genocide was in the 1600s, when the Ottomans surrounded Mount Sinjar and slaughtered forty thousand Ezidis. And again in the late 1800s, the Ottomans killed thousands around Sinjar. More recently, Saddam Hussein declared the Ezidi to be devil worshippers and initiated genocidal attacks; in one, around two hundred and fifty villages between Sinjar and Mosul were eliminated.

Reaching their cousins' village, after kisses and hugs between the cousins, Aunt Ezna welcomes them to lunch, a welcomed meal after the travails the Khatum siblings faced in getting there. Afterwards, Soran goes to help his aunt Ezna organize materials they want to move from their outside shed.

And the "girls" begin to play. Just for a moment, they return to the innocence of their wonderful childhood together. Diyar puts on music from their teen years as Rona shows them memorabilia from their days in Duhok Province. Zara pulls out her Erdil dress for fun. Rona and Diyar get theirs. Can they still fit into these? Reliving the girls that they still are inside, they slip into them, putting on a private miniature fashion show. They laugh about the flesh they are showing, with Zara describing how much more the Americans show on the mildest of summer days.

The bliss pops as the front door is knocked down. Two heavily armed men have Soran at gunpoint, and another holds Ezna at bloody knifepoint with her dress and undergarments ripped open. Soran is beaten, stabbed, and bleeding, but must have had a great fight with these two as they both sport deep, bleeding cuts on their cheeks. Soran, the veteran soldier, battled in vain to protect his aunt.

Zara stands defenseless, naked as far as they are concerned, knowing that they are in the wrong place at the wrong time in the wrong dresses.

CHAPTER 34

*This is my simple religion. There is no need for temples;
no need for complicated philosophy. Our own brain, our
own heart is our temple; the philosophy is kindness.*

—Dalai Lama

8500 BCE
Site of modern-day Karahan Tepe

I, Amanta, high priestess of the Followers of Illyana, am soon to be their last high priestess. As my mother told me, as her mother had told her, our priestess ancestry dates back five thousand generations to the revered and divine Nanshe, who first touched the object and first communed with the voice. I am the great-granddaughter of the fifteenth Nanshe, the great mother. I am granddaughter of the seventh Ki, the great huntress.

Today I celebrate my thirtieth sun cycle. Like my mother and her mother before her, I decided on my own not to marry until later in my life. Most women of our times first bear children after fourteen to sixteen sun cycles of age. My mother waited until she had twenty-six cycles to give birth to me. Like me, she wanted to find the right partner, not wanting to be forced into the choices of afflicted dreamers prescribed by the Followers of Illyana.

I remain unmarried, for I do not care for any of the men presented to me who claim to suffer the dreams. These men only want me to use our ancient comforting methods on them. I believe they are only looking for pleasure and do not truly desire our destined contact with the dreams and the voice.

My grandmother, Ki the seventh, told me that I must produce the purest children with the highest ancient affliction. Children who will show the strongest dreams and possess the strongest connection to the voice. But what does all this make me? No more than a vessel for breeding? To what end? What does it matter anymore?

The values of Nanshe and Ki are not of worth to today's generation. They were strong women who led with vision, ethics, and compassion. Today, in the lands away from our temple, women have become little more than farm animals. There are few pairs of one man and one woman. Now only a select few powerful men rule, having secured the most productive farming lands. A woman who wants to prosper will be one of many wives for these few men. And everyone else? They are the desperate, the poor, the people with no champion or hope.

Yes, those giants of Nanshe and Ki's time no longer exist as they did then. We are no longer victim to giants rampaging the villages, violating the women and enslaving the men to build their temples. Instead, their descendants settled into the farming life. Their blood is now diluted over generations, but their smaller progeny own the most important lands. They now fight over land to raise crops and animals. They fight over water. In essence, the monsters of the past, their villainy, have merely changed into another form.

The gift of Nanshe's family, farming, turned out to be no gift to women. In her time, equality existed between man and woman, dividing the tasks of hunting and finding food. In her times, women bore fewer children. Today, the needs of the farm and harvest favor larger families. Women have been pushed into domestic roles, raising child after child until they can bear no more. The great vision of the matriarchy of Nanshe could not compete with the farming patriarchy, as fathers pass land to sons and women are traded like cattle. The Ki warrior of peace and faith will never happen again. Not in my lifetime.

The harvests, the long grass grains, the oilseeds that are now common to our diet, changed us. Women, that is. I studied the statues they made of my ancestors, their bodies much leaner. They bore fewer children. And over time, these statues show how women became rounder and curvier with each passing generation. Something changed in our bodies as we ate more grains and seeds, and we became more fertile. Women of Nanshe's time bore only two or three children. Today, they are forced to produce as many as they can bear, as many as the richness of the man who owns them can afford.

And the faith of Nanshe, so wonderful in idea, so beautiful for those who express patience, has waned, save only the last faithful around our temple. Very few today possess the want or will to worship the God of Nanshe, my God, my voice. As they did before she arrived, they want to worship the goddess of fertility, so they can spawn more children to work the farms. They want to worship the goddess mother earth for prosperity of crops. And they want their goddesses to bare their bodies and promote sex, promote having more children to farm and to fight for the men in control.

I should be happy to be high priestess at this temple. I have heard the stories of a giant of the past who raped one of my ancient ancestors and raised his own lineage of priestesses. But without the object, what were they to become? I cringe, knowing they succumbed to the pressures I face. They had been forced to become conduits to not only the mother earth goddess, the fertility goddess, but the love and sex goddesses. And what some of them were made to do, I do not wish to be forced with such a dilemma, nor should my daughters. I stay faithful to the voice, the God of Nanshe, the one true God.

Perhaps if our great mother Nanshe had not prescribed we be people of peace—perhaps if her oldest warrior daughter Ki, the obedient and the faithful, had not advocated defense only if attacked—the great mother's matriarchy might have prevailed across the lands. But I know, my mother knew, and her mother knew, the beauty and purity of our faith, the wisdom and guidance of the voice, would not exist if we had done otherwise. Words of peace.

I have only heard the voice twice in my thirty cycles. As a child of a family of priestesses following the faith of Illyana, I have heard my mother, her mother, and her mother talk of the voice. They raised me with Ki's ideals of duty and devotion. I too obediently prayed with them always, until one day, in my fourteenth sun cycle, the day after my first monthly bleed, I heard the voice while praying with my mother at the object. The voice was as beautiful and harmonious as I had been told, and it asked me if I would help. After I said with all my heart I would do anything, the voice said I would not know what I could do until I became one with my other half. The voice thanked my mother for all her efforts and obedience to help our people understand her words. Words of peace.

And several times each moon cycle, my mother and father would present new men who promised to be my other half. How could they know who is my other half? What if I had no other half? Was I never to hear the voice again? Why did I need to have another half, especially one I did not love?

The second time I heard the voice was last sun cycle. The voice expressed sadness that I had not united with my other half. I asked why this was so important, and the voice explained that, without uniting with my other half, I could not be as close to the voice as had my mother and my grandmother. I have only eaten an apple a few times. Why are two halves of an apple so important?

The voice was saddened that, despite my ancestors' faithful guidance to the people across these lands, the masses no longer heeded, no longer needed the words of the voice. And they continued the old ways—their violence, their wanton lust, their selfishness, their intolerance of our ways. Our people will forever be small, forever be lonely if they will not hear these words. We will not become the people of peace we had the potential to be. And someday, our failure to be so will lead to our demise.

But what the voice said next surprised me the most. Bury the temples. We should bury the object. Our time was not right for the words of the voice. I thought to myself, this was why I could not find that other apple half. The voice heard me, of course, and said my other half waited out there for me in patience and faith. I simply needed to find him. Generations upon generations from now, there would be born those who might be ready to bring the message forth, during an age in which the words of the voice were needed the most. Ones who could bring peace to the people and beloved children of the voice. And if not, they would possess the means to return the object to the voice.

Obedient as the words of Ki said we should be, eleven moon cycles ago, I relayed the words of the voice to the faithful at our temple, who began to fill in the temples here. I made the dangerous trip to the ancient temples three days from here. And I saw how the giants of the oral tradition had desecrated the temples of Ki and An. I looked for where it was said my ancestors were buried and kneeled to pray for their forgiveness of our people's disrespect.

After Illyana, the daughter of Tallia, the granddaughter of Sarpani, had left the ancient temple with the object, the giants came back to use the faith Nanshe had built for their own purposes. For they had found that faith was more powerful than their spears and arrows. They continued the worship ceremonies the local people had followed, but with their priestesses and to their gods. And they commanded that animal gods, star gods, any god of the local peoples be carved into the stones of the temple.

But I know the truth about what happened here. They turned the great faith of Nanshe, the great temple of Ki, into a place where they could promote the desecration of women. My distant cousin priestesses were denigrated in perpetual public demonstration of the power of the giant descendants of the stars. They claimed their priestesses to be the rightful ones to reach the gods on the giants' behalf, the giants who descended from the stars themselves. They used these ceremonies as thinly veiled disguises for their orgies, with false shamans and their potions that induced hallucinations. And the people believed these hallucinations to be the same as the visions of my ancestors.

These shamans abused the priestesses in public as their right given by the gods in the name of fertility and crop prosperity. These fake shamans offered the priestesses as sexual gifts to leaders of other lands to gain the alliances the giants sought. And the giants built more temples so they could promote more simultaneous orgies. The more sex, the happier the people. The more sex, the stronger the alliances.

I stand here today next to the object. We have only known peace at this temple, as most of the giants lived in fear of the object, and of the power the priestesses of the object might wield. Ki and Illyana made sure of that, killing that giant with lightning. I can only hope my prayers could bring forth lightning if we were ever attacked.

But the influence of the giants found its way into my own temple nonetheless. The people wanted many of the indulgences they found at the other temple. And so, my great, great, many times over, great-grandmothers were forced to emulate the debauched priestesses of the other temples. We have faithfully endeavored to maintain the principles of modesty as taught by Ki. But somehow, for our ceremonies, we succumbed to forces making us disrobe and show our organs of fertility.

This faith somehow became the Cult of Illyana. As my mother has told me, Orzu's nightmares, his dreams of his sister Illyana, her heart between her breasts where he needed to shoot his arrow through, became a fixation for the afflicted men who suffered the same dreams. And somehow, men in power distorted and demeaned our faith into a worship of the female breast. That is, my breasts, which I am forced to show in ceremonies. They made statues of my mother, my grandmother, every woman in my matriarchal lineage. Statues unclothed focused on our organs of fertility, focused on our breasts in the name of their worship of Illyana.

Today, in my thirtieth cycle, I end this madness. I will not parade my body in front of these people. I will not procreate with their pick of my other half in public. My body is mine. My life is mine. The temple here is buried. I have made my last prayer at the object. And the last faithful Followers of Illyana, the true followers of Nanshe's original faith, are burying the object.

If I had children, I would create an addition to the oral traditions of Orzu, Nanshe, Ki and their descendants.

The voice is beautiful, but we were not ready for beauty
When you are once again ready to know beauty
Not the beauty of the skin, but the beauty of the soul
The beauty in the collective in all of us
Then you are ready to seek the object
It is said it must be man and woman
But it must be man who loves woman
Not for her skin, not for her fertility, not for her family

But for her
For her inner beauty seeking to be with the voice

And as we bury the object, I turn away from the tail of the bird star to go away from it. My head covered, my arms covered, my legs covered, I leave here no longer a priestess, but a simple humble woman.

CHAPTER 35

*If, for example, tomorrow an expedition of Martians
came, and some of them came to us, here... Martians,
right? Green, with that long nose and big ears, just
like children paint them. And one says, 'But I
want to be baptized!' What would happen?*

—Pope Francis

8:00 p.m. GMT+3, May 22, 2022
Karahan Tepe, former Turkey, now Anatolian Kurdish State

She closes her eyes again, only to relive her failure. Failure as a daughter to her mother, who obviously wants her to start a family with this man. Failure to her sisters as her carelessness, her poor choice of a moment to let her guard down, her straying from her faith, led Rona and Diyar to a fate worse than death. She cried inside not for herself, but for the savagery they committed upon her sisters in front of her. Her heedlessness, her laxness, her recklessness made her and her sisters into slaves

She had killed so many like those two men, but she was now defenseless in front of this man. Had she only left the YPJ a day earlier. Had she not gone to her mother's house. Had she not played little girls with those dresses. Zara's guilt broke open as she sat paralyzed in front of this strange man from

California. And the façade of strength she had created seven years ago in order to survive, so stone hard and cold, crumbled.

Trembling and in tears, she pulls back from Peter. "I cannot do it. I just cannot," she says, barely able to speak. She turns from him and pulls her headscarf up to wipe her tears. She shakes uncontrollably.

Peter reaches out to comfort her but stops short of touching her. Practicing Dr. Beverly's therapeutic advice, he whispers, "I respect you, Zara. I care about how you feel. I want to give you the comfort you need, but I think you need your space now more than comfort." She nods yes, and Peter gets up to check in with Jean-Paul, who is calibrating his last lonely EM detector.

"Jean-Paul. Father Jean-Paul, I need your advice," says Peter.

The good Father puts down his material goods to attend to the affairs of the soul. "Peter, Zara is a very special person, as are you. She has led an extraordinarily complicated life, and thus conflicting emotions run extremely deep in her. Only her inner scars run deeper. Give her time. You did the right thing by giving her space and time, and more importantly, your trust."

Peter finds consolation in Jean-Paul's affirmation that he did the right thing. He asks, "What did you show her that made her try the algorithm again?"

The good Father pulls the medallion off the chain around his neck and shows Peter, explaining, as he had done with Zara, that it was six to seven thousand years old.

Looking first at the woman and the apple, Peter exclaims, "How on earth? A banana slug?" He looks at Jean-Paul. "My Proto-Greek is rusty, but this says something about her and the voice of God, doesn't it?" Jean-Paul nods.

Peter stares at the woman hearing God, holding the two halves of the apple, and then the banana slug. He peers back at Zara, who is curled in a sitting fetal position in tears, so different from the warrior she had presented herself as. And he finally gets it. This mission is not about him. So self-centered, so full of self-pity, he did not get it. Everything is really all about her. About Zara.

Peter turns the artifact over, points to the giant, and says, "Aliens did this. They did this to us, Zara and me. They are speaking here on this medallion."

With a serious face, he looks into Jean-Paul's eyes and asks again, "What are you going to do when we talk with the aliens? The moment of truth is coming shortly. Are you going to ask if they are God? Are you willing to cross that line, admitting that thousands of years of religious belief is simply about 'beings from another world,' as Professor Schmidt said about these giant figures?"

Jean-Paul replies, "Maybe the question should be, 'Did God make them too?' Peter, for all you know, we might be worshipping the same God together, mankind and your aliens."

Peter asks skeptically, "Why did the pope commission a group studying extraterrestrials, anyway?"

The Jesuit teacher in the good Father comes out as he says, "One would like to believe the idea we all evolved from one common source. We are truly special creations of God. But the question should be if we are His only creations. And if we are not, then can we learn from His other creations?"

"So His Eminence wants you to be the Zefram Cochrane of our time," Peter asserts, regaining his cocky self.

"Who?" asks Jean-Paul, a puzzled simple man from France who obviously did not own a television at home.

"The inventor of the warp drive in *Star Trek*. He makes first contact with the Vulcans, the pointy-eared aliens."

His eyebrows pointed inward as he ponders Peter's odd comments, Jean-Paul goes back to analyzing the EM data he has gathered today. Peter looks to find out how Zara is doing, for he really does care about her, how she feels, her well-being, in a way that he cannot explain. He sees her in the midst of Maghrib prayer in the evening, the second to last of the day. He begins to realize that her attentiveness to her faith, to her rituals, is vital to her maintaining her strength.

She comes back to the truck, not saying anything to either of them, takes her night vision goggles, and walks the perimeter, holding her rifle as a child does their safety blanket. Peter searches on his MoxWrap for something. Something special.

After Isha prayer, the last of the five daily prayers, Zara tells Jean-Paul she will take the first watch. The good Father, knowing how stressful last night and today have been for her, tells her to take the second watch, which she does not debate, for she could sleep standing up at this moment.

Later, as she takes the second watch, she comes over to check on Peter. She looks at him, utterly confused. How does this man of the banana slug play out in Xwedê's plan? Closing her eyes, she envisions that image on the medallion, the woman touching the object, and the ancient text: "She hears the voice of God."

She looks again at Peter's lean, twiggy body and cannot fathom how he is the other half of the apple. Why did Sara, Roza, or even her own mother not tell her? Why did she need to find out among complete strangers?

Her thoughts are interrupted by this other apple half rolling over and murmuring something. And it dawns on Zara that he is not fighting something tonight. Why? She tiptoes closer to listen to what he is saying. "Amanta, please don't go. Amanta, you mustn't go. We need you. We love you."

The next morning, Peter awakes. And he is actually somewhat rested. This must be what a good night's sleep feels like, he muses. And there is no fog in the Anatolian Kurdish State! He goes over to Jean-Paul and Zara to tell them about how great his sleep was. Jean-Paul says this may mean the object is very close.

Zara, knowing he had been dreaming, asks, "Peter, do you remember your dreams?"

Shaking his head, Peter laments, "No, that part of my head isn't so clear. But I could get used to getting up every morning of my life and feeling this good."

Zara looks at Jean-Paul suspiciously and asks, "And, priest, how was your sleep last night?"

The former priest blinks twice rapidly and says, "Um. It was good. I am refreshed. But the effect might not be as pronounced as it is with Peter, as I am less afflicted."

Watching his eyes, Zara is now certain she has only one person she can trust. Not her family. Not Alexander. Not Mei. And now, certainly not this lying priest. Only a silly man, half an apple, who does not know better than to lie to her.

Jean-Paul, very reflectively thinking, proposes, "Perhaps we can narrow down where the object may be by the two of us sleeping in different locations each night. Between our sleep barometer and the EM readings, we may be able to triangulate a narrow zone where we can dig."

Zara, shaking her head, both at his veracity and his suggestion, says back, "Priest, maybe it could take a couple more days, but maybe it could take a few weeks. I just do not know how much time we have before we are found and attacked again."

Encouragingly, her MoxWrap shows the AC focused around Sanliurfa and not coming across the Harran Plain to their position. She would feel better if she could call for more help here. She debates if she should call upon the Kurds to help her, weighing their own safety against the possibility of more security breaches.

Zara walks away, tapping her MoxWrap as she goes to higher ground to scan the horizon. Jean-Paul heads off to perform more EM scans, tapping his MoxWrap. And Peter smiles as he watches the animation of Sammy the Slug he finally found last night. Sammy is dancing, singing, doing flips, all things Peter hopes he can do soon, somewhere safer than here. Peter gets up to walk around the site, hoping he can "feel the Force" like Luke Skywalker and divine where the object is hidden.

At noon, he comes back to the truck, with no more of a clue about the object's whereabouts. Zara gives him fresh water, then takes him by surprise. She asks, "Tell me about your girlfriend, Amanta?"

"Who?" responds a very confused Peter.

Zara, knowing full well she can trust his answers, tries a different question. "Okay, so Amanta does not sound familiar. What were the names of your past girlfriends?"

Unsure of where she is going, Peter meekly answers, "Sarah was my last girlfriend, but you already knew that. And before her were Ciara and Tara. Do you need a longer list?"

Zara repeats him. "Sarah, Tierra, Dara, yes?"

"No, no, Zara. Sarah, Ciara, and Tara." And as soon as Peter says this, he realizes what he just did in front of her. She does too, by the look in her eye.

Zara pursues her lips. She gets it now. "And Alexander knew the names of your last three girlfriends, did he not? He knew them before you told him." Peter, head down, nods yes.

"And you saw the medallion, did you not?" Zara asks more forcefully, at which Peter nods.

She shakes her head and mutters, "I cannot imagine we are two halves of an apple. We are entirely different. Alexander, he has no scruples about forcing two people to mate. No better than cattle are we. And my meddling family. They are like the old Kurds, trying to set me up with a man they want to have sire their next generation. Am I merely breeding stock for the world?"

Peter taps his MoxWrap, and Zara's beeps. She looks at it and sees a banana slug singing, dancing, doing back flips. It hits her in the right spot, for it was something her silly little brother would have done to her when she was despondent at the world.

"I cannot understand you," she admits. "You appear so innocent. You appear so weak, so silly. And yet you stood up for Mei. You were willing to take a bullet instead of her. And you couldn't pull that trigger when I asked you to kill me instead." She looks at his silly banana slug dancing, and for a moment, a wave of warmth passes through her. Not long enough for her to mount a defense. But enough for her to notice. And she smiles.

Reading her body language, Peter holds his hands out to her in the same gesture Jean-Paul made to her on the plane ride out. She nods her approval, and he hugs her. She revels in the warmth. The same warmth she felt as a child, but here now with this banana slug man.

She whispers in Peter's ear, "I am not marrying you. Not going to have sex with you. We are not right for each other." She then strokes his face and says, "But let us try again. This time standing up, so if it gets too strange, I can run away."

After Peter nods in agreement, she tells him to close his eyes as she takes his hands under her headscarf, removes it with him, and strokes her hair with him. She gently places his head to smell her hair as she touches his head. She blows on his ear, licks it, and then lifts his head so she can brush her lips with his, licking his lips.

She unbuttons his tunic shirt, exposing his chest. She rubs his heart while holding his head into her neck, saying for him to smell her. While still rubbing his heart, she licks his forehead in circles, around and around. He begins to murmur, "Nanshe." And then he stops.

And the moment arrives where she needs to close her eyes to find her strength. The strength to do what Mei did. Her hand hovers, shaking, above his crotch, in deep debate as to what to do next. She shivers. She cannot do this. Not even to save the world. She cannot do this with Peter.

The image of their rough hands dissipates as she senses something. Something so very different from any feeling before. Peter is with her. But how? They are seeing together. She feels him taking her hand, to put not on his crotch but to his lips, and he kisses it so ever gently. And as if the spirit of her father has come, she senses the warmth of hands on her cheeks and kisses on her forehead. She remembers her father doing this from when she was so very little to the day before he died. How did he know to do this? And the terror of those other men continues to fade into the past where it belongs.

He leans in to smell her cheek, and she pulls back, covering her scar with her hand. As if he was in her mind, he kisses and licks her hand, covering her disfigurement, and then gently moves it aside. He kisses and licks her scar and whispers, "Your face radiates with your inner beauty. You have no need to hide."

He hugs her, squeezing and surrounding her, giving her that sense of safety, of security, of being his little Zara. Her mind reveals in the joy she thought had been lost. Again, how did he know to do this?

Minutes later, he kisses her lips lightly and licks them as she did to him. He rubs her forehead, and her mind becomes completely clear of the negative images of the past, filled only with the joy and happiness she once knew. He lightly rubs her heart over her tunic shirt, and she feels his closeness to her, not just physically, but within her. She takes his hand and rubs her chest even more deeply.

She starts seeing a vision of many temples, with many pockmarks from lightning strikes. She kisses him, opening his lips for her tongue. And the vision becomes clearer. She sees the northern knoll of these grounds. She sees that he sees the same. She wants him to know her heart. She wants to put his hand onto her left breast over her heart. Not to do what Mei had been tasked to do, but because she has grown close to him and wants him to. Once again, her fear of what she hides within overcomes her. She cannot let him know what has happened to her.

He senses her and whispers, "I see the knoll too. Let me help you."

He puts his fingers on her shirt buttons around her bust. As she anticipates his intimate touch, to her surprise, his fingers trace up her clavicle, away from where she thought he would touch. Up along her neck, wet with perspiration, to her cheeks, and then to her temples, where he gently rubs. She can feel the radiance of his heat, his moisture emanating from his fingers down into her heart, her head, and deep within, even to where she hides her deepest secrets. She can sense her whole being opening up. She spots the place on the northern knoll, pocked where the lightning has struck over and over again.

He tries to put his lips upon hers, but she is frightened at where this might be taking them and puts her finger upon his lips. For she is deformed. They took her beauty away from her. Not what she shows on the outside, but inside. She pulls back, turning away from him. He turns her back towards him, puts his warm hands around her cheeks, softly kisses her forehead, and hugs her. And after what seems like eternity, she is home again. She is Zara again. She feels family.

With a deep sense of bliss, with the rage gone for now, Zara slowly pulls back from her apple half and smiles, gazing at Peter with eyes with dilated pupils, so differently than she looked at him in Luxembourg. They both look over to the northern knoll and flag Jean-Paul. Peter helps her put back her headscarf and straightens out her tunic. She smiles and clasps his hands in hers, taking him to the truck to get the excavation equipment.

As the three of them walk over to the northern knoll, the good priest comprehends very well what has just happened. Just as the traditions said. Only man and woman together. They arrive at the place Zara and Peter saw together in their visions. Jean-Paul verifies the spot with science, not mystic visions, as he points out the shattered rocks engrained with straight parallel lines. These lines are usually associated with shock lamellae created by meteorite strikes, but have been known to happen with lightning strikes. This one spot of earth on this desolate hill is littered with pockmarks and shattered rocks from millennia of repeated lightning strikes.

And they dig as the archeologist in Jean-Paul cringes with each of Zara's rough, deep shovel thrusts. Her shovel uncovers something, and she doubts her sanity as an image from her teen visit to the Ka'abah arises. She seeks a black stone. Peter comes and puts his arm around her, assuring her he saw the same stone in his dream. She is overwhelmed, and to the surprise of her apple half and the priest, she kneels and kisses it.

Peter gently asks, "Should I kiss it too?"

Very embarrassed, Zara says, "No. No. I was just overtaken by a memory. A very important spiritual memory." She turns to Jean-Paul and makes the first religious joke of the mission. "Priest, come here with your cross. You may need to bless this stone."

The archeologist in Jean-Paul takes over as they carefully expose more of the stone. Black, with many round indentations. Peter stares at it. Not what he and Alexander had imagined. He says to Jean-Paul, "How do we know this is it? It isn't a monolith. Is this just some weird stone?"

He puts his hand on it and says, "Kirk to Spock. Come in. Bones misses you. Beam down here and we can have a family reunion."

Touching the stone with her palms, Zara asks, "What?"

Peter, thinking she just isn't a Trekkie, or they simply did not own a television in her village either, says, "I was calling Spock, the friendly pointy-eared Vulcan alien."

But Zara shushes him and repeats herself. "What? What did you say? Yes. Yes, I understand. How? I will."

She leans back in astonishment. Stares up into the heavens and breathes slowly. She looks over at Peter, then at Jean-Paul. She glances back up and says, slowly and serenely, "I heard a voice."

She turns to both of them and says, "And she was beautiful."

And the three of them go silent—Zara in deep reflection over what she has just heard, Peter rubbing the object to get it to talk to him as well, and Jean-Paul tapping away on his MoxPad+.

Zara breaks the silence, turns to Jean-Paul, and says, "She is the same voice for all of us. There is only one voice. And she is sad. She did not say so, but I felt it—disheartened. She has attempted many times over many thousands of years to talk with us. Each time, her word is heard, and then distorted. Mankind takes her words for other uses. She asked if I understood. She asked if I would help her. I asked how, and she said I will know soon. She asked again if I would help."

An internally disheveled Zara looks at Peter and adds, "And then she told me I would not know how to help as long as I was only half."

Peter, missing his cue to truly bond with her in the way that would bring them both closer to the voice, lets the editor in him spoil the moment. "If that's true, and God is She and not He, the copyeditors of the world will rejoice as there will be decades of revisions that need to be made."

Not amused at Peter's insolence, Jean-Paul simply states, "God might present as different genders to different people. Just as He, well, as God may speak in the native language of different people."

Zara is indifferent to the two of them and says, "She is She and that is that."

She leans down and kisses the object again. She cannot leave the object, as she feels compelled to sit in its presence. Her MoxWrap gently taps on her wrist, signaling the time for Asr prayer. She turns to the object and kneels down. And at a spiritual dilemma, she debates for a minute. Moving to the side of the object that puts her in line with Mecca, she then performs her prayer while the two men set out to search for dinner.

After a vegetarian dinner, they work on digging a ramp around the object so they can roll and lever it up to the level ground. Jean-Paul is fascinated with the geologic structure of the rocks around the object. He takes samples of the rocks as well as more EM readings of the area.

The next day, Zara spends her time in meditation on the object, taking breaks for her routine of daily prayers. Peter tries to be her companion and sit on the object with her, but he is not getting any signals, vibes, or anything special from being near the object, other than his newfound contentment at simply being next to Zara.

While Jean-Paul continues taking samples and obtaining readings, Peter decides to walk around the other excavated areas of this temple complex. He notes the number of goddess statues unearthed by Alexander's excavation team, all unclothed. He brings back six of them to show Zara. He taps her shoulder, but she is not amused by his interruption over a bunch of statues.

"But, Zara, there are literally dozens and dozens of these in the excavation trenches," exclaims Peter. He looks to check if Jean-Paul is nearby, and then shows her two, the leaner two. "Look at these two. Don't they look familiar?"

"No. What was wrong with my ancestors here? Did they not understand what modesty was back then?" says Zara dismissively.

Peter backs away out of hitting range, gulps, and then says his piece. "Zara, you have their body."

That "Zara glare" comes back. She winces at him. Not only has he interrupted her meditation on the voice, but he is fantasizing about her naked body. "Little Boy, what makes you think you know what my body looks like?"

Very embarrassed, Peter timidly says, "Well, they match your calves, and their breasts show the same proportion to the rest of the body as yours."

Zara is outraged and lets him have it. "I let you touch my bra and suddenly you are an expert on my breasts." She crosses her arms across her chest. "I don't care if World War Three is starting. You are not going to touch me there again."

Peter leaves the six statues on the ground in front of her and finds more friendly grounds to ponder his existence. Zara at first is dismissive. But then she sees what he saw. One statue in particular is anatomically close to her proportions. Not exaggerated as four of them are.

Thankful he was not physically harmed by his other apple half, Peter searches around the excavation trenches for something other than that which would offend her highness. Thinking he has sunstroke, he rubs his eyes to look again. Isn't that the same kind of stone as the object? And Peter brushes dirt off a two-and-a-half-inch black stone fragment protruding from the side of a trench. He finds another rock to dig the fragment out. It is eight by three by one inches and looks the same on the surface as the object.

He runs back to Jean-Paul, yelling, "I found something. It's part of the object."

Jean-Paul looks at the fragment with Peter. Finds where it might have fit on the object, and remarks, "This may mean that the object could have split over time. There may be more fragments or even more sizeable pieces of the object here, or anywhere along the path of the descendants of the originators." Incredibly excited inside, but his serene self on the outside, Jean-Paul takes his MoxPad+ and EM detector back to the truck to chase his idea.

Peter makes a belt by ripping up his undershirt, fastens the object fragment securely around his belly, and puts his tunic back on. He has what he has come for. A fragment of the object to bring back to Pappy. His mission is done here. He looks back to the northern knoll and spies Zara sitting on the object. He bites his lower lip, for he has another mission here to fulfill.

Zara opens her eyes again to see her Little Boy has come back, hopefully not with more statues. She recognizes the apology in his face and she signals for him to sit next to her. He cautiously does so, watching her carefully.

"Stay here with me," she implores. "I know you mean well. You must understand I am fearful of a man who is that close to me. Who might know me. It has never gone well in the past."

She closes her eyes again. Minutes later, she opens them and says, "What I am sensing becomes stronger as you are near." She takes his hand into hers and closes her eyes again to commune with the object.

Another vegetarian dinner later, Jean-Paul explains how he has confirmed his theory that another object piece might exist. He noted the magnetic and structural changes created by the multiple lightning strikes where the object lies. Now understanding this, he confirmed that the grounds at Göbekli Tepe Enclosure C showed the same. Much to Zara's alarm, Jean-Paul has tasked Alexander's satellites with looking at the lands and shallow seabeds around the Black Sea. There are a number of places where this object and potential other ones could have existed. On his MoxPad+, he shows the dots, which look like a road map of the originators' migration from the northernmost dot in the Crimea.

He points to the ones near the Turkish-Georgian border. He says these are the most suggestive of an object resting between the ports of Rize and Çayeli. He shows Mount Kaçkar Dağı, the highest mountain in the region, where the signature lightning and EM convergence appears as well. This could be consistent with the oral tradition of another group of originators trying to find "the mountains past the hill of obsidian rocks."

The late evening arrives. Jean-Paul leaves the two of them to their privacy with the object as he takes his post at the truck. Peter pulls out a surprise for Zara. He brought her prayer mat from the truck when they were searching for things to eat. She is pleasantly surprised. She holds her hands around his cheeks, kisses him, and invites him to sit with her as she performs her Isha prayers.

They sit on the object, looking into the north to find the tail of the bird star. She leans over and softly says, "I apologize for my doubt about you. My family was once again wise in their assessment of you."

With that, they touch each other. Not only the skin-to-skin touch, but truly and deeply touch each other in the way the tradition said. Peter repeats for her the tradition prescribed twelve thousand years ago for them to hear. *Only with the two together can you find peace. The Object. You might see in sleep, might hear. But only as man and woman.*

She takes his hand into hers. "It is so very difficult for me to express this part of my being, this part of my life that has long overshadowed what you have touched in me. What I have done, no person should have done. Because I strayed, I was made to pay the price. And I pay the price today, for I can never be a woman to a man anymore. My bad deeds led to my body being destroyed in ways that no man would want." And she puts her hands over her face to muffle her cries.

Peter remembers the words of warning from Roza. Perhaps her grandmother was using their faith as a graceful way to save her granddaughter from facing humiliating requests of her sexuality. He so wants to let her know how beautiful she is. He has seen her from within. He remembers what Maryam said to him, and he whispers in her ear the poem little Zara recited to her mother after the gas attack so long ago.

A moment of happiness,
You and I sitting on the verandah,
Apparently two, but one in soul, you and I.

Taken by surprise by what he has said, Zara lifts her head out from her hands, rivers streaming down her cheeks. She murmurs through her tears, "Where did you learn that?"

Peter puts his hands on her waterlogged cheeks. "Your mother told me you said that to her at the moment when she needed to hear you the most. She said I should memorize it, for someday I would need to say this to you too."

She puts her head against his chest and cries. He strokes her head. She whispers for him to remove her headscarf, for her grandmothers were right. He is blood family somehow. Once her tears subside, she kisses him open-mouthed. As their moistures mix, that chemistry, that magic boils over into the rest of their beings. That sense of peace spreads. He brings her head to his chest again and tells her to smell him, opens his shirt and tells her to taste him, and puts her ear to his heart and says to hear him.

She is swept up by the moment. Her mind is at peace. Her fears dismissed. Her angst subsided. She wants him to be in her, with her, around her. Overcoming her fears, her apprehensions, the dark visions of her tormentors, she reaches to open up his pants. Not because Alexander said she needed to. Not because her family said she was destined to. But because she wants to. Because she has fallen for him, wanting his love, his warmth.

But he takes her hand in his and puts it onto his heart. She takes his hand and puts it to her heart too, as she says she wants him to know who she is. She whispers for him to close his eyes as she opens up her shirt, taking his hand onto her heart over her bra cup as his palm gently rubs. He touches part of a deep gouge on the side of her breast and pauses. She flinches and says she understands if he will be repulsed, for what she lost here is only symbolic of what has happened within.

He continues rubbing her on her outer wound in gentle circles as he whispers in her ear, "What I touch is not the definition of your beauty. It is what I touch deep inside that makes you so beautiful. Beautiful in the eyes of

God. Beautiful in my eyes." And she trusts him and guides his hand under her bra cup and truly close over her heart as she lets him in, for better or worse.

As they kiss, they see the peace. They are overwhelmed by the peace. The peace that Nanshe saw. The peace that Sarpani and Zirbani saw. The peace that Illyana saw. And in this peace, they fall asleep in the bliss of each other's arms.

Drifting in a wondrous state, free from the pains of her life, free to love again, free to be herself again, Zara is awakened by the hand. That rough hand that haunted her nightmares. How can this be after she had been freed?

She is dreaming and must open her eyes to stop the horror. As her eyes open, she sees his face with the cheek scar her brother carved. The face attached to the hands taking her bra off. She is restrained by another as she sees Peter also restrained by a dark figure.

It is happening to her again.

CHAPTER 36

Strive to discover the mystery before life is taken from you.
If while living you fail to find yourself, to know yourself,
How will you be able to understand
The secret of your existence when you die?
—Farīd ud-Dīn Attar,
twelfth-century Persian Muslim poet

3:00 a.m. GMT+3, May 23, 2022
Karahan Tepe, former Turkey, now Anatolian Kurdish State

This can't be happening again.

The object gone. Her weapons gone. Has she failed herself again? Has she failed another person she cares about again?

She knows this man. Aymen. And she knows him in all the wrong ways. He is here again, about to do what he did repeatedly each and every day for nearly a year, he and his brother.

Aymen, with the scar carved by Zara's dead brother, a full head taller than her, with those dark piercing eyes, long ears, and those huge, imposing hands, screams at his victim, "You thought you could hide from me, but I have finally found you, the disobedient property of mine and my dead brother Skander. You are my rightful property, rightful wife, rightful slave, and I have come to collect what I am owed."

He grabs at her pants. "*Dêlik*. You donkey slut whore. You are not a good woman of faith. You never were. We stopped you from having sex with this kafir." He rips opens the belt to her pants. "I will enjoy my rights to you in front of your boyfriend like I did in front of your brother."

Zara breaks a leg loose from his grip and lands a solid kick into him, missing his groin. Aymen takes his gun, shoots between Peter's feet, and says, "He will suffer the worst death a man can have if you do not cooperate as the obedient wife should." He looks at her with those dark eyes. "I know you. You will cooperate the same as you did to save your two Ezidi devil women from the torture they deserved."

Shaking more than a heroin addict in withdrawal, Peter looks to the heavens and begs to anyone who will hear. *Please take me and spare her.* But his physical struggles lead to nothing.

Zara relents, for she knows he would not kill Peter quickly, but would make Peter die slowly over days while he takes her in front of him, over and over again. As she glances quickly at Peter, that micro-moment in time arrives where everyone else slows to a crawl. A voice speaks with her, but not the one she heard before. A steady, firm woman's voice that says, "My daughter, Ki, in the brief moment when the giants grab you or your sisters, you must not hesitate. You must not heed their demands. Someone will die and you must decide who. You must be strong."

And in this moment, Zara is touched by an ancient inner strength. She will not fail this time. For she is a different Zara than the victim he once terrorized. She is willing to die today.

With a renewed venom, she spits back at this monster, goading this giant. "You are not even Iraqi or Syrian. You had no right to fight in our lands. You and your brother were desperate poor men from North Africa who could not afford to have a woman of your own. So you had to join the Daesh to steal women for your sadistic needs."

That did it. She has gotten under his skin, and he slams his fists into her stomach. In sheer anger, he unbelts his pants and rips hers down enough so he can finger her with his giant rough digits. But looking at what is smeared upon his fingers, he yells in disgust, "You are unclean."

Peter, still pleading inside for some superpower to be granted to him, suddenly recalls Roza's words. And he rallies his inner superpower. With the voice of the incensed editor, he yells out the vilest words he knows. "Die, you plagiarizing, adverb-abusing, sentence-inflating, monotonal, repetitive cliché-flinging prima donna! Eat my pencil!"

Aymen's total revulsion that his slave is in the middle of her period turns to rage, and he takes his anger out on Peter and shoots him in the gut.

Bad move on his part, for in that brief microsecond in time, Zara decisively kicks him, knocking him down. She rolls backwards, wrapping her leg around the neck of the brute holding her arms down, and rolls him backwards, grabbing his pistol as she goes over the top of him.

Bang. She shoots this brute as Aymen gets up to come back at her. The man holding Peter drops what he thinks is now a corpse to run and help Aymen.

For the first time in his life, Peter has kept his head under fire as he faked his dying moments receiving Aymen's bullet. The object has saved him, or at least the fragment did. As his captor tries to help Aymen, Peter trips him up like he did Zara when they wrestled. To the ground he goes with a thud as Peter rushes Aymen from the back with the object fragment.

Just as Aymen has his arms around Zara's neck, ready to snap it, Peter slams the fragment into the side of his head. Aymen is stunned for but another microsecond, long enough for Zara to aim at his thigh and shoot. *Thud*, down goes her tormentor. And she does the same to Peter's captor. All three taken care of.

Zara is in the zone. High respiration rate. High heart rate. High cognition rate. She turns in a circle and scans around herself with the gun out in a combat position. There is no one left. She sighs and nearly collapses as Peter catches her. She cries into his shirt.

Uncannily calm and composed, he kisses the top of her head as she lets loose a decade of the deepest, darkest emotions. Images of helplessness as they forced her to watch the violation, torture, and mutilation of Rona. As they did the same to her in front of Diyar. She searches within her soul for redemption now that she has shot the last of their tormentors. And all she encounters is blackness, loneliness, and icy coldness. She shivers, with her arms around Peter and the gun dangling from her hand.

As her tears subside, she looks at his hands and whispers, "Peter. Your hands."

Incredibly embarrassed, Peter takes his hands away from her chest as he realizes she is almost as undressed as the statues he showed her. He strips his tunic shirt off and gives it to her, putting his hands over his eyes to show his respect for her modesty.

Peter peeks through his fingers to see if she is modest again. She is his Zara once again except for one detail. As she checks the downed assailants, he searches around and finds it. Her headscarf. The sign of her protective outer persona. He gets it and places the final mark of modesty around her head as she pauses in collecting the assassins' weapons. She smiles, in a more special way than she ever has before with him, and she kisses his cheek affectionately.

She stands over Aymen, whose wound does not allow him to get up. She points one of their rifles at his crotch. "Why should I not rid you of this as I did to your brother, who begged me like a child before I exterminated him from this Earth?"

Aymen looks at her with the same dark piercing eyes and spits at her. "You donkey slut whore. You deserved everything we did to you, and so did your pathetic ugly Ezidi friends."

Zara shakes her head. And to Aymen's surprise, she shoots on both sides of his crotch, leaving his organ intact but disabling his adductor tendons, then knocks him unconscious with the rifle butt.

Peter watches this. He has only imagined until now how fierce a warrior she must have been. And from what little he has heard in their exchanges, this monster deserved to be ripped apart for what he did. Why didn't she take her rightful revenge?

He puts a comforting arm around this complicated person he is halved with, and she takes his other arm around her to get his bear hug. And she cries again, but with tiny tears. The grief of saying goodbye to something that has been with her for too long. Something that is now gone. Something she needs to let go of.

The other two assailants start to move around. Zara breaks from their embrace and shoots both of them in the legs again. They will not be chasing after anyone anytime soon.

Peter stares at her, wondering how she could go from tears to cold killer in a nanosecond. He is compelled to ask her, "Zara, after what they did to you, your friends, why do you leave them alive? They will just do their horrible things again to someone else."

The cold, efficient Zara melts a little as she answers, "Peter, you simply do not know what I have done in my life. I stopped killing people four years ago. Killing does not right the wrong. Only leads to more killing."

She gives him a pistol. "You kill them."

Peter looks at the gun. He thinks about what they were about to do to Zara. He thinks about what they must have done to her. They must have been the ones to have inflicted those scars, those deep wounds on her breast, on her upper and lower inner thighs, which he tried not to stare at. He points the gun at Aymen's head. Staring down the barrel, he begins to shake. And he cannot pull the trigger. He does not need to do so to be a man.

With the tiniest of smiles through her tough façade, she takes the gun from him. "You are not a killer, Peter. Maybe that is why you are my other half."

As they leave the wounded to fend for themselves, Peter watches the large dark birds circling, ones resembling the big birds carved on the pillars at Göbekli Tepe, now a pile of dust thanks to them. With object gone and no sign of the priest, at the truck, Zara says, "Gloves off. No more nice girl," as she ducks under her wounded vehicle to access a secret compartment. Out comes a Russian AK-9. Then comes a box with a Russian VSS Vintorez. "My old friends," she says as she checks them.

Peter knows these weapons as well. "Zara, what are you doing with Spetsnaz special operative weapons?" He points to the AK-9. "Old-tech assault rifle. Shoots without a sound but can pierce bulletproof vests." He points to the VSS. "Old-tech sniper rifle. Sound suppressor and the same subsonic bulletproof-vest-piercing rounds."

She grins like a kid after Halloween. "Old tech. But highly effective."

"And why do you have Spetsnaz special operations weapons?"

She flashes a mischievous smile at him and replies, "Mei is not the only one who can get what she wants out of men. Back in the day, I did too."

Even having the advantage of having been inside her soul for a moment, Peter still does not fully understand this woman. In his confusion, he has to ask, "But I thought you didn't kill anymore?"

"I am going to make an exception for killing a priest. A two-faced, lying man of the cloth who sold us out to the AC, who stole the object for his buddies in Rome," Zara vents as she gives Peter the VSS to carry.

Looking puzzled, a common face he has around her, Peter asks, "Are we going to chase Jean-Paul on foot?" He points to her truck.

Shaking her head, Zara surveys the front tires of her poor truck. The assassins have flattened them.

Peter looks at the punctures, then the writing on the side walls, and says, "You have the top of the top here. Self-inflating, self-sealing run-flat tires. These babies run over a thousand a tire." Seeing her surprised face, he says, "You must not be a car person either."

After reading the truck manual in the glove compartment, Peter, sitting next to Zara in the front seat, punches the needed sequence on the MoxWorld center control console and the tires are fixed. Just in time, as Zara's MoxWrap lets loose an ear-bursting shrill. She yells, "Hang on," as she punches the accelerator and the first bomb obliterates the area where the object was. The second one craters where their truck was parked as Zara pushes these tires as fast as they can stand.

And the bombs keep falling on Karahan Tepe, cratering even all the unexcavated areas. Someone seriously wants no trace of any leads to the object ever to see the light of day. As they descend the ridge that was once home to the object, Peter is particularly proud he did not panic and cower in the fetal position. Was it the object, or was it Zara who did this to him?

As Zara appears to be driving for the sake of driving, Peter asks, "Not to destroy your concentration, but do you know where you're going? The faster you go, the more likely those tires will fail. So hopefully we have a specific place in mind."

Without a flinch, Zara responds, "I planted a tracer in Jean-Paul's

MoxWrap." She taps the center console screen, bringing up a map. "He is fifty klicks from here, heading towards the AC lines. I cannot believe the Catholic pope would be conspiring with the Arabic Confederation. Sending an assassin team, even."

She glances at Peter for a second. "You know he was lying to us all along. His blinks told all. He never had the dreams like you do. He never renounced his vows. And he transmitted our information to these beasts, the ones who raped me, and who stole my object." She reflects a second and amends, "Our object."

Peter points to the screen, where the tracking blip has taken a more southerly direction into New Kurdistan, and not into the Arabic Confederation lines. Zara is exasperated. "Why? It does not make sense. They are going to take the object to the Kurds." She tries to accelerate, but the tires begin to vibrate horribly.

She laments, "They are moving thirty kilometers per hour faster than us. Unless a miracle happens, we are going to lose them." She glances at Peter. "Once they cross the Turkish border, we have lost them. The Turkish border guards are not going to let me pass with my history, and certainly not with these weapons."

With that Little Boy look, Peter says, "Zara, you know I want to help you any way I can. I felt so helpless back there, and they almost… almost… to you."

Since she met this Little Boy, this man, a part of her has begun to regrow. Her compassion. And her compassionate self says, "Peter, your odd yelling distracted them just enough that I could subdue them. You were not so helpless."

Happy that perhaps he was meaningful to her, Peter asks, "So maybe I helped save you? I was a little bit of a knight coming to your rescue?"

Hiding her chuckle, she says, "Yes, you were, Peter. I will forever be grateful."

But deep inside, she knows that her oddly timed period saved her more. For Muslims, even Aymen, vaginal intercourse with a woman during her period is forbidden by the Qur'an. And his disgusted pause, along with Peter's bloodcurdling scream, allowed her to subdue them.

Still, she ponders how her period came so early. Her last one ended only six days ago. And the bleeding stopped as soon as she subdued these beasts.

Peter interrupts her thoughts, asking, "Zara, do you believe in miracles?"

"Why, Peter? Why do you ask?"

He holds up the fragment. "I should be dead from Aymen's gut shot. But I put this on my belly for safekeeping, and it kept me safe." He points to the area where the bullet ricocheted off him.

As Zara ponders these questions of miracles, Jean-Paul's dot stops moving on the center console screen. She looks and says, "They have stopped outside of Harran. Why? It is near neither the AC forces, nor the Kurdish, nor the Turks. They are dead in the middle."

Peter mumbles, "Maybe they don't want anyone to interfere."

Interfere with what? is the question Zara ponders.

Peter takes her hand in his and rubs softly. She looks at him, wondering why. He ponders Dr. Beverly's words about not pressuring PTSD suffers to talk about past traumas, but he is nonetheless logically compelled to ask gently, "I don't mean to probe a topic that might bring back past pain, but what did Aymen mean when he said he and his brother owned you?"

Zara turns away from him, wanting to take her hand back from him, wanting to hide her tears. As her mother trusts him, as her grandmother trusts him, as he is the only man yet who has not lied to her, she finds the courage to trust him too.

She purses her lips and then replies, "They kidnapped me and my sisters, Rona and Diyar. They kept them as their sex slaves for nearly a year. And they coerced them to submit to their perversion by torturing me in front of them. And then they claimed I too was a Ezidi heretic as an excuse to sexually abuse me as well. Finally, I escaped, killing Skander in the process."

She looks to see Peter's expression and determine he is okay to hear the rest. "For years, I hunted down all the men involved in the kidnapping and raping of the women of my sisters' village. I killed each and every one of them in the most heinous, brutal way possible. Only Aymen I could not find. That is, until today."

She takes several deep breaths and rubs Peter's hand. Their moisture on each other helps comfort her to finish her story. "Peter, revenge has no redemption. I thought I would find solace in their brutal and savage murders. But there was none. I was left desolate after I had done the unspeakable back to them. I was lost. Only the words of the Prophet comforted my dark soul. Only his words would be my salvation."

She rubs his hands some more and then takes her hand back, saying, "I do not want to talk about this anymore."

Wanting to be the one she can lean on, Peter refuses to let her retreat into her sorrows. Something must be said, and he is the one who must do so. "I'm no expert on your language, but didn't that Aymen guy call you something exactly the same as Rohat did?"

Her first instinct is to hit him, but it finally dawns on her. Why did Aymen say that to her? How did Aymen know that Rohat had called her a donkey slut when she fled with Zengo, and again when she was home a few days ago? She now comprehends what Peter is suggesting. Not tormenting her for her mistake, for her punishment, but to raise the question of why Aymen and Rohat would get together and why they would want the object. And that priest—where does he fit in, much less the Vatican? Jean-Paul had a gun on Rohat, but maybe this was merely another part of his act.

She reaches out for Peter's hand again, and he flinches, afraid of what she is going to do. She gives him the look, saying, "With all we have been through together, you should know I am not going to hurt you. I want you to be safe." And he slowly offers his sweaty hand. They touch. And the peace, the beauty, the harmony climbs up their arms into their souls.

Softly Zara apologizes. "Peter, I treat you so hard sometimes, and I should not. It means so much that you still come back to my side, to my aid, no matter what I might do to you as the pains in my soul lash out. Please, never stop. Please."

Hours later, as dawn tries to break over the mountaintops demarking the Kurdish lines, the roosters' crowing hides the sounds of Zara and Peter positioning themselves behind a rise just under five hundred meters out from the truck carrying the object. The assassins have their trucks parked near the edge of a farm, one whose residents have fled due to the impending invasion of the AC. Zara sets up her once-retired Spetsnaz sniper rifle and night scope while Peter puts on the headphones attached to her parabolic microphone.

Zara whispers that she sees two trucks and eight, maybe nine assassins. As she scans, she stops and gasps. Peter asks what she's found, and she replies that she sees a cage, and Jean-Paul is being held captive in that cage. God forgive her for what she was thinking about him, for they have tortured him. She whispers for Peter to focus the microphone in that direction.

Peter whispers back they are taunting him over his faith. That they will burn him if he does not renounce his false faith and submit to the true Creator. They pour gasoline over his head, and he cries from the pain in his eyes. Zara spies one of them flicking a lighter. She adjusts her scope and readies to fire.

A panicked Peter pushes down her rifle. "He's innocent. Don't shoot him."

Zara removes his hand and reaims her sniper weapon. "Jean-Paul fears being burned alive. I need to shoot him now out of mercy."

Peter is conflicted. Is this what Alexander meant when he said that Zara was one of the most compassionate people he'd met? Is killing out of mercy part of that compassion?

Her finger about to pull back slowly on the trigger, she sees the lighter being put away. What happened? Something happened. And then she sees him. Unmistakable. Her cousin, speaking with someone who looks American.

She asks Peter to listen in. He gasps, "That cheeky bastard. I can't believe it."

Zara puts down her rifle and sits up. "There's too many of them. I cannot take out enough of them before they light up Jean-Paul." She puts her head down in resignation.

Peter puts his arms around her and hugs her. He brings the object fragment out and puts it in her hands as she looks at him, very puzzled. He kisses her forehead and begins to undo her tunic buttons.

"Peter, what are you doing? Not now. You men. You get into battle, your hormones rage."

Putting his hands around her cheeks, he says, "No, not that. You need to go back with me to see that woman at the temple. She did something there, but I can't clearly picture it. You need to do what she did."

She stares at him in disbelief. Does she trust him on this, or are they just going to kiss while Jean-Paul is flamed? Her instinct is to start shooting and kill as many as possible. She stares at him for but a brief moment, and the innocence in his eyes, his face, overwhelms her. Against her instincts, she joins her hands with his around the fragment, leans in and kisses him. She lets him rub her heart over her shirt as she rubs his. And as their minds enter the zone of peace, of harmony, of clarity, an image becomes clear, and she knows what she needs to do.

And she prays. She prays with Peter in her. With her.

As the sun rises, what should be warmth and clarity is obscured by rapidly forming dark clouds. Zara breathes deeply in synchronicity with Peter, and day becomes night.

Zara looks up. "Get in the driver's seat of my truck."

The epitome of horror flashes across Peter's face. "Zara, I don't know how to drive. I take the bus."

Once again stunned that this person is her other half, she says, "It does not matter. Aim my truck at the one carrying the object and push the right pedal down all the way."

As she literally has to shove him into the driver's seat, the clouds, dark and angry, beg to speak. Beg to bark. Beg to spit out their fury. And as Zara gets into the passenger seat, sniper rifle in lap, she knocks out the windshield with her rifle and tells Peter to punch it.

Her mistake putting him behind a wheel. As the rain begins to pelt them through the open windshield, Peter punches the gas pedal, then lets up, then punches again. Yes, indeed, he did not lie. He cannot drive. She yells at him not to use the brakes and to ram their truck, and just then, the first lightning bolt cracks down, striking the object, and the gas tank of the truck it sits upon explodes. Blinded, Zara stretches her foot down on his and jams the accelerator to the floor, shooting out the front at anything that looks human.

A moment later, her poor truck smashes into the flaming truck, overturning it, sending the object flying. Airbags deployed, Peter is smothered while Zara claws her way out into a torrential downpour with her two Spetsnaz weapons spewing death. The assassins flee, clearly in a panic. Lightning out of nowhere, and then the truck overturning. Zara shoots as many as she can as she runs to Jean-Paul's cage, where the downpour is rinsing the gasoline off the good Father, who looks up into a veritable waterfall washing out his eyes.

She takes a defensive position as the remaining mud-covered assassins take cover in the farm. Peter finally claws his way out of the airbag maze, retrieves Rohat's gun from the backseat, and slips and slides to Zara's position. He shows her proudly that he has a gun. Little consolation to her, but she pats him on the back.

Peter will follow her anywhere, and where it is now is not so good, as she tells him to get Jean-Paul out of the cage. She lays down suppressing fire as Peter helps a very battered Jean-Paul limp to cover behind the object.

He asks Zara, "Now what? I think we've run out of lightning bolts."

Zara, quite perturbed—not at him, but at herself for the rashness of this plan—says, "We hold out here until our next miracle comes. If not, you are going to need to fire that gun shortly."

The sound of several single shots rings through the air. Zara tries to identify where these shots are coming from, and then it goes silent. A haunting pallor overcomes her anguished face. Her teeth clench as she scans the farm with her sniper scope and sees a dark figure running away. She knows this profile. She aims and fires, nicking his buttocks. He falls but scampers away on all fours. She laughs. "That should smolder your burning fires to enslave your poor cousin into a pitiful marriage with you. Second wife, indeed."

From the farm emerge men covered head to toe in black commando suits, with their weapons and arms raised in the air. The leader says, "Don't shoot us. We are on Jean-Paul's side. We are his friends."

With her aim on them while still staying behind the object, Zara says for them to come forward. They remove their black masks and approach. At twenty meters, she tells them to stop and identify themselves.

394 | MAXIME TRENCAVEL

Jean-Paul weakly clambers up on the object and says, "Zara, they are my friends. As you had suspected, I did signal for them to come and save us if a situation like this arose."

And so his comrades come forward to help support Jean-Paul. Major Buchli of the Swiss Guards introduces himself to Zara and Peter, followed by Petrus, Guillaume, Pedro, and Simon. Peter chuckles as they introduce themselves. Former Jesuit priests just like Jean-Paul. *That means they are still priests*, Peter muses as he calls each of them Father.

The major signals for Pedro, Guillaume, and Simon to secure the area as he and Petrus check Jean-Paul's condition. The major says to Jean-Paul, "You need immediate medical attention in a hospital. We can have a helicopter here in twenty and fly you to Ankara and then back to Rome. His Eminence would want to see you and affirm that you are well."

Jean-Paul shakes his head and replies weakly, "My mission is incomplete. I need to remain here with Peter and Zara. Take me to where Zara specifies in her hometown. His Eminence will understand. I still work for MoxWorld Holdings."

As the rain begins to let up, Guillaume and Simon bring back a guest, a mud-covered, cowering one. Peter cries out, "Mr. Ivy League himself. Fancy meeting you out here. Tell me, please, the final test results are in and I'm fired and released from my contractual obligations with MoxWorld."

Zara is not as amused as Peter, but then again, she did not interview with this miserable mole for five hours. Mr. Harlan Chapwell the Third stands slouched in his bulletproof vest in front of her. She puts her AK-9 in his chest. "Peter, why do you not explain to your friend here what happens when a subsonic nine-millimeter is fired at a bulletproof vest? Or maybe you should tell me who you are working for. Alexander?"

Harlan shakes his head. "That man has no respect. He lets losers like Peter on the payroll. And he lets his mistresses like you run the roost. I know for a fact that you are on the payroll under CEO personal expenses. Don't play coy with me."

Infuriated at his accusation, Zara hits him in the gut with the butt of her rifle. As he folds over, she demands, "Who wants the object? Who is bombing us? Who are you working for?"

Harlan lifts his head, groaning, and peers at Peter. "How can you blindly follow a woman with severe PTSD? Everything she has told you is half reality, half protective fantasy. How can you truly believe in what she is telling you? She's only using you to placate her disturbed fantasies."

Not amused, Zara hits him again with the butt of her rifle. "Stop stalling. Tell us who are you working for."

With a cough and a look at Jean-Paul, Harlan replies, "Ask your Vatican friends here. Did you ever wonder why there are so many priests with guns in the midst of Kurdistan and Turkey?"

And before Zara can stop him, he crunches his molars, says goodbye in Russian. Harlan froths at the mouth as the cyanide hidden in his molar begins to take effect, and he crumples to the ground. Zara searches him and finds items of interest only to Jean-Paul, which she palms. She takes his MoxWrap, which is still transmitting, and stops it, searches for where it was transmitting to. Her heart stops when she spies two MoxWrap addresses, both belonging to men she knows, Anatoly and Dan.

She woefully glances at Peter. "Why? Why? They want the Americans and Russians to go to war."

As they wait for Major Buchli's helicopter to come and take Jean-Paul to receive proper medical care, a dusty rose pickup truck, the same model as Zara's crushed red one, appears on the horizon. The major signals for the former priests to deploy in defense, but Zara says it is only her friends, bringing her backup truck. And Peri, Rana, and Firya exit the truck armed to the hilt and run to hug Zara once they affirm all is well.

After a heated debate with the major, who explains that the object can be lifted by his helicopter, the group loads the object onto the second assassin truck, to be driven by Zara, with Rana and Firya riding literal shotgun.

In the pink backup truck, Peri will drive Peter and ex-Father Petrus. Two of the other ex-priests will drive their vehicle, while the major and Guillaume fly Jean-Paul in the helicopter, an old one at that. Peter wonders if the rumors of the Vatican riches are indeed false if they could only send a sixty-plus-year-old helicopter to save Jean-Paul.

In the pink mobile, it is very clear Peri has taken a liking to Petrus, who sits between her and Peter. She has her hand on his thigh, squeezing it, and lets him know in no uncertain terms in what ways she likes him. She asks, "So if you are no longer a priest, you are free to be with the woman of your choosing, no? Ever thought of marrying a nice Kurdish woman? Your French accent is so sexy."

Peter comes to this poor ex-priest's rescue by interrupting, "Petrus, how do you know Jean-Paul?"

"Jean-Paul and I came from the same military school in France," Petrus answers, relieved for the moment not to have to answer Peri's proposal. "And then we were together teaching in the Philippines, and again in Mali with Guillaume."

And Peter gets the same background on the others. Pedro and Simon were in the Congo and Nigeria with Jean-Paul. As Peter probes further, he realizes that the dates when they were in each of these countries coincided with wars or military actions. Soldiers of the pope, he quips to himself.

Peter asks, "So, Nigeria—what was Jean-Paul doing there?"

Petrus smiles and says, "My dear Jean-Paul has a soft spot for redheads, especially ones with good singing voices."

"Oh, you mean Mylène," Peter replies proudly, showing he knows something of Jean-Paul's predilections.

Petrus shakes his head. "Mylène Farmer? *Non, mais non.* Not the singer, but Sister Magali. I thought they were having an affair in the Philippines when he was nearing the end of his Regency, but in the end, they both took their full vows. But he never stopped loving her. She was teaching in Nigeria, and the Boko Haram took a busful of her kids. It took one phone call, and twelve hours later, Jean-Paul is down there with Pedro and Simon. Fourteen hours later, the kids were returned safe and unharmed."

Mystified, Peter says, "I never heard of this incident."

"The good Sister explained to the kids later that it was a training exercise for them to know what to do if the Boko Haram ever came. And their kidnappers—well, Jean-Paul is very thorough about disposing of waste. Magali, he loves her so much, he would do anything for her."

Now Peter understands better his love of Mylène. She is his safe substitute, as his love for the redheaded Sister is of the untouchable kind. The stuff of the romance novels he tried his best to edit.

Peter just has to ask, "Father Petrus, ex-Father Petrus, please tell me this—why would priests operate like Special Forces commandos?"

Petrus simply smiles, so serenely, as Jean-Paul would do. "The work of the Lord takes many forms."

CHAPTER 37

The things that we love tell us what we are.

—Saint Thomas Aquinas

5:30 a.m. GMT+3, May 23, 2022
Siirt, former Turkey, now Anatolian Kurdish State

Peter slowly opens his eyes, never having felt better. No fog. No haze. Just peace and beauty. He tries to remember this really important dream. But alas, that has not changed, as he cannot. Blurry-eyed, he spies the ceiling of Zara's brother's room.

But then, a fuzzy black head pops over him. *Slurp.* And here's a lamb greeting him at the gates of heaven. Was that all a dream? Did they save Jean-Paul or did he really die in a hailstorm of bullets? But then he feels the heat. Was his mother right? He didn't confess enough and he's headed the other way.

Then his eyes pop wide open as he senses the body heat next to him. Zara is in bed with him. She was that dream? Did they really do it last night? He lifts up the bedcovers to find out.

Zara glares at him lifting the covers, hits him, and covers herself. "What are you doing? What did you think we did last night? Certainly not that."

And before he can reply, the other lamb, the white one, crawls under his bedcovers to look at what he was looking at. With a white woolen tail wagging under his nose, Peter sneezes and then uncontrollably laughs as Zara's little friend tickles him.

Years and years without laughter. True laughter. Zara breaks open as her lamb's assault of this banana slug man is the funniest thing she has seen in years.

But her little lamb, never having heard such noises, hides under Peter's armpit while the black one dives under the covers as well. He lifts the two quaking creatures up and hugs them, much to the delight of these woolen balls as well as to the woman next to him.

"They both like you. That is a good sign," Zara asserts, petting the heads of her surrogate daughters. "I raised them to be picky about the boys they cuddle with."

After much petting, Peter starts to say, "Not that I mind at all waking up to your friends, or you, at all—"

"I heard you fighting in here," Zara interrupts, still smiling. "I though you deserved a peaceful sleep after what we have been through." She pauses, glances aside, and says, "And with you saving me yesterday, I thought you deserved to sleep well."

"I've never felt better. But I had this dream," says Peter. "I thought it was about us. Maybe not. But it was very, very important."

Zara watches her lambs, the young ladies of great discrimination purring in the arms of the man next her. And to his surprise, she takes her petite puffballs out from his arms to lay them on the floor. She then leans over, kisses his forehead, and rolls the bedcovers down to his waist. She kisses his chest over his heart, wets her palm, and rubs this special spot slowly with her palm as she kisses his forehead. She pulls his head to her neck, letting her hair drape over him. She whispers for him to smell her.

At the risk of forever losing this long-awaited cherished moment, Peter pulls back from her when her hands reach lower. "Zara, you don't need to do this to access what is in my head, my dreams." He touches her temples and says, "You can touch me here and the same will happen."

She smiles and touches his temples. "Are you happy now?" And she lifts his head and kisses him, softly, and then with her mouth open. She breaks for but a moment and says, "I do this because I want to." And Peter returns her kiss.

As peace transcends and their minds clear, they both observe images of a woman being tortured by giants. Zara wants to flinch and pull away as she has seen too much of the same, but for real, in her life, but Peter holds her tight, with the warm hug that has always settled her. They listen to the lead giant call the woman Ramana, daughter of Ki, the killer of their father. They see Ramana's memory of her mother shooting an arrow through her oldest daughter out of compassion and mercy, another image that forces Zara to pull back in tears. Zara pulls her head away from Peter and cries, "I cannot watch this. I cannot."

From laughter to tears, Peter quickly reframes and tries to put his hands around her tear-covered cheeks, but Zara bats them away. She tries to get up out of the bed, but Peter grabs her and wrestles her back down. He is on top of her, and she fights her instinct to knee him in the groin as she says, "Do not do that with me. You do not understand what I have been through. Do not pin me down with your weight."

He rolls back. "Then come back with me to the dream. We need to understand what your voice is trying to tell us."

She sits up, staring at her nightgown covering her legs. Minutes pass as she finds courage within to witness another woman suffer what she did, what her sisters did. She reengages with Peter with the touches that bring them closer to the voice, to the dreams. She finds that he is there with her, and his warmth and strength bolster hers to watch this tormented woman being forced to tell the giant what he wants to learn about the object.

Ramana says there is another object from her granduncle Namu, whose son married her aunt Sarpani. Namu's boat had been crushed upon the rocks arriving on this side of the lake. With the object lost in the shallow waters off the coast, Namu became so depressed that he drank wine for the rest of his days until, at his wife's request, his sons built a boat to trawl for the object. After many sun cycles, they snagged part of the object, which had split on the sea floor.

Her granduncle again heard a voice that told them to bring the object away from the lake to a high mountain overlooking the fertile plains where their descendants would create a new, prosperous world.

Zara flinches again as the images show the giants gathering to violate this woman. Peter holds her tight as the lead giant turns and shows his face. And the vision reveals the face of Alexander, who yells to the others that he wants this object. He wants to rule the new lands with this object. The other giants cower in fear of the lightning god who strikes those who defile the object, and they proceed with their defilement of Ramana, away from the object.

Having relived the trauma that she had buried deep in her psyche, Zara breaks down in tears, soaking Peter's bedclothes, once her brother's. He tries to comfort her, whispering, "You are my beautiful and wise Zara. You were so brave."

Peter strokes her head as her tears subside. He empathetically says, "I can understand if your relationship with Alexander makes this dream even more terrifying. I can understand if your relationship with him means you cannot be close to me. I have come to know your soul. And there is a spot I cannot touch, your most private thoughts about Alexander."

Her eyes red, from the tears, but now more out of anger at his implications, Zara scolds him. "What do you think? I am having sex with Alexander? Is that how shallow you think I am?"

Sitting back and putting his hands on his belly, Peter meekly replies, "I meant no disrespect. You are everything to me. I want you to know there is no shame about your relationship with Alexander. I just wanted to say I understand and respect your privacy."

She teeters on being mad. A red flush passes her cheeks. The *mehhhs* of her daughters interrupt her thought. She sighs and inhales. "He is not my lover, and I am not his mistress, his sex thing." She glances away from him. "He is like what you would call a godfather, of sorts. He is Sara's nephew, her brother's son who married a Russian woman."

She turns back to him, her arms folded in front of her chest. "He sent me to school. He sent rescue teams to save me from those monsters. He looked out for me as I recovered. He still looks out for me."

Peter is floored. But now Alexander's parting comments to him in Luxembourg start to make sense. He loves her, as he would his own daughter, and thus he envisioned Peter as the prospective son-in-law. Thinking Alexander implied Peter was always destined to be with her, Peter reaches out for Zara, who turns away from him. Peter softly asks, "Why? If it's not Alexander, why?"

Avoiding looking into his eyes, she says, broken up as she stares into his chest, "For the voice, I must let you in. I am so vulnerable with what you can touch in me. The woman in your dream, she witnessed her mother kill her daughter and niece. Killed out of mercy. How do you think her mother felt doing that? The guilt of killing your most cherished ones. The choice of death or worse. The same I had faced with Jean-Paul."

"But you didn't need to kill him. You prayed for the rain instead and you saved him," Peter says, trying to comfort her.

Pursing her lips, she struggles to hold back the tears, which are like high tide destined to come ashore. And the waters let loose as she turns to cry again into Peter's already damp chest.

In time, she composes herself; glancing at Peter, she purses her lips again and says, in as flat a voice as she can muster, "When I escaped from those two monsters, I freed my two cousins. We had scars from having tried to use battery acid to make our faces so hideous they would not want us, but this did not work. Rona had tried to starve herself to death, finding no other way to end her suffering.

"When a message from Alexander got through to me, saying he'd fielded an escape plan, I took Rona and Diyar with me. We were being chased by Aymen and his friends, who were furious, as I had killed his brother Skander. But Rona was so weakened that she stumbled and broke her ankle."

Zara stops, sniffles and buries her face into Peter's hair as she holds him closer. And she continues. "Rona begged me to leave her there and save her sister. She cried about what those monsters would do to her. She could not take any more. We all were so disfigured already." Zara pauses, touching her bedclothes over the deep scars on her inner thighs. "And then Rona looked at me, her eyes saying what she wanted me to do. To shoot her. But I could not. I just could not. She was my sister."

Zara stops again and grips Peter's hand very tightly. "Rona was my sister. She knew all my secrets, and I hers. How could I shoot her? But Diyar was also my sister. And as we saw Aymen and his goons getting closer, I aimed Skander's gun."

Clenching Peter's hand ever tighter, until he felt like screaming, she says, "I cannot get the image of Rona out of my head. In my nightmares forever is this image. Like the rabbits you saw me kill, I blew her head apart. Splattered across eternity. This is the place you could not touch in me."

With that, Zara loses it and cries in Peter's arms in near hysteria, muttering about how bad she is. Peter embraces her tightly, kissing her hair, kissing her ear, and whispering how much he knows she is a good person.

The door to the room opens ever so slightly as Maryam peers in, having heard the laughter, then crying. She spies her daughter in Peter's bed in a lover's embrace, and she smiles as she lets the little lambs out and closes the door so quietly and discreetly.

Zara, wet as a dolphin, kisses Peter tongue to tongue as they continue their embrace. She whispers to him, "There are so many reasons why I cannot love you and you should not love me." With that said, she gets up, straightens out her soaked nightgown, and leaves for her room.

CHAPTER 38

However rare true love may be, it is less so than true friendship.
—François de La Rochefoucauld

1:30 p.m. GMT+3, June 1, 2022
Siirt, former Turkey, now Anatolian Kurdish State

Petrus sits next to Jean-Paul, who is in a private ward in a hospital in Siirt as per his request. On the television plays the MoxWorld News, showing this morning's invasion of northwestern Turkey by three armored Russian divisions. Video shows the air battle between the Turkish and Russian air forces. Sahir talks about the US and Russian fleets facing off in the Black Sea, and the ultimatum the US president gave, demanding a withdrawal date of one week from today, or the US forces in Turkey would engage Russian air and ground forces. Rhonda shows Sanliurfa, which is now under an encircled siege as Turkish forces withdraw. She discusses the third day of Turkish paratroopers' occupation of buildings in Diyarbakır, the capital of the Anatolian Kurdish State. The Turkish tanks that were moved up from Sanliurfa to break through Kurdish lines and join forces with these paratroopers have been stalled by advanced weapons now possessed by the Kurds. The US president accused the Russians of supplying these arms and has sought the approval of Congress to mobilize the most advanced US weapons to Turkey.

Jean-Paul watches, shaking his head while his old friend Petrus gives him a message from the Father General. Petrus asks, "Jean-Paul, do you understand what he is asking?"

Jean-Paul acknowledges.

Petrus says more forcefully, "He expects your obedience."

His eyes puffy and red from the exposure to gasoline, Jean-Paul peers at Petrus. "I have renounced my vows. Everyone knows that, including the Father General."

Staring back at the television screen, Petrus states, "You can never truly leave. You know that."

Zara enters the room dressed in a yellow cotton gown with colorful flowers and gold trim over beige pants with a beige-and-gold headscarf. Jean-Paul asks Petrus to leave and give them privacy.

"How are you doing, priest? You are a hard man to kill," Zara says.

"I am recovering. Thank you for asking, Zara," replies the suffering Father. "Forgive my voice, as the fumes eroded my throat and my lungs have been injured. It is good you did not come yesterday, as I was still in confusion." He points to his hands. "And my skin is sore all over. But I am happy that you and Peter came to save me."

She takes his hand and puts his crucifix in it. He smiles and clasps her hand. "Where did you find this? I thought it lost. Lost like my soul."

"Where? On a dead mole," Zara replies. She pulls out a new white gold chain, puts the crucifix on it, and places the chain around the good Father's neck. "It looks good on you."

Jean-Paul cries through his puffy eyelids. "This means so much to me. I stepped away from my faith. I renounced."

"I know. You renounced your vows," says Zara in her most sympathetic tone.

"No, not renounced my priesthood, but my belief in Christ," Jean-Paul laments. "I thought I was strong. I was once the soldier who braved death without fear. But in that moment in that cage, with gasoline soaking into my soul, I recanted Christ as my savior. As they held the lighter closer and closer, I recanted Christ as the Son. I traded my faith for my life." And he cries through puffed-out crimson eyelids.

Zara leans over and hugs him. A hug such as he has not experienced since the Philippines. She whispers to him, "To me, you will always be the priest of faith in God, faith in Christ." She kisses his forehead.

"You are so kind, Zara. You are who we thought you would become," the saved priest praises.

Zara reflects on those words for a second, and her anger at the men who kidnapped them arises. Not only at her traitorous cousin, at that mole who Alexander trusted, at the men who kidnapped and raped her and her sisters, but at men who tried to burn a priest in the name of her faith. She is furthered saddened that these few misguided savages are why many in the Western world malign her religion.

Kneeling beside his bed, she gently covers his hand with hers and begs, "Please, Jean-Paul, please do not judge these men as representatives of Islam. A true modern Muslim would not have asked you to recant your faith at the point of imminent death."

The good Father, former Father, puts his hand on her head and replies, "I value your words to me. Please be assured I would not have thought poorly of your faith. But you are mistaken. They did not ask me to convert to Islam."

In complete surprise, Zara's back straightens. "But we heard through the parabolic mike, they asked you to renounce Christ in the name of the true Creator."

And oddly, Jean-Paul smiles. "And there lies your answer. Who is their true Creator? Please do not tell Peter what I am about to reveal to you. These assassins, as you call them, they wanted me to confess my true belief that God, as we know him, as we have expressed in our writings and in our traditions, was created by beings not from this planet. They had a cell phone camera recording my confession, which they were going to show to the world to discredit the Church, given my close connection to the Holy Pontiff and my positions on his extraterrestrial commissions."

With a gasp, Zara sits back. "But even the Islamic extremists would not sponsor such a blasphemous, heinous act like this. Who did?"

"Whoever did found people in your past who hated you, who hated Alexander, and men from the Boko Haram, the Congo, Bosnia, who hated me. All had no political alliances with any of the countries about to go to war around us, which is why they stopped in no-man's-land to record and transmit my confession. Whoever assembled this group chose mostly would-be assassins of Islamic faith and, in doing so, may have wanted to fan the flames of worldwide religious tension and drive the world deeper into a global holy war."

She looks away for a minute, reflecting on the implications of the revelation, then leans forward, kneeling again, and offers, "I too have a confession, if you would hear it."

The good Father, happy she has confided in him, leans down, delicately places his hand back atop her head, and says, "Please. I would be so honored."

She looks into that tiny space between the red balloons that have replaced his eyelids and says, "I was going to blow your head off before they could light you up. I thought you might have wanted someone to do that."

A strategic pause as she stares coldly into his eyes. "I thought for sure you were the mole. At first, I thought you were simply the device of the Vatican spying on us. Then I thought you were the one informing the assassins of our every move. So I had no compunctions about blowing your head off.

"But then I heard how they tortured you," she says with eyes turned soft and compassionate. "As they did to me. And as I would have wanted, I thought the most merciful, most compassionate act I could give to you was to cleave your head off."

He slowly raises her head, lightly clasps his hands around hers, and says, "Thank you. I know you would have done so out of love and mercy for my soul."

"Jean-Paul, you must understand that it was not an easy thing for me to do to aim a sniper scope at your skull. I know you must think me a cold-blooded murderer, about which you would be correct for most of my kills. But what keeps me awake at night, what I most suffer from, is the memories of the last time I had to kill someone I loved out of mercy and compassion. It is not so that you feel you did the right thing. You lose and they lose. And there is no redemption. Only the pain that you killed them haunting your dreams, night after night after night, like a cancerous nodule in your soul."

She takes his hand from hers and opens it. "I hope you are not offended. I would not have thought twice about blowing your head off. You would be in heaven, watching me here, suffering in my pain over killing someone I love." She then places his medallion in his hand.

Jean-Paul breaks down in tears again. "I thought this had been lost. Forever gone. And my dear Magali would have been so devastated. There are so many things I have done that she would not be able to forgive me for, but losing this is much worse."

Sensing his deep love for this woman, Zara asks, "Why do you not go back and reunite with your Magali? You found the secret of her medallion. Your mission is over. You have delivered your promise to her."

Jean-Paul grimaces, not from the pain of the gasoline, but from his unresolved guilt. "We almost did not take our final vows once. It would be a shame to ask her to break hers now." He looks into Zara's eyes as best he can. "I hid things from her. I did not let her into my soul completely. I lied to her."

Realizing his parable for herself and Peter, Zara glances momentarily to the side. "If you are not a priest anymore, why not go back and tell her now? She must love you still, as much as I see you do her."

She looks at him and winces as she adds, "And if you truly are still a priest, then you should go back and talk to your friend, the pope, and ask him to change the rules about priests and marriage. Think about how much better your religion would be if priests could have normal, natural human relations with women."

Jean-Paul tries to protest her accusation about his priesthood, but she will not hear any of it. "Your secret is safe with me. I know you do not suffer the affliction. You lied to me as you likely lied to Magali. I will not tell Alexander, but you should tell her. But what I cannot understand is what your true interest is in the object. For a number of hours there, I was going to kill you because I thought you had stolen it for the pope."

"Zara, please trust me about what my motives are," says Jean-Paul.

"Priest, that is a tall order, for me to trust. Peter trusts you, so I will trust in his trust in you," Zara states.

She takes his hands into hers again. He flinches from the pain and she loosens her touch. She asks, "What do you know about miracles?"

The good priest is feeling well again as she asks him to dwell upon theological concerns. "A miracle is often something that neither natural nor scientific law can explain. In Catholicism, a miracle is thought to be an act of God."

"My great-grandfather, a Sufi imam, once told me stories of Sufis being clairvoyant, taming wild beasts, and producing food and rain in seasons of drought."

Jean-Paul lightly rubs Zara's hand with his thumb and asks, "Why do you ask about miracles?"

Zara puts her other hand on her lower belly. "My period. It was not time for it. But it came during the moment of their attack on us and saved me and Peter. And then it disappeared as mysteriously as it arrived. Is that a miracle? Or only my biology acting up under stress?"

As Jean-Paul reflects upon her words, Zara touches the top of his head. "The rain that washed the gasoline off you. Peter's touch allowed me to envision what someone did ages ago. I prayed. And the rain came and saved you."

Jean-Paul again reflects upon her words, then speaks. "You must continue whatever it is you are doing with Peter. I do not want to encroach upon your privacy, but you must continue whatever it is. Apparently, your connection with the voice is getting stronger as you are with him in that way, just as the traditions said would happen."

She looks at him with a mix of compassion and dismay. Begging him, she says with flushed cheeks, "Please. Do not break my trust. When we touch, I see what Peter sees, and he sees what I see. What I have heard. We touched this morning after he had a dream and saw a giant who looked like Alexander, who wanted the object to rule the lands."

Jean-Paul reflects. "This is a difficult situation. You are asking if we can trust Alexander. You are closest to him—what do you believe?"

"Do not go there," Zara says. "Peter did that with me this morning. There is no intimate relationship between us. None that would allow me to know whether to trust him or not after a dream like that."

Pointing to the television, Jean-Paul says, "As he did in the Crimea and Ukraine, Alexander persuaded the Russians to invade the Turkish coast, where the other object lies. One must ask why he needs both. Have you heard the voice again, Zara?"

Zara simply shakes her head.

Taking both her hands into his, Jean-Paul says, "You need to be as close to Peter as your morals will let you. Only you can know what line you are willing to cross or should cross. Only by being as close together as two humans can be will you reveal the truth. You need to let Peter in. Wherever that is."

Now Zara reflects. "Priest, I will make you a deal," she replies. "You call Sister Magali and tell her in no uncertain terms how you still feel about her and let her choose if she wants to be closer with you. And I will do the same with Peter."

He nods. Not wanting him to procrastinate, Zara looks up the good Sister on his MoxWrap and dials her for him. She stays long enough to hear the Sister's delight that he called her and not the other way around, as their long history has shown.

The compassionate one, Zara, leaves the room knowing indeed she has saved him.

CHAPTER 39

*Marriage is a long conversation. When marrying you
should ask yourself this question: do you believe you are
going to enjoy talking with this woman into your old age?
Everything else in a marriage is transitory, but most of the
time that you're together will be devoted to conversation.*

—Friedrich Nietzsche

5:30 p.m. GMT+3, June 1, 2022
Siirt, former Kurdistan of Turkey, now Anatolian Kurdish State

That dusty rose pickup truck of Zara's pulls into the bomb shelter adjacent to Sara's ancestral home. Does such a feminine color for this tough woman bespeak something else in her soul that she does not desire to be known?

As she gets out, Zara laughs as she watches her mother trying to show Peter how to milk a goat. Roza is laughing too, in a way Zara has never seen from her before. And they laugh together as the goat is winning, standing over Peter flat on the ground. She avoids eye contact with him as she wipes the tears of laughter from her cheeks.

That night after everyone is in bed, she sneaks into her brother's old room again. Peter, having just put his head to his pillow, looks at her with great confusion, as he thought her last words to him meant they would not sleep together again, ever. As she crawls in under the covers with him, she affectionately pecks him on his forehead.

He softly says, "I promise not to press you for areas you wish to hide. I want you to know how much I deeply respect you and your need for privacy."

Zara hugs him, her nonverbal way of saying thank you.

Peter, though, needs to ask another question, one that has rattled within him ever since they saved Jean-Paul. "Zara, if you don't mind, I do wish to ask you another very personal, maybe private question."

She looks at him cautiously, then nods yes as she kisses his nose.

Summoning all the bravery he can, Peter asks his burning question. "Why do you own a pink pickup truck?"

She laughs. He is so much her Little Boy in all the good ways. She looks serious and replies, "The Daesh soldiers were afraid if they were killed by a woman, they would not go to heaven. My rose truck would nearly always send them running, and many times we never needed to fight."

Peter touches her hair, pushes it back behind her ear, and strokes her neck. "That's one of the reasons why I have come to love you so. You are so smart."

Zara takes his hand and puts her hair back over her ear. She swallows. "I cannot do with you what a man and woman who are very close do. They took that away from me. It is impossible for me to have sex, to enjoy sex, to have children. But we need to be together. We need to sleep together."

She turns around in bed away from him. "I have done very bad things, and I was punished for it. Each time I was with a man, bad things would happen afterwards. I went against my faith. And I was punished so that I could never be with a man again. My brother was tormented by what he saw happened to us, the bad things that happened to my sisters, their mother, and me because I was careless. He fought with the PKK out of his penance for not being able to help us. He died from guilt over not being able to help us. In reality, my bad actions led to his death.

"I killed my sister, and it was my fault she was taken. My other sister, Diyar—a year after she returned to her father's family, she set herself on fire out of family shame and dishonor for what they did to her, what my misdeeds did to get all of us punished in the worst ways imaginable."

Peter puts his arm around her, offering her comfort. She pets his arm as she says, "That is the box I did not want you to see. I am a very bad person. And I live in perpetual punishment for it."

Turning her around to face him again, Peter caresses her cheeks in that special way that demonstrates to her familial love. He hugs her tightly and deeply for a long while. She feels peace in his arms. He whispers in her ear, "I am willing to take vows of chastity, the same as Jean-Paul did, still deeply in love with his Sister Magali. What is important is my love for you, which transcends the physical."

She caresses his cheeks and says, "I cannot love you back. Such a thing is no longer possible."

He kisses her lightly, then deeply. He whispers again in her ear, "I can love you without you feeling that you need to love me in return. I think I now know what unconditional love means. You have shown me. And for that I will be forever grateful." They kiss deeply again.

Peter then dares to ask, "Zara, will I ever be more than a little boy to you?"

She smiles, so deep throughout her being, and replies, "You will always be my Little Boy." She hugs him and they embrace. And they feel the peace that bonds them—to each other, and to the voice.

In the middle of the night, Maryam sneaks a peek into her daughter's room. Empty. Not even the bed touched. She then peeks into her son's room. And there they are in a lovers' embrace under the covers. She looks up and thanks Xwedê.

The next morning, Zara takes her Little Boy out for a hike in the hills behind her great-grandmother's village. Not quite the mountains of Duhok, where she grew up, but she still loves the outdoors and the freedom to go as she pleases. As they begin to leave the compound, her little black lamb comes running up to rub against Zara's leg, making the cutest of sounds. Zara picks up the lamb, her child. She asks if she missed her. She hugs and kisses her and rocks her like a baby, and then her other little lamb comes over. She picks this white one up as well with hugs, kisses and rocking along with the black one.

This side of this mysterious woman does not escape Peter's attention. Is this the soft-eyed, compassionate Zara Sasha referred to?

Putting her little children down, she says to Peter, "If we could all be in submission to Xwedê as well as are my lambs, all would be better."

And the black and white lambs follow her up the hill with Peter in tow. Many kilometers later, the black lamb finds her way into Zara's arms again. And much to Peter's surprise, he ends up carrying Zara's white surrogate daughter on the hike back. Zara does not fail for a second to notice that her little lambs approve of Peter, for lambs do not lie.

On the way back, they pass by a house. Kilda's, says Zara as she asks Peter to wait while she talks with her. Peter plays on the doorstep with the two lambs, and a teenaged girl comes out wanting to play too. They play until the lambs seek their adopted mother's attention. Peter finds some white rocks and two black ones and plays wolves and sheep with the girl. Something that does not escape Zara's attention either.

After the young girl's sheep surrounds the last wolf, the soft-eyed Zara sits down with Peter and they play with her wooly children. Seeing how they have adopted Peter, she hugs him, gives a peck on his cheek, and takes his hand to stand. And they leave for home without a word said.

After lunch, Roza and Maryam take Peter outside to teach him to whirl. This whirl is simply the worst for Peter, never one to dance. Zara laughs at Peter's attempts to stay upright and not hit anyone or anything. Seeing how amused she is, Maryam invites her daughter to whirl with Peter. Zara smiles and shakes her head no. Her mother relents as it is only a matter of time.

That night, the same thing happens again. Zara sneaks over to Peter's room after everyone has gone to bed. Maryam peers out and watches her, so happy her little Zara has put the tenets of her faith aside for the moment as this man is the right man. But then she hears them leaving his room. Maybe she is finally taking him to her bed? She peeks again and is puzzled as they leave the house with blankets.

Outside, Zara and Peter sit with the object. She whispers to him, "It means so much to me that you do not talk of the aliens. You show your respect of the voice. Of me. And I feel that much closer to you."

Peter replies, "Alien or God, I do not know. I know my obedience is to you." They touch, embrace, kiss, and Zara leans her head onto his soft shoulder.

Closing his eyes, Peter searches for his bravery gene. For he is about to reawaken the dragon. Willingly.

"Zara, who was the woman you stopped and talked with earlier?"

Stiffening a little, Zara replies, "Oh, Kilda? Roza babysat her when she was young."

Peter shifts his position. "And Waja, her daughter—she has scars on her."

Zara sits straighter, her eyes starting to darken. In a deeper voice, she laments, "In some traditional Kurdish families, young daughters are betrothed to men of power or wealth for the benefit of the family. Kilda's daughter, Waja, was thirteen years old. About the same age as my aunt Leyla and my best friend Peri when they were essentially sold off by their families. None of these marriages worked, and the poor girls were left suffering, traumatized, abused by their supposed husbands, as was Waja."

He reflects on Dr. Beverly's advice. Be patient. Be a good listener. Build trust. And do not pressure them to talk about what they do not want to talk about. But now, having touched this troubled soul in their time around the object, Peter cannot sit back and let her suffer so either. Inside he is coming to understand that his new role in her life will require him to be courageous.

And so, Peter takes her hand into his and delicately continues his line of questioning. "And what happened to Waja? She's safe now, right?"

Zara shifts a few times, stares down, and quietly replies, "Waja escaped from her tormentor, the man who paid her father for her body as his third wife. And this man wanted his property back."

Squeezing his hand tightly, she pauses in the midst of many conflicting emotions, in the midst of dark memories of so many lives to be forgotten. "And I solved the issue. He will never torment Waja again."

He hugs her in the way she has missed, wanted, and so needs now. Zara feels the recovered bump on his head, the one that bled at their first meeting. "I suspect you have done the same in your life," she says as her hand descends to his right arm, to a spot she had felt when she taught him how to aim his pistol on the shooting range.

He puts his hand upon hers at that spot on his arm. "My little sister. They had her pinned against a wall, and she was only in middle school. I was bigger than they were, but there were more of them than me. But she got away while they took out their anger on me. Lucky for me, she got help, and before those boys could do real damage, they ran." He rubs his right rib cage.

She strokes his hair back, kisses him on his forehead, a wet one—the kind that bonds the likes of them. "Your little sister, your Mrs. Harrison, your Mei, and then me. You fool people when they meet you. They think you foolish, weak, and cowardly. But underneath that veneer lies a brave, clever man who arises when a woman he cares about is in need. Tell me I am wrong about this?"

They hug and she whispers into his ear, "Who arises when I need you most." And she kisses his ear.

Sensing the moment, his hand under her chin, Peter lifts Zara's head up to make eye contact. "Zara, do you trust me?"

Given her history of trusting men with her intimacies never resulting in a positive outcome, she first tries to turn away, but a newfound strength in Peter's hand holds her fast and steady.

He wraps his arms around her, transmitting a warmth she so needs at this moment. She relaxes and sinks into his embrace. With eyes closed, a sense of security envelops her. The same as when her father held her. The same as when her first Little Boy wrestled with her.

She opens her eyes and says, "I trust you."

Sitting up straight, nearly choked up, she adds, "But don't break my trust, Little Boy. Or I'll have to kill you."

Her words no longer transmit fear to Peter, as he has come to appreciate this is how she says, "I love you." Hands again on her cheeks, he plants a wet kiss upon her nose, a lip-grazing one on her lips, and then a deep tongue-laden kiss into her mouth.

Zara braces herself for what she would expect men in her past life to do after a kiss like this. Intimacies that she has not had for many a year. Intimacies she physically cannot fulfill for him. Intimacies she had forestalled having in her life by choice in her pursuit of her faith. But now she wants him. Somehow he knows how to fill that void within her. As with their past touches, the sense of peace, calm, and harmony overtakes all her proclivities. She accepts that what will happen now must happen and puts her destiny in his full control.

And although her desires would want otherwise, Peter's hands do not go down to her chest, nor down between her legs, but instead push her hair behind her ears. He licks the fingers of both his hands and begins to massage her temples, driving the wetness into her. Peter's superpower of assembling diverse abstract information into a simple statement has led him to understand that the exchange of their fluids is a way to activate something very ancient in the both of them.

Rationally acknowledging her new mate is not simply after intimacies with her body, she does the same to him, massaging his temples with wetted fingers. And they meld in the presence of the object. A lightness. A dissociation from the external as all sounds slowly disappear. A floating within a growing warm light.

And she begins to feel free at last. Until she senses him reaching for the black zone buried deep within her. She opens her eyes, pulls her hands back, and yells, "You promised you wouldn't touch me there. You promised to respect my privacy."

Catching herself and not wanting to lose him as well as the only other two men in her life who made her feel so secure and safe, she decides she will let him cross another line of hers. A compromise she might live with, even though he will be disappointed. So, she takes his hand down to the growing warm wetness between her legs and says, "Touch me here instead, but not where you tried."

He shakes his head, taking his hand moist with her lower essences, to his lips. He licks her wetness on his hand and then plants another deeply throaty kiss upon her lips and mouth. She calms again.

"The voice. What would the voice want you to do?" Peter whispers quietly. "Know that I am totally committed to you. And I believe that the oral tradition is clear. Only man and woman together. And we two, truly together, can solve anything."

She logically comprehends that he is correct, but past precedent has shown otherwise.

Gone is the quivering young man hiding in the fetal position as the bombs fell around them. He has discovered a new sense of courage around her and this object. He wets his fingers again and massages her temples. She closes her eyes with the growing warmth, but a little piece of her still remains tense. He kisses her again, licks his fingers again, but this time places them behind her neck, upon that special bump their lineages share. And his soft digits lightly rub there.

And total surrender happens. She lets her strong will to protect that dark place in her dissipate. She surrenders all as she wets her fingers and places them on the same place behind Peter's neck and rubs.

As they lose themselves into their new surrender, their new release from earthly bonds, their willingness to follow the light, the memories of an ancient time come back to them. An aged, solidly built dark-haired woman lies on a mat covered by blankets. She is dying. Kneeling at her side, holding her hand, is a lithe yet strong woman with long straight black hair, crying for her mother. Normally the epitome of strength, this daughter is distraught at the impending death of the true source of her inner strength.

"Ki, my child," says the dying mother. "Please do not fret for me, for I will go to another place of beauty. I fret, though, for you. Your obedience and faith are inspiration to all of my grandchildren, your children, your nieces and nephews. But I am saddened that you cannot touch what your sisters and I have touched, no matter how much you pray."

Wiping her uncustomary tears, Ki replies, "Please do not worry for me, Mother. I will continue my faith in your god. I will continue to lead prayers along with my sisters many times each day for all in our village. I have come to peace with the fact that I was not gifted as you three to hear the voice. I can live with this because of my love for you and my sisters."

"My dear Ki. My dearest. You are the most faithful, the most obedient of all who do not hear. But I fear you will not join us, not because you do not hear the voice, but because you have not fully let go, not fully surrendered. Only when you do can you truly be with the voice, and with me after my death."

"But, Mother, I do not understand. I am obedient. I am humble to your god and to all. I live in modesty and respect."

The older woman signals for her daughter to lean towards her. She strokes her daughter's face. "You are the one with the greatest compassion of all our lands. I love you so. In your compassion, you have internalized a hatred of those who killed your father and grandfather, who raped your grandmother, your aunt, and me. All of this darkness resides in a tiny place deep within you that you show to no one. You must release yourself from this bondage, which restrains you from fully following the voice."

As the dying mother closes her eyes, Ki signals for her sisters to come in prayer around her. And the elder woman's facial features become clear to Peter and Zara. Hers is the face of Zara, at which Zara opens her eyes in shock.

Knowing what his other half needs at this moment, Peter kisses the forehead of the woman in front of him, the one with the face of the ancient matriarch, and gives her a deep hug.

Comprehending fully now that Peter does this out of respect for her father's and brother's love for her, Zara hugs him back. She leans them both gently down to the ground and pulls the blanket around them. She so wants to tell him she loves him. And maybe she did, but she is too enraptured to remember. And they fall asleep once again in each other's arms.

Maryam tiptoes out and covers them in their blankets as a good mother should with her sleeping kids. She hears Zara saying in her sleep, "I have beauty inside, Mama. Yes, I do." And Maryam knows that this man has truly brought her little daughter back to her. The beautiful little Zara, full of love and joy.

For the next number of nights, the same pattern happens again and again as the two sneak out each night to bond in presence of the object. And Zara's love reemerges and grows. In the daytime, Zara is now willing to teach Peter the Sufi whirl. He tries to whirl but keeps crashing into her, finally knocking her over. He flinches, thinking she is going to hit him, but she just laughs and teases him for his lack of balance.

One evening, Zara knows she has followed the words of the voice. She has let Peter in. And she senses something has grown in her. She tells Peter, "I have let you in. I hide nothing. You have touched me and truly know all there is to me. The horror in my brother's eyes as he was forced to watch my rape. The horror in my heart as I killed Rona. The darkness in my soul as I brutalized and mutilated her tormentors. The hundreds I have killed for my lovers."

She kisses him, and pets his hair. "And you have been with me without judgment, only seeking to comfort my soul. And in that, you have brought peace, joy, light, and warmth back into my soul."

She knows that with this Little Boy, this man, she finally can share and talk about her darkest secrets. She so needed to let these out, to verbalize her fears, her anger, her doubt, her guilt, and not be judged. And she now knows what halves of the apple truly meant. He would listen to hear each night, see with her as they touched. And listen again he does as she takes him hiking in her mountains, little baby lambs and all.

And then one night as they touch, seated at the object, she says, "What?"

"I didn't say anything," Peter says back.

"Shhhh," she says sharply to Peter. "Yes. Yes, I am listening." She pauses, then says, "You are right. I see and understand. Thank you."

Another pause and she asks, "But how can I? Yes, I will. Yes, I understand."

So curious about her ability to talk with this voice, Peter asks, "Was that the voice? What did she say?"

"She said we, all her people, all her creations, must exercise greater patience with each other. For true peace will only come with patience, which leads to understanding, the basis of tolerance."

Taking his hand into hers, she gently rubs her thumb along his palm. "In combat, you must make instantaneous decisive judgments. But in normal life, you have the liberty to wait before making judgment. I jumped to conclusions about Mei because of how she looked. I thought the worst of Jean-Paul because he was a Jesuit. And you. I thought you superficial because of where you came from. And the prejudice, the stereotypes, the intolerance I despised as a teen, I find that I have displayed myself. It stops when you stop and show others how to be tolerant."

She kisses him on his forehead and peers into his eyes with hers, so soft, large, and brown. "And you. That is one of the reasons I have come to love you. You are special among the special. You judge not. You watch, you probe, and you seek to understand. You did with me. And you see me, know me, and share love with me."

Zara hugs him. The kind of hug you give your savior. She then adds, "She said I need to forgive myself as she has forgiven me. To forgive is to be tolerant. She said I did well allowing you to touch me in those places I needed to forgive. And she knows you have forgiven me." Zara kisses Peter. "And she says we should keep doing what we do with each other. Your dream tonight will tell us the rest."

She takes his hand and leads him back into the house, to her room this time.

As Zara closes the door to her room, Maryam peeks out of her own room, so happy that Zara has finally brought this nice Peter to her bed. She prays, *Let Zara bear a little girl as nice as she has been.*

As morning comes, Peter awakes, seeing Zara looking at him. He knows this look. Sarah did that with him the morning after their first night of passion together. But he is sure *that* did not happen last night.

Zara touches his face, kisses him, and pulls his head to her neck, asking him to smell her essence. Much to his surprise, she pulls up her nightgown and puts his hand upon her naked mounds. She guides his fingers over the deep indentations in her left breast where those monsters seared her tissue away in anger over her obstinacy about fulfilling their pleasures. She does not want to hide anything from him any longer. Neither outside nor in.

He feels her loss, much like partial mastectomies he saw in a book he edited. As he continues to rub his fingers over her heart, he looks her in the eyes and says without saying how truly beautiful she is to him. And their minds begin to clear.

The images from Peter's dream last night appear to them. The two halves of the object were put back together. And sheer, utter devastation happened.

They break their embrace and look at each other. They cannot let Alexander have the object.

CHAPTER 40

To one who has faith, no explanation is necessary.
To one without faith, no explanation is possible.
—Saint Thomas Aquinas

5:45 a.m. GMT+3, June 9, 2022
Siirt, former Turkey, now Anatolian Kurdish State

In shock. Once again. He lies in Zara's bed next to her. She has let him in. Another step in their growing intimacy. But that intimacy together only led to a vision of the ending of the world as they know it. They both gaze at each other in silence. Not the gaze of lovers, but the stare of the bewildered, assimilating what they envisioned together.

Peter slowly gets up, straightens out his nightclothes, and tries to sneak out of her room and back to his. But as he silently closes Zara's door, Maryam comes around the corner on her way back from the prayer room. He freezes, but she takes his hand and leads him back to her son's room, closing the door behind them.

Maryam whispers, "My future son, I thank you for bringing back my little Zara. She is who she has wanted to be again. Thank you." She kisses his cheek. "I am so happy you are sleeping together finally. She needs that in her life again too."

Hands waving in front of him and shaking his head side to side, Peter says, "No. Roza told me that was off-limits. We aren't sleeping together that way."

Taking his hands into hers, Maryam grimaces and says in a reassuring motherly voice, "It is okay. I will talk to Roza. Zara needs you to be with her in that way."

And to their surprise, someone knocks on the door. Maryam says, "Quick, start twirling."

Zara comes in and sees Peter twirling with her mother chanting. Peter stares at Zara with tremendous apprehension. Maryam says to her daughter, "Forgive him, please. He wanted me to teach him to whirl more correctly."

Zara simply smiles, kisses her mother good morning, and takes Peter's hand to show him how to balance better.

Late that morning, the family welcomes Jean-Paul, brought back from the hospital by his Jesuit friends. Zara has spent the morning preparing lunch. Peter comes up behind her in the kitchen, puts his hands around her waist and teases her about preparing food for the men. She turns and puts her arms around him and says, "I will when I want to apologize to holy men for mistrusting them." And she pecks him on the lips and returns to preparing the food.

After Zara's sumptuous lunch, the Jesuits leave. Leyla offers to go back to her apartment to allow Jean-Paul to stay at the house. He is too humble and says he will sleep with the object outside. Leyla says this is not proper and she will leave after spending dinner with the family.

That afternoon, the trio gather around the object. Zara discusses the dream Peter and she shared with Jean-Paul. They agree they should contact Alexander, all three together. Zara sets up a 3-D projection call.

Alexander appears. His back is turned to them. He lets them wait, then slowly he turns and demands, "Why have you been out of contact for so long? This is not normal."

Zara says, "We had nothing to report. Many unforeseen factors have intervened since our last message."

The tall Russian with the long face and piercing dark eyes glares at each of them in turn. "My team retrieved another object from the ocean floor." He peers at Jean-Paul. "I saw your findings and was extremely disappointed you did not communicate them to me personally. I had to use my own initiative to learn that this was another object."

Alexander turns away from them, looking upwards. "I had a dream. In my dream, you three conspired against me to keep the object for yourselves." He turns and glares again into each of their eyes. "Is this true? I would be so disappointed with each of you if this were so. I have monitored your movements. Who wishes to be truthful with me about what is really happening?"

"Sasha, we were attacked three times, and the object was destroyed at the temples of Karahan Tepe." Zara aims her stern eyes into his. "Our deal was that I get them there, object or no object. You will deliver my requests of you."

"Zara, Zara, Zara," Alexander bemoans. "You should not lie to your Sasha. Did the priest teach you how to do that? Or was it your new lover, Peter?"

Not amused, Zara states back, "The deal is the deal. Do not renege. You should know more than anyone what I can do to those who fail to deliver what they have promised."

Alexander stares straight into Peter's eyes. "You know you should not lie to me about what happened."

Peter, clearly mad at how Alexander has treated Zara, asserts, "You never said I would be attacked in your jet. Nor anything about being bombed three times by unknown aircraft, and then taken captive by radical assassins—much less your Mr. Ivy League HR guy ratting on us. *You* tell *me* what is happening."

Like a proud father, Alexander smiles at the backbone his boy has developed, but like the proud father, he pushes his boy again. "Whatever happened to that meek boy I interviewed in San Francisco? The one who knew how to speak properly to his elders."

Alexander glances at Jean-Paul. "I am not talking with the priest, who is a traitor to you all. I have monitored his transmissions with the Vatican. Zara and Peter, do not trust him." He turns back to Zara. "Contact me when you have decided to be honest with me." And the transmission ends.

Quivering, Peter says, "Mei said Alexander is always two steps ahead. He knows everything." He turns to Jean-Paul. "Was all of this really for your Sister Magali and her medallion? Or is this all about the Vatican wanting to hide the object three hundred yards down in the catacombs?"

With her stern maternal face, Zara admonishes Peter. "Peter, stop it. Alexander is only trying to play us off each other. He is expert at this. We fail to stand together and we lose. And we can lose big."

The good Father speaks up. "Zara, Peter is right. I have to earn your trust. Please, judge me by my actions. I will have your backs as you did mine outside Harran."

Zara nods and excuses herself to change into her Sufi whirling dress. Jean-Paul makes his first close examination of the object. He sees the pitting all around this black stone, softball-sized and larger indentations.

Peter says, "It resembles a meteorite."

John Paul concurs. Peter glances around to see if Zara is back yet. "I wouldn't say this in front of Zara, but is this just a rock? Or is there something hidden inside that connects to the aliens?"

John Paul smiles, which turns into a quizzical expression. "After all you have seen and been through with Zara, you still think this is all about aliens?"

Zara returns with the full complement of the women of her matriarchy, Maryam, Leyla, and Roza, dressed for dance. She and Peter demonstrate the Sufi whirl, with Peter still wobbling and the onlookers apprehensive he will crash into them. Maryam extends her hand to Jean-Paul to join her in whirling as Peter and Zara step back to admire them. She joins her mother, spinning her dress up as she did as a child, no longer feeling the need to hide, deep scars and all.

That evening, Zara and Peter sneak out again to sit with the object. As they complete their touches, kisses, and hugs, they enter their zone of peace, bliss, and clarity. And much to Zara's surprise, she hears her again. "Yes," says Zara. "I understand. What? Now?"

Zara breaks away from Peter, who reaches to touch her forehead. "I felt her presence in you," he says.

She takes his fingers from her forehead and kisses them. "She said we need to be together very closely so we can be her agents of peace. And this must happen right now."

And Zara peers up and around. "Listen."

Peter glances at her and says, "I can't hear the voice, remember?"

"No, not Her. The buzz," says Zara as the child in her starts to shake, remembering the terror Saddam's helicopters brought upon her village and her family. She gets up and runs to the house, saying, "We need to get everyone out and flee now."

With much effort, everyone is rapidly loaded into Leyla's car and Zara's pink truck. Sara was very distraught about leaving her family heirlooms and history. She refused to leave, but with Jean-Paul and Roza's help, they collected most of her most treasured items into Leyla's car. Zara fretted about how to move the object, but the Jesuits arrived with Peri and loaded it into their truck. Peri told Zara that paratroopers were landing at key strategic locations in Batman and Siirt, exactly like what happened in Diyarbakır, or so she thought.

Their vehicles are just ready to leave when Zara hears the buzz again, and she fights the frights of the fearful child within her. She stares up, and the helicopter is almost upon them. She signals to Peri and grabs her AK-9 with the bulletproof-vest-piercing rounds. She unloads an entire magazine, knocking down the black-clad soldiers rappelling down from the helicopter.

In the back of her mind, she stores the information that there are no insignias on these attackers, nor on the helicopter. Peri fires a grenade launcher at the helicopter, which flames from the hit, twirling around out of control. The three vehicles with Zara's family and friends zoom along a dirt back road as fast as they can without killing great-grandmother Sara in the process.

A taxing forty minutes later, Zara and Jean-Paul stand overlooking the Botan River valley. She gives Jean-Paul her night scope as she goes into the safe spot cave she provisioned when they first moved to Siirt. Inside, Sara is exhausted, and Zara shakes her head, thinking maybe she should have honored her great-grandmother's request to be left behind. Peter is searching about curiously, seeing how well equipped this cave is, with cots, blankets, chairs, canned food, stainless steel drums of water, elevating his respect for Zara even further. Evidently people here take fleeing very seriously.

Assured all is under control in the cave, she reemerges outside to join the good priest. She laments, "Still no sign of your friend's truck? And our object?"

Jean-Paul shakes his head no.

And for the first time since they left Luxembourg, Zara loses it with Jean-Paul. She yells at him, her finger pounding on his chest. "I trusted you. I trusted your friends with my best friend Peri. Did your priest friends steal the object? And I trusted you." And she breaks down into tears, the emotional stresses of the past few days finally catching up with her. He offers to hug her, but she flat-out refuses.

Jean-Paul simply says, "I know no more than you do. I am sure they are safe."

Zara just wants to scream at someone. The pressure of the past weeks has come to a head within her. Instead, she cries, "But what if we have nothing? After all this, we have nothing." She stares at him with her dark, angry eyes. "Why are you here? Peter was right. Why are you here? To taunt us? To watch us suffer while you and your Vatican friends play with us like we were pawns in some grand game against Alexander?"

Jean-Paul puts his hand out for Zara's hand. She first refuses, but then relents and allows him to hold her hand. "It has never been about the object for me, Zara," the good priest insists.

He puts her hand on his chest, over the medallion. "I am here for you. From the very start, this has always been about you."

CHAPTER 41

If words come out of the heart, they will enter the heart, but if they come from the tongue, they will not pass beyond the ears.
—"Shahāb ad-Dīn" Yahya ibn Habash Suhrawardī,
twelfth-century Persian philosopher and mystic

8:00 a.m. GMT+3, June 10, 2022
Hills overlooking Tigris River, southeast of Siirt, former Turkey, now Anatolian Kurdish State

Now it is Zara's turn not to sleep well. She tossed and turned all last night worrying about Peri. Zara stands weary-eyed, staring down the road into her cave of refuge in smoldering self-doubt. Did she get careless again? Did the rapture of the voice cloud her judgment? Did she just get her last best friend Peri hurt, by rebel Jesuits of all people? But what bothers Zara the most is whether she got close in the wrong way to a man again. In her past, her dalliances always led to something bad. If Peri was okay, she should have gotten a message from her by now.

She closes her eyes, hoping to hear something. Will she never hear the voice again? A hand touches her shoulder. A soft, gentle hand. The kind a mother has with her daughter. And Maryam says, "We are safe here because of your foresight and planning. We thought the days of fleeing from helicopters, planes, and tanks were over. But you insisted we be prepared. And here we are, safe because of you. I love you, my daughter."

Maryam hugs her, knowing Zara needs her mother at this moment. Zara cries into her mother's arms. She has cried more since meeting Peter than she has in the last five years.

Standing guard at the entrance road to Zara's safe spot, Jean-Paul watches, hoping, maybe even praying, he did not misjudge his friends, his comrades in so many acts of salvation of souls and lives. At his side, Peter tries his best to emulate and repeat every step told to him by Zara on how to load, aim, and shoot her cousin's 10mm gun.

Jean-Paul notes with fascination how Peter will follow Zara word for word with utter obedience, just as he predicted from his studies of the traditions. Historical records are obscure concerning the full role of the matriarch in this genetic descendancy.

Emerging from the cave, Zara glances at Peter, with her cousin's gun. Peter is expecting her warrior woman mission leader eyes to return. Instead, with her large dilated eyes, she says, "We should put your gun to good use." Peter is puzzled as she takes his hand. She looks at him in a new special way. "What is wrong? We need to get lunch."

An hour or so later, Zara leads Peter back into the cave. He is carrying four rabbits with their heads intact. One shot by him, proudly so. The other three by Zara, the huntress.

Pointing to his MoxWrap, Jean-Paul says, "I have a quick message from Petrus. He is coming back with Peri. He is asking me to save him. What does that mean?"

Entirely relieved, Zara leans over Jean-Paul to see the message and just shakes her head. "I told Peri no touching the merchandise." She looks at Jean-Paul very apologetically. "I am afraid for your friend."

Very puzzled, Jean-Paul asks, "Why? Is he in mortal danger? From whom?"

Grimacing, Zara replies, "If he is still a priest, then his chastity vow has been broken." She checks the time on her MoxWatch. "And by now, broken a dozen times."

Dinner arrives with four more rabbits who came in with their heads intact. To Peter, it is now clear Zara no longer feels compelled to blow the heads off cute animals. Something has profoundly changed in her. And more, Peter is very proud he can finally shoot, although the rabbit he shot is missing most of its meat compared to Zara's. But he is proud nonetheless. More importantly, he no longer feels the need to go back to Sarah and show he can carry a gun as well as Sam. Something has changed in him as well.

As Peter cleans the rabbits with Maryam, Zara glances at her MoxWrap, now getting very worried about Peri. The perimeter alarms sound, and the threesome exit the cave armed to the teeth. Up the road comes the Jesuits' truck. Out pops Peri, who runs up to Zara and hugs her, saying she got sidetracked.

Zara looks at her best friend sideways. "I got so worried about you. I thought you would have sent a message at least. What took you so long to get here? I thought you would be here by morning at latest."

Peri glances back at Petrus, meekly getting out of the truck, and with a maliciously playful smile, she replies, "Oh, that priest needed a little extra not to take the object here before we knew it was safe."

Jean-Paul walks with Petrus, making sure his old friend is truly unharmed as he notes the rope burns on Petrus's neck and wrists. He asks softly, "Were you mistreated?"

Petrus, very flushed and embarrassed, answers, "No. Not at all. Quite the contrary. Zara's friend, she is really kinky. Do you think Zara is like that?"

Of course Jean-Paul shakes his head with a definite no.

Looking back at Peri, Petrus asks his old and trusted friend, "What did you say to the Father General when you told him you wanted to leave? I think my turn has come."

During dinner, Peri sits next to her new beau, who is trying to hide his rope burns as Roza keeps staring at him. Peri tells the latest news. "The invasion of Siirt was short-lived. Once the men in black uniforms realized they could not find the object, they left. It should be safe for all to return to Siirt."

Zara appears very pensive and then says, "It is very bothersome that these soldiers were without insignias. Who sent them? They timed their attack for just after the same style of attack was made by the Turks in Diyarbakır and Batman. The helicopter, also without identification, looked American, but the AC uses American equipment that ISIS captured from the Iraqis."

She pauses to think while Peter serves her more of his rabbit. She says, "Peri, if you would go back and let us know if it is truly safe to return, I would feel better about the security of my family."

Peri nods as she smiles and squeezes Petrus's thigh. She says, "Only if a strong manly priest comes to protect me."

That evening after Maghrib evening prayer, Zara and Peter go to sit together with the object. As Peri and Petrus observe them from afar, Jean-Paul explains to them that something very divine is happening to them.

Petrus asks, "This is all about the medallion from your redheaded girlfriend, isn't it?"

Turning a noticeable shade of rose, Jean-Paul says, "From the good Sister Magali, if that is who you mean."

Peri, getting warm from being a voyeur, spying on her best friend Zara seemingly making out with her new man, pinches Petrus's lower cheeks and whispers in his ear with a little lick to boot. Petrus turns the same shade of rose as Jean-Paul and says, "You must excuse us. I am clearly this woman's prisoner. And it is time that I must go back to my captivity tied to her bed."

The next morning arrives. Peter awakes to see Zara staring at him with large eyes. He finds once again they are covered by a blanket. He says, "Did you notice how each morning we are covered?"

Zara peers over into the cave at her mother and says, "My mother did that to me all the time when she would find me asleep on the couch or floor with a book open on me." She touches Peter's nose. "You must be like a good book for me."

They sit up next to the object and Zara asks him, "What did Maryam say to you? Do not hide it. I saw in you that you talked with her."

"She said she was so happy that her little Zara has come back," Peter answers. "You two enjoy a very special relationship. You are so fortunate."

"That is not all, Peter. Tell me. Why does she think I have changed? The object?"

Peter is embarrassed to have this conversation, but is ultimately faithful to Zara and replies, "No. She thinks it is because you took me into your bed."

Zara pauses, looking over to her mother, and then says, "She said the same to me too. And what else, Peter?"

Peter gulps and touches Zara's heart. "She hopes that you and I have a daughter as nice as you."

And to Peter's surprise, Zara puts her hands on his over her heart and gently says, "She said the same to me." She peers into Peter's eyes with all seriousness. "Would you be happy if that could never happen?"

He kisses her lightly and gently and says softly, "I will be forever happy and in peace just being with you." He puts her hand on his heart. "And you know this to be true."

Her hand upon his, forehead against his, she stares down and says, "If only it could be true. Us together. Forever."

She kisses his forehead. "We need to see your dream. She said it would tell us what is next to come."

They kiss, embrace, rub temples, touch bumps, and their minds once again clear with that peace, harmony, and beauty that comes with the union of two halves of an afflicted apple. They envision the last high priestess of the Cult of Illyana, Amanta, who buried the object after rejecting what the people of her lands had distorted in the words of the voice. They hear her memory of her last conversation with the voice: "Ones that could bring peace to her people and her beloved children. And if not, they would find the means to return the object to her." As Amanta walks off, leaving her priestess life behind her, she morphs into Zara, aiming her gun in between her sister Rona's eyes. And Rona is begging, pleading for Zara to kill her.

Zara flinches and tries to pull away from Peter, who holds her even tighter, for they must see this dream no matter what. And then Rona morphs into Illyana, who is begging her brother to kill her. Then Zara in the dream morphs into Orzu, aiming his arrow between his sister's breasts. Illyana begs and pleads for her brother to kill her. Kill her now. And then Orzu morphs into Peter, aiming his gun at Alexander, who has his gun at Zara's head. And Zara is begging, pleading with Peter to let him kill her.

Peter pulls back in horror, crying, "No. No. This cannot be true!"

Zara, knowing how true this will be, stares down, knowing that her time has come, knowing why her time has come, knowing the voice told Amanta as much, knowing that the world is not yet ready to listen to the voice.

She puts her hands on Peter's cheeks and gazes into his eyes. "Listen to me, Peter. If the time comes when I must die for the good that the voice asks of us, then I am ready. It has been my destiny for thousands of years. Listen to me. You must kill me. You must let me be killed."

"I can't, Zara. How can you ask me that? How could I kill you? I love you too much," says a mortified Peter.

"Peter, listen to me. The time has come. My time has come. I am ready to meet my death with a contented soul and a faithful heart," she says with eyes wide.

Like the boy at the grave holding his mother's hand, Peter holds hers, shaking before the darkness. "I cannot kill you. We are destined to be together, you and I."

With an aura of lightness surrounding her, she strokes his wet hand. "Please promise me something, Peter."

"Anything Zara. Anything but killing you."

With a gleam in her eyes, she asks, "My lambs. I would be at peace if I knew they were safe in your care after I die."

Peter searches for the right words and finally speaks. "We are destined to raise your baby lambs together, you and I. Know they will grow to be faithful sheep and we will raise their little lambs too. We can take them to visit my mother, who will be in joy over our children."

She snorts a little laugh. "You are so sweet, Peter. I could love you. My Little Boy."

As Zara rises to go to sunrise prayer with her family, she says, "But you must. You must kill me."

After breakfast, Peter sits catatonic while Zara discusses his dream with Jean-Paul. They both conclude they must meet Alexander with the object. It is clear what the voice is asking for.

Peter breaks his silence. "We cannot win. He will kill all of us for betraying him."

And Zara's killer face comes back in full force as she places her hands atop his cheeks, not the gentle touch of just an hour ago, but the firm, rough touch of a woman determined to meet her death. "Little Boy, I know Alexander. I killed for him. I set up meetings like the one he will want to have with us. I killed his meeting invitees. I know how he will set us up for our deaths."

Peter shudders. Somehow fate has mated him with the compassionate woman of mankind's future peace, who can, in less than a microsecond, flip into a malevolent, merciless murderer.

Zara walks off with Jean-Paul to discuss her plan. They come back later to see Peter sitting on the object, watching Sammy the Banana Slug singing and dancing on his MoxWrap. As he sits on the object, Zara sets up the 3-D videoconference with Alexander.

Alexander's image looks around at Jean-Paul, then at Peter, sitting on the object they said was destroyed, and finally at Zara. "My dear little Zara. You have found the object, haven't you? I must presume, then, that you have heard the voice. What did he say?"

Not expecting such a direct question about the voice, she checks with Jean-Paul, who gives her a nod. "Alexander, She said there is only one voice. And She seeks peace for us all."

"Come now, Zara. He must have said more. Please share what he said with your dear Sasha."

Peeved that he is not taking her gender specificity seriously, Zara replies, "*She* says emphatically you owe me what you promised. *She* will not take kindly to those who break promises."

With a giant frown, Alexander states, "My child, no need to be flippant with me. You are like a daughter to me. Have I not always been there for you? Did I not pay millions in bribes to the Iraqis to free your father from captivity when you were little? Did your mother tell you I paid millions more in bribes to free him another time before you were born? Why would you deceive me now? Lie to me?"

Zara almost flinches at learning another thing her mother never told her, but stands defiant and replies, "Alexander. State your terms and let us get on with this."

Staring at her body language, Alexander says, "I know what your stance means all too well. So, you want me to take the gloves off and spar bare-knuckle now? Tell me, did I not locate you after those men abducted you and your sisters? And as soon as I found you, did I not get that message to you about how to escape and meet my extraction team? Did I not take care of you with the world's best psychiatric and neurological care after we saved you? Did I not train you and equip you to hunt down those monsters and to punish them as mercilessly as they had destroyed you?"

He pauses to let his words eat at her. He stares at Peter and then winds up his hardest hardballs. "Peter, ask Zara, did I not support her all her life? Through all her schooling? Did I not make sure she was assigned to the same Peshmerga unit as her boyfriend, Zengo, so they could fornicate all night long in defiance of her religion, in defiance of her family's traditions? Did I not send her to Georgetown to chase her married boyfriend so she could cheat with him behind his lovely wife's back and those adorable children of theirs? Did I not send her to Moscow so she could further learn the arts of intimate seduction from the Russian Spetsnaz?"

He pauses while Peter's forehead furrows and his lips quiver. "Peter, did she tell you the sordid details of what she did with them? My boy, my son, have you not wondered why she did not perform upon you all those delightful perversions which she had given to those men, who are, in my opinion, so much less deserving than you? And Peter, why is it she denies her body to you, the man who has loved her the most?"

As Alexander's image seemingly gets darker and darker, he turns to Zara again and demands, "Tell him now. Tell him exactly what you did with these men. What you withhold from Peter. Tell him and see if he still stays with you. Tell him he should go back to Sarah, who you know deep inside would be better for him than you could ever be."

Zara's face shows no reaction other than to bespeak her determination to bring this mission to its final resolution. She stares back into his dark and piercing eyes with her equally dark and piercing eyes and firmly says, "Sasha, none of that matters. You owe me what you promised. This is all that matters. I delivered these two to the target and then to one more. This was all that was required of me."

Alexander shows an insidious smile as if proud, like a father, and turns his back to them. He says, "I had a dream last night. My little Zara set up a meeting and tried to double-cross me as she has done with so many others."

He turns and stares at each of the three, one by one, ending with Zara. "I possess the other half of the object. They are meant to be together, the same as two halves of the same apple are meant to be together. So destiny calls me to have your meeting so you can double-cross your dear old Sasha. And Peter will kill either me or you. I know you know this to be true. These are the coordinates of where you will meet me tomorrow at four p.m."

Zara shakes her head no. "Alexander, we will meet you there at four forty-five p.m. Send your helicopter to pick us up at these coordinates at two thirty." And she terminates the call.

Both she and Jean-Paul begin tapping on their MoxWraps. She peers at Peter, who grimaces back at her, deeply scared of her again—this time for many new reasons.

Zara steps towards Peter, who steps backwards in deep apprehension. Her eyes are as dark and ominous as Alexander's at his worst moments. And using the voice of the Zara whom Peter first met in Luxembourg, she says, "Everything he said is true. I am not the woman you think I am. I am not the woman you wish I were. I have been very bad, and you will need to kill me tomorrow. And you should not think anything of it other than Xwedê wills it."

CHAPTER 42

I warn you against shedding blood, indulging in it
and making a habit of it, for blood never sleeps.
—Saladin, Kurdish founder
of the Ayyubid dynasty

1:15 p.m. GMT+3, June 11, 2022
Hills around Siirt, former Turkey, now Anatolian Kurdish State

Finished with her last Dhuhr prayer with her family, Zara rises to leave the prayer room in her beloved great-grandmother's home. She searches to find the courage within, to find the right words within, for the time has come to say her final goodbye to her mother.

As the menfolk wait for her outside with the object already loaded onto her pink truck, Zara brings her mother into her brother's room, the memory of his fate so symbolic of the same death she faces today. Her mother looks at her daughter with great curiosity as to what she has to say privately, hoping this will be the day.

"Mama," says Zara, "the time has come for me to leave you."

Maryam's expression turns to one of joy as she clasps her daughter's hands, so happy for her. She says lovingly, "Yes, I knew this moment would come."

Zara peers back at her mother, more than a little confused. "And you are understanding of what must happen to me today?"

And to Zara's surprise, her mother cries and hugs her. But these are not tears of sadness, of impending grief, but ones of a mother overjoyed for her daughter. "Yes, my little Zara. For you have grown to be my big Zara, ready to leave with your husband to live with his family as women do in our tradition. I will miss you so, but maybe you could arrange for me to visit often. I have heard California is a beautiful land."

Zara takes a deep breath. She knew this day would be emotionally challenging, but her mother has just made it even more so. She puts her hands on her mother's cheeks. Maryam is surprised Zara's soft warm hands of only yesterday are now so chilly, cold and rough. Zara says, "Mama, today is a good day to die. Today I leave for my death. I want you to know how much I love you for all that you are and all that you have done for me and my brother."

Maryam puts her warm hands around her daughter's frosty ones, trying to bring back the warmth into her being. "My child, do not talk this way again. These are the words of the Zara of four years ago. What you and Peter have done together is nothing short of a miracle. You, the Zara you have sought to find again, has returned with the arrival of this man. Whatever it is you are going to do, he will be there to protect you. To save you. It is his destiny."

Taking her mother's hands off hers, Zara stares down and sadly replies, "Mama, you do not understand. Peter will kill me today. That is his destiny. That is why Xwedê brought him here." She kisses her mother for the last time. "But do not be sad for me, Mama. For my death today will make the world a better one. Make your future a better one." And Zara leaves for her truck.

Her MoxWrap shows 13:57 hours as she follows the telltale signature of an inbound helicopter on her MoxWrap's satellite surveillance app. Around the encampment, she has deployed her four most trusted former YPJ friends, Peri, Firya, Beri, and Rana, who stand guard armed with Russia's best MANPAD handheld missiles, equipped of course with Alexander's latest electronic warfare tech. With the pink pickup truck, the good priest waits with the object and with arms around his AK-74XM, ready for the eventuality of things to come.

And Peter. He stares into the skies, extremely pensive, still bewildered at his last conversation with Zara. She has not talked with him directly since asking him to kill her yesterday. Is this why he was destined to be here? To find her, to help her find herself, and just when she has, to cold-bloodedly kill her?

As the helicopter arrives, Peter identifies it as a Russian Mi-28NM, a low-radar-signature attack helicopter that can fly at speeds of up to six hundred kilometers per hour and was introduced only a year ago. Of course, as with all things of war today, it is equipped with Alexander's latest tech. Whatever is about to happen, Zara's plan brings to bear the best firepower in the world on her side.

He watches a sole Russian officer, bold, bearded, and broad, exit the craft carrying a large case. Zara goes up to greet him and, much to Peter's surprise, he looks down and puts his hands under her headscarf, open-mouthed kisses her, and then, lowering his hands, squeezes her buttocks tightly.

Zara pulls back, pursing her lips. The Russian removes his sunglasses and gazes at her with eyes of deep familiarity.

"That is all, Anatoly. That kiss was your payment," says Zara. "A little reminder of why you owe me."

He tries to hug her, but she pushes him back, saying, "That Zara does not exist anymore."

Dejected but not yet deterred, Anatoly relents. Zara points to the case he has brought and says, "Show me the goods." She waves Jean-Paul and Peter over.

With Zara's clear signals that this Russian is friendly, Jean-Paul lowers his assault rifle and comes over. Peter on the other hand has watched this Russian with keen eyes. His focus is on Zara. And he is ready to step in if she shows any sign of being hurt by her past. Peter puts Rohat's gun into the front of his pants and follows.

Anatoly glares at him and laughs. "Yankee, you are going to shoot off your wee-wee with that little gun placed like that." He laughs some more, turning back to Zara while pointing at Peter's crotch.

A microsecond and Peter dallies with the full and deep agony of Sam and Sarah. But the idea evacuates his mind as he focuses on the only person who matters and replies, "Just do as the woman has asked of you. We all owe her our faith and obedience."

After a quizzical glance at Peter, Zara signals for her former Russian paramour to open up the case. On one side is a kilo of Semtex, a highly malleable plastic explosive. Anatoly points to the other side and says, "And as you have requested, three kilos of trifluoroheptanitrocubane, the most advanced malleable explosive Russia can offer, which means the best in the world."

Happy to see Zara finally grinning, he points to the object and adds, "I had these made in the color you specified. It matches your stone there perfectly."

Nonplussed about her former lover who has come back into Zara's life at her call, Peter has stood fast until now. But his voice wavers as he says, "But won't this blow up in our faces before we get to Alexander? I'm not a suicide bomber!"

Anatoly laughs at him again and taunts, "You cute American. Trifluoroheptanitrocubane is extremely stable. That is, unless detonated by a highly focused explosion such as this Semtex will provide. Other than that, maybe a trillion watts of electricity might do it, but where are you going to find that around here? You planning on blowing up a power plant?"

Peter's back stiffens, and his nostrils flare. But then, his hands upon his chin, he says, "You're a genius, Anatoly. No wonder Zara called for you."

The Russian, jaw down with a vapid stare, is pulled at by Zara, who says, "Stay to task, soldier. Time is burning."

While Anatoly cozies up to Zara as they apply the explosives around the object, filling in the pocked indentations, Peter watches intently as Zara touches her old lover's hands, which are full of explosives. Alexander's words begin to permeate his inner vocabulary. Does she just use men for her purposes? Him included? No, he has to have faith.

He walks up to Zara and asks her if she could step aside for a minute.

Zara walks with him and says, "If this is about Anatoly, you should not think there is anything between us other than that he owes me and is paying up now. And if you're worried because you think he was my lover and still may be, then I have grossly underestimated you."

Ashamed of what he thought for but a moment, he stares down at her feet. "No, not that. Please understand. I have come to understand you are a fiercely free and independent woman. And I love you for it. I would never ask you to restrain or restrict what you wish to do in life."

Zara is taken aback, for no male who is not family has ever said that to her. But she knows she needs to be prepared for what must happen, no matter what declarations of love he may be making.

Peter peers into her dark eyes. "I just thought we should talk about what happens if the object is destroyed. If we blow it up, will you still have contact with the voice? I can only surmise that your relationship with the voice is growing. If we blow it up, you'll never know what she really wants from us to create world peace."

Staring back into his big puppy eyes, Zara reminds herself that every time she has let a man get close, bad things have happened. No matter what she might think she feels for Peter, she cannot let herself go there.

"Peter, you have a long life ahead of you," she replies. "Many women more deserving than me want to be with you. You have the blessing of having so much choice. And if not them, then there will be many more, I am sure. For I know how kind and gentle your heart, your soul, your very being is. I am sure you will know love all your life."

He casts his eyes down and exhales. Zara takes his hands into hers as she says, "I will always love you for opening up my soul to the beauty I once knew. For teaching me how to let go of my darkness. For bringing the old Zara back to my mother. Back to Roza and Sara as well. You will be forever in my heart." She tries to kiss him, but no longer as brave, he turns, walking away with his hands in his pockets.

With her mission face back on, Zara returns to finish business with Anatoly, who followed her interactions with Peter with great interest. Anatoly purposefully touches her hands in a way that reminds Zara of what he hoped they once were together. He holds her hands, about to say something, but she puts her fingers to his lips, saying, "You better be about to tell me that you have brought the rest of the gear I asked for." Anatoly shakes his head in final acknowledgment, glum, dour, and disappointed.

He brings her back to the small cargo space in his attack helicopter and shows her two vests and pairs of pants, and another long case. Zara touches the vests, ironclad strong without the bulk, and says, "These better not be the crap they gave you Spetsnaz people in Chechnya. You remember, the ones bullets passed right through."

Anatoly finally laughs again. "Who do you think I am? These are the latest prototypes. Class six vests and class five pants."

She waves Peter and Jean-Paul over. Out of the case, she pulls out a black cassock for her dear priest and says, "These vests will fit nicely under my dress and your new Russian-made cassock. Thank Catherine the Great for the Russians' love of you Jesuits."

Peter asks, "Where's my vest?"

Zara glares at him with unsympathetic eyes and replies, "You will not need one. For if they shoot you, the object will detonate. It is for you to let them know this fact. Otherwise they will shoot you by accident."

Anatoly takes two ASh-12.7 urban assault rifles out from the case. Peter's jaw drops. Hitting power of fifty-caliber bullets built for the FSB, Federal Security Service.

Jean-Paul picks one up and asks, "Why would the Spetsnaz be helping us here? Aren't the Russians in Alexander's back pocket?"

Anatoly laughs. "Not everyone in Russia is a fan of Alexander." He winks at Zara and adds, "Like me." And he hands the other ASh to Zara, who refuses it, pointing to the AK-9 and VSS in the back of her truck.

And the Russian laughs even harder. "You insult me about Chechnya, and look at what you are using. My old gifts of love to you."

With a hint of a smile, Zara says, "Old tech, yes, but they do the job. Do you have the grenade launcher I asked for?" And Anatoly pulls that out of the case as well. She says, "Okay. I think we are ready. I am going to find a little privacy to put your fancy vest and pants on under my dress."

Anatoly puts on his best version of puppy eyes and begs, "For old times' sake, please, let me help you put these on?"

Zara peers back at him with unempathetic dark eyes. "Anatoly, did I not tell you before that the shop is closed? No more touching the merchandise."

Her downtrodden Russian glares at Peter, who is busy trying to flex his arms and chest, and says, "Are you telling me you are turning me down for this silly bespectacled American twig?"

Zara smirks at Anatoly. "Remember Zakhar the Crazed Crusher? That silly bespectacled American twig is the CIA's equivalent. But even more crazed. He has a hairpin trigger between silliness and super limb-ripping monster." She winks at Peter. "They sent him here to keep me in line." With skeptical eyes, Anatoly looks at Peter, practicing with his gun, as Zara goes behind her truck to change.

As Zara gets ready to meet Alexander's helicopter, Anatoly comes to her again, still undeterred by her off-putting behavior. He begs her to allow him to take her to the rendezvous with Alexander, for they would both be heroes of the State if they were to kill Alexander. She informs him it is not his destiny to bring her to her death. It is Peter's. And Anatoly leaves in his attack craft to return to Georgia in complete despondency, scorned by this woman who somehow still controls his life.

Two thirty p.m. comes, and Alexander's helicopter arrives with full Russian air escort flying overhead. In the helicopter, Zara sits next to Peter. She takes his hands in hers as it takes off, squeezing as she confronts her childhood fear. She leans over to him and says, "I will never stop being afraid of these beasts."

Sensing maybe her compassion has returned, Peter leans over and asks, "Zara, please tell me, what did I do wrong? You've become more distant from me. It's as if all that's happened between us has disappeared."

Zara touches his cheek. "Peter, it is time for us to become distant. This is for real now. For keeps. This is that moment that will define all time to come." As she sees him withdraw further in his sorrow, she takes his hand and punches it into her armor-clad breasts. "You cannot kill me with a shot here."

She takes his pistol, tucks it in his hands, and then places it against her head. "You have to shoot me in the head. The same as I did to Rona. It is what must happen to me for all that I have done."

Peter's lips and chin quiver. "I can't do that, Zara. Why do you need to die? What does Alexander want the object for, that you have to die to prevent him from getting it?"

She replies, "He needs me for what I can do now. For my connection with the voice. You cannot let him have me and the object. It is one or the other. Or you may have to detonate the object so he has neither."

He cries out, "I love you, Zara. I can't shoot you. We need each other."

The shop, once full of compassion and empathy, is now closed as Zara coldly takes out a detonator switch. "Remember the one I showed you when we landed in Siirt? Flip the knob this way, and it becomes a dead man switch. Your finger comes off, and it blows up the object. Flip it that way, it becomes a normal switch that you push to detonate."

He leans in to cry into her hair, but their helmets only clank. "But then if I detonate the object, we all die, don't we?"

Sensing he needs her compassion at this moment, she leans in to kiss him, but shaking his head, he pulls back away from her. And as if Alexander was in his head, he says, "That's what you did with Anatoly. And what else did you do with him? And all the others. Did you use me like you used them? Except I was the stupid one who you denied sex. Was I only a way for you to talk to the voice? And now, it's just time for all of us to die?"

Zara licks her finger, touches his forehead, and rubs. As she sees him calming, she says, "I should be offended by what you have said, but I know you now, like you know me. The muscle I love most in you is here. In your head. You need to remember that when the moment comes that you need to pull the trigger."

Seeing his mouth still downturned, she touches his heart. "You ask if what we have been to each other since we found the object is nothing? You have to look into your heart and decide what you trust, and what you will do when the time comes. I love you for your heart as well. You are the only man I trust who is not family. And my family feels the same. Roza and Maryam say you are family. What are you, Peter Gollinger? Family or foe? Or just a scared Little Boy?"

She puts her hands back into her lap and stares forward.

Peter takes her hand and says, "I would rather die than let you die. You must live through this. Only you can talk with the voice."

Zara, forever the mission leader, tests him and replies, "You mean I can talk with the aliens."

Peter shakes his head. "You talk with the one who will save us all. Except me, as I will die instead of you."

She takes a fresh magazine out and replaces the one in Peter's gun. "This is a full fresh set. Repack rounds, as we poor Kurds cannot afford factory rounds. The top one has my name on it. You will know when that time comes. It is Xwedê's will." She pats his hands, picks them up, and licks and kisses his palms. She puts his hands back down and looks forwards, putting her game face back on.

As their helicopter approaches Alexander's appointed meeting spot, Jean-Paul, reading his MoxWrap, yells from the facing seats, "It has started. The Russian invasion fleet has sailed. The Americans have entered into war with Russia. The US fleet is taking positions. The Russians are readying bombers to attack the US fleet. The American F-35 and F-16 fighters are readying to launch. Alexander has timed this perfectly. Any later and our helicopter would have been shot down."

They disembark from Alexander's helicopter as the crew unloads the object onto an awaiting forklift. Zara glances at her watch. Four forty. Perfect timing. Fifteen minutes to get her plan in play.

Zara, Peter, and Jean-Paul follow the truck along a stone jetty jutting out into the Black Sea to where Alexander is waiting. His yacht is docked past a few white wooden buildings. Perfect cover for his men. The sky is cloudy with the smell of salt water mixed with the smell of impending death, which the residents of the multicolored five-story buildings across the highway from this jetty are oblivious to.

Zara cautiously walks holding her AK-9 and carrying the grenade-equipped VSS in her backpack, Jean-Paul with his 12.7mm urban antiterrorist weapon, and Peter with a detonator in his pocket and a carpet rolled up under his arm.

Alexander awaits with the other object. Zara scans around and spots the multitudes of guards he has deployed in the same pattern as she designed for him for his other ambushes. With their object deposited next to Alexander's, they stop within ten meters of Alexander when Zara raises up her MoxWrap, pointing at it. "Alexander, it is four fifty-eight p.m. In six minutes, it will be time for the Asr prayer. You cannot deny me honoring my faith."

As Alexander nods his consent, Zara rotates with her MoxWrap and then points towards Mecca. She signals where Peter should place the prayer mat. She signals Jean-Paul, who kneels with her to join her in prayer. And for the next ten minutes, Zara, the devout Muslim Kurdish woman, recites her prayer in silence with her Jesuit priest companion.

Most of Alexander's guards are standing up to watch this spectacle. As Zara finishes reciting her Asr prayer, she peeks around at Alexander's protectors and nods at the black-cassock-gowned priest. Jean-Paul yells back at her it is only respectful that he performs the prayer aloud in Arabic. Zara retorts that only imams perform prayer aloud. As they get into a loud, heated theological debate, all of Alexander's guards begin to laugh at this spectacle of a Catholic priest asking to perform an Islamic ritual in Arabic. Zara spies that even Alexander's snipers have risen, even one with a distinctive double cleft chin, to get a better look at their performance, their circus, their very well-timed distraction, as four ninja-like ghosts slip around the pier, having risen out of the Black Sea.

Zara concedes to the priest in black and proclaims, "I have heard the voice Alexander seeks. And She assures us there is only one voice. Hers. One voice who guides all of us. One voice for my people, the people of this Jesuit, the people of this American. The same voice with the same message." And she and Jean-Paul perform the Asr prayer together again while the ninja ghosts silently and discreetly whisk away guards one by one.

As the pair prays, Alexander has his two closest guards place the two halves of the object adjacent to each other but not yet touching. He walks around the newly arrived other half of the object and smugly smiles. His lifelong search, his father's lifelong search, is finally over.

Rising from the prayer mat, Zara nudges Peter to play his part. She whispers, "Just as I told you in my truck this afternoon."

Twisting the detonator switch to the dead man position, Peter holds it up, stares at Alexander, whose eyes now turn dark at seeing him, and declares, "Alexander, our object is surrounded by enough high-powered explosives to make dust out of both of them."

And the clicks of many guns ring through the air as Alexander's remaining guards take aim at him. Peter turns around slowly so the guards can see his thumb on the detonator and yells, "This is a dead man switch. You shoot me and you all die." And as Peter talks, more of Alexander's guards slowly disappear.

Alexander waves his hand in a big arc to the side, and his guards drop their rifle aim off Peter. He puts on a fatherly face. "My boy, you have done well. Remember our conversation in Luxembourg? We are more alike than different on a deep intrinsic level. We both needed to find that woman on Jean-Paul's medallion. We both needed our other half of the apple, who we found was Zara."

He looks at Zara with a loving face. "There was not a Zara of my generation, so I took Zara as my daughter. Peter, you have a sibling relationship with her, but you would like so much more. I forgive her for all of her misdeeds, for her follies, and even for her treacheries." Alexander peers into Zara's eyes with a loving smile, which then melts into something more sinister.

He turns back to Peter. "You forgave her for all of her past sins, as she had said to you. You forgive her now, even though you know she has held back sex from you, the sex she freely gave to men who are your betters. You forgive her now even though she has used you, just as all the other women in your life used you. I love her very deeply for all of who she is, good and bad. You want to love her very deeply for all of who she is, but she won't let you fully be with her. And you stand here in front of me now, still not knowing who she really is. And yet you hold my object hostage for a woman you do not know."

Alexander pauses to check Zara, who has not changed her game face, only watching the events happening around Alexander, one by one by one, in her peripheral vision.

Focused solely on moving Peter to side with him, Alexander puts his hands out to Peter in an open gesture to join him. "My boy, Peter, you are like the son I could never have. The son with shared genetics of the originators. The son with whom I can help change the world for the better. Do you trust me, Peter, your alien genetic father? Or would you rather trust a priest who renounced his vows only to lie to you, to Zara, to the love of his life, poor Sister Magali?"

Alexander now points to Zara. "Or a seemingly needy woman who hides her past from you, who hides her true motives from you? Who uses you without returning your love for her? I have done for you what I said I would. I have foretold to you things that have happened. Am I not the one you should trust the most here?"

His eyes darken like the depths of the sea behind him, glaring into his surrogate daughter's eyes, which reflect the exact same darkness. He asks, "Zara, what do you have to say to Peter? Tell him that you will take him to your bed for real tonight. Like you did Anatoly. Like you did Dan. Like you did Zengo. Tell him that he will have with you what even his Sarah would not do."

Dead still, Zara does not drop her game face or her focus on what is happening around Alexander, weakening his position with each minute he pontificates. For she knows his need for soliloquies and eggs him on, saying, "Keep talking, Sasha. Peter knows how bad I have been. He knows why I must die here today. He knows that I must die today at his hand."

Realizing Zara has "vaccinated" Peter by asking him to kill her, Alexander tries a different tack. "Peter, my boy, my son, who do you love the most in your life? Your grandfather, no? Why are you here? For me? For Zara? For your pappy? Your motives are the most noble of the three of you standing here. These supposedly newfound friends of yours are standing ready to kill me, ready to deprive the world of the wonders of these objects. In sharp contrast, you, Peter simply want peace for your pappy. Tell me, when Pappy dies, will his agony over his father and what he was, what he did or did not do, be gone? He will die with the agony that his father will forever be known as a Nazi conspirator, a war criminal, a pain he has harbored for all his adult life. So shameful he hid it from you until only three weeks ago. Which is more important to you? Freeing Pappy of his guilt-ridden pain? Or chasing the unrequited love of a woman who will not truly let you in? A woman you have only known for a few weeks?"

Peter glances over at Zara with different eyes. Alexander has clearly gotten to him. But Zara does not take her focus off the situation around her as she says, "Peter, you know what we have seen together. You know what you have seen in me. It is all real. It is all true. You know what you have to do. Do it."

Peter looks back at Alexander with resignation and says, "That's a lot of talk. What can you really do for my pappy?"

Alexander smiles and replies, "I can exonerate the father of your dear anguished pappy of all wrongdoing. You can bring proof to the world that your dishonored great-grandfather was in actuality a Nazi resistance fighter, a hero of his times. My father and your great-grandfather discovered the secrets, ones with which we, you and me, Peter, can together bring true peace to mankind. Your pappy will die with the greatest inner peace knowing this. Your pappy does not believe in heaven, so all he has is the peace he might have upon his death. Let me help you in your mission, the reason why you are truly here today."

Peter looks at Alexander, who has just appealed to him on a level he cannot deny. He stares down at his arms, chest and belly, so much more muscular and toned than three weeks before, with the gun in his belt, and then at Zara, who has had her eyes closed, saying something in silence, maybe her last words before she dies. He so wants her to compel him with her love and compassion into believing that everything Alexander is saying is mere lies. But Zara only peers at him with deeply cold, dark, piercing eyes, the same as Alexander's, and says, "We are ready, Peter. Tell him what you want."

Alexander senses the cold-bloodedness in her voice and, knowing Zara all too well, scans around. His guards have disappeared. He turns back to Zara and smiles. "You have done well, my little Zara. I have trained you too well."

Zara answers, "Peter has more character, more resolve, more ethics than you give him credit for." She looks at Peter just as coldly as she did before and glances upwards. "Peter, do what you believe is right, but do it now before it is too late."

Peter looks at the skies and the clouds that have gathered. Grey sad ones. Not angry ones, but sad, grieving ones, mourning the death to come of someone he loves so much. He glances back to the object and asks his pappy's forgiveness for what he is going to do.

He says to Alexander, "I will detonate our object if you don't withdraw from here now. You lose. I lose. The world loses."

Alexander doesn't flinch. With his frigid black eyes piercing into Peter's soul, he says in a firm, fatherly tone, "I know you, son. You cannot destroy our world's best hope for peace. You cannot kill Zara, no matter what she has asked of you. You only parrot her words, which she has beguiled you into saying. My son, Peter, why do you think you follow women around like you do? You followed Mei without a thought. You followed your beloved Sarah like a good puppy. You follow Zara blindly, no matter how she treats you. Your mother trained you to do so. It is what the mothers of the afflicted do. They make sure the male half of the apple is fully under the control of the female half. It is a pattern that has prevented mankind from truly benefiting from the full power of the objects. You can break this pattern, Peter."

The towering man, projecting his protective father figure to Peter, points at Zara and says, "She tells you not to believe that the aliens have left this object for us to find. She misleads you so she can retain full control, so she can retain power over all of us men. Break the pattern, Peter. Let us, you and I, father and son, work with the aliens, and bring into this world what we as a species deserve."

Peter looks at Jean-Paul to his left, then Zara on his right, then down at his feet. As Peter is distracted, Alexander holds his hand up, and the two guards to his side shoot at Jean-Paul and Zara. Jean-Paul is down but shoots the guard, who shoots him back. And the same happens to Zara, who is down but shoots her guard as well. Apparently these guards have the same vests the Spetsnaz were given in Chechnya, as their bodies are ripped in half by the duo's subsonic rounds.

Peter feels brave as he watches Zara's plan playing out exactly as she had said. He boldly says, "Alexander, you've run out of guards. Leave here in peace and no harm will come to you."

Annoyance on his face, Alexander raises his right hand.

Crack. Crack. Jean-Paul is taken out by a sniper. He is down flat and bleeding, his weapon thrown to the side.

Peter, in a panic, yells what he was told to say. "Alexander, tell them to stop or I'll detonate the objects. You lose. I lose. We all lose."

Alexander yells something in Russian into his lapel mike.

Crack. Crack. Zara is taken down by a sniper too, her AK-9 sent flying. She is bleeding as well, but with inner resolve still running strong, she rolls over, taking her VSS out of her backpack and aiming the grenade launcher at the sniper.

Boom.

Alexander, more than annoyed she has killed his sniper, points his revolver at Zara.

Peter breaks from what Zara told him to do. He has to save her. It does not matter if obedience is what his mother programmed him to do. It does not matter if Zara loves him back. It only matters that he loves her so much he will die today to save her. He flips the detonator knob to normal push function and fiddles with his gun in a panic, trying in vain to load the first bullet. Finally, he cocks back the slide hard twice to get it to click.

Too late. Alexander fires off several rounds at Zara.

And Zara is down for good this time, her dress bodice ripped to shreds, showing her vest plates shattered into many pieces. She weakly tries to yell, "Peter, kill Sasha! Rapid-fire rounds. Into the chest, like I showed you."

With detonator in one hand and gun in the other, Peter aims at the giant monster, following what Zara had shown him to do. His hands shake as he fights the images of his father's death with that gun that have hampered him all his life.

Until now. For only Zara matters as Peter says, "Alexander, I will kill you if you move any muscle at all. Believe me, I have the resolve to do this. I know you know so. Somehow you know things about what Zara and I have said. Maybe you have our MoxWraps bugged. And so, you know I have changed. I can and will shoot you."

"Peter, my boy. Tell me, did you dream last night that you would be killing me today?" Alexander yells back, still focused, with his revolver now aimed at Zara's head. "Because if you didn't, then Zara here will die needlessly. Your choice, Peter. Kill me and kill Zara at the same time, or simply push that button and blow us all up. What did your dreams say you would do? Mine said you're not the kind of person to kill."

"Peter, shoot him. Ignore him. It doesn't matter if I die. You know what will happen if he puts the object stones together. You know what the voice from the object told us," Zara says weakly as her head finally slumps to the ground.

"Peter, my son. You have been a loser, a failure so many times in your life up to now. Did I not say that you and I were more alike than different? Be a winner this time. Be a winner with me. We both need the object intact. Put down the detonator," pleads a fatherly Alexander.

Peter's mind freezes. But maybe not. He is now in that microsecond between choices. Between his love for Zara and his love for his pappy. He is no longer the panicked, sheltered man-boy hiding behind his computer screen. He is now fully aware in this microsecond as the world around him moves in ultra-slow motion. He has changed so much since he first met Zara. He has found his destiny with her and through her. What is happening is so surreal, just like the dream he had three weeks ago. He only wishes he had not awoken before finding out what he did in his dream. Now he has to decide whether to cross that line or not.

"Peter, my boy, my son," Alexander says softly. "Spare Zara. It's obvious how deeply you care about her. I don't want to shoot her either. I care about her too. Put down the gun. Put away that detonator. And you and Zara can walk out of here as man and woman together, just as you are destined to be."

Zara makes one last appeal. "Kill him, Peter. Let him kill me. If you love me. If you truly love me, let him kill me. Just kill him."

"Okay, Alexander, here's what we're going to do," says Peter.

He aims his gun at Zara's head. "I'm going to kill her, and what do you have? Nothing to bargain with."

Prone on the cold pier, Zara stares at him in disbelief. He is clearly off script. That is not what the dream foretold. She is helplessly furious at him.

Alexander stares at Peter with his deeper-than-black piercing eyes, which are harder and harder to see with the darkened clouds. Then he smiles. "Are you happy now, my son? You have grown a pair. You would have never said that three weeks ago. You would have never had such confidence with a gun three weeks ago. Have I not done for you what you wished when you left Sarah's brownstone with deep envy, that day you watched the man who replaced you in her bed?"

Peter looks up at the now-blackened clouds. He looks at the blackened anger in Zara's eyes. He looks up and sees that same anger in the near-night-colored sky. What did Anatoly say? And he gets it. He looks at Zara again, putting his hands together as if he were praying.

She nods back at him and closes her eyes.

As the rain begins to fall, Peter says, "Alexander, my new father, if only you could have given me pecs and abs, everything would be perfect."

And to Alexander's surprise, Peter walks over to him, turns the detonator switch to off, hands it to him, turns his gun around, and hands it to him too. He bows and says, "I counted. Yours is empty. Our fate is in your hands."

Alexander drops his other gun and takes Peter's gun, aiming it at Peter's head with a tight two-handed combat grip. "My son, you should have listened to Mei more attentively. I had a son once. Zara spurned him as she did you. And he betrayed me like you have done. I killed him, as I do to all who fail and betray me."

Peter, with deer-in-the-headlights eyes, slowly backs up. Alexander lets Peter simmer in fear for several steps and finally pulls the trigger. Rohat's gun violently explodes in his hand, making the round miss Peter's head. Alexander drops his gun, bending over and holding his bleeding hands.

Knowing his one goal this morning was to defy Zara's declared destiny, Peter runs to get Zara, who screams in agony as he lifts her up to walk. The black-clad figures come out of the shadows and pick Jean-Paul up.

Zara yells at Peter, "Look at the sky." His eyes are pelted by the falling tears. She demands, "Leave me here. You know what is going to happen. Stop Alexander from putting the objects together."

Peter moves his hand to support her better. He says, "No, I won't. I will always be with you."

As the reunited lovers and the black-clad priest hobble down the pier, Alexander, with injured hands and other puncture wounds, pushes the two objects together.

Boom.

He is thrown off the pier fifteen meters into the Black Sea. Peter and Zara are thrown several meters to the ground. Peter looks up and sees the angry black clouds again ready to discharge. He pulls Zara up, kisses her, and says, "I love you. The bad you. All of you." And then he throws them both off the pier into the water and pulls her away from the pier.

Flash-boom is the last thing they see and hear.

PART III

He may be clearing you out for some new delight.
The dark thought, the shame, the malice, meet them at the door laughing, and
invite them in.
>Be grateful for whoever comes, because each has been sent as a guide from
beyond.
—Jalāl ad-Dīn Muḥammad Rūmī, thirteenth-century Persian Sufi mystic

CHAPTER 43

For true love is inexhaustible; the more you give, the more
you have. And if you go to draw at the true fountainhead,
the more water you draw, the more abundant is its flow.

—Antoine de Saint-Exupéry

Peter awakens, eyes not yet open. He remembers sensing the love of his life stroking him adoringly, fondly, passionately. Ready to be with him for eternity. But the fog he has known until recently still surrounds him. He cannot think straight. His head hurts and his body is fatigued.

His eyes attempt to open in vain, yelling as he tries to budge his eyelids. He peeps through the small slit he is able to muster between the screaming lids. He is not in Zara's room. He is not in Zara's brother's room.

No. It can't be. Is he still in his room in San Francisco? It wasn't just a dream, was it? Zara, was she just a woman in his dreams? Was he so emotionally fraught, unable to overcome his dismay at seeing his Sarah with Sam, that he dreamt up a divine romance with an extraordinary woman, the descendant of those who made Pappy's oral tradition?

On his forehead, he feels the warmth of fingers stroking him in the exact right spot. But these fingers are too large to be Zara's. His eyes pop open in panic. Alexander? His vision is still fuzzy. There through his fog, a large black-clad figure starts to appear. As the fog that blurs his eyes dissipates, Peter spots the medallion hanging next to the crucifix. He reaches for Jean-Paul's hand and grabs it.

Jean-Paul, so serene once again, says, "You have had a rough two weeks. But we knew you would be okay."

Peter hears the word *we* and looks around for Zara. But there is only an empty bed next to him. Oh no. Did he really kill her? He tried his very best to find a way to save her. Did he end up fulfilling her destiny to die that day? Maybe if he had only conceded more and prayed to her voice, maybe, just maybe, the voice would have had mercy on them.

The good priest sees his distress and can only imagine what is tormenting him. He says compassionately, "She was here in the bed next to you for the past two weeks. She prayed next to you, holding your hands in hers. Last night, her great-grandmother died, and she left early this morning."

Peter rubs his strained eyes and laments, "But I didn't even get to say goodbye to her."

His large hand lightly touching Peter's head, Jean-Paul says reassuringly, "You should know she was at your side every day, every night, stroking you. Very lovingly so, if you were to ask me. She kissed you many times. But as I let you two share each other in privacy, I cannot tell you more."

As Peter's vision begins to clear, he can discern Jean-Paul wearing a black cassock. Peter asks, "Didn't you get a chance to change out of that Russian imitation cassock?"

Jean-Paul smiles and says, "This is mine, from my residence here in Rome."

"I'm in Rome?" asks a bewildered Peter.

"Yes, Major Buchli was on standby and flew us all here for medical care. Zara and I were spared major internal injuries thanks to her old friend's vests and pants. We suffered broken ribs and armor impact wounds, which bled, but nothing deeply penetrated past the armor. You, on the other hand, took a major concussion hit due to the blast."

Peter touches around his head. "What blast?"

"When the lightning struck our object, it detonated," Jean-Paul explains. "But oddly so. Most of the explosive force went straight up, sparing the town next to us. You were hit in the head by debris from the pier. Zara kept your head above water until my friends were able to retrieve you."

Peter looks up at the TV screen in his hospital room. Rhonda is talking with almost no makeup or accessories. "Experts are still unclear as to the source of the mysterious explosion in northeastern Turkey a week ago. The area is still recovering from a massive electromagnetic pulse that spanned out a thousand kilometers from this blast. The face-off between the Russian and US air forces was averted as all modern military equipment ceased to function."

Sahir comes on screen and adds, "Shortly following this EM pulse, a massive earthquake measuring 10.6 on the Richter scale occurred in the Black Sea. Experts are at a loss to explain the fifty-meter-high tsunami that overturned both the Russian and US fleets but mysteriously only ran south to north, sparing the Turkish coastline. Religious groups, moderate and fanatical alike, are calling this a divine miracle that averted the start of what appeared to be a Third World War. Major religious leaders have called for a multifaith summit to discuss this miracle and how they can work more closely together in the future to further ensure world peace and promote interfaith and intercultural tolerance."

Peter stares back at Jean-Paul. "But how did we get out of there?"

But he remembers his own observation. "The sixty-year-old helicopter. It wasn't equipped with modern digital circuitry. It came from the end of the tube age, didn't it? You knew all along, didn't you?"

The Father shrugs. "I deduced from the traditions that the object might have produced a large EM pulse twelve thousand years ago, but I had no idea that it could be of such an enormous magnitude as we just experienced."

A Catholic Sister dressed in blue arrives at the door, carrying a box. She says, "Father Jean-Paul, His Eminence is ready."

Peter could swear he sees a wisp of red hair under her blue veil. He looks at Jean-Paul and says, "Father Jean-Paul, eh? You never renounced. I knew it."

Jean-Paul smiles and rapidly blinks. "The Father General, with the blessings of His Eminence, was gracious enough to allow me to return to my

Order. Any sins I committed while I was away have been forgiven."

As Peter's fog finally clears, he bemoans, "And the object? Is it totally destroyed? After all that, I got nothing to bring back to my grandfather. I failed him."

And Jean-Paul says sadly, "As the voice had asked for and Zara had planned, we blew the objects into dust, straight back into the heavens. One would not even find a fragment of it."

With that word, Peter remembers. "And my fragment I had found at Karahan Tepe—where is it?"

The good Sister comes forward, gives the box to Peter and says, "She said to give this to you when you asked for it."

With great relief, Peter finds the fragment in the box. He can go home and give this to his pappy. As he studies and fondles the fragment, he notices something odd on the back of his left hand. It is a heart, scratched into his skin in ink. He spots a note in the box that had been placed under the fragment. He reads it.

Am I all that Alexander said?

Did I do to you what he said?

Did I withhold from you what he said?

You did not know for sure.

And yet, you still loved me.

And below this, a heart is drawn. The same as on the back of his hand.

The good Sister smiles at him. "I know a woman in love when I see one."

And she looks up at Jean-Paul with that very look she spoke of, takes the good Father's hand, very affectionately so, and says, "His Eminence is waiting for us."

Peter raises his eyebrows. "He's meeting the two of you? Is this the first time he's seeing you, Jean-Paul? You and Sister Magali together?"

Jean-Paul, a little flushed, stammers a bit until Sister Magali, less abashed than her friend, says, "His Holiness has seen Father Jean-Paul every day since his return to Rome. Today, His Holiness was to see your Zara. But in her absence, he has requested the two of us meet him to discuss a very important topic."

With that, Sister Magali takes Father Jean-Paul's hand, very passionately so, and slowly leads him to the door.

Peter stares again at the TV, which shows the world leaders pointing fingers in blame at each other. Rhonda says that MoxWorld News hopes the world's political leaders can follow the lead of their religious counterparts and work together to rebuild this region, to help these people, and to do so not by proxy war, but by showing true compassion, providing the resources needed to rebuild their towns, cities, places of worship, and their health and educational infrastructures.

Peter looks back at the Sister and the Father in the doorway. He could swear she had just stood on her tiptoes and kissed him.

CHAPTER 44

Dear Friend, let me plunge in the sea of love,
Let me sink into that sea and walk on.
Let both worlds become my sphere where I can
Delight in the mystic glee and walk on.
Let me become the nightingale that sings
A soul freed from the dead body's yearnings;
Let me bury my head in my two hands,
Take the path to unity and walk on.

—Yunus Emre,
thirteenth century Turkish poet and Sufi mystic

10:20 a.m. GMT–8, July 15, 2022
Skyline Boulevard, California

Michaela hangs on for dear life as her crazed older brother whips the hearse he convinced her to ride in around a sweeping mountain turn facing into the fog-covered Pacific. They had paid homage to Pappy's fog at a grove of fogbound redwood trees, where the banana slugs emerged, enjoying the mist of their beloved ocean. In the back, the casket of their pappy rattles around, and she dearly hopes that these excessive g-forces Peter is placing on them doesn't throw her dear grandfather out of his final resting box.

Glancing behind, Michaela scans to see if her nutty brother hasn't lost the procession. But her mom, just as nutty as her brother, is right on their tail, with the biggest grin as she is simply loving this too. The apple does not fall far from this tree. Right behind her mom's car, Mei is whipping around too in her purple Mini Cooper rental.

"Peter," yells Michaela. "What did that crazy Kurdish woman teach you? I can't believe driving laws in Kurdistan are that much different than here."

Grinning from ear to ear, Peter replies, "Pappy wanted us to drive him through the fog one last time. He so wanted to say goodbye to the fog that clouded his brain for the last nine decades. That object fragment worked wonders to rid him of the fog."

Unsympathetic, Michaela yells back, "Peter, you could slow down a bit. I've read of the gory things that happen to people who misjudge these turns. You only got your driver's license a week ago. You aren't in that armored pickup truck with your crazy Kurdish girlfriend shooting some assault gun out the windshield. Those stories your priest friend told at dinner were beyond belief. Slow down now. Please."

Just as unsympathetic, her brother replies, "I can't slow down. We need to be on time to meet Jean-Paul at the cemetery. He said we need to time everything precisely, for reasons he couldn't reveal. You know those Jesuits— they always have something up those long black sleeves of theirs." He smiles, remembering all the mysteries surrounding his tall black-clad friend, and adds, "And you can count on whatever that is to be something good."

As Peter drops the speed down just a few kilometers per hour, he fondly remembers his last moments with Pappy. After his convalescence in Rome, Peter went immediately to see his beloved pappy, not even stopping at his own apartment to change. Pappy's condition had deteriorated in Peter's absence, and when Peter entered his room, he was fully bedridden, with tubes coming out of his nose and mouth and everywhere else.

Nine decades of restless, physically draining nights of dreams that could not be remembered had taken their toll on poor Pappy. Barely able to see, he was elated as he heard his grandson enter his room at the Angel's Rest convalescent home. He was even more elated as Peter told the complete story of the oral traditions, the lineage of those afflicted like the two of them, and how Pappy's faithful teaching of the oral traditions assisted Peter's search across the lush, beautiful Anatolian hills and mountains.

As Peter opened his backpack and showed him the object fragment, Pappy came back to life again. He'd never truly believed he would see the object in his lifetime, or even part of it. He had even given up his faith in Peter's success, knowing his final days were coming.

Pappy held the object. Fondled it. Caressed it. And then kissed it. He asked Peter gently if he could sleep with it. Of course, replied Peter, knowing without the fragment, Peter would have the anxious violent nights again.

Pappy had faithfully taught a lifetime of reciting the oral traditions, suffered through tormented nights with never-ending turmoil, and endured the mornings after mornings of misery, sorting out dreams that couldn't be touched. And for Peter, giving his pappy the first and final relief of his life was worth all that Peter had been through over the past two months.

The world had been at the edge of war, and Peter couldn't care less. World peace was at hand, and Peter couldn't care less. Only Pappy's chance at peace, which was finally here, meant anything to Peter. Except for one other person, whom Peter kept the memories of to himself.

The next morning, Peter came back to Angel's Rest, groggy and head hurting from some dream—something he could no longer recall without his other half comforting him. Wide awake, sipping his morning tea and smiling, Pappy went on and on about how good it was to have real sleep. And the dream, not the horrible dream, but the clear one, was something worth waiting a lifetime for. If only his ancestors had known what he now knew.

He held Peter's hand, looked him in the eye, and said, "Peter, you have to repeat after me and memorize this for you and your children."

Peter, having thought the oral traditions were over, slumped back in his chair. "Yes, Pappy, what's the story?"

Pappy, with a great smile, recounted his dream of a great mountain, the object, and the quest to find another mountain. Peter could only groan. But while the joy of his grandfather transcended and buoyed his spirit, Peter thought to himself, "It's time to settle down."

A few weeks of blissful sleep later, Peter's beloved grandfather passed away during his afternoon nap, smiling like a cherub, peaceful and happy. Peter had fulfilled his pappy's quest.

Now, as the hot rod hearse comes to a screeching halt at the cemetery, Michaela sighs with relief, exiting the vehicle with haste to stand motionless on terra firma. Peter, in his state of joy, scans around. He spots his mother, Michaela, and Mei exiting their cars and Beverly waiting at the open grave with a Catholic priest in full regalia. Pappy was an atheist and didn't want a service at his funeral, but Peter's mother absolutely insisted on a Catholic service. After much debate, Peter consented, but only if the service was given by his new lifelong friend, Jean-Paul.

But Peter continues to search the area, and he cannot find her. His joy dissipates into his first tingling of grief, for it has been seven weeks since he last saw her as she pulled him to safety in the waters off Çayeli. He tried to get messages through to her. But there were no answers, only the note she left for him in Rome, which he has carried in his pocket every day since. Only through Jean-Paul did she confirm she would do her best to come to Peter's grandfather's funeral. Peter sadly guesses she couldn't make it work, even for him.

Standing with his mother and sister, Peter listens to Father Jean-Paul conducting the Catholic rites. A priest once again, he came in his black cassock with a white surplice and black-and-gold cope—so different from the bulletproof vest and black commando pants in their final showdown with Alexander.

Jean-Paul nears the end of the service, saying, "May the love of God and the peace of the Lord Jesus Christ console you and gently wipe every tear from your eyes."

Peter's mother is the most vocal in response. "Amen."

Jean-Paul continues, making the sign of the cross. "May almighty God bless you, the Father, and the Son, and the Holy Spirit."

And while he speaks of the Trinity, a black government SUV arrives. Three men dressed in black step out. Since that afternoon on the pier, Peter now recognizes when someone is packing a weapon, and all three of them are carrying. And much to Peter's delight, one tall, dark woman emerges, adorned in a loose-fitting opaque black ankle-length abaya with a high neck. Around her head is wrapped Mei's black silk scarf with the red-and-gold embroidery. He glances at her feet and sees she's wearing Mei's gift to her, the flat black bow tie suede ankle-wrap sandals. Peter so wants to run over and hug her, kiss her, tell her how much he has missed her, and how much he truly loves her. But the ever-vigilant Samantha grabs his hand tightly, holding him back.

Jean-Paul, also peeking over at Zara, smiles as he speaks again of the Trinity in concluding the rites. "May the love of God and the peace of the Lord Jesus Christ bless and console us and gently wipe every tear from our eyes. In the name of the Father, and of the Son, and of the Holy Spirit."

Samantha, Michaela, and Mei provide their final "Amen." Seemingly, Zara mouths the same.

Jean-Paul looks to the sky and concludes: "Nikolas Peter Gollinger, may you go in the peace of Christ."

Samantha, Michaela, Mei, and even Zara all give a final "Thanks be to God."

After final words from the Gollinger family, Father Jean-Paul waves Zara over and asks if she has any words she would like to say. She thanks Jean-Paul and offers the following from her, and her mother's, and her grandfather's favorite poet, Jalāl ad-Dīn Rūmī:

You mustn't be afraid of death.
You're a deathless soul.
You can't be kept in a dark grave.
You're filled with God's glow.
Be happy with your beloved.
You can't find any better.
The world will shimmer
Because of the diamond you hold.
When your heart is immersed
In this blissful love
You can easily endure

Any bitter face around
In the absence of malice.
Her soft, dark eyes gaze into Peter's as she finishes the poem.
There is nothing but happiness and good times.
Don't dwell in sorrow, my friend.

Finally, she adds, "I have learned with you, Peter, and you, Jean-Paul, that, as people, we are more similar than different. That our beliefs are more similar than different. And that to achieve the peace we all seek, we need tolerance. And the willingness to know and accept each other for who we are.

"And most important, I have learned with you there is one voice. Only one voice. Be that the Father, the Son, the Holy Spirit, Elohim, Parvardigar, Krishna, Xuda, or Allah, or Xwedê, only one voice. And I am thankful to have learned from you, Peter, the voice of Nikolas Peter Gollinger. His voice that spread the word to you of a quest now concluded, which led to the friendship of our families. For this, I thank you, Nikolas Gollinger. *Amin.*"

Samantha's eyes well up in tears and she goes and hugs this strange woman of wise words, giving her motherly kisses. "That was so beautiful. Thank you. Thank you. And bless you." They hug, crying in each other's arms.

Holding Zara at arm's length to get a better look at her, she remarks, "You must be Zara. We're so happy you could come and join us. Father Sobiros has told us so much about you." Her last comment is strategically placed, intimating her son's reluctance to share his true feelings on the subject.

Wanting to talk with Zara, Peter turns to address her as Mei tries to get his attention. But Doctor Beverly beats her to the man of the moment. "My condolences, Peter. Your grandfather was a fine man. He loved you so and talked about you every time I came to visit while you were gone." She takes his hand into hers.

Peter rubs her hands. "Thank you so much, Beverly. That means so much to me. Both for his words and, more importantly, your friendship in taking such good care of Pappy."

"It was my honor and my pleasure. By the way, your grandfather left some things for me to pass on to you. Maybe we can do that later this week? Dinner at my place? I have a draft outline for my new book," she says.

As Beverly walks away, Mei quickly comes back to see her sweet savior Peter. Once again with no makeup, no earrings, she is a little fuller than he last saw her, dressed in a simple black ankle-length dress with purple accents and embroidery, covered by an elegant black silk lace shawl, black silk stockings, and black flats, also with purple accents, matching her Mini Cooper. And she matches Michaela's outfit, which differs only in having light blue accents and embroidery. She too clasps his hands and says, "And how is my sweet, silly Peter doing?"

Peter leans in and lightly kisses her lips. "I owe so much to you, Mei. Without you, I couldn't have navigated what faced me. You were so right about Alexander."

Mei smiles at the mention of his name. "Speaking of Alexander, you are not on his list of most favored people at this moment. You are a very clever man, Mr. Peter Banana Slug. No one has ever denied him what he wanted and lived." She kisses him back lightly on his lips. "Your sister, Michaela, she is so much like you. Funny and charming. She makes me laugh like you made me laugh. You two have brought such joy into my life. You make me feel like family."

Peter smiles at her, gazing into her beautiful eyes. "And I can't thank you enough for making sure Michaela, my mother, and Pappy were all safe while we were being hunted down by those assassins. And Michaela is ecstatic she's been able to room with you in Shanghai and have access to all your designer contacts. That's so nice of you."

Mei smiles right back at Peter with that special shining smile of hers. "It is the least I can do for my favorite banana slug man." She purses her lips and glances down and then back into his eyes. "Remember what we said when we parted in Luxembourg?"

A snicker and Peter rubs her hands in his, smiles, and replies, "Someday maybe we could go out? A date?"

She ruffles his hair affectionately. "My, you still are rash. I think you have found the answer to who is that dark-haired woman. The one Michaela said she guided you to. The one who you saw in the fog of your mornings." She glances over to Zara.

Mei tilts her head, gazing into his eyes, and says, "And the rest? I'm there for your sister helping her in Shanghai. She's already raising eyebrows at the Shanghai-Paris Fashion Institute with her innovative designs. Who knows, maybe she'll be designing Rhonda's wardrobe soon."

She kisses him on his adorable dimple and goes back to Michaela.

Peter turns to Zara and thinks, *What was that Kurdish proverb she said? What the heart thinks, the mouth speaks.*

Zara, desperately trying to appear as if she was not focused on Peter and Mei, says to Jean-Paul, "It was quite an honor that the Holy Pontiff appointed you to head the Catholic relief mission in Turkey. That electromagnetic pulse sent all our lands back to the Neolithic Ages. Little did we know how dependent we were on such fragile microcircuits."

"And your role in helping the Anatolian Kurdish State come to the negotiation table with Turkey about terms of reunification is equally of honor," responds the good Father.

"You honor me too much," says the humbled Kurdish woman. "As much as it pains me to say so, most of the credit should be given to Mr. Murometz, who, as always, pulled his puppet strings among many governments to nicely or not so nicely persuade them to the negotiation table. I only helped my new government understand the possibilities of working with Sasha's agendas."

Clasping his hand, she says, "I do appreciate your arranging a private meeting with your pope. But why would such an important person want to spend time with me? I am clearly not Catholic, and I am sure he has many more pressing issues than a simple Kurdish woman."

The good Father says, "As I said to you in the hospital, this whole mission has always been about you. Not Peter. Not the object. But you. Alexander and I shared that goal together. Your newfound humility hides what you know so well. The object only served to unleash within you what you have always yearned for, what you strived for, what you have now but are only starting to understand. Be that through Mei's theory of dormant gene activation or through more simply the act of the divine. You were the true goal of the oral traditions. And now, you are changing in many profound ways. My agreement with His Eminence was to help you make this change, which meant finding your other half, bringing you two to the object, and most importantly helping you let Peter help you. And now His Eminence would like to meet you, honor the changes you are going through, and hear of your experiences with the voice."

As Peter arrives, he compliments Jean-Paul on the service and on his new post in Ankara and asks if he could have a moment alone with Zara. Jean-Paul nods of course and walks over to Samantha. Peter beholds Zara's face, her scar still present, but somehow her beauty inside shining through.

Peter faces Zara and takes her hands into his, an act that once had so much meaning between them. That first touch in the airplane. That first moment of peace, harmony, beauty, and bliss between them. He has missed her so much, in such profound ways. He can only hope she feels the same way too.

With dilated eyes that emanate innocence, Peter says, "Zara, I am so grateful, so delighted, so happy you came. It means so much to me."

Head tilted up, he leans in to kiss her, but she turns her head. And that feeling he has fought so hard to suppress wells up. That growing tinge of grief. That empty sadness of the loss of a loved one. That hint of separation angst. The one he thought he had lost as they dived off that pier as he tried to save her. The one he thought he had lost when she left him that note with the fragment in Rome. The one who stands in front of him is about to tell him she is lost to him. Forever.

In great despondence, he puts his hand into his pocket and pulls out her note to show to her. She looks at it and says, "It is all true." And she looks away.

He touches her cheeks. And she lets him. He says, "And what is most true of what you wrote, *I still loved you no matter who you really are.* I still love you now. And you do not have to explain to me who you are or what you have done."

She touches his cheeks back, holding them with both hands, shaking as he has never seen before. "And you were not certain whether everything Alexander said was true or not. And yet, you still saved me. You could not kill me no matter what he said or what I said. You found your own unique silly Little Boy way to save us all. How could one not love you back for that? I have asked myself this question for many weeks."

She places her fingers on his chest and rubs lightly across the fabric of his shirt. "Alexander pushed every button he could find on you. And I thought you were going to give in until you placed your hands together in prayer."

Putting her finger under his chin, she lifts his head so he can peer into her dark and still piercing eyes. "He and I are cut from the same cloth, the same bread, the same apple. I pushed your buttons the same way he did. I am no better than he in that regard. What he told you, though, is the biased interpretation a patriarch puts on a woman's actions. The same acts as I would tell you a matriarch would interpret differently. For when a woman chooses celibacy, what is she withholding from others? Did the good Sister Magali withhold from Jean-Paul? I think not. How she chose to live was her choice, as the way I have lived has been my choice. You have to decide which version you wish to believe. Which version you want to remember me by."

Peter points to the back of his hand and says, "I don't want to remember you at all. I want to be with the woman who drew the heart. I want to be with her heart. I know her heart. And she is not the bad person she says she is."

For the first time since their time in Rome, Zara starts to shed tears, the ones that soaked Peter on so many occasions. She looks down as she cannot bear to look him in the eyes. "I know you desire to know my love. I know you desire to feel my love. And I want to tell you of that love. But our time together has come to its end. The thousands of years of destined forces pushing us together disappeared as we sent the objects back to heaven. There is no earthly or heavenly reason for us to continue. I cannot hear the voice anymore. And you should have seen by now, your dreams are becoming less and less severe."

Not ready for dejection, Peter valiantly tries to save the situation as he saved her once before. "But if we have love, why do we need the object as our reason for being together?"

Recognizing she is not responding to his plea, he says, "Remember our last special touch, the one where you saw my dream of the last high priestess of the Cult of Illyana? What did she say in her new oral tradition? 'It is said it must be man and woman. But it must be man who loves woman. Not for her skin, not for her fertility, not for her family. But for her. For her inner beauty seeking to be with the voice.' That is me to you she spoke of."

She purses her lips, still looking down. "Peter, we had a few weeks together. We became close in ways normal people will never know. Alas, it was only a few weeks. Here in America, in your films, a man and a woman meet. They have an adventure for a couple of weeks. And it's love for life. Happily ever after."

Pointing back at her chest, she says, "I do not live in an American film, Peter. Love is something that happens over years. Over decades. Over a lifespan. And my love is for my mother, my family, and my country."

"But I am family. I am your family. Your mother, your grandmother, both feel that way," implores Peter. "I am still your silly Little Boy." He puts his hand under her silk headscarf, moving it back a bit so he can stroke her dark hair.

Finally, Zara smiles and touches his forehead lightly. "You are like my brother, my other brother. And I love you like my brother."

Hoping for much more than brother status, something far more intimate, Peter concedes and says, "Your brother. I would be happy with being in your life as your brother. I just want to be with you, Zara. Object or no object."

She smiles even more deeply, knowing her mother was right about this man. But she lets her logic override her personal feelings. She has made a commitment she feels obliged to complete, and so she explains. "Peter, what afflicted men would want you to believe is that they are the holders of the oral tradition. They held power over women that way. What I should not tell you, but I will because we are close in a special way, is that the afflicted women in secret passed down their own oral traditions. Not even our expert sleuth Jean-Paul was able to discover that."

Peter's jaw drops. When will her surprises ever end?

Her face turning more serious, Zara says, "Promise me you will not repeat this. Not even to Jean-Paul. Sara taught me the following, which she said came from the first matriarch but then was suppressed by men who had other ambitions thousands of years ago. *'God asks us to be people of peace. Find ways to have peace and harmony. Find ways to create bounty to share and create community. For those who are close to God, they can find peace with ease. But for those who are not close to God, they need to have abundance to find peace. For without abundance, there is want, need, jealousy, intolerance, all things that stand in the way of peace. And avoid killing if at all possible, but defend people's right to peace.'"*

She waits as her other half absorbs the whole new paradigm she has dropped on him. "My late great-grandmother Sara taught me this oral tradition while I was in the midst of vengeance, killing all those who defiled me and my sisters, while I was repaying Alexander by killing all his enemies. And after I sat with her, listening to her retelling of the matriarch's view of history, of the object, of what our mission truly should be, Alexander asked one last act of me. I killed his son."

Pausing again, she brings his head to hers as she looks to the sky. "In that moment, looking into his son's eyes as he begged me for mercy, I realized what I had become. I made the decision to stop killing. To seek redemption. I renewed my commitment to honor Xwedê again with my full and complete submission."

Pulling his arms lightly around her, she says, "That was, until Sasha abducted me and told me I had to meet you. And I had to pick up arms again. To my surprise, the old violent hateful Zara came back, all too easily. I do not want to be her. I do not." She kisses him lightly. "And I cannot be with you. I cannot be that Zara ever again."

She turns away from him but keeps his arms around her. "I never told you what Sasha had promised when he abducted me from the Sugar Fest. What he finally promised to give me in return for taking up arms again and meeting you. As the matriarch advised twelve thousand years ago, I asked him for 'abundance.' An abundance to create peace in my lands, for my people, and most importantly for the women of Kurdistan."

She turns again, facing Peter and taking his hands into hers. "You will be very expensive for Alexander. And you should feel proud of it. He has committed to help the economy of my people. Until we are self-sufficient on exporting goods other than oil, we will not have a truly independent and strong country. One not suffering from proxy wars and violence both from within and out."

Peter sees his fierce, bold woman once again as she continues. "Alexander promised to build three new plants for making his Mox devices in Kurdistan. One each in the former Turkish, Syrian, and Iraqi states. He is even adding one more outside of Ankara as a peace offering to the Turkish government. And to help elevate the labor force in Kurdistan, we have developed a remote university program through his Mox devices to train Kurds, even those in remote villages, on the latest in advanced digital technologies. He is upgrading the tech in leading universities in all three territories, and we will be able to broadcast the first classes in Kurdish in a couple of months."

Peter's mind boggles. She's doing it all over again. Rationalizing every external reason not to touch that part of her that they intimately shared together. The real Zara. All he can say at this moment is, "I don't know what to say, but I love you, Zara, for the good you bring to those around you as much as I love Zara in all her forms and emotions."

Putting aside his plea for emotional engagement, she proudly states, "The best part of the deal? I got him to commit to education and employment of women in my country, who otherwise have no access to such. There are many functions within MoxWorld that trained women can fulfill remotely from their rural villages. We will at last allow Kurdish women to advance to their potential. And my friends, Beri, Firya, Peri, and Rana, will be traveling and teaching physical fitness and self-defense. Kurdish women will no longer be economically enslaved, nor physically. No more honor killings. No more suicides," Zara says emphatically, with idealistic zeal in her eyes.

"That was my quest, Peter. And that is why I agreed to meet you. I am sorry I used you like all the other women in your life have used you." She pauses, gauging his reaction.

But Peter is calm, waiting on her every word. "And I thank you, and I love you with all my heart for helping us Kurds to regain control of our destiny." And she gives him the kiss he has long sought from her, so reminiscent of the ones they shared sitting with the object.

But instead of addressing her diversion away from her inner self, her true essence, curiosity pops up in Peter, not letting him fully enjoy what might be their last kiss together. He asks, "But why would your Sasha still do this for you? You double-crossed him. Through me, you tried to kill him. You told me to kill him right to his face."

She simply smiles, then says, "Sasha and I have a perverse familial relationship. He tried to kill me once, like he did his son. He has no qualms about me trying to kill him back. That is his form of family. He only loves and respects me more for trying to do so."

And then her smile goes away. Not knowing how to end this on terms Peter can accept, Zara turns to her Kurdish upbringing. "Sara taught me the wisdom of Rabi'a al-Adawiyya, a great woman, a great Sufi mystic, who wrote, 'In my soul there is a temple, a shrine, a mosque, a church where I kneel.' I seek love, Peter. But I seek the love of God inside me, as did she."

Peter stares at her pensively. Samantha, once at a distance, has moved nonchalantly within eavesdropping distance.

"Peter, I know you. Better than you think I know you. The energy of the object, it affected us both. I saw your soul. And much to my surprise, you saw mine. Bare, naked, and vulnerable. A bare soul is far more disarming than the bare body. My soul was there for you to see, touch, and do with as you would. I was deeply frightened. I tried to push you away. I held back from you, exactly as Alexander said. But not what he lewdly suggested. I thought I was honoring my vow of celibacy. But I must be honest with you. I withheld letting us become intimate out of fear of losing myself loving you."

Zara brushes her fingers down around Peter's heart. "Our souls have different paths. Your soul still yearns to find ET. Perhaps when an alien sits in front of you and points you towards God, you may be ready. I cannot be distracted from my mission to better the world for my people, so that other women will never suffer in the ways I have, the ways that our women have suffered for generations upon generations. I cannot be distracted from my love of God."

She gives him one last kiss. Not for his lasting memory, but for hers. "Maybe someday we—"

And before Peter can try to persuade her he is willing to abandon the aliens, he lives to be hers, and only hers, one of the men in black interrupts and says, "Ms. Khatum, it's time to go. The plane is waiting."

Zara gazes at Peter with those dark piercing eyes. But not dark and angry ones. Dark and loving ones. Her hands caress his hair. She gives him a peck on the other cheek. "Peter, I must go. Know that I love you. I should say goodbye to Jean-Paul as well." She nods for Jean-Paul to come over.

Peter, looking at the men in black, asks, "So you're Alexander's new henchmen, eh?"

The first man gives him his business card, which reads, "Dan Connelly, Director, US Department of State, Near East Bureau." Peter glances at the card and then at Zara, who demurely says back to him, "What did I say? What Alexander said was true. But what he did not say is how Mr. Connelly here owes me for not showing certain evidence to his wife, for not breaking up their marriage, for letting him see his children through college with dignity, for leaving him so he could return to ask his wife for her forgiveness."

Peter asks, "So who is the other guy?"

Zara responds jokingly, "He's the true crazed CIA agent with the hairpin trigger." Zara gives a rare giggle. "Peter, seriously, they're taking me to Air Force Two to meet your vice president."

Jean-Paul has come over to say goodbye, and she gives him a hug. "And through Jean-Paul, the vice president and I will be meeting with the pope tomorrow. The good Father says His Eminence wants to know this humbled Kurdish woman."

Looking at Mr. Connelly from the State Department, she adds, "And after Rome, your vice president will take me home, pick up my mother and my aunt, and we will go to Mecca. It is time for me to perform the Hajj again. I have some repentance to make for many of my actions in the last few months.

"It's obvious your government wants in on the Kurdistan action. Kurds have no friends but the mountains. That is, until they have something everyone else wants to be close to. So, we Kurds have many friends at the moment. But we are wise enough to know that could change," she says as she nods at her old State Department contact.

For one last time, Zara clasps his hands in hers, and says, "No matter where you go, your destiny follows you."

She kisses him lightly on his lips, for she too cannot bear the thought of how long it might be before they will touch again, feel that peace again, if ever. Peter closes his eyes and savors the moment, which lasts for eternity, and yet ends too quickly.

Releasing from the kiss, she readjusts her scarf back into a nice respectful and modest headscarf. And into the government-issued black SUV Zara goes, assertively saying to Dan the shop is closed. And she goes.

The last Peter is to see of Zara. Ever. He cries inside so sadly.

CHAPTER 45

*Try to keep your soul always in peace and quiet, always
ready for whatever our Lord may wish to work in
you. It is certainly a higher virtue of the soul, and a
greater grace, to be able to enjoy the Lord in different
times and different places than in only one.*
—Saint Ignatius of Loyola

*1:200 p.m. GMT–8, July 15, 2022
Colma, California*

He saved the world, and yet his world has just abruptly ended as the black SUV leaves the cemetery.

Seeing Peter needs his mother, Samantha comforts her oldest child in the only way she knows how. With a lick of her palm, she takes his hands into hers and says, "Lost your newest girlfriend, did you? She seemed like a real keeper too. You really blew that one, Peter. Didn't I teach you to leash that curiosity? When a woman is in that moment where she needs to hear you know her, see hear, and accept her, you don't go asking about some monstrous multibillionaire and her."

She keenly watches as Peter strokes the laminated piece of paper in his hands, the paper with a heart on it. She takes his hands and says, "Peter, here's some more motherly advice. When a woman tells you she has bared her soul to you, when she tells you that your soul will wander away from her, when she says she is afraid of loving you and makes up reasons to leave, she is exposing to you her deepest fears, her deepest self. And what did she want from you? She wanted you to love God with her. All that nonsense about this Sasha committing to help her country. Come on. You're smart enough to see she is only trying to talk herself out of loving you. You really should rethink your relationship with God. You may never truly be with your other half until you do."

A lick of the palm again, and she takes her boy's hand. The one she held so tightly in front of her husband's grave. The one that so needed her assurances through the moisture of her hand. And she walks him back to her car. The good Father has just finished tapping away on his MoxWrap.

His eyes on all of Peter's interactions with the women in his life, Jean-Paul comes over and puts his arm around Peter, walking him a few meters away from his mother's car. "Peter, we have been through a lot together in a very short period of time. Sometimes it takes a while to sort through one's feelings. And for you, the other half of the apple, it may take a long time before you make sense of what has happened."

Peter hugs his priestly friend and says, "Thank you, Father. As always, you know exactly what to say."

"It's just Jean-Paul. Simple, humble Jean-Paul to you, my friend."

And the good Father glances into the sky, pursing his lips. Nodding his head, he looks back to Peter. "My friend, I told many lies in my time working for Alexander. I have one of a number of confessions I need to make to you."

Wondering if the good priest is finally going to admit the Vatican's acknowledgment that aliens do exist, and maybe even that the Church has been in contact with them, Peter says, "Jean-Paul, simple, humble Jean-Paul. I'm ready to finally hear what you haven't yet said."

The good Father slowly blinks. The blink of utter and faithful truth. He says, "Peter, I apologize for not fully expressing my beliefs. I am not noncommittal on the subject of aliens. I believe our Lord has created many creatures throughout the galaxies and we are one of his many. And no less loved because of this. The love you seek, the love Zara seeks, underneath it all is the same. But she is willing to say it out loud. And it is you who hides behind the notion of aliens controlling us all. I suspect that is what she was trying to tell you."

Samantha interrupts them, pointing at the time on her MoxWrap, and grabs the good Father's hand. She says, "Well, Father, I think we've become close enough that I can call you Jean-Paul. We're going to be late for our date down at the Mission in Santa Clara. It's so awe-inspiring walking in the rose gardens."

Before Peter can say goodbye, his mother gets in her car with the good Father. She yells out the window, "Don't forget, Peter, I'm expecting you for lunch tomorrow with the good Father, your sister, and your 'simply beautiful' friend Mei." And she drives off.

Left standing with a hearse he needs to return, Peter looks around. And he is alone. Just as he was alone two months ago, on that day when he swore he would change his life for the better. He has sure changed his life. He looks up and says, "I'm waiting for the better."

And then his MoxWrap sounds.

"Mr. Gollinger," says the elegantly attired lady on the screen. "Mr. Murometz would like to speak with you."

Stunned, Peter's mind races again. *What do I say to someone I just tried to kill?*

"Peter, my boy," exclaims Alexander. "My condolences for your grandfather passing away. I know how much he meant to you. And what his words meant to all of us."

Peter stares at Alexander's image. A scar on the temple, arm in a sling, and lightly splinted and bandaged hands, which he delicately holds together.

"Yo, Alexander, how are those hands of yours? Did I blow them off, or do the fingers merely dangle there?" replies Peter with the most bravado he can muster.

Alexander shakes his bandaged hand at Peter. "My boy. That was a very, very bad thing you did back there. Trying to kill your boss is illegal under US corporate governance laws. I hope you know that." The giant man purses his lips, then smiles.

Putting on a fatherly air, he adds, "The doctors say my hands and fingers will nearly fully recover in another month or so. But I will always have these painful twinges to remind me of you. That kind of love is forever, Peter. You and I are bonded through the douleur in my hands."

"Sasha, it couldn't have happened to a nicer guy. As I recall, you were going to kill us over some piece of rock."

"Peter, my son, you were simply brilliant on the pier back in Turkey. That priest was certainly right in his assessment of you. You are the best yet. Even better than my little Zara," Alexander beams like a proud father.

"Was I at a different fight than you? Didn't you have a gun pointed at Zara's head after you had fired several rounds into her chest?" asks a very puzzled Peter. "And by the way, you pointed my gun, which I voluntarily surrendered to you, at my head and pulled the trigger. Should I be feeling warm and fuzzy about you right now?"

Alexander howls in laughter. "That is what families are for. You fight a little. You make up. And you are still family. That, my son, is unconditional love. We are family, you and I, Peter. Exactly as I said."

He stops for a second, watching Peter's reaction, and recognizes what is wrong. "And Zara is your family too. She knows this all too well. Did I not tell you she was the most compassionate person I have ever met?"

Peter looks at him, quite puzzled.

Alexander smiles and says, "What is compassion, if not the willingness to put one's own concerns aside to end the suffering of others? Was she not compassionate when she killed her closest friend and relative, her sister of love, rather than let her be taken back into savage captivity? Was she not willing to give up her life to save you? Was she not willing to sacrifice her life to save the world?"

He pauses again, assessing his protégé. "Give her time, my son. What the object did to you and her was much more profound than anything I would have anticipated. She needs time to cope with her changes and how much she will still be changing."

Peter is still unmoved by Alexander's prognosis.

His grief begins to overwhelm him as he stares downwards. "Alexander, I am not ready to talk about this. Especially with someone who was going to destroy the world."

With a frown and eyebrows forming a V, Alexander says, "Peter, let's look at things in a different way. So many people want to, they need to villainize others. They need a clear bad guy who suffers the consequences of violating their morality. But isn't this the essence of intolerance? Isn't that your own intolerance not seeing who I really have been? Ask yourself, who equipped the world's greatest militaries with the most advanced tech ever to be invented? Albeit, tech incredibly fragile to the most frightful electromagnetic pulse known to mankind. And who sent you and Zara out there to find the object? And at the risk of his own life, who pushed the two object parts together to create their momentous evaporation into the heavens, which wiped out the specter of warfare in the most conflict-ridden region of the world? Are not the leaders of the world now under pressure to talk about true peace, having been denied their tools of proxy war?"

Peter glares at this giant, this perpetually lying, masterfully manipulative monster, with a very distrustful look. Is it possible he was that many steps ahead of the entire world, just as Mei had said? And all Peter can say is, "Alexander, it's been a really emotionally difficult day. You need to go."

With a sinister grin, Alexander asserts in a deep, booming voice, "Peter, you forget. You still work for me. You signed a contract. And no one breaks their contract with me. Not even my son. I expect you to be in your new office at MoxWorld USA headquarters by eight a.m. tomorrow, where we can discuss your new job. Be there or suffer the consequences." And the monstrous giant signs off.

Alone and in disbelief, he looks around at the empty cemetery. *Incredulous* is the only word this editor can come up with for this day. He saved the world, and he doesn't get the girl. Any girl, as he stands alone once again.

What should he do with his last free afternoon before he goes back to work for the man he tried to kill and who tried to kill him? Maybe a run along the Pacific? No, where did that get him?

And then he remembers it. Back at the hearse, he finds the object fragment he left under his seat. He takes the blackened grey thing from another world back to his grandfather's grave, kneels down, and plants the last remnant of the object in front of him. He looks about again, seeing no one anywhere around, and ponders what he should do next. What is the right thing to do?

He prays.

❧

Waiting for a sign, an image, a sound, a voice, the voice, he silently tries to replicate the peace, the beauty, the wonders of what he once shared with her. But like Ki in the dream, he laments he was not gifted with hearing the voice. He cannot touch the voice. He cannot be one with the voice. He can only be faithfully obedient to her concept.

He continues to pray.

A brush of the grass. He hears the near silence of expertly light footsteps nearby. The cemetery was empty except for him. Who so skilled would be sneaking up on him? Assassins? Did the monster Alexander play him again, only to buy time for his newest henchmen to arrive and kill him in some hugely prolonged, inhumane, painful, excruciating, and torturous way?

He prays to God for forgiveness of all his idiotic claims that aliens invented Him. Or Her. He prays he can still go to heaven today. He prays his death will be quick.

With eyes closed, he hears his killer kneeling next to him. How bizarre. It must be a Russian style of execution. Waiting for the bullet, the knife, the lethal injection, Peter tenses, finally sensing warmth near his hand. Alexander has sent someone to remove his hand. A hand for a hand. How biblical.

A touch.

A wet touch. A touch that brings back the peace, the joy, the beauty. Did he die and go to heaven?

And then he smells her. Kneeling next to him, she takes his hand into hers, moistly kisses them, and rubs. He opens his eyes to see his angel smiling at him. His divine cherub in her beautiful black abaya. She removes her headscarf and touches her ear. For adorning her lobes are those yellow mollusks. She innocently shrugs her shoulders, looks at her watch, showing two fifteen p.m. and the direction of Mecca, and says, "The vice president will just have to wait. It is time for Asr prayer. Will you pray with me, Peter?"

Peter raises an eyebrow and returns the smile, as he has been studying a certain subject. Asr prayer is not for another three and a half hours.

But time has no importance nor meaning for these two halves of the apple as they come together into a whole completeness. Man and woman together. In prayer.

Thank you for reading The Matriarch Matrix.

Turn page for preview of The Matriarch Messiah

PREVIEW — THE MATRIARCH MESSIAH

PROLOGUE

Theirs not to make reply,
Theirs not to reason why,
Theirs but to do and die…

—Alfred, Lord Tennyson

1944
German-occupied Crimea

Irony is a poem handed to us by a dark god. So his mother has told him every day since her husband, his father, left for the Eastern Front, where millions of German soldiers have died already.

Irony was why his mother told him that. As he was her only child, she had to tell him what her grandmother had said to tell only her granddaughter.

Irony was why Nikolas was born male. A gender not endowed with the verbal abstraction to make sense of what his mother has told him to memorize. "Someday her daughter would return. Two women will fight for the light. One must die. For only in the death of life can one be in the chamber of the blue light." Nevertheless, she said that these legendary phrases might one day save his life.

Two months after turning sixteen, Nikolas Gollinger mulled over his mother's last words to him before he took the train from Austria to Odessa, then a boat to Sevastopol, to join his father, Professor Gollinger, and the German paranormal research unit he'd voluntarily joined.

Now, as the Russian troops close in on the last Germans defending this odd peninsula jutting into the Black Sea, the lanky blond Nikolas waits in an oak grove near the hidden mouth of a cave for the return of the stout black-haired Ghurdzi, a native from the local Jewish community, the Crimean Krymchaks. The distinct smells of gunpowder and blood waft through the air around them.

Like Nikolas, Ghurdzi suffers dreams of an ancient torment. Like Nikolas's, Ghurdzi's male lineage has passed along an oral tradition of an ancient mystery. And like Nikolas, Ghurdzi has been taught by his father that life is, first and foremost, a chance to solve the mystery.

The oral tradition passed down from dream-afflicted father to dream-afflicted son talks of an ancient star falling to earth, enslaving giants of the north, the bright star in the Cygnus constellation, and a black object that will save the world—but only if the destined man and woman find the object together.

Every Gollinger man dedicates his life to solving the mystery of the all-powerful black object. And thus, Ghurdzi pleaded, part of the mystery could be solved if he could enter this cavern before the Russians retook Crimea. The reason why Nikolas now waits for this Crimean Krymchak outside these secret caverns.

A half hour passes as Nikolas paces back and forth, wearing a new trail into the ground before he lets out a juicy curse in German, one his mother would not approve of. At last, he enters the cavern to find Ghurdzi, to find the truth of the mystery. Minutes into the cavern, Nikolas's torchlight illuminates ancient skeletons. All male, from the tilt of the pelvic bones. All signs that men were not to survive the trip into this cave, just as Ghurdzi's wife said. His breathing slows as he notes these bones belong to men nearly three meters tall. Nikolas's first hard proof of the ancient oral traditions.

The narrowing sandstone-lined cavern shakes with thunderous booms, dropping bits of sand onto his head. Nikolas waffles between going back outside and descending further to get Ghurdzi. Why did he say he had special permission to enter when all other men died? More booms rock the cavern. But the skeletons, evidence of the giants of the legend, compel him to brave death to find out the truth.

One would think the air would be only stale. Perhaps with a tinge of the dank, dark smell of death, given these skeletons. But from further down the passageway comes a different smell. Like the air after it rains. Like the first morning of spring after a long, cold winter. It is the smell of life, and it calls him to descend further.

His nose plays tricks on him, then his eyes do the same. A blue glint? Or is he going blind in these endless passageways? He turns off his lamp, and a tiny glint of blue shimmers on another symbol on the wall. A bull's head. Didn't Dr. Murometz, the Russian physician working with his father, wear a pendant with a similar bull's head?

Blue. The color of the light in that chamber his mother described. He must keep going. For his mother. For every Gollinger who has tried to solve the legend.

He descends further, and his torch illuminates another engraving on the wall. The tail of the bird star, the brightest star in the Cygnus constellation, same as the legend says. He takes out paper and pencil and traces the inscription, written in a language no longer known. A dozen more twists and turns, or was that three dozen? Nikolas is lost as he comes back full circle to the tail of the bird star on the wall. Ghurdzi better still be alive, or Nikolas's mother's last words to him were truly the last.

In the distance, he hears a woman's faint voice. She says Ghurdzi's wife must spread the word to her daughters. Must tell the woman's side of the story. That he must sacrifice all so that these teachings can be passed to their children. Ghurdzi's voice says, "I believe in the light. I believe in you. I will not fail you. She will return to you. She will. But you must trust what I ask."

A bright blue flash blinds Nikolas. Before his eyes fully recover, Ghurdzi emerges, skin crispy and burnt, shirt off, wrapped around something glowing blue. The Jewish Krymchak says they must protect this blue stone at all costs.

Hanging from his neck is a pendant built around a small black stone, one of a pair Ghurdzi's wife brought out of these caverns when Nikolas stopped here with her, helping her escape the impending Russian onslaught.

Nikolas asks who he was talking with. Ghurdzi says the same who gave his wife the essence of the vaccine Dr. Murometz injected them all with three months ago.

Emerging from the darkness comes an elder woman in a long beige robe covering her body neck to ankles, head covered by a pure white headscarf. She ignores Ghurdzi, addressing only Nikolas, who is holding the injured Krymchak. "Men are forbidden in here. Why should I spare you the fate of your friend who dared intrude upon our sanctuary?"

As Ghurdzi's oozing burns begin to seep upon Nikolas's clothing, the young Austrian's mind races. Knowing he has only moments to save his life or become one of those male skeleton, he blurts out, "Because my mother sent me to say that one day, the daughter would return here. That only in the death of life as one knows it can one be in the chamber of the blue light."

Glancing at him, she puts her hand on his forehead. A blue aura emanates from the juncture, a color Nikolas prays is not the beginning of scorching pain.

She says, "Your mother is wise. You must leave and raise children with a woman of purity like us. Teach your descendants as well as your mother did you. For one of them will help the right woman return to the chamber of the blue light. You will know which one. Tell no one but your child, their child, and only after they have known the truest love of their other half."

Thankful for his mother's wisdom, thankful for his life, Nikolas now faces too many twists and turns to remember as Ghurdzi describes how to leave the cave. When finally they emerge, they find the SS outside with machine guns pointed at Ghurdzi.

Dr. Murometz has his hands up as the SS commander says he is a traitorous spy playing doctor among the German ranks. Nikolas's father, Professor Gollinger, stands behind the SS soldiers in a German Ahnenerbe uniform, his machine gun aimed at Dr. Murometz as well.

The SS commander says to Ghurdzi, "Hand over what is in your hands. It belongs only to the Aryan race. We have been searching for the past year for this holy stone from Orion, which transmitted cosmic energy as described in the captured logbooks of a Russian researcher."

With a look of resignation, the destined-to-be-executed Jewish Crimean freedom fighter tosses the blue aura stone to the ground. The SS commander picks it up, inspects it, and then drops it, seeing his hands crisped. Howling curses in German, the red-faced SS commander shoots Ghurdzi. Once, twice, thrice in the chest as Nikolas cries out, "No, no! He is innocent."

An artillery shell explodes nearby, and dirt pellets and rocks shower them. While the SS soldiers are distracted, using their hands to protect their heads, Professor Gollinger guns them down, an act of betrayal if the SS command finds out he killed them to save a Russian.

Nikolas kneels to Ghurdzi, hearing his dying words. "My real first name is Ya'akov. Only my wife knows that. Take this stone pendant and return it to my Ariella. Only the destined man and woman can reenter the grotto in the cavern. Only with these can they both navigate the pathway through the caverns."

No time for Nikolas to mourn the dead, as Russian soldiers are heard. Dr. Murometz says, "They will not like Austrians any better than Germans. You must flee or be captured."

Nikolas cries out, "But how are we going to hide the blue stone from the Russians?"

With a smile, Dr. Murometz says to the professor, "You can run away and live, or die with this rock of no significance."

The Russian doctor takes Professor Gollinger's gun, shakes his hand, and says, "May God bless our children and our grandchildren with the genetics to finish this."

Paralyzed, Nikolas wants to tell this doctor what he heard in the caverns, but his father grabs his hand to flee into the forest.

The Russian soldiers enter the grove from the woods, astonished to find this physician scientist with a smoking submachine gun surrounded by a dozen dead SS soldiers. The senior officer says, "You will be a hero of the Motherland. Stalin will reward you handsomely."

Around the doctor's neck, an in-field medal for the Defense of the Caucasus is hung. It dangles next to another pendant. A bull's head.

CHAPTER 1

O my Lord, the stars glitter
and the eyes of men are closed.
Kings have locked their doors
and each lover is alone with his love.
Here, I am alone with you.

—Rabi'a al-Adawiyya,
eighth-century Persian philosopher and mystic

Skyline Boulevard above Silicon Valley, California
6:30 a.m. GMT-8, January 2, 2022

She never realized it would be this long. She never, ever thought she would be holding his, his…his thing. Yes, she has seen one before. She is certainly not that innocent. But it enchanted her, it called to her, as it seemed to purr in her two hands.

This moment is exactly what he has been waiting for since they first touched. And finally, here she is with him. Outdoors in his redwood forests, amidst his mountains. He referred to a game children play. *I'll show you mine if you show me yours.*

Zara gently squeezes his dearest thing and says, "Like a ripe banana with a brownish tinge and little reddish spots."

As she squeezes again, Peter lets out, "Oh, yes. Do that again."

"Oh, yes, you are so much like my silly little boy brother. Playing with your…your…"

As the two gaze down at the seven-inch-long banana slug wiggling in Zara's hands, wisps of drifting white fluffy fog float by, swarming the majestic redwood giants in the grove they have found by this mountain crest drive overlooking the San Francisco Bay.

Peter has been such a dear. Zara mentioned how much she missed the mountains of her childhood in Duhok province in Iraq. And so, he suggested they spend time in the mountains of his childhood. It was time for her to know what drove his fondness for these yellow creatures.

As Peter draws his fingers lightly across his beloved banana slug, they land upon Zara's fingers. And her finger purrs as much as the slug does.

Six months ago, she was about to leave Peter at his grandfather's grave. They had completed the mission her Sasha had coerced her into, the search for the black object of the ancient matriarch. She smirks as she recalls how that malevolent Sasha got what he wanted. And he certainly got what he deserved when he took Peter's gun, which ironically exploded in his hands as he tried to kill them.

She should be more thankful to Sasha, "The" Alexander Murometz to the rest of the world, she muses, as it was at his insistence that she met Peter, a man who has surprised her at every turn and twist.

After she left Peter that day, intimating that they were parting forever, he went back to pray at his grandfather's grave. The man-boy, who believed in aliens over God when she first met him, found solace in praying. Not because his mother told him to do so. Not because she would have wanted him to. But because he had an inner calling. At that moment, she thought, maybe, just maybe, he would be different from any other man who had sought her love.

Her mother said she first noticed Zara's father as they were on the same worship schedule together. Already, they shared a belief in common. A bond that made their marriage so wonderful. A bond that created Zara and her little brother. And maybe that is why Zara has come back many times over the past six months to visit Peter.

Peter touches her banana slug earrings. Zara responds by rubbing her scarred cheek with his hand. A drop of dew from the giant redwood above them lands on her nose. She puts her nose upon his to wipe away the drop, followed by a light affectionate peck on his lips.

"This means so much to me," Peter whispers in her ear. "You being here with me so early in the morning—the most likely time to catch banana slugs slithering out to bathe in the mists. Most women wouldn't dream of doing this."

Another dewdrop forms on the brow of Zara's dark plum headscarf from the dampness of the passing fog drifts. She passes the wiggling object of Peter's second fascination back to him so she can brush the drop off her headscarf before it lands in the eye of Peter's first fascination. Her.

"So, am I to assume an outing into the cold damp woods before sunrise is not your typical first date?" muses Zara.

"First date, huh? We're so far beyond first date, aren't we? Only the women who count in my life come here," Peter asserts as he puts his treasured yellow friend back onto the forest floor, matted with fern leaves and redwood twigs and needles.

"My father took my mother, my sister, and me up here on family outings," says Peter. "I fell in love with these denizens of the Pacific coastal forests. They are so peaceful. They hurt no one."

Peter glances at the broad trunks of the surrounding redwoods towards the road. "Except if someone hits them as they cross the road. But no one would be driving so fast out here at this time of morning."

She gazes into the branches above, the drops hitting her eyes as she stands among his beloved banana slug in his most sacred place on earth. *In this regard, he is like me*, she thinks, as she has her sacred place on the mountain back at her childhood home. A flattop rock next to the twisting trail where her beloved father would take her hiking. The place where she found her greatest peace. That is, until she met Peter.

Her fingers touch her ears, on which hang the banana slug earrings Peter so adored. Her tribute to his love for these creatures. She gazes at him. Eyes and nose so relaxed. His face devoid of lines, so serene. Her grandmother Roza was right again. She needed to be open to his culture and his ways to truly understand him.

Peace comes from tolerance. The root of tolerance is mutual understanding. His communing in these woods with his yellow mollusk friends is his source of deep mysticism. No different from Roza's father's Sufi twirling dance. Both ways to understand Xwedê's world and be closer to Her.

Her eyes close as she revels in her realization about why she has made the long journey from the Anatolian Kurdish State to California many times since his pappy's funeral—the culmination of their two-month mission together searching for the mythical black object of his family's legends. Because there is more to this man than his silly demeanor would portray. In their first meeting, Peter's penchant for Sammy the Slug, mascot of his alma mater, led her to form a less-than-complimentary first impression. But his composure, his placid eyes gazing in unity with nature, remind her so much of her father on her mountain back home. Perhaps he really is a man seeking the Divine. Like her. Like what her mother had with her father. *We shall see*, she thinks.

"So, I showed you mine," Peter challenges, brushing a dewdrop from her nose as the fog intensifies. "Time for you to show me yours."

Having grown up on the other side of the world, both geographically and culturally, from this man who now asks her to show him something most intimate of her inner being, she purses her lips as she stares at him, unsure what he is truly seeking. Their several-month relationship had already transcended the physical, the emotional, the limits of what she has had with previous boyfriends. What could he have not already seen in her, given their ancient ability to bond spiritually?

Her hand tugs her headscarf more tightly to her head. Shelter from the cold fog? Shielding her most intimate thoughts from this man? Or simply her instinctive subconscious action?

Knowing not what drives her action, she turns back to him, facing the redwoods. The negative-ion-charged Pacific air passes quietly as it flows through these monolithic beings. Ones who have seen a millennium pass. Ones whose family has seen the passage of time since the ancients. Seen the mysteries of the ancients. Like the mystery they encountered because of their descendancy from the ancient matriarch Nanshe's family. Through their solving the mystery of Nanshe's words, passed from generation to generation.

The words that Peter's pappy, Nikolas, made him memorize. The words that her Sasha knew would lead to an ancient monolith, the black object. Known to the rest of the world as Alexander Murometz, her malevolent Sasha built the world's most powerful, politically invasive private enterprise so he would have access to the resources needed to find this object. The black object that spawned Zara's prophecies. This stone could destroy the world. And this silly man in front of her had outfoxed, outargued, outwitted the most manipulative man in the world, her Sasha, to prevent Turkey, the US, China, and Russia from starting a world war.

Another dewdrop hits her nose. But this time, she does not wipe it off as it mingles with the drops from her eyes. She searches inside for the strength to remember that which remains unresolved in her life, with her family, with her destiny.

"My great-grandmother was our link to the wisdom of generations of spiritually inspired women before her," Zara says, still facing away from Peter. "Sara liked you. She saw something in you when she first met you. That first dinner at her ancestral house, when we were staging for our mission to retrieve the object."

Turning back to Peter, she says, "Sara told me that you harbor the same light her husband, a Sufi imam, had within him when they first met."

She points to his eyes. Blue ones that naturally go with his once-blond and now-sandy light-brown hair. "Sara said the light we should seek is blue. The world thinks the light is white. But the one we seek, we yearn for, we die for, is blue. She so feared dying before she could find the blue light. For in the blue light, we shall return, she said."

Peter, who knows so much trivia because he is an editor of all sorts of topics, papers, and books, is speechless. Finally he mutters, "Blue? Where did that come from? I'm not getting the connection to the mystery of the ancient matriarch we solved."

Turning back to Peter, she replies, "As you had with your grandfather Nikolas, who entrusted you with an ancient oral family tradition, passed from mouth to mouth, from generation to generation, as far back in time as that temple, the world's oldest temple, which our follies led to be destroyed, so there is a line of similar wisdom passed down in my family line. But through the women. Mother to daughter and to granddaughter."

She sucks in her cheeks, then continues. "I had always thought the wisdom originally came from Rabi'a al-Adawiyya, the saintly woman whose beliefs inspired the Sufi faith. A woman who dedicated her life to the love of God, of Xwedê. The woman who, since I stopped working as Sasha's mercenary, I have strived to emulate. But after meeting you, meeting Father Jean-Paul, whose research says these oral traditions come from an age twelve thousand years ago, I can only wonder if I should tell you the other side of the story."

Eyes aside for a moment, she says, "That ancient pendant hanging from Jean-Paul's neck next to his crucifix is thousands of years old, portraying a woman praying to God who had a worm next to her. When Jean-Paul stated that worm was in fact an image of your beloved banana slug, he shook my spiritual paradigms. The text next to the carving, in an ancient form of proto-Greek, said, 'And she hears the voice of God.' This ancient woman with two halves of an apple, standing next to a spotted banana slug, became my clear sign from Xwedê to unite with my other half so I could speak with God."

Alone in this ancient grove, she moves to place a peck upon his lips, but stops just short of lips touching as she glances for the time on her MoxWrap. Instead, she smiles and says, "Who would have thought that a pendant would foretell a five-thousand-year-old prophecy of our relationship?"

He tries to return a peck on her forehead, but her fingers push his chest back as she points to the time. Nodding his acknowledgment of her faith's need for a certain cleanliness, Peter says, "Imagine if you hadn't realized our meeting had been prophesized? You wouldn't have bonded with me in the ways of the ancient matriarch. We wouldn't have found the black object that gave you the ability to hear the voice. Her. Who you believe is Xwedê. All because of an image of my friends here. My banana slugs."

Her eyes close as she thanks the voice for guiding her openness to ultimately allow the spiritual intimacies with him, which she would have never otherwise permitted. Intimacies that conflicted with her traditions of modesty. Just as she had chosen to wear a headscarf out of respect for her family's traditions, her modesty, she had chosen celibacy as her path forward. That was before meeting Peter.

She exhales long and deeply and turns to face her other half now. She unbuttons the top of her jacket and then the top of her shirt. She spies Peter staring intently as she quips back, "Showing you 'mine' does not mean that."

With a light scoff, he smiles and retorts, "That, coming from a woman who sleeps with me every night we've been together, for the months since we found our bonding accessed the powers of that black object that empowered you to talk with Her."

He stares at her long earlobe and adds, "And how many men do you know who could go through the intimacies of the night next to you, under the bedsheets with you, and not look or touch?"

She moves closer to him, coming short of putting her forehead to his as she exhales. "You do look, you do touch the nakedness of my bared soul, as I do yours. This intimacy, one far more revealing than physical intercourse, is the gift of our touching the object and the genetics that the ancient matriarch left for us."

Head canted slightly down, she gives him a playful lascivious smile. "If you must see my chest, you can look now."

Out from under her shirt, she pulls a slim gold chain with a pendant. An ancient stone emblem. A circle atop a crescent. "My mother thought you the man the prophecies spoke of, and she first entrusted this family heirloom to you. A secret they had not even shared with me. And to my doubt, you fulfilled all of their expectations. And mine, by giving this back to me."

She rubs the pendant, kisses it, then puts it up to his lips. "After the blast that destroyed the object and knocked you out, I left you in that hospital in Rome only because my great grandmother was near death. I made it back only hours before she left us. She could no longer speak. In her hands she held a parchment I was to have, or so she told my mother. Mama said her last words were that I must carry on with what this parchment said. I took her hands in mine and cried and cried. What happened next, I have not talked of until now, as I thought it only for the women of my family. But my grandmother, my mother, and me, we have not made any progress in understanding this parchment."

Her finger gently wipes a teardrop as she continues. "In her last moments, I rubbed my tears on her hand. And she miraculously spoke. 'Seek the light. Blue light. She awaits you.'"

He opens his arms for a warm bear hug. The type her father gave her. The type that endeared him to her. The kind that gives an inner warmth. An inner glow.

At first leaning in to revel in the warmth of his arms, she closes her eyes and exhales as she gently pulls back with uplifted edges to her lips. "You trying to be like all the other lovelorn men in my life? Baiting me with a hug?"

Crinkling his nose, he replies, "Hey, the game is 'I show you mine and you show me yours.' Don't get shy on me now and not show me yours."

Glancing down, edges of her lips now downturned, she says, "Truly, I do not know. Sara waited decades before showing my great-grandfather the writing. He had said it was an ancient form of Kurdish."

"Did you ask Jean-Paul? With his expertise in biblical archeology and ancient languages, he should have been able to discern something on the parchment."

"No, these sayings from Sara were given to her by her great-grandmother, only to be shared with by a woman with her husband if absolutely necessary, after several years of marriage and children."

A wee bit of a snort is emitted through his nostrils as Peter says, "And you are sharing this with me because? Do I qualify for that 'H' word? Your mother thinks of me as such. Is this the secret you're sharing with me in our little show-me game? You only need to say the word and we're onto the next phase of our relationship."

She bats him on the chest. "Be happy that I come back as often as I can. You should know by now I am not one to be rushed along. At least anymore."

Turning away from him again, she adds, "I do not know why I do keep coming back. We are so different. Night and day. Dogs and cats. Goats and sheep."

A quick flip back towards the impetuous Peter, she adds, "But I have no one else to turn to. I do not understand what my great-grandmother has asked of me. From the visions we have when we touched in that special way near the object, you and I are like the reincarnations of the ancient matriarch and her husband. Mei, Sasha's biogenetic and fashion executive, says we are the two people on Earth whose DNA most closely resembles the ancient matriarch and her husband. In that, you are like my husband. The one my Sara said I should turn to. The one whose dreams, whose visions could shed light on what I need to do."

He makes a fist and lightly taps her chest below her neck. "That's more of a tease than pretending to strip off your shirt. But I'll take it. I'm your ancient husband who will wait at your side, will support you, and will be there when you are ready for someone more than a husband-like brother."

He leans in to give her a peck again, but she pulls back shaking her head. He smiles as he knows why, and then he reaches for their gear on the ground and pulls out her prayer mat.

Tucking her family's pendant safely under her shirt, she glances at her MoxWrap around her wrist, the never-needs-charging, nearly cost-free device that offers 12G data anywhere in the world where a satellite connection can be made. It's the omni device that propelled MoxWorld Holdings to become the dominant global digital platform company it is today.

Zara says, "You remembered. Sunrise. You know I appreciate your respect of my traditions, my faith. My need for wudu, purification."

He holds out an unopened bottle of spring water, which she uses to wash her face, her arms, her hands. She then pulls her headscarf around her neck again and loosens her jacket so she can supplicate in prayer.

Peter smiles back and then points across to the road. "That way is Mecca, no?" He kneels, clearing a place among the redwood twigs and fern leaves matting the forest floor to place her prayer mat.

She watches as his hands gently moves along his beloved slug friends who dine on the forest floor flora. She now feels it, understands it. His serenity in his grove. His deep meditation here. Not on the mollusks, but his deep connection to something more transcendent. She was right at the cemetery— he is a man of prayer. But a prayer of his own derivation. He does not wear his faith on the outside.

"Peter, you do not have to pray with me to show your respect of me." She glances around at the banana slugs moving through the leaves. "I see in here your place of worship. You pray in your own way. And I respect that."

Patting the place on the mat next to him, Peter replies, "I do so because I want to."

And with that attestation, they pray together. Man and woman, as the prophecy of the ancient originators foretold.

Prayer completed, Zara rises to roll up her mat. She rubs her foot through her boot as Peter intently stares. "Still find my feet arousing, do you?" she says, staring back.

"You'll never let me live that down. The first time you caught me staring at your feet on the plane ride to Kurdistan to find Alexander's object. You didn't seem to mind so much after you found out what a wicked foot massage I can give."

"Now is not the time or place for one, but my feet. I have spent years in military boots, fighting Saddam with the Peshmerga, then Assad and then the Daesh with the YPJ," laments Zara. "I do not understand why they hurt now. These boots you bought me are the exact size I used to wear. My feet must have grown soft."

A tender moment, literally for her feet and figuratively for their relationship. Her vulnerabilities exposed, and yet she still feels safe. A safety with a male she only ever truly felt with her father and brother.

And she leans into him to give him that peck on the lips she has so wanted to give but did not in deference to her need for spiritual ablution before prayer. Their lips barely touch when the tender moment is shattered by the sound of crunching, snapping, and a woman's screams coming from the road.

The runner in Peter comes out, and he springs up, racing to the road to aid those in need as if he were in the Olympic hundred-meter dash. But when he gets there he screams, "Oh my God. The poor slugs."

By the time Zara catches up to him, her ancient genetic husband is helping a cyclist, a lycra-fleece-clad woman, off the ground. Her carbon fiber bike is shattered in many places. A couple meters up the road, she sees Peter's friends, or what is left of them, smeared across the road. This woman hit and slid through a herd of banana slugs trying to slither across the daunting damp descent.

A blood-curdling scream comes from the other direction—the type of cry she heard all too often in the battlefields of Iraq and Syria. Three meters downhill, another cyclist, a man in a bright yellow lycra jacket with a torn left sleeve, shrieks in torturous pain. The type of scream she heard when one of her soldiers took a bullet in the abdomen. The type of scream her Ezidi cousin, Rona, let out as the Daesh, who had held them as sex slaves, mercilessly violated both of them.

The woman trying to untangle herself from her trashed bike tells Peter to help her fiancé first. Zara hears tires at high speed coming around the corner from them. As the lights of the oncoming car come into view, Peter, like the proverbial rabbit caught in the headlights, bolts up. Faster than Zara has ever seen him move, he dashes in front of the oncoming car, shielding the screaming rider on the ground, waving his jacket as a signal flag.

The charging red Mini Cooper slides diagonally across the road, smashing into the grey steel railings meant to prevent vehicles from rolling down the mountain towards the San Francisco Bay.

Zara yells to Peter, "Check the driver. I have the screaming guy covered." Her field combat medical training comes into play as she determines the wailing guy has dislocated his shoulder and likely has a broken wrist along with a good deal of road rash lacerations.

Peter assists the Mini Cooper driver out of his mangled motorcar. He's okay, but furious at the situation as he taps his MoxWrap for road service. Peter returns to help the woman cyclist. He scans around and is saddened. At least half a dozen banana slugs were killed because two cyclists were joyriding down a mountain road at a time when it wasn't safe. For man or slug.

Zara says, "This man will be okay, but he needs medical attention. I called 911, but it will be more than an hour for emergency medical assistance to reach our location because of some sort of traffic congestion this morning. His injuries do not warrant an airlift out."

After determining the woman has only road rash and a snapped three-hundred-dollar handlebar, a shattered two-thousand-dollar carbon wheel, and a smashed seven-thousand-dollar bike frame, Peter asks, "What were you two doing racing down this road at this hour?"

The woman cyclist taps her MoxWrap. Up comes a 3-D projection of a contest for fastest time down this mountain road, good only until 7 a.m. The prize? Free trip for two to the Tour de France. She says, "My Harold wanted to win this so bad. So, we had planned our equipment perfectly for the fastest descending speed just after sunrise."

His arm around the woman, Peter brings the black-fleece-clad woman down the road over to Zara and the injured man. Zara says, "I can reset this shoulder. I did this a number of times in the battle for Kobanî."

The man's panicked eyes are alit, and his fiancée cries, "We have to get my Harold to an urgent care facility sooner than the ambulance can. If you could kindly give us a lift in your MoxMover, we can make our appointment with our wedding planner and then the church at noon. The whole family is coming into town tonight. Harold has to be ready."

Shaking her head so ever slightly, Zara contrasts this woman's dilemma with those of her people she fought for. She battled Saddam, Assad, and the Daesh for Kurdish freedom. And now, this woman's wedding plans are more important than anything else in the world. Such is love. Or at least life in love.

Zara and Peter help them into their MoxMover. Between them, their bikes and Peter's gear, there is only room for either Peter or Zara. She offers to stay up here as she calls for another MoxMover. There is one only minutes away that can pick her up. She is acutely aware that Peter also needs to be back in the city to prepare for his special day tomorrow. The launch of his first book, his first creation.

She pecks Peter's forehead and says, "I will see you later at your mother's house. Take care."

And off Peter goes with the killers of his beloved slugs. It is a great person who helps out those who mercilessly murder the ones they love most.

Standing with her prayer rug, Zara tightens her jacket, chilly in the damp fog as her adrenaline rush subsides. She rubs her pendant through her shirt. Did she do the right thing, opening up to Peter? He is not her husband. He may never be her husband. The tradition said the words were only for women.

Only shared with their lifelong mate, their forever husband, if absolutely necessary. Is being her ancient genetic match enough to be her husband? Oh, what did she do? Does she really feel that way about Peter?

When the MoxMover she called for arrives, its gull wing door opens, and his face appears. "My little Zara. I thought you would never call for me."

Sasha.

To find out more about The Matriarch Messiah, please go my website:

www.tailofthebird.com

ACKNOWLEDGMENTS

The inspiration for *The Matriarch Matrix* came a few years ago, when I read a pop archeology article on an ancient monolith site in southern Turkey, Göbekli Tepe. The authors postulated that this site must be a sanctuary, perhaps a religious site, as there were no signs of houses nor sources of water. And that gave rise to creating an epic tale about who these people were, what they believed, who they worshipped, and what of their world has been transposed into today's world.

I would like to thank the many people who offered comments, encouragement, and suggestions. In particular, I would like to thank my alpha readers, Elaine and Lucia, who reviewed the earliest drafts as well as recent ones and cover art. And once again to the latter for asking me to challenge the stereotype, as history is often written from a man's perspective, and change the story from one about patriarchy to one about matriarchy. And my appreciation to the dozen-plus anonymous beta readers from many countries and cultures whose comments helped guide the editing of the story.

I would also like to thank my editor, Eliza Dee (clioediting.com), for patiently and nicely holding my hand through the process, from first draft to final proof. And my gratitude to Ava Homa, author of *Echoes from the Other Side* (avahoma.com), for her expert Kurdish cultural advice and general editorial counsel. And to G.D. Dess, author of *Harold Hardscrabble* (desswrites.com), for sharing his journey, advice as an author, and expert opinion on cover art. Finally, to the good folks at www.covermint.design for their many wonderful book cover options.

Surtout, merci à ma femme bien-aimée pour son soutien à travers cette dernière année. S'assurant toujours que je trouve une table pour taper mon texte partout où nous avons voyagé. Pour supporter le bruit de frappe constant sur le clavier. Pour me donner l'inspiration en faisant passer à nos filles les sagesses belges reçues de ses parents et grands-parents. Peut-être que ces déclarations proviennent d'il y a 12 000 ans. Qui sait?

To learn more about the history and culture described in *The Matriarch Matrix*, please visit my website: www.tailofthebird.com

Thank you for reading my book. Maxime.

ABOUT THE AUTHOR

Maxime has been scribbling stories since grade school, from adventure epics to morality plays. Blessed with living in multicultural pluralistic settings and having earned degrees in science and marketing, Maxime has worked in business and sports, traveling to countries across five continents and learning about cultures, traditions, and the importance of tolerance and understanding. Maxime's debut novel was written and edited in different locations in Belgium, including the Turkish and Kurdish neighborhoods of Brussels, in Peru, in London, and on the two coasts of the United States.